# Rocks and Shoals

## The Seventh Carlisle & Holbrooke Naval Adventure

Chris Durbin

Chris Durbin

To

William Durbin

Royal Navy

Rocks and Shoals

Rocks and Shoals Copyright © 2020 by Chris Durbin. All Rights Reserved.

Chris Durbin has asserted his rights under the Copyright, Design and Patents Act, 1988, to be identified as the author of this work.

No part of this book may be reproduced in any form or by any electronic or mechanical means including information storage and retrieval systems, without permission in writing from the author. The only exception is by a reviewer, who may quote short excerpts in a review.

Editor: Lucia Durbin.

Cover Artwork: Bob Payne.

Cover Design: Book Beaver.

This book is a work of historical fiction. Characters, places, and incidents either are products of the author's imagination or are used fictitiously. Any resemblance to actual persons living or dead, or to events or locales is entirely coincidental.

Visit my website at:

www.chris-durbin.com

First Edition: May 2020

# CONTENTS

| | Nautical Terms | vii |
| --- | --- | --- |
| | Principal Characters | viii |
| | Charts | xi |
| | Introduction | 1 |
| Prologue | Nudging the Ice | 3 |
| Chapter 1 | In the Nick of Time | 8 |
| Chapter 2 | A Happy Meeting | 21 |
| Chapter 3 | A Williamsburg Christmas | 30 |
| Chapter 4 | A Man of Consequence | 42 |
| Chapter 5 | Halifax | 47 |
| Chapter 6 | Prizes in the Ice | 56 |
| Chapter 7 | The Surveyor | 69 |
| Chapter 8 | The Wilderness | 78 |
| Chapter 9 | The Pilots of Bic | 87 |
| Chapter 10 | The Coudres Channel | 100 |
| Chapter 11 | The Quartermaster-General | 110 |
| Chapter 12 | Hogsheads and Luggers | 120 |
| Chapter 13 | The Great Traverse | 131 |
| Chapter 14 | Infernal Engines | 142 |
| Chapter 15 | Running the Gauntlet | 152 |
| Chapter 16 | The Admiral's List | 164 |

Rocks and Shoals

| Chapter 17 | The Whitby Cats | 176 |
| --- | --- | --- |
| Chapter 18 | A Bloody Repulse | 186 |
| Chapter 19 | Bilged and Stranded | 198 |
| Chapter 20 | Flotsam | 208 |
| Chapter 21 | The Deserter's Tale | 218 |
| Chapter 22 | Anse Au Foulon | 228 |
| Chapter 23 | A Shattering Volley | 240 |
| Chapter 24 | A Ship of the Line | 249 |
| Chapter 25 | Stolen Moments | 257 |
| Chapter 26 | The Wide Ocean | 267 |
| Chapter 27 | The Channel Fleet | 277 |
| Chapter 28 | A Rising Gale | 286 |
| Chapter 29 | Quiberon Bay | 297 |
|  | Historical Epilogue | 307 |
|  | Carlisle & Holbrooke | 311 |
|  | Bibliography | 317 |
|  | The Author | 319 |
|  | Feedback | 321 |

Chris Durbin

# LIST OF CHARTS

| | |
|---|---|
| 1759 American Campaign | x |
| The Saint Lawrence River | xi |
| Quebec City | xii |
| Quiberon Bay | xiii |

# NAUTICAL TERMS

Throughout the centuries, sailors have created their own language to describe the highly technical equipment and processes that they use to live and work at sea. This holds true in the twenty-first century.

While counting the number of nautical terms that I've used in this series of novels, it became evident that a printed book wasn't the best place for them. I've therefore created a glossary of nautical terms on my website:

https://chris-durbin.com/glossary/

My glossary of nautical terms is limited to those that I've used in this series of novels as they were used in the middle of the eighteenth century. It's intended as a work of reference to accompany the Carlisle & Holbrooke series of naval adventure novels.

Some of the usages of these terms have changed over the years, so this glossary should be used with caution when referring to periods before 1740 or after 1780.

The glossary isn't exhaustive. A more comprehensive list can be found in Falconer's Universal Dictionary of the Marine, first published in 1769. I haven't counted the number of terms that Falconer has defined, but he fills 328 pages with English language terms, followed by a further eighty-three pages of French translations. It is a monumental work.

An online version of the 1780 edition of The Universal Dictionary (which unfortunately does not include all the excellent diagrams that are in the print version) can be found on this website:

https://archive.org/details/universaldiction00falc/

Chris Durbin

# PRINCIPAL CHARACTERS

## Fictional

**Captain Edward Carlisle**: Commanding Officer, *Medina*

**Lady Chiara Angelini**: Captain Carlisle's wife

**Patrick Moxon**: First Lieutenant, *Medina*

**John Hosking**: Sailing Master, *Medina*

**David Wishart**: Master's Mate, *Medina*

**Enrico Angelini**: Midshipman, *Medina*. Cousin to Lady Chiara

**Able Seaman Whittle**: a follower of Captain Carlisle's from his home in Virginia

**Black Rod**: Chief-of-Household of the Angelini family, real name unknown

**Matthew Gresham**: First Lieutenant, *Dartmouth*

**Arthur Beazley**: Sailing Master, *Dartmouth*

## Historical

**Admiral Edward Hawke:** Commander-in-Chief Channel Fleet

**Hubert de Brienne, Comte de Conflans:** Commander of the Brest Fleet

**Vice-Admiral Sir Charles Saunders:** Commander-in-

Chief North America

**Rear Admiral Phillip Durell:** Commanding the squadron at Halifax during the winter of 1758

**Major-General James Wolfe:** Commander of the British army at Quebec

**Pierre François de Rigaud Vaudreuil:** Governor of New France

**Louis-Joseph de Montcalm:** Military Commander in North America

**Louis-Antoine de Bougainville:** ADC to Montcalm

**James Cook: Sailing Master:** Pembroke

Chris Durbin

# 1759 American Campaign

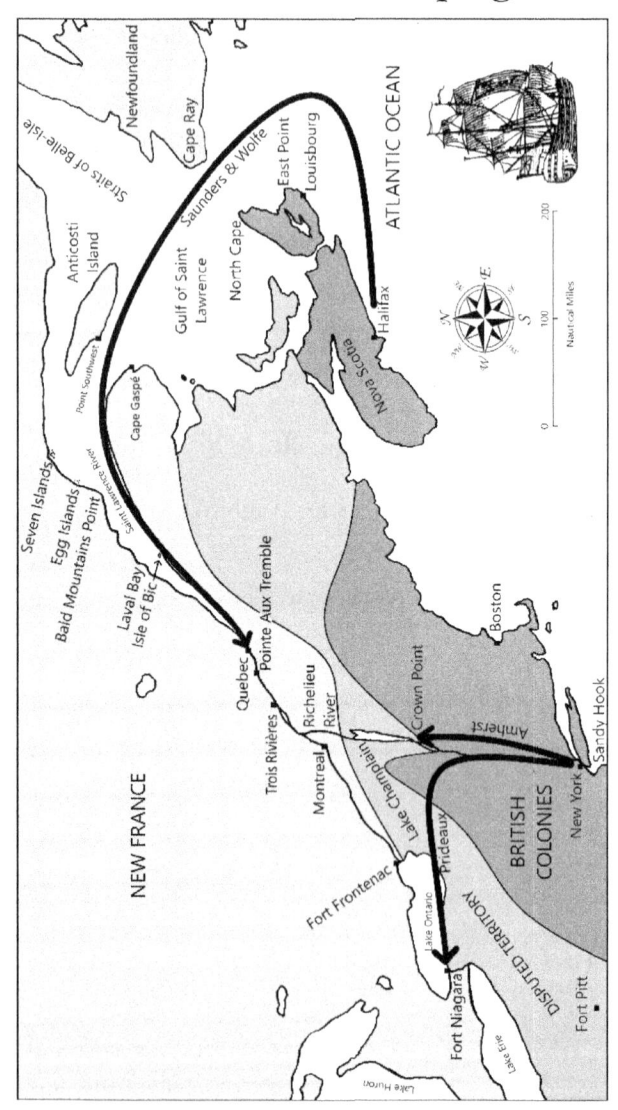

Rocks and Shoals

# The Saint Lawrence River

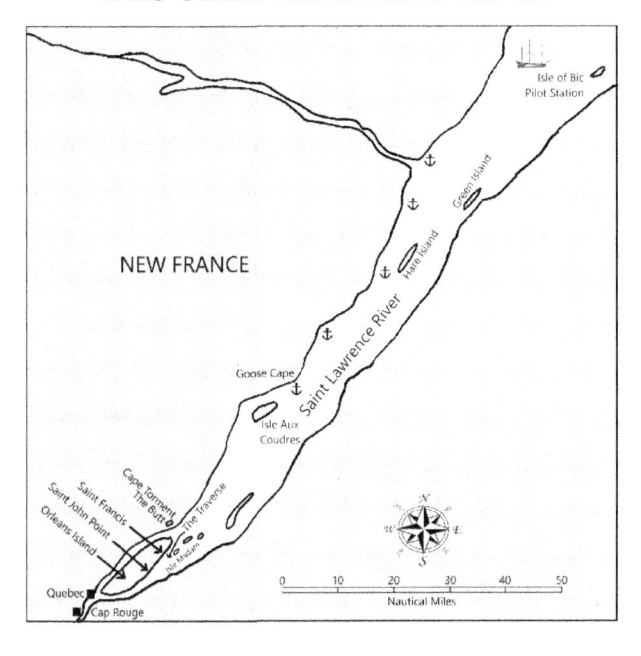

# Quebec City

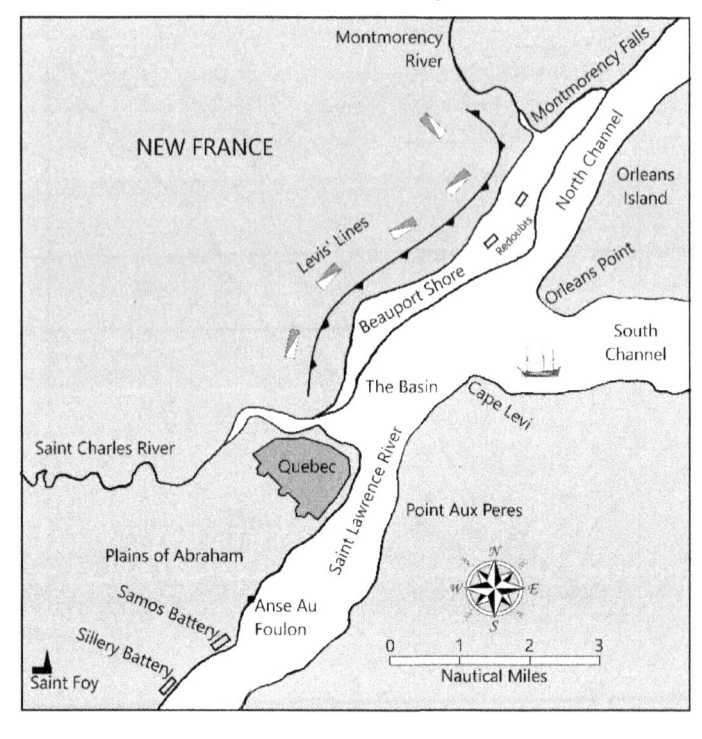

Rocks and Shoals

# Quiberon Bay

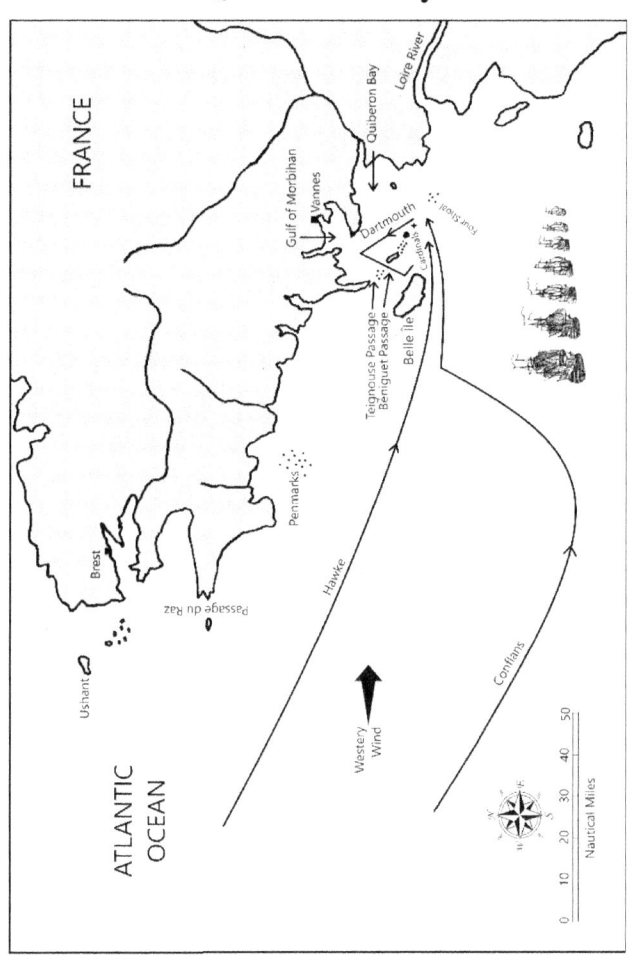

Chris Durbin

*'The punishment of death, or such other punishment as a court martial may adjudge, may be inflicted on any person...(who) suffers any vessel of the Navy to be stranded, or run upon rocks or shoals...'*

\*\*\*

*Articles for the Government of the United States Navy*

# INTRODUCTION
## The War in North America

William Pitt had planned that the end of 1758 would leave him in command of the Ohio Valley, Lake Champlain and the Saint Lawrence as far as Quebec, so that in 1759 he could squeeze Montreal and force the surrender of all New France. However, the year didn't turn out as well as he had expected.

The campaign season started with a defeat as a powerful force led by General Abercromby failed to capture Fort Carillon at the southern end of Lake Champlain and suffered heavy casualties at the hands of Montcalm's troops. As a result, Abercromby was replaced as Commander-in-Chief North America by General Amherst. To William Pitt's great frustration, the French would hold Lake Champlain for another year.

Further west there was a surprise victory when Fort Frontenac, located at the point where Lake Ontario empties into the Saint Lawrence, was taken and destroyed, briefly disrupting French communications between Montreal and Quebec and their western territories.

In November, a mixed force of British regulars and colonial militia advanced on Fort Duquesne. They had learned the lessons of the disastrous 1755 attempt and after an initial repulse they took possession when the French destroyed the fort and withdrew to the north. The British rebuilt it and named the new structure Fort Pitt.

However, the best news was the taking of Louisbourg which fell to General Amherst and Admiral Boscawen in August. It was welcome news indeed, but it fell so late in the year that the army couldn't push on up the Saint Lawrence River to lay siege to Quebec, as Pitt had intended, before the end of the campaign season. Amherst left a garrison at Louisbourg and Boscawen left a squadron at Halifax, and the remainder of the British forces withdrew until the next year.

While 1758 wasn't an unqualified success for William Pitt's strategy, it did lay the foundations for 1759. This time there would be no mistakes. General Wolfe and Admiral Saunders were to sail up the Saint Lawrence and take Quebec. Amherst was to advance up Lake Champlain while a separate force was to cross the wilderness to attack Fort Niagara. If the strategy worked, then Montreal would be isolated, unable to communicate with France and unable to support its western possessions.

## Carlisle and Holbrooke

In 1758 *Medina* had been part of Admiral Boscawen's fleet at the siege of Louisbourg, where Carlisle gained renown for his leadership in cutting-out two French ships-of-the-line. When the fortress fell, *Medina* was sent south with a convoy and Carlisle reached Williamsburg just hours after the birth of his son.

Meanwhile, Holbrooke's *Kestrel* joined the Inshore Squadron of the Channel Fleet under Commodore Howe to take part in Pitt's strategy of descents on the French coast. His hopes of being made captain – and with them his prospects of marrying Ann Featherstone – were dashed when he was captured on the beach at Saint-Cast, as he was covering the withdrawal of the army. When he was exchanged and returned to England, he found that *Kestrel* had been given to another commander. There was no ship for him, and he was sent to North America to command the boats for the advance on the French fort at Niagara.

# PROLOGUE

## Nudging the Ice

*Vendredi, quatrième mai 1759.*
*Machault, au large de Point des Monts Pelés, Fleuve Saint-Laurent.*

Jacques Kanon could not help looking back over his shoulder; he did it often, casting uneasy glances down the mighty, frozen river towards the sea. He knew that it irritated his passenger, but it was an automatic action. He found it impossible to believe that the British would let this vital convoy through to Quebec unmolested.

Kanon had a strong force; four large privateers and four frigates of the *Marine Royale*, although three of them were armed *en flute*. They had landed their guns to take three hundred and fifty recruits for the regular battalions, as well as sixty sappers and artillerymen with their necessary powder, arms, and provisions. He had set sail from Bordeaux with seventeen merchantmen under his protection, carrying food and supplies to sustain the garrison of Quebec until Versailles could muster a proper relief force. But three of the ships had lost contact in the perpetual fogs off Newfoundland, and now he had but fourteen. Still, it was a colossal achievement to bring twenty-two ships across the Atlantic and this far up the river with the loss of only three.

'Monsieur Kanon, if you believe the British are chasing us then be so good as to deploy your ships in defence. If not, then I would be grateful if you would look to the river ahead. God knows it holds enough dangers without the officer in command looking in the wrong direction.'

Louis Antoine, Comte de Bougainville shook his head in despair.

Kanon had been placed in command of this convoy even though he wasn't a King's officer; he was nothing more than a Bordeaux privateer, albeit a successful one. He should be able to tell his passenger to go to the devil, and two months ago he would have done just that. However, de Bougainville's mission to Versailles – to plead for support for New France – had made him something of a national hero; he'd been promoted to colonel and made a chevalier of Saint-Louis. His star was in the ascendant, and it wouldn't help Kanon to make an enemy of such an influential person. Oh no, not with the certainty of being bottled up in Quebec for the summer and probably the autumn, winter, and next spring as well. In Quebec, de Bougainville was the favourite of General Montcalm, and in a city under siege the army had limitless powers to commandeer ships, goods, and people. He'd just have to curb his apprehensions and rely on his lookout.

The other cause of his nervousness was this very same man. De Bougainville was a soldier, and yet he was continually asking the most technical questions about the ship, about navigation and about the sea. Kanon objected to sharing his hard-won knowledge and did it only reluctantly, when he was cornered and couldn't escape with a plea that his duty called. Why was de Bougainville so interested in the sea and ships? There was something unnerving about a colonel – a chevalier of Saint-Louis no less – studying the arts that soldiers and nobility so often despised.

Kanon stamped his feet on the deck to warm himself. It was chilly – no, it was downright freezing – and the temperature had only briefly risen far enough to melt the frost on the deck. Spring was late in the Saint Lawrence River, and at Bald Mountains Point the floes were coming down thick and fast. Not just the small bits of ice that scraped along the hull, but sometimes much bigger pieces that could stove in the side of a ship.

Kanon's crew was thoroughly fed up with the cold and the labour. Half of his men were stationed on the fo'c'sle and along the gunwales with massive sweeps to fend off the ice; it was heavy work and they'd been at it all night. They hoped for some relief now that the sun was reluctantly rising, they wanted to be allowed below to get warm. However, their captain had decided that they must press on and test the water. *Nudging the ice*, he said. It meant setting just enough sail to move forward against the river's current and bump the ice aside, always looking for a clear passage. This morning they were helped by an easterly wind, but the ebbing tide meant that they had to make about four knots just to stand still, five knots to move forward. None of his men, if asked before, would have believed it possible to fend off massive ice floes at five knots, but that was what they were doing, time and time again.

'Captain, look there, two points on the larboard bow,' said the sailing master, waving his arm, 'perhaps…'

Kanon looked carefully then reached for his telescope. He didn't hope for much; old Henri was forever sighting leads through the ice that turned out to be fleeting wind-blown gaps that closed ahead of them as soon as they drew near. However, this one looked a little more substantial. As Henri said, perhaps…

'Steer for it,' he said curtly.

*Machault* was at the lead of the convoy with his friend Nicolas-Pierre in *Chézine*, another Bordeaux privateer, close behind. The other two privateers and the frigates of the *Marine Royale* were at the rear in case the British should be sighted. It was a gesture, no more. Two privateers and one naval frigate could hardly hold off the force that they could expect. The three flutes may give the impression of a stronger rearguard, but only until the British drew close enough to see how high they rode. Kanon was confident of one thing: the British weren't ahead of him. Nothing could have come up the Saint Lawrence yet. But where were they? Everyone knew that they planned an expedition against Quebec this year, and a squadron of ships-of-the-line and frigates had spent the winter in Halifax. It didn't take much in the way of zeal and energy to send a part of that squadron to patrol the limit of the ice as it retreated upstream. By rights, he should be fighting his way through now. Where were they?

The familiar sounds started again. The monstrous, hairy rope fenders that festooned the bow were compressing with a grating, wheezing noise as they encountered the larger floes, and the bosun was shouting at the men who wielded the sweeps. But worst of all was the heart-wrenching sound of the knees as they twisted against the timbers, the sound of a ship slowly tearing apart. And it was relentless, as *Machault* probed and nudged, trying to find a way through, and all the time Kanon was aware that his time was running out. Soon, inevitably, the British must come.

'Ease the sheets,' shouted the master urgently.

Crash! Kanon staggered as the ship nudged aside a massive floe. There was a splintering sound as the blade of a sweep was crushed between the ice and the hull. A man was down, hurled to the deck by the leverage of his sweep. His broken arm dangled uselessly at his side, and all the time the bosun was cursing in his fluent Bordeaux dockside patois.

Kanon braced himself for the next impact and spared hardly a glance for de Bougainville who was picking himself up from the deck. He braced, but there was nothing, no sound of timber against ice and no more shouts from the bosun. He looked over the gunwales, first one side then the other. He hoisted himself onto the main lanyards and looked ahead.

'*Mère de Dieu,* we're through,' he said, looking in astonishment at the river ahead.

There was ice, for sure, but it was a slushy, pallid imitation of the solid white blocks that they had forced their way through so far. He looked astern. There was *Chézine*, with clear water between the two ships. Beyond *Chézine* he could see the other twenty ships following obediently. *Machault* and her convoy were running free. They were through the ice, and there were no British in sight! Jacques Kanon could look forward to a juicy bonus for his six weeks of labour, yes, and one in the eye for the high and mighty Chevalier de Bougainville.

***

# CHAPTER ONE

## In the Nick of Time

*Sunday, Third of December 1758.*
*Packet Lord Halifax, at Sea. Saint Augustine west 70 leagues.*

George Holbrooke woke with a start, his sailor's instinct alive with the knowledge that something had changed. They'd been reaching with the constant trade winds broad on their starboard quarter for the past three weeks, and barely a sheet or brace had been touched. At some point in the next twenty-four hours, Holbrooke knew, the packet would have to bear away for Savannah. Then the yards would be braced in and the sheets eased, but Jonathan Harley, the profoundly conservative master, would certainly leave that for the change of the watch. In any case, there was far too much shouting and running for such a routine manoeuvre. His friend, David Chalmers, was still asleep and didn't stir through Holbrooke's blind struggle into his breeches. He ran up the ladder onto the deck, remembering just in time to slow to a walk to maintain the dignity of his rank. It would never do for a King's officer to show alarm on the deck of a mere post office packet.

The brig was hauling its wind, and with half of the crew still struggling up the hatch the watch on deck was making heavy going of it. The mate was in full flow, shouting at all and sundry and urging the men to their sail handling stations. Harley was staring earnestly to leeward. Holbrooke followed his gaze, fearing the worst.

'It's a privateer, I reckon,' said Jackson, unseen against the dark mass of the main shrouds. Trust the navy bosun to notice the unusual movement on deck a full half-minute before the commander. 'A schooner, French by the look of her.'

There had been no candle or lantern in the cabin, so Holbrooke and Jackson had better night vision than those whose sight had already been affected by the loom of the sun over the southeastern horizon.

The schooner was lying hard on the wind. She'd evidently seen the packet before the Englishmen had seen her, and now she was clawing to windward to cut her prey off from the land seventy leagues to leeward. Harley's snap decision to keep to windward rather than attempt to cross the schooner's bow had been a bad choice in Holbrooke's opinion, but one that couldn't be corrected now. If the master had immediately put up his helm, he could have escaped to leeward before the privateer had cleared away his guns. His square rig would have given him the legs of any fore-and-aft rigged schooner with the wind abaft the beam. Committing himself to a luffing match with a vessel that could steer at least a point higher was a poor policy.

Holbrooke and Jackson exchanged knowing looks. They'd sailed together for four years now, the last year as captain and bosun respectively, in the sloop-of-war *Kestrel*. They knew each other and trusted each other's judgement, and they could both see that Harley had put them in a dangerous position.

Charles Lynton was on deck now, buttoning his breeches and trying to look as though he hadn't just turned out of his cot. He'd been Holbrooke's first lieutenant until a few months ago and was—in a way – still Holbrooke's first lieutenant; second in command of this unusual enterprise with no ship and a total complement of six.

'Mister Jackson. Be so kind as to shake Mister Chalmers, Chips and Serviteur. There's no need for them to hurry, but you may inform them that we'll be prisoners before dinner unless a guardian angel heaves over the horizon.'

'Coffee, sir.'

That was Serviteur, Holbrooke's servant. He must have heard the commotion and decided that his best contribution would be to offer sustenance. There was no question of him worrying about the packet's officers, they messed separately and had their own steward.

This crew of Holbrooke's was top-heavy: a commander, a lieutenant, a chaplain, a warranted bosun and a carpenter, and one servant. He must be careful to avoid resentment, but so far they had all found their places and were rubbing along well with each other.

'What do you make of her, sir?' asked Harley, still studying the schooner through his telescope. He looked worried, more so than when they'd been chased by the privateer in the Chops of the Channel a month ago. Holbrooke could understand his concern. A privateer whom he knew, based in one of the French channel ports, was an entirely different proposition to this unknown schooner that must have sailed from one of the French Caribbean islands, or perhaps from the Louisiana coast in the Gulf of Mexico. It had been many years since the heyday of piracy, but there was a sense that different laws governed the West Indies. The term, *no peace beyond the line*, was still commonly heard to justify commerce raiders even when there was no war raging. While a privateer in European waters could be relied upon to obey the rules, in general, that was most emphatically not the case on this side of the Atlantic and this far south.

Holbrooke took his time answering. There was something unpleasant about that schooner.

'I take her to be a privateer but judging by the haphazard way she's rigged – look at those patches in the mains'l – I'd say she's privately owned, perhaps with a letter of marque from one of the smaller French islands. Six guns, by the look of her.'

The master nodded. They both knew the danger from these irregular privateering affairs, often sailing close to the wind where the law was concerned. They all looked at each other. No words needed to be said. They would fight this privateer, however long the odds.

'You'll help with the guns, sir?' Harley asked, looking at the navy men stood before him.

The *Lord Halifax* carried six four-pounders on oak

carriages. They were in good order as Holbrooke had determined early in the voyage. The packet had no gunner as such, but one of the hands had been rated quarter gunner in the fourth rate *Canterbury* in the last war, and he'd taken on the care and maintenance of the guns and the powder magazine.

'With great pleasure, sir.' He replied, still studying the schooner. 'Mister Lynton, clear away the larboard guns and perhaps you could give Mister Chalmers a shake and request his assistance.'

'There are cutlasses and pistols aplenty. I'll have the mate open the arms chest now,' the master added.

\*\*\*

Harley was thrashing to windward as close-hauled as his vessel would sail. He'd lost the opportunity to escape to leeward; now he was delaying, for as long as possible, the moment when the schooner's guns were in range. Anything could happen at sea, and it was always worth playing the game through as long as possible.

'We can't let him board. He'll have four times our number, and they'll be a ruthless crew,' the master mused.

The details of the schooner were clearly visible now, and they could both see the crowds of people clustered on her deck. No, they certainly couldn't allow the packet to be boarded.

'It's not my place to advise you, sir…'

'And yet I'd be grateful if you would,' the master interrupted. 'If you don't mind me saying, I may have a few more years at sea than you, but you're a fighting man and in my heart, I'm not. Any advice at all…'

Holbrooke was taken aback for a moment. He'd never perceived himself as a fighting man. Of course, he recognised that combat at sea was the core of his profession, but privately he'd always thought of himself as an imposter, pretending to a real understanding of the art.

'…your bosun has told me a tale or two,' Harley added. 'Your fight with that big French frigate off the Caicos

Passage is almost legendary.' He jerked his head over the starboard quarter, towards the south, 'and then Emden and Saint-Malo. Yes, I'd appreciate any advice you'd be kind enough to offer.'

Holbrooke looked up at the main tops'l and then all around the horizon.

'I take it we're some two hundred miles or so offshore.'

'Yes, give or take, and we've perhaps two hundred and thirty miles to Savannah if we could get to leeward of this gentleman.'

'If we try that he'll fire into us and throw himself alongside.'

The range had closed while they had been talking. The schooner had run out its guns and now there were men out on the tops'l yard, readying the grapnels to bind the two vessels together.

'Do you have boarding nets?' asked Jackson. He'd learned the hard way never to risk a close engagement without the nets rigged, and certainly not if the enemy had the advantage of numbers.

Harley looked momentarily startled. He'd forgotten about that elementary defensive tactic.

'Bosun!' he shouted, 'rouse out the boarding nets, there's no time to lose.'

The packet's bosun came rolling aft. He was an older man, and he'd served decades in the post office packet service. He'd been lucky in a way; in all that time he'd never come to close quarters with an enemy. His rigging was immaculate, and he kept good order in the brig, but he was no fighting sailor. He looked shamefaced.

'I put 'em ashore in Falmouth to be mended,' he said, 'and when we were sent up-channel to Plymouth a week ahead of our schedule, I clear forgot to collect them from the rigging store.' He stood there before the brig's master, fidgeting with his cap and looking down at his shoes.

'Is there anything else we can use?' asked Jackson, 'seine nets, cargo nets, anything?'

## Rocks and Shoals

'Nothing,' he replied, 'the biggest cargo net is just a fathom-and-a-half square.'

They all looked blankly at the wretched bosun.

'Well, there's no use crying over spilt milk,' said Holbrooke. 'I doubt whether boarding nets would keep them out in any case. We'll just have to keep our distance. Now, here's what I recommend…'

Holbrooke outlined his plan. First, the packet had to keep to windward of the privateer for as long as possible. That was the master's task, he knew his brig's sailing qualities better than anyone. But they could all see, from the narrowing gap between the two vessels, that it would only be an hour or so before the schooner was alongside them and then…

\*\*\*

Holbrooke stood beside the larboard quarterdeck four-pounder. He was eyeing the approaching schooner, estimating the distance, and watching the pattern of waves that were running under the brig's starboard bow.

'I'll warm the guns and get some idea of the range,' he said to Harley.

The packet's gunner captained the fo'c'sle guns, and they appeared to be in good hands. Jackson had taken command of the midships guns and Lynton had the quarterdeck guns.

'Fire when you're ready,' he shouted against the keen northeasterly wind.

He watched the fall of shot. Not bad, he thought. Two of the three guns had fired at the first attempt, so at least some of the powder hadn't been allowed to spoil, and the touchholes were still clear. The fo'c'sle gun was well-pointed, but the gunner hadn't allowed enough elevation and the ball fell a cable short. Jackson's had fared better, just half a cable short, which was evidently the maximum range of these guns. Lynton's had misfired. It was almost certainly damp powder, and he had already run it in, removed the wadding with the long-handled worm and depressed the barrel to let the ball roll out. Now he was using the worm again to extract the useless cartridge.

'Try again when you're ready, Mister Lynton.'

The schooner hadn't answered the packet's fire. Probably they had nothing larger than two-or-three pounders and would need a to be a lot closer before they had any chance of reaching the brig. Perhaps they had no intention of using their guns at all. They could be confident of boarding before they took substantial damage and there was no point in knocking their prize about and reducing its value.

The other two guns were loaded long before Lynton had completed the frustrating process, but at last he raised his hand. Gun ready!

'Again, fire as you will.'

Bang! Jackson's gun fired first at the top of the brig's roll, and a spout appeared close alongside the schooner. Then Lynton's gun fired, a little after the optimum moment and the shot fell a hundred yards off the schooner's weather bow. There was a pause, then the brig's gunner looked up guiltily. His gun had misfired, and he knew why; it was his responsibility to take care of the powder magazine.

Holbrooke stamped his foot in exasperation.

'Mister Lynton. Take over the fo'c'sle gun. Chips, can you manage the quarterdeck?'

Abraham Sutton looked uncertain, then reluctantly shook his head. He'd learned his carpentry trade in the dockyard and had rarely been to sea. This was his first time he'd seen guns fired, either in anger or for practice.

'I'll do it, sir,' said Serviteur.

Holbrooke looked at Jackson, who nodded his agreement.

'Very well. Run down to the magazine Mister Gunner and bring up a dozen of the driest cartridges you can find. Centre tier is usually best.'

Holbrooke knew that there was little hope. If these cartridges were damp, then probably the whole magazine had suffered the same fate. One misfire out of three was

## Rocks and Shoals

unacceptable in a man-o'-war, but most likely normal for a post office packet. He'd sent the gunner away more in hope than expectation, but also because he'd already lost the confidence of his gun's crew. It was better if Holbrooke's own people handled these guns.

Things were moving more quickly now. The schooner was in range, and Lynton, Jackson and Serviteur were keeping up an irregular fire, hindered by the frequent interruptions to draw misfired cartridges and to organise the unhandy gun crews. They'd hit the schooner at least once, and they could see that a piece of the gunwale capping abaft the mainmast was missing, but it hadn't slowed its inexorable advance. Nor was the schooner firing, despite having her guns run out.

Closer and closer. Now they could see the five-or-six individuals clustered around the privateer's wheel. The remainder were all out of sight below the gunwales. It was most unlikely that the packet's four-pound shot would penetrate the thickness of the gunwales, and the Frenchman's boarders were quite safe if they stayed low. Holbrooke knew that his best chance was to shoot away the wheel. The spars and rigging were attractive targets, but the packet had no chain shot, no grapeshot, and only a limited amount of canister and the range was still too short for that man-killing ammunition. Lynton, Jackson and Serviteur knew where they should be aiming, but it was a difficult target with both vessels pitching and rolling and with the spray flying across the deck as they butted into the northeast trade winds.

\*\*\*

The schooner was only a cable to leeward, and Holbrooke was waiting for the ideal moment to execute his plan. Too soon and the privateer would be able to react at leisure, too late and he wouldn't have enough room to complete his intended manoeuvre before the schooner came crashing alongside.

'Are you ready?' Holbrooke asked the brig's master.

He had a moment to consider how their respective roles had changed with the need for violent action. Two hours ago, Holbrooke had been nothing more than a passenger with no authority whatsoever. Now, he was effectively captain of the packet until the action should be over. Harley – it's legal commander – was acting in the same role as a sailing master on a King's ship, handling the brig under Holbrooke's direction.

Holbrooke was gambling that the privateer would expect him to tack any time now. If he left it any later then the schooner – like all its breed, handier in stays than a square-rigged brig – would be able to luff up and crash alongside before the brig could gather way on the new course. Yes, tacking now, without delay, was the brig's logical manoeuvre, and all things considered, it was the safest. And yet it merely postponed the inevitable. With nothing on the horizon, the value of a delay was diminishing by the minute. There was still a chance that the brig's fire could disable the schooner, but it was unlikely. Holbrooke could see the men on the schooner creeping towards the sheets, staying low but ready to come about the instant the brig put her helm down.

It was past the optimum moment. Soon the privateer would start to suspect that the packet had something other than tacking in mind.

'Now! Up helm, master!'

The brig may have had a small crew, and they may not have been very warlike, but even with half a dozen at the larboard guns, there were enough real seamen to wear the ship in a flash. The brig's bows swung rapidly to larboard, and the massive driver came crashing over as the stern swung through the wind. The schooner had not been expecting this, and in truth, it was a profoundly un-seamanlike move. In seconds, the brig's bows were pointing at the schooner. In wearing, the brig had hardly lost any way at all, and she came rushing down upon the startled schooner, more like the pursuer than the prey. Too late, the privateer realised that the correct reaction was to wear also, but wearing a tops'l schooner needed preparation, and his crew had been expecting to tack. He made the best of a bad job and tacked right into the path of the brig. It was a desperate move and a collision looked imminent as the schooner's bows came through the wind and she paid off smartly on the other tack. A collision under these conditions could be to nobody's advantage; both vessels could be crippled, sunk even, and any commercial benefit from a capture lost in an instant.

The brig's bows came around as Harley tried desperately to keep away from the schooner's jutting bowsprit. At one moment it looked as though it might work, then the schooner's jibs filled on the larboard tack and she came hurtling down upon the brig. Her solid, stubby jib-boom caught the brig's mainsail sheets and, in an instant, the lower block tore away from the taffrail. The mainsail split from peak to clew, and the mainsail boom slammed forward against the shrouds.

'Watch your helm!' shouted the master at the steersman. The unexpected loss of pressure aft was affecting the brig's steering most fantastically, and she was careering downwind almost out of control. But at least she had stolen a march on the privateer. Then there was a crash aloft, and the mainsail gaff parted company with its jaws.

'Get that mainsail down,' screamed the master.

Holbrooke left Harley to the task of bringing the brig back under control. Now they were heading for the land to leeward, but the schooner was hard on their heels. The privateer had suffered no serious injury. Her fore-staysail and jib were still drawing, and until they could repair the brig's mainsail, the schooner had the advantage both on and off the wind. He looked aft again. Yes, she was gaining on them, and now there was nowhere to go, no scope for maneuvering against a faster adversary who had the weather gage. He looked forward at the guns. The starboard battery was being made ready, and with a glance, he knew that the larboard battery could be brought into action in seconds.

Then he saw it. A flash of white on the horizon, four points off the larboard bow. It was only visible when the brig soared up onto the crest of a wave, but there was definitely something there. Holbrooke's heart started to beat faster. It could be another privateer, or a lone French merchant vessel, or possibly even a French man-o'-war on passage for the Saint Lawrence. But with a global war raging, and Britain reigning supreme at sea, the chances were that it was a British ship. At this point anything would do; man-o'-war or merchantman, together they could see off this schooner.

Here was the master, gloomy resignation written all over his face.

'We should strike, sir, while we can still garner some goodwill from that gentleman,' he looked aft towards the menacing bows of the schooner, not four cables away and closing fast. 'It's my responsibility; it can be my decision. You've done all you can, and you needn't be implicated. I must think of my men now, and myself. You'll have a few minutes to make your preparations.'

Holbrooke smiled and pointed over the larboard bow. The small white dot had been joined by others. That made it almost certainly a British squadron or convoy.

'I wish you happiness in our deliverance,' Holbrooke said.

\*\*\*

The packet rose and fell as the long Atlantic rollers passed under her keel. On her starboard bow, the privateer schooner was reaching away to the southeast, having taken one look at the approaching ships and knowing them for what they were, West Indiamen under the escort of a frigate and sloop. The privateer captain was having nothing to do with any escorted convoy. He knew well enough that on his own, he had more chance of being the prey than the predator. He was putting plenty of distance between himself and the British navy and heading back to his natural hunting ground among the reefs and cays of the Bahamas.

Holbrooke felt as though he should be doing something more productive. All five of his crew were busy. Chalmers was in his shirt-sleeves, assisting Abraham Sutton in replacing the mainsheet block on the taffrail. Lynton and Serviteur were with the sailmaker putting a new cloth into the leach of the mainsail. At the base of the mainmast, Jackson and the brig's carpenter were taking two feet off the mainsail gaff to re-attach the iron jaws. Holbrooke was merely watching the approaching convoy through his telescope. There was something familiar about that frigate to windward of the eight-or-so merchantmen and the sloop.

'Mister Lynton, can the sailmaker spare you for a moment?'

Lynton hauled tight the seizing around the cringle that he had been working into the peak and handed over the rawhide sailmaker's palm to its rightful owner.

'What do you make of that frigate?' Holbrooke asked, offering his telescope.

'Why, it's the old *Medina*!' Lynton replied before he'd even looked through the telescope. A smile of wonder spread over his face.

'I haven't heard of Captain Carlisle being superseded,' said Holbrooke, 'so this may be a happy meeting.'

As they watched, they saw *Medina* hang out two flags, clearly a pre-arranged signal. The brig-sloop came about on a course to intercept the privateer, to warn her off.

The convoy came on boldly through the sparkling winter sunshine. *Medina* spread her stuns'ls and, as though happy to be free from the slothful merchantmen, she bounded across the sea and came to on the packet's leeward side.

Her captain was a tall, lean man in a frock coat with his own brown hair tied in a queue.

'What ship?' he shouted. Then he looked hard at the brig's quarterdeck and gestured behind him for a telescope. He raised it to his eye and trained it on the equally tall, slim, uniformed man at the taffrail. He lowered the glass, wiped the lens, and looked again.

'Mister Holbrooke!' he shouted, a broad smile transforming his face. 'Well met, and just in time, I see. Where are you bound?'

\*\*\*

# CHAPTER TWO

## A Happy Meeting

*Tuesday, Fifth of December 1758.*
*Medina, at Anchor. Savannah River Sound.*

With the wind on its beam, the convoy made short work of the reach to Savannah. They ran into the Sound late in the forenoon watch two days after the incident with the privateer and dropped their anchors in the thick mud of the river estuary. The wind had been too advantageous to waste in transfers from ship to ship, so it was only when they were safely at anchor that Carlisle sent a boat for Holbrooke and Chalmers.

The three men looked each other up and down. It was a year since they last met, a year in which much had changed for each of them.

'And they haven't posted you? Not even after Emden and Saint-Cast? I heard of your capture and exchange,' Carlisle asked after they'd swapped all the news.

'You know more about this than I do, sir,' replied Holbrooke, 'but it appears that neither Commodore Holmes nor Commodore Howe saw me as part of their family, if I can put it that way. I was an accidental addition to their commands, and neither had much chance to get to know me. When they came to share out their goodwill at the Admiralty, I passed through the sieve.'

'Hmm, and that's the way the patronage works, regrettably. I assume you weren't acting truly independently either, not sending reports directly to the Admiralty Secretary?'

'Only one or two before I came under Mister Holmes' command, not enough to establish a relationship with their Lordships.'

'Then you've been trapped between the devil and the deep blue sea. I'm sorry for it. But what is this mission you've been sent on?'

'I'm afraid this offers even less prospect for promotion, sir. I'm to join Brigadier-General Prideaux in an expedition to take Fort Niagara.'

Carlisle raised his eyebrows. He knew all about Fort Niagara; it was the vital connection between the French colonies in New France and Louisiana. It was part of Pitt's grand strategy, and the counterpart campaign to the operations on the Saint Lawrence and Lake Champlain. If the French lost Niagara, then they would have no waterborne route to the Great Lakes, and they would have to strike overland to reach their forts and settlements on the Ohio. As Quebec was the gateway to French Canada, so Niagara was the gateway to their interests in the west of the continent. Nevertheless, it was an essentially military affair, and the Admiralty would hardly notice a sea officer who distinguished himself in such a campaign.

'They need boats to pass up the Hudson River and the Mohawk, then down the Oswego to Lake Ontario. There's a precedent, although it's not very encouraging. There was a sea officer with Braddock at Monongahela in '55. Charles Spendlow. He was killed.'

Carlisle nodded silently. It was hard to find the positive in his friend's appointment, and his knowledge of the geography of that area was sketchy. He knew that there had been a fort where the Oswego River met Lake Ontario and that the French had taken it two years ago. But of the terrain – the rivers, the swamps, the mountains, and the hostile tribes – he knew almost nothing, except that it had earned its reputation as a wilderness.

'Then there's a rumour that a pair of French brigs are being built on the lake, or down the river towards Montreal. I'm to build and command the boats and give the brigadier naval advice,' Holbrooke added, suddenly feeling overwhelmed by the magnitude of the task.

Carlisle changed the subject. 'I saw Mister Lynton and Jackson and Serviteur on the deck. Are they with you?'

'Yes, and a carpenter from Plymouth Dock. There are six of us. We're to take passage in the packet as far as Hampton then make our way to New York.'

'Then you'll be my guests, I trust, at least as far as Hampton. That's where this convoy is bound after we've discharged some of the cargo here. We sail on Thursday, come hell or high water.'

'That'll gladden the heart of the master of the *Lord Halifax*,' Holbrooke smiled. 'If you can take all six of us and a few bags of mail, he has no other reason to go as far as Hampton. It's not on his normal run, so he can sail for home as soon as he's repaired his gaff and mainsail.'

'Then we'll make it so. Mister Chalmers, my people are in a desperate state of irreligion, perhaps a few of your Sunday sermons would set them back on the right path.'

Chalmers bowed and held his silence. Jests about his religious duties on a man-o'-war rarely went down well.

'Have you heard from Lady Chiara, sir?' asked Holbrooke.

'Not since I sailed from Hampton in October, but mother and child were doing well when I left. I'm hoping there may be some mail waiting for me here; it's the first place that I could decently expect news.'

Holbrooke always used Chiara's hereditary title, even though on marrying Carlisle it became merely a courtesy honorific, and a foreign one at that. He'd heard by letter about her staying in Williamsburg for the birth of their child.

'I've been lucky. After Louisbourg, it could have been the East Indies or the Channel Fleet, instead of convoy duties down to Jamaica and the islands. But I'm to pay for it now as I suspect I'll be joining the expedition to Quebec. Who knows, we may meet again somewhere on the Upper Saint Lawrence.'

'Is Lady Chiara enjoying Williamsburg?' asked Chalmers, joining the conversation for the first time.

'I believe so. She's lodging with my cousin Barbara and her husband, but in October she was talking about having our own place in the town. She appears to like it there. We'll see. It's not the most convenient place for a post-captain to set up home.'

Carlisle thought for a moment.

'But then where is? The fact is that this life, for all its advantages, takes its toll on families. If we settled in London or Portsmouth, I could be sent to the far side of the world, and not see them for months or years. On reflection, Williamsburg seems no worse than anywhere else. And I expect my time in frigates will soon be at an end. Sooner or later I'll be sent to a ship-of-the-line, a fourth-rate at least, then who knows what the future will bring?'

\*\*\*

Holbrooke was alone in the great cabin for a few blessed moments and at last he had the leisure to put his thoughts in order. He'd been lucky, he knew. His tactics to evade the privateer had failed. If *Medina* and her convoy hadn't appeared when they did, he and his people and packet would be in the hands of the privateer now. He felt a chill as he thought about it. It wasn't the fear of semi-piratical villains, nor of being held captive, he'd faced both before; it was the realisation that his gamble had almost ended in disaster. The packet's master had been good about it, but there was no doubt that for a few minutes the packet and all those aboard had been put in a dangerous position by Holbrooke's intervention. He'd thrown away any goodwill by firing into the schooner, causing casualties for all he knew. It wasn't inconceivable that the master of the privateer would have offered no quarter when he boarded, it wasn't without precedent.

Where had he gone wrong? He knew the answer; hubris leads to nemesis. He'd been guilty of over-confidence. He'd become accustomed to his gambles paying off, as they had when he'd boarded the French frigate *Vulcain* in the Mediterranean, and when he'd fought the Dutch pirates in the Caicos Passage. There was an element of luck, he knew, but he suspected that he'd pushed his luck too far.

## Rocks and Shoals

Was that how reputations and careers ended? A few fortunate engagements then one where his luck failed? Even if he'd survived being captured by the privateers and returned quickly to service, his character would have suffered. Word would soon get around that a King's officer had offered advice – no, he'd absolutely taken command – of a Falmouth packet, and it had ended badly. It was food for thought, and it piled another layer of doubt onto the misery of his ship-less state.

***

A keen wind from the nor'-nor'west blew across *Medina's* deck as the convoy butted its way up the coast. They'd left the trade winds behind the day before they'd sailed into the Savannah River and now the North American winter had them in its grip. It was only five hundred miles from Savannah to Hampton, but with this foul wind and their convoy of unweatherly merchantmen they were forced to stand well out to seaward until they could fetch Cape Henry on a single tack. For four days they'd been fighting their way northeast, four days in which the wind never backed to the west of nor'west, and more commonly came screaming down from the north or nor'east.

Carlisle, Holbrooke and Hosking, *Medina's* sailing master, were gripping the weather mizzen shrouds, trying to keep their footing on the tossing and plunging deck while cowering behind the meagre shelter of a scrap of canvas secured to the lanyards. The motion was at least predictable. As each wave approached the larboard bow, the frigate's forefoot rose to meet it. Then, just before it reached the crest, a sheet of spray burst over the fo'c'sle rail and flung itself the length of the ship, soaking everything and everybody that hadn't found shelter. The watch on deck had adapted themselves to the weather and found refuge behind gunwales and under tarpaulins. But the officer of the watch, the quartermaster and the steersmen had no such protection. They'd been discussing when they could tack to make Cape Henry and the entrance to the Chesapeake Bay.

'I've had no sight of the sun since we left Savannah,' said Hosking, 'so this is necessarily a guess, you understand.'

Holbrooke stole a glance at Carlisle. They both knew Hosking of old, and this was just one of his little ways. He was preparing his defence in case his navigation should be less than perfect.

'I've run our dead reckoning from our last sight of Tybee Island, sir. Cape Henry's sou'west-by-west fifty-six leagues, or as near as I can tell.'

'What did you allow for the stream?' asked Carlisle.

It was a crucial navigational decision. If *Medina* had been alone, then it would be easy to put in another tack if they found they couldn't weather the cape. However, with an assorted gaggle of merchant ships and brigs in company, any manoeuvre necessarily took hours, not minutes. Even then, some of them would botch it and take even longer to find their right course. It was infinitely preferable to put in just a single tack, but on the other hand, they didn't want to prolong the voyage by beating further north than they needed to.

'Two knots, which may be on the low side. In any case, if the stream's running more than two knots, we'll be to windward of the cape.'

'Then let's hang out a signal for the convoy now and call all hands to tack the ship at the change of the watch. I expect in this weather the merchantmen will wear, but we're to windward, so it hardly matters.'

Hosking turned away to talk to the officer of the watch, a master's mate by the name of David Wishart who'd sailed with Carlisle since his first command, the smaller frigate *Fury*, three years ago. Wishart was ready for his Lieutenant's examination, and Carlisle was giving him all the responsibility that he dared. Perhaps whichever Admiral was carrying an army up to Quebec would see fit to hold a local examining board; there would certainly be enough candidates.

'The last time I came north through these waters – it was

in March – you could see the boundaries of the stream as clear as a mountain torrent emptying into a broad river. There was a most pronounced colour variation, and then there was the broken water at the edge, and the seabirds, great flocks of birds diving and snapping up the sea creatures that come to the surface there.'

Carlisle looked wistful. There was no chance of seeing that transition today; there was no sunshine to bring out the colours, and the howling wind and blown spray kept the birds away. Holbrooke was aware that Carlisle had a deep fascination for birds. It wasn't a philosophical interest, more an aesthetic pleasure in watching them.

'Before we sailed for Saint-Malo, I had to test the flatboats up Fareham Creek near the tidal mill,' Holbrooke said. 'They're ungainly craft, and I was trying to think of what they resembled. Then an old grey heron flew overhead. You know the way they roll and yaw in their flight, it's just like a flatboat with a moderate lop slapping on its bows.'

He imitated the flight of a heron with the flat of his hand.

'Aye, there are herons on the James River,' Carlisle replied, looking thoughtful. 'I expect you'll have a few days before you can find a passage to New York, so you'll see them when you visit us in Williamsburg.'

Holbrooke could tell that Carlisle was ready for some time ashore with his family, his wife and baby son. They both knew how unlikely that was with a new campaigning season soon to start. The army would need a massive fleet to support it, and every ship already on the west side of the Atlantic could expect to be drawn in. It was highly likely that Carlisle would have orders waiting for him in Hampton, and he'd be lucky if he had a week at home.

\*\*\*

There was mail at Hampton, so much mail that it delayed Carlisle's departure for Williamsburg by a good two hours. Here was a letter from Chiara, the fifth in a sequence since he'd sailed, no doubt the first four would catch up with him in the next month or so. He left that until he'd read the official mail.

'This one is the most important, sir,' said Simmonds, his clerk. 'It's from Admiral Durell at Halifax.'

He passed over the letter without another word.

Carlisle read it through quickly, then again more slowly. It was as he'd expected. Here were his orders to join Durell's squadron at Halifax in preparation for an early advance up the Saint Lawrence. Just like a year ago, but then it was Alexander Colville who overwintered at Halifax. So, another spring of bitter cold as he probed through the ice and fog and the cutting winds of the Gulf of Saint Lawrence. The difference this time was that they would have to go right up the river, or at least far enough to prevent any early French relief convoys from running the gauntlet to Quebec.

Carlisle knew Philip Durell. He'd commanded the sixty-four-gun *Trident* at Minorca in '56. It was arguably his action in backing his tops'l to cover the damaged *Intrepid* that had destroyed Byng's line of battle. It led, with the inevitability of a Greek tragedy, to Byng's execution at Portsmouth a year later. At least Durell knew Nova Scotia and the Gulf of Saint Lawrence; he'd been present at both successful sieges of Louisbourg, in '45 and '58. But did he know the river upstream from the Gulf? Unlikely, Carlisle decided, and it would be a daunting prospect to bring a squadron into that frozen wasteland before the thaw.

But here was the critical part. He was to refit at Hampton and sail to pick up a convoy from New York to Halifax on the first of February. He did a quick calculation. Even given the worst luck and the most extreme winter weather, it wouldn't take more than a week to reach Sandy Hook. He could sail from Hampton on the twenty-fifth of January and have a clear six weeks with his wife and son. He had an excellent first lieutenant in Patrick Moxon, and he could leave the refitting entirely to him. This was glorious news, the best of good fortune, far beyond his expectation.

He was startled from his reverie by a knock at the door.

'Ah George, how timely.'

Holbrooke could see that Carlisle was bursting with good humour.

'I have a whole six weeks here in Hampton! Isn't that wonderful? I'm to collect a parcel of transports and merchantmen at Sandy Hook on the first of February, so I don't need to sail until the twentieth, at the earliest. It's sheer idleness for me, for six weeks!'

'My congratulations, sir. Lady Chiara will be delighted, I'm sure.'

'Yes, and the rest of this mail can be handled by Simmonds. I wash my hands of it. Call away the longboat, Mister Simmonds; I want to leave within the half-hour. Can you and Chalmers be ready in that time, Holbrooke?'

'Oh, certainly. But my news gives me a more pressing schedule. We must leave for New York before the end of December. I've sent Lynton to inquire about a passage, but I regret that I won't be able to spend as much time in Williamsburg as I had hoped.'

'Never mind, never mind, we'll have two weeks and Christmas to round it off.'

***

# CHAPTER THREE

## A Williamsburg Christmas

*Tuesday, Twelfth of December 1758.*
*Medina, at Anchor. Hampton Roads, Virginia.*

Frost lay thick on the ground, and the wheels of the coach crunched through the ice-covered puddles as it lurched into Williamsburg. The town had a glazed look to it. The roads, the roofs, the fields, the ponds, all were covered in a silvery-white encrustation. In the dead air the smoke from the chimneys rose vertically until it merged with the leaden sky. Carlisle was reminded of a calm sea with a mist lying upon it when there was no discernible horizon. It was disorientating.

'Snow before long,' said Carlisle, looking out of the window at the familiar sights. He was nervous, as all sailors are returning home, not entirely sure what they will find and bearing the indefensible guilt of separation.

'Does it last long, usually?' asked Chalmers, recognising Carlisle's need to talk.

'It can do, but it's generally gone in a few days. It's hardly likely to interfere with my visits to Hampton. I can always send for the longboat if the roads are impassable. Souter knows the way to Princess Anne's Port by now, and Enrico can remind him if he's forgotten.'

Midshipman Enrico Angelini smiled from his place in the furthest corner of the coach. He was Chiara's cousin, an ensign in the Sardinian cavalry on leave of absence to follow his cousin's husband. As a subject of King Charles Emmanuel and a catholic, he could never take a commission in King George's navy. Yet, the rank of midshipman was otherwise entirely populated by young men whose sole immediate aspiration was a lieutenant's commission. The French navy was more honest about the status. There they were called *aspirants*. Enrico, therefore, was an enigma,

## Rocks and Shoals

neither a dilettante follower nor a serious sea-officer.

Enrico had been with Carlisle back in September when they had arrived unannounced from the siege of Louisbourg just hours after the birth of the captain's son. With no carriage available, the frigate's longboat had sailed up the James River and then rowed through the gathering darkness along Archer's Hope Creek to Princess Anne's Port. Yes, Enrico knew the way as well as did Souter, the captain's coxswain.

The coach lurched past the capitol – an austere towered building behind a brick wall – and onto Duke of Gloucester Street. It was late in the afternoon, and the lamps and candles were starting to be lit in the homes and taverns and shops that lined the broad thoroughfare. The coachman drew up outside Shield's Tavern. They were expected; news of *Medina* anchoring at Hampton Roads had outpaced the coach and the landlord's boy had spotted them at the edge of the town and had run to warn the tavern. The last thing the landlord wanted was for these valuable customers to pass him by for one of the other establishments further down the road. He was at the street-side muffled into a colossal coat to greet his hoped-for guests, a rare commodity in these untravelled winter days.

'You'll call on me tomorrow?' Carlisle asked as Holbrooke stepped stiffly down. 'Mister Angelini knows the way. It's only a few steps down the street, shall we say eleven o'clock?'

An interested crowd had gathered around the tavern. The whole town knew about the famous Captain Carlisle – their very own King's sea officer – and most had heard that *Medina* had anchored at Hampton Roads that morning. Carlisle had to lose a few moments acknowledging old friends, but the coach was soon on its way to the printer's shop a hundred yards down the road. It was an unlikely lodging for a successful post-captain's wife and son, but it was owned and run by his cousin's husband and the private apartments at the back of the shop were both spacious and comfortable.

The innkeeper ushered Holbrooke, Chalmers, and Enrico into the tavern. It was an in-between time for trade, and there were few other customers. He'd finished serving dinner an hour before, and the coffee drinkers hadn't yet left their places of work to fill up the front saloon.

'I have three nice rooms looking over the street if that would suit you, sir,' the innkeeper said, looking at Holbrooke, the man with the most elaborate uniform. And I expect you'll be hungry, so I kept back some of the joint from dinner for you. Ham, and winter greens with mustard. I can serve it in your rooms or here if you prefer,' he waved an arm at the almost deserted saloon where just two men sat in a corner, talking in low voices.

Holbrooke realised that he was indeed hungry. They'd left Hampton without a thought for food along the way, and the roadside inns were all closed, or they had an out-of-season look about them. He cast a glance at Chalmers, who nodded his agreement.

'In the saloon if you please,' said Holbrooke.

They had spent too many days at sea to wish for their own company any longer than was necessary. Holbrooke took it for granted that Enrico would agree, being at that permanently starved age. He didn't spare a thought to the reality of the very, very few years between him and the midshipman. That was the effect that command had upon him; unless he stopped to think about it, he saw himself as almost a different generation to the youngsters who inhabited the cockpit.

Any ham would taste good to seafarers lately come ashore, and this was the best of Virginia ham. However, it was the greens that made the dinner, fresh vegetables that tasted of the earth from which they had so recently been plucked, and real cow's milk in their coffee. A Lucullan feast after an Atlantic passage. After a couple of glasses of wine and a baked bread pudding for dessert, they felt mellow and well-fed.

# Rocks and Shoals

\*\*\*

Enrico spent two days in Williamsburg before returning to his duties in *Medina*. Carlisle had already determined that he would leave the management of his ship to Moxon. He had no intention of making the journey back to Hampton Roads until he was ready to sail, and that would be at the last possible moment. He'd keep in touch with regular messages sent overland to the frigate, or by river if the snow blocked the roads.

Holbrooke and Chalmers had no duties of any kind and could take their leisure in Williamsburg until after Christmas. It was a delightful time, the calm before the storm as people of Virginia knew so well. Here the war was both immediate and personal. Few felt that their colony had a future if the French remained in Canada and continued to spread down the Ohio and Mississippi, and they had no illusions that the colonial militia could stand up to the French without British support. It was soon known that Carlisle was bound for Quebec and Holbrooke for Niagara, and they were the present and tangible proof that the mother country hadn't deserted her children.

\*\*\*

Carlisle woke early and slid noiselessly out of bed. The slight draught that stole in as he parted the drapes barely woke his wife whose eyelids fluttered once and then relaxed again in sleep. He crept the length of the still-sleeping house and through the printing premises at the front to get a view of the street. As he'd expected, the bright winter sun hadn't yet risen far enough to melt the last of the slushy snow on the sidewalks, and glistening puddles of water surrounded the remaining patches.

'I'll tell the coachman that he's required, sir,' said the deep, soft voice from behind him. Carlisle hadn't noticed the silent approach of Black Rod, Chiara's servant. It would be a good half an hour's walk in the cold for the tall, austere Sardinian, but he would likely avoid that by finding a boy on the street who would run the errand for a penny.

Carlisle nodded. 'Let him know the necessity of being on time; it won't do to be late at the church on Christmas day.'

Black Rod was another enigma. He was the chief of the household staff for the Angelini family, ordinarily resident in Nice. However, he'd accompanied Lady Chiara when she'd announced her decision to follow Carlisle across the length of the Mediterranean and the Atlantic to faraway Antigua. When they married in Saint John's, the capital of the island, Carlisle had assumed that Black Rod would return to Sardinia, but it appeared that his secondment from the family home was more-or-less permanent. But the real mystery was his name. If Chiara knew it, she wasn't saying, and he'd never volunteered the information. When they'd first met, the officers of Carlisle's old frigate *Fury* had given him the nickname of Black Rod, after the Gentleman Usher of the House of Lords, such was his bearing and demeanour. That nickname had stuck.

Carlisle still had his reservations about Black Rod. He suspected – no, he was sure – that the Sardinian knew more than he cared to admit about the Tunisian merchant who claimed to be Chiara's godfather. Hassan Ben Yunis had been cleared of the charges of piracy, but Carlisle just wasn't sure, and it coloured his relationship with the imposing Sardinian servant. Nevertheless, Black Rod had repeatedly proved his loyalty to his mistress. In that narrow respect, Carlisle trusted him.

'I believe Lady Chiara would prefer the carriage,' said Carlisle with a wry smile. Chiara's refusal to walk to important social events was well known.

'I do not doubt it, sir,'

Black Rod's English had always been adequate, but constant practice had perfected his grammar and vocabulary, and his accent had vastly improved. He and Chiara spoke mostly Italian when nobody else was in the room, but otherwise he had perforce to become proficient in English.

Carlisle retraced his steps to the rooms at the back of the

house that he shared with his wife. They'd arrived at Williamsburg nine months before with Chiara coming to the end of the first trimester of her pregnancy. They'd intended to stay only a few days while the merchantmen that Carlisle was convoying discharged their cargoes at Hampton. However, Chiara had fainted during a reception at the governor's palace and under a barrage of medical advice had conceded that she should stay in Williamsburg for the birth. Carlisle's cousin, Barbara, had offered her these comfortable – almost elegant – rooms in her family home that doubled as a printing and bookselling business. Here she had stayed while Carlisle had sailed north for the siege of Louisbourg and then south to the West Indies on convoy duty.

Not for the first time, Carlisle wondered at his wife's motivations; he still had no idea of how she saw her life developing. In fact, he really had no idea why she had married him when she had unlimited suitors throughout the Italian states. He'd always been nervous that she'd want to return to Sardinia and make the Carlisle family home there, an almost impossible arrangement for an officer in King George's navy. London would be a more practical base in every way, but she showed little interest in even visiting that great city. Yet – and he still wondered at it – she appeared to be happy here in the capital city of the English colony of Virginia. Did she see this as the future of the Carlisle family?

He had always assumed that he would never settle in Virginia. One of the few biblical passages that he retained from his youth put it succinctly: *A prophet is not without honour, but in his own country, and among his own kin, and in his own house.* But now, he wasn't so sure. When he walked in the street, folk hailed him as a man of substance, and it was clear that his contemporaries looked upon him as one who would take his place in Virginian society, a man to be watched and courted. He could be a big fish in this relatively small pond, while in London he would struggle to raise enough support for even a seat in the House. He was reluctant to raise the subject with Chiara for fear of breaking this pleasant truce.

\*\*\*

'Does this dress look well?' asked Chiara regarding herself critically in the looking-glass. She turned from side to side, rotating her neck at that impossible angle that women accomplish when wishing to see themselves from all aspects. This was her first outing without her baby. It was like a debut into society, and she wanted to be sure that she looked her best.

'It looks perfect, dear,' Carlisle replied, touching his wife's waist affectionately. In truth, she hadn't completely regained her before-pregnancy figure. However, Carlisle knew that there was nothing to be gained in telling her so, and much to be lost. In any case, she would still turn heads in this or any other town.

'Will the carriage be here in time?' she asked, taking one more look over her shoulder. 'It wouldn't look well to be late for the Christmas service, and I dread that the box pew may be taken if we're not there on time.'

'Never fear, my dear…'

Carlisle paused, a look of mischievous delight spreading over his face.

'Ha! It rhymes, did you hear it? Never fear…'

Chiara gave him an affectionate yet pitying look, much as she would have given to a small boy stumbling over his reading.

'Well, never mind. George and David and Enrico will certainly be there on time, and they'll hold the pew for us,' he continued, still smiling foolishly.

'It's good of Mister Wythe to offer his pew while he is away. Elizabeth and I are great friends, you know. I believe she feels some sympathy for me with her own maiden name.'

Carlisle looked blankly at his wife. He'd known George Wythe most of his life, they were only a year apart in age and they were both raised in the vicinity. However, he'd been absent from Williamsburg since he was fourteen and hadn't kept up with the news.

'Before they married, her name was Taliaferro. I believe, incidentally, that the letter *g* should be in the name.'

She spelt out *Tagliaferro*, letter by letter.

'The name is quite obviously from Tuscany, she's practically a kinswoman. Yet the family has been here for generations; they've become important planters, I understand.'

'I don't believe I know them,' Carlisle replied. And yet he was surprised. He thought he knew all the old planter families.

Chiara laughed and patted her husband's arm affectionately.

'Does the name *Tolliver* mean anything to you?' she asked, pronouncing it in her best newly-acquired Virginian accent.

'Yes, certainly, I've known the family for…'

Light dawned upon Carlisle.

'You English! How you mutilate good Italian names. Somehow you can misspell *Tagliaferro* and then pronounce it as *Tolliver* without the slightest hint of shame. After a decade it becomes accepted, and after two the original spelling and pronunciation are lost forever. I shall make a point of saying it correctly – and spelling it in the Italian manner – whenever I have the opportunity.'

Carlisle was sure that she would. He was also confident that her natural grace and charm would allow her to get away with it.

\*\*\*

The coachman arrived fifteen minutes early. He used the time polishing away the mud that the coach had accumulated over the half-mile or so from the livery stables where he, the coach, and the horses were lodged. He shook his head in wonderment that anyone would need a coach to travel a mere four hundred yards down the main street. Nothing of the sort would happen in his more rustic home of Hampton, but then this was the colonial capital, and they did things differently here. Nevertheless, he was happy for the employment and didn't at all mind a month away from a perpetually harassed wife, an overbearing mother-in-law and a clutch of wailing children. After all, he was being paid for the hire of his coach with his lodgings and victuals thrown in. In the depths of winter, when he was usually idle, that was no trivial matter.

The parish church in Williamsburg was full. Each prominent family and the more prosperous traders had their private stalls, and the students from the College of William and Mary had their own gallery. The common people packed into whatever space was left.

The Wythe family pew was a spacious affair in the north transept, yet it struggled to take the eight adults who rapidly filled it. Elizabeth Wythe was already ensconced with her feet on the wooden cricket over the box of hot coals. She, at least, was warm. Holbrooke, Chalmers and Enrico had made their introductions and being unaware of the local customs had not provided themselves with any heating arrangements. Carlisle and Chiara arrived with Cranmer and Barbara Dexter with still ten minutes to spare. Black Rod ceremoniously led them to the pew and installed the coal boxes and crickets as though he'd been doing it all his life.

Elizabeth Wythe was alarmingly young. She couldn't be yet twenty, Carlisle thought as Chiara introduced her. She was short and slim with a pretty, youthful, yet in no way beautiful face. She was enjoying this outing without her husband or servants, and although she couldn't hide her shyness, she greeted these unfamiliar faces with grace.

The introductions were cut short by the arrival of the lieutenant governor. Apparently, it was the local custom for the whole congregation to rise when he made his entrance. Carlisle may have been the senior King's officer present, but he was eclipsed entirely by the monarch's personal representative in the colony, and Francis Fauquier was aware of the dignity of his position.

The liturgy of the Church of England was not over-long,

and the rector's sermon recognized the fact that these good people had dinners waiting for them. They filed out in order of seniority, rather like a gaggle of captains leaving a flagship. Fauquier paused as he passed Carlisle.

'A word perhaps, Captain Carlisle, before your duties take you away from us. Would Thursday be convenient? Very well, shall we say eleven o'clock?'

Carlisle felt that every eye was upon him. There were men there who would sell their souls for a private meeting with the lieutenant-governor, and Fauquier had a loud voice. As Carlisle left the church with his beautiful wife on his arm, he felt for the first time like a man of consequence and honour in his hometown.

\*\*\*

The evening had drawn in, the lit candles glowed in their pewter holders, and the outside world was silent. The Dexter family and their guests were playing whist and talking quietly, wondering who would be the first to announce their retirement for the night, for it was already late, and half their number had to walk back to the tavern.

'Where is Mister Chalmers,' asked Chiara, 'I was hoping he would give us his blessing before we bid each other goodnight.'

'He's probably taking his evening constitutional, dear,' Carlisle replied.

Then, as if in the script of a play, the door to the printing rooms opened and Chalmers appeared. Enter stage left with sparkling eyes and an excited smile, which wasn't at all typical for that most composed of men. He swept his gaze across the room and saw that everyone was looking at him.

'Lady Chiara, Mrs Dexter, my apologies for intruding.'

He paused for effect.

'It's a day late, yet still within the feast of the nativity,' he said mysteriously. 'I have a phenomenon to show you that you would regret missing. Do come outside. No not into the street, there are too many candles in the windows. Follow me to the back of the house if you please. The ladies will need shawls; it's bitterly cold out there.'

Chalmers was unusually mysterious, but his manner was so sincere that they all dutifully followed him into the chill air of the back yard, wondering what could have caught his attention. It was a still night, and the wind had dropped to a whisper. The sailors in the company knew that the moon wouldn't rise until sometime in the middle watch, a few hours away. The constellations were clearly visible, and the milky way was a blaze of light arching across the sky.

Chalmers led them over to the pump at the centre of the yard.

'Now look up there,' he said, pointing, 'just to the right of the dovecote, perhaps a hand's breadth above the weathercock.'

The sailors were used to the night sky, the stars in their fixed relations to each other and the planets in their ordered rotations, but tonight there was something not quite right. There was a new light in the sky. It wasn't in the right place for any of the planets, and it was too bright to be a star. And its illumination was diffused, it had an almost opaque look to it.

'*Where is he that is born King of the Jews? For we have seen his star in the east and are come to worship him.*'

Chalmers quoted from Matthew's gospel as he gazed at the light in wonder. His reason told him that there must be a philosophical explanation for this phenomenon. Nevertheless, on this of all days…

They stood together, gazing at the sky, trying to make sense of what they saw.

'Then Edmond Halley was correct,' said Holbrooke, breaking the spell. 'That's the return of the comet that he predicted.'

Carlisle looked sideways at him; he'd forgotten about the famous comet.

'That's the same as was seen last in 1682, and roughly every seventy-five years before that,' Holbrooke added still staring earnestly into the sky. 'He corrected for its near pass to Jupiter and today is quite close to his estimate. It's said to be a harbinger of the fall of dominions.'

'Yes, I remember now that you mention it,' said Carlisle. 'It was seen in 1066 when Duke William defeated Harold. What a triumph for Mister Halley to predict its return, and he cold in his grave these many years.'

'An omen for the year to come, perhaps,' said Cranmer, 'the fall of France in the New World.'

'I do believe, Mister Cranmer, that you might open one of those special bottles you've been hoarding,' said Barbara hugging her shawl around her shoulders. 'You have a dozen, enough to toast this comet and still have sufficient remaining to raise a glass to these gentlemen's victories when they return. Don't hold back now. If Mister Holbrooke is correct, then none of us except young Joshua Carlisle will see this emissary from the gods again. Let's go back indoors; the chill is seeping into me.'

With last lingering looks, they returned to the warmth of Dexter's parlour and the wonderfully smooth Madeira that he'd been hoarding. All of them raised a glass, all except Chalmers who kept his lonely, cold vigil beside the pump, thinking his thoughts and praying his prayers.

***

# CHAPTER FOUR

## A Man of Consequence

*Thursday, Twenty-Eighth of December 1758.*
*The Governor's Palace, Williamsburg.*

Chiara stamped her foot. 'You cannot seriously intend to walk…' her fingers made little airborne trotting motions in mockery, '…to walk, to the governor's palace! Edward, I believe you are teasing me.'

'I fail to see why you should be concerned, my dear,' he replied as he struggled to smooth his stock, 'after all I'll be alone, and the walk will do me good.'

'Look out of the window if you please. What do you see? Please tell me.'

Carlisle knew very well that a good inch of dirty-looking slush covered the road and the sidewalks. He had a carriage at his disposal, and it would be sensible to use it. Nevertheless, having made his decision – however unwisely – he was determined to stick to it. He could wear protectors for his shoes, and he was sure that the palace servants were quite used to dealing with damp visitors at this time of year. It was time that he stood up against domestic tyranny.

'The road looks perfectly reasonable for this time of year,' he said, trying to sound convincing.

Chiara strode over to him. She could look frightfully tall when she was in this mood, and she forcibly turned him around so that she could get at his stock and neckcloth. With deft fingers, she twisted and twitched him into sartorial perfection. Carlisle was touched, even though there was little affection in her brusque movements. He could hear the normal sounds of the street muted by the slushy snow, the jangle of wheels and harness as some vehicle, perhaps a cart bringing supplies for one of the inns, rattled down the side road and turned onto Duke of Gloucester Street.

## Rocks and Shoals

'There, now at least you will look like a gentleman, a man of consequence, from your knees upwards. You will not entirely disgrace me. However, if you persist in this mad notion that you should walk to the palace – really, Edward, one does not walk to the governor's palace even on a bright summer day – then I can do nothing for your shoes and stockings, they will look like they belong to the boy who empties the night-soil. La! Let it be so.'

The strength of Chiara's feeling showed in her reference to the vulgar aspects of family life. Under normal circumstances, her breeding wouldn't allow her even obliquely to refer to such an item as night-soil.

She was right, of course, and Carlisle had known it from the first moment that he'd declared his intention to walk, but he was unable to find a way of backing down. Perhaps he'd been too long in command of King's ships and had become accustomed to having his way. He looked at his watch, fifteen minutes to eleven.

'Well, it's too late to call the coach now,' he said.

To Carlisle's surprise, Chiara offered her cheek for a kiss. Usually, when she had lost an argument, she was cold and aloof for an hour or so. Carlisle hated that. It wasn't worth winning to be subjected to his wife's cold shoulder.

He walked down the stairs and through the print shop. Black Rod was holding the door open for him, and that was a little unusual. Then he saw why. He should have recognised the sounds of the traffic, and he should have been suspicious when Chiara hauled him away from the window. For there, outside the front door of Dexter's Print Shop, stood his own carriage with the driver standing at what he imagined might be the attention position. Chiara had sent Black Rod to the livery stable in defiance of his wishes. A dark look crossed his face, then the sun peeped from behind a grey cloud and cast its healing light upon him. He saw the absurdity of his position and laughed, and behind him, he heard the delicate answering laughter of his wife.

***

'You know, Carlisle,' said Francis Fauquier as he nursed his coffee, 'when this war is over, when we've thrown the French off the continent, Virginia will have a great future, a great future indeed.'

He placed his cup on the polished wooden side-table and walked over to the back wall of the library. Every other wall was covered in shelves and loaded down with books, but the north wall was reserved for maps, and half a dozen were on their rollers ready to be displayed. He chose the widest, and with an implement that looked like a small boathook, he pulled it down and secured the lower part on a brass bracket set into the dado rail. Carlisle stifled a smile when he saw a servant unobtrusively replacing the lieutenant-governors coffee cup on a cloth coaster.

'This is what I mean, Carlisle. The first Virginia Charter only imagined a colony along a narrow coastal strip, but the second gave the colony the rights *up into the land throughout from sea to sea*. Those are the actual words, *from sea to sea*.'

Carlisle knew that very well; it was as common knowledge to a Virginia schoolboy as the Glorious Revolution of 1688 was to his English counterparts. Still he said nothing, just nodded his head.

'Now, we've lost much of the original coastal strip to the Carolinas, Maryland and Delaware. Virginia is smaller north-to-south, but we still retain that *sea to sea* clause, and it will become particularly important when the French no longer control the Ohio Valley. Nobody knows what lies in the interior of this enormous continent, but it gives us room to grow. As the century moves forward, and old Europe becomes more crowded, that will become a valuable commodity.'

Carlisle studied the map. It was a magnificent example of imperial optimism, drawn up by a clerk in a dusty office with no concept of the immense spaces involved. Somewhere beyond the Ohio Valley lay the great Mississippi that drained into the Gulf of Mexico, and beyond that, there was a vast land, untouched by Europeans, that stretched to the Pacific Ocean. One could calculate the distances from the known longitude of each coast, but the nature of the country was a mystery. Whether it was suitable for settlement had yet to be determined. In any case, it was already populated by native Indians, even if they had little use for the European sense of land ownership.

'The fact is, Carlisle, that Virginia won't forever be held in such a tight embrace by the mother country. Oh, we'll always be an English colony,' he said, raising his hand to forestall Carlisle's instinctive objection, 'but you can already sense the desire for more autonomy. For example, I can see the taxation situation changing so that the people of this colony have a say in how they contribute to governance.'

If it wasn't the lieutenant-governor speaking, then this would almost be seditious talk. If he'd heard it in a tavern, as a King's officer, Carlisle would have felt obliged to distance himself.

'After the war,' Fauquier continued, 'the colony will need good men to represent it. My question to you, Carlisle, is this; will you be one of them?'

Fauquier stood dramatically with the grand and hopeful map of greater Virginia behind him, watching Carlisle as he struggled for an answer. Carlisle remembered the entry describing Virginia in *Diderot's Encyclopedia* that he'd read in the Angelini house in Nice.

> *The theorizers of this century made lots of objections against these distant settlements and predicted that, after having drained their mother country of inhabitants, sooner or later they would be seen to shake off the yoke in order to form an independent state in America.*

He hoped not, but he too felt the first stirrings of a wind of change that he was sure would only grow stronger when the French threat was no more. He cared deeply about Virginia, even though he wasn't sure that he wanted to live there. Perhaps there was a role for him; as a moderating voice in the colony, a conservative with a broad experience of the world who could articulate the benefits of being part of the growing British Empire.

'It's an interesting question, sir,' Carlisle replied, thoughtfully. 'However, for now I'm a King's officer, and the war goes on, probably for many more years. I haven't yet given a thought to my position when it's over.'

'Then you should think about it. I'll need all the loyal Virginia-born men I can get, King's men who support the relationship with the crown and parliament. Your stock is high in Williamsburg and – you'll excuse my frankness – you can hardly be known at all in London. And if I understand matters correctly, Lady Chiara enjoys our city. We married men must take that into account, mustn't we?'

\*\*\*

# CHAPTER FIVE
## Halifax

*Monday, Thirtieth of April 1759.*
*Medina, at Anchor. Halifax.*

Captain Carlisle was in a foul mood. He'd been hurried away from his wife and child in Williamsburg in January to take part in the blockade of the Saint Lawrence River, yet he'd spent most of those three months swinging around his anchor at Halifax. His only useful contribution had been to sail as far as Louisbourg to carry dispatches and to check on the extent of the ice. He stared hard at *Princess Amelia*, the eighty-gun third-rate flying Rear Admiral Philip Durell's flag. If looks could kill.

'I'll be in the cabin,' he growled at the master's mate who had the anchor watch. 'Pass the word for Mister Moxon,' and he stamped his way below into the relative warmth of his quarters.

Moxon had learned much about his captain in the past year. For example, he knew that he detested slovenliness in his officers' dress and personal appearance. That's why he shaved every morning, come howling gales or summer zephyrs, and that's why he took a few minutes to brush down his coat before knocking on the cabin door. He didn't look at all like a man who'd been taking a late forenoon nap only minutes before.

'Come!' shouted Carlisle.

'Ah, Mister Moxon. Take a seat, please.'

Already Carlisle's mood was improving for the better. He liked his first lieutenant, and he still felt lingering guilt at the way he'd treated Moxon in his first few months in the frigate. The problem had been the age-old one of comparing the new man with his predecessor, and Carlisle hadn't made enough allowance for that.

'Did you receive any letters?' Carlisle asked pleasantly.

He knew his first lieutenant's situation well.

'None, sir. My uncle appears to have forgotten me. He could have died for all I know. I'm in the unusual situation of having nobody in the world outside this ship. However, I'm used to it,' he said with a shrug.

Carlisle nodded. They'd discussed this before, and there was no point in hiding Moxon's difficult situation. There was a modest inheritance from his father, but it was held in trust by an uncle who was lying low, presumably hoping that his nephew never returned from the Americas. Other than that, he relied entirely upon his pay, although that wasn't unusual for sea-officers. No, the problem was that he had nobody to speak for him in England. Nobody to lobby for a promotion at the Admiralty, nobody to plead for a ship when his time in *Medina* was over, and nobody to wrangle with the lawyers over an inheritance. Only Carlisle could influence his fate, and both men knew it well.

'I'm sorry to hear that,' he said. 'Have you thought of writing to the local magistrate?'

'I think it's coming to that point, sir, although I'm at a loss for a name and address.'

'This has gone on long enough. With your permission, I'll have my agent investigate the matter. At your leisure, tell Simmonds all that you know and have him draft a letter to Hawkins & Hammond.'

'Yes, sir, thank you.'

Over long years of disappointments, Moxon had cultivated a strangely impassive face, but now he smiled at the thought that his captain was taking up this fight for him.

'However, that's not what I called you here for, Mister Moxon.'

Carlisle looked a little uncomfortable, as though he was about to raise a discreditable topic.

'A month ago, you started to tell me something you'd picked up ashore about the admiral's orders, but I cut you off.'

'Yes. sir,' Moxon's face betrayed nothing of his feelings.

## Rocks and Shoals

'Well, like your problem with your uncle, this hanging around in Halifax is now at the point where I must take some unpleasant measures to understand the situation. I stopped you before because I had notions that it was rather dishonourable for a captain to be told his superior's orders in that way, but now I feel I must know. Are you prepared to give me a second chance?'

'Of course, sir. Perhaps I should start at the beginning?'

Carlisle nodded and leaned forward eagerly. The past three months had come close to destroying his soul, and the letter he'd received that morning from Chiara, with its talk of the spring in Virginia and the growing intelligence and strength of their child, had sealed his resolve.

'Well, there's a sort of informal meeting of lieutenants once or twice a week in the tavern, and I often speak to one of the flagship's officers. You'll excuse me, sir, if I don't tell you his name.'

Carlisle nodded.

'He berths with the admiral's secretary, things being so tight onboard, and naturally, they talk. It appears that the secretary is – how can I put this? – he's surprised at the admiral's interpretation of his orders.'

Carlisle shifted uncomfortably. There was no reason that he should expect Philip Durell to have told a frigate captain the content of his orders; they were a private matter between their Lordships and the admiral. And yet it appeared to be common knowledge among the lieutenants. They were sailing in dangerous waters now.

'The orders, as far as I understand, are for the squadron to patrol in the Gulf of Saint Lawrence, covering both the Straits of Belle-Isle and the southerly route, in advance of the thaw.'

'Then we should have been at sea two months ago?' asked Carlisle.

Moxon didn't answer, and Carlisle made a gesture indicating that he didn't expect a response. It was one thing to discuss an admiral's secret orders, but quite another for two King's officers to pass comment on the implementation of those orders. Byng's trial and execution were still fresh in everyone's mind.

'Apparently Mister Anson's particular concern is to prevent any French supply ships making the passage up to Quebec before Admiral Saunders arrives with the main force.'

'Just as I would have expected,' said Carlisle, almost to himself.

'Then as soon as practicable, the squadron is to sail up the river to the point where it narrows enough to establish a blockade. The orders mention the Isle of Bic.'

Carlisle had studied the charts; the Isle of Bic lay some hundred and thirty miles below Quebec and a little over five hundred miles upstream from Louisbourg. It was a good position for a blockade. The channel at Bic was less than five leagues wide and could be covered by two men-o'-war in fine weather and no more than five in thick. Durell's squadron could certainly stop any French reinforcements passing that point if they could get there as soon as the river was navigable, and before the French made their ascent. The plan appeared sound, but what the hell were they doing loitering in Halifax? True, the passage up to Bic was probably only now clearing of ice, but if the French were in the Gulf already, they would steal a march and get the all-important provisions up to the city. The Gulf of Saint Lawrence was broad, and it offered plenty of opportunities for a supply fleet to keep out of sight while waiting for the thaw.

'There's one more thing, sir,' Moxon continued. 'There are supplementary orders for the squadron to survey as far as the Great Traverse, and beyond if it can be achieved. The general opinion is that Admiral Saunders wishes to take the battle fleet all the way up to Quebec.'

Now that was interesting, Carlisle thought. The French had never taken ships-of-the-line up to Quebec. In Queen Anne's War, a disastrous British expedition had lost eight ships and over a thousand men in the Gulf of the Saint Lawrence. He'd assumed that only the frigates and transports would make that dangerous passage and leave the battle fleet in the Gulf, with perhaps a squadron off Bic.

'That's all I learned, sir. Those who know or guess at the orders are all surprised that we haven't sailed yet.'

As well they may be, Carlisle mused. Durell had overwintered in Halifax, just as Colville had the previous year, explicitly so that he could be on hand when the ice broke. He had ten ships-of-the-line and some frigates, and they were all ready for sea. Halifax was still not a regular navy yard, but its facilities had improved immeasurably over the summer and autumn of '58 and Durell's problems of maintenance and supply had been far less than those that Colville had faced.

'Thank you, Mister Moxon. It's perhaps better if we keep this conversation between ourselves.'

\*\*\*

Carlisle called for coffee while he turned over in his mind what he'd learned. Yes, the admiral had kept a frigate in the Gulf since January; *Medina* had taken her turn along with the others. But that wasn't what their Lordships had ordered him to do. A single frigate patrolling between North Cape and Cape Ray could carry the news of the thawing ice and could give warning of a French squadron if it came from the south. However, no single ship could cover both the southern passage and the Straits of Belle-Isle. The southern passage was fifty miles wide, and although the northern was less than ten miles across, it issued into the Gulf many, many miles to the north. Blocking the way into the Gulf of Saint Lawrence was a job for squadron, not a single frigate. Even if the watching frigate should sight the French, it was three hundred miles back to Halifax, and if the wind blew from anywhere between sou'east and west, it could take days to get the message back to the admiral. It was inexplicable, and Carlisle had to force himself to banish the words *dereliction of duty* to the furthest recess of his mind.

His gloomy thoughts were interrupted by a knock on the door. His standing orders were that messages from the officer of the watch should not wait on ceremonial, and the door was opened immediately after the knock.

'Mister Wishart's compliments, sir, and he says there's a longboat rounding George's Island. It looks like a third-rate's boat, he said, and it's flying three flags for pilots.'

The midshipman was new, a King's Letter boy who'd joined a week ago. He'd been foisted on them by the admiral, and he hadn't yet been to sea in a frigate.

'Very well. Tell Mister Wishart that he's to send a lookout to the masthead to watch the passage…'

'He's already done that, sir,' the boy interrupted, 'Able Seaman Whittle'.

'… and inform him that I'll come on deck.'

Carlisle gave the midshipman a withering look. A simple, *aye-aye sir*, would have sufficed. His response bordered on being glib. He'd have to ask Moxon to correct his attitude; it was no job for a post-captain.

\*\*\*

*Medina* had anchored at the northeast side of the harbour, the furthest from the town and the yard. It was an inconvenient berth, but it gave the best view of anything coming up the difficult channel into Halifax. The wind was keen on the quarterdeck, chilly but refreshing, and a pale spring sun showed fleetingly through the hurrying clouds.

'Whittle thinks he can see a third-rate's tops'ls now, sir,' said Wishart, 'just to the right of Cornwallis Island, but still far out in the offing.'

If Whittle thought he could see tops'ls, then that was good enough for Carlisle. Able Seaman Whittle had been raised on the Carlisle family plantation and, not caring for a rural life, had gone to sea to follow the fortunes of the plantation owner's younger son. He'd made a name for himself as a superb lookout, a man who could identify a ship from a glimpse of her main t'gallant masthead truck. This third-rate was either Saunders' squadron of ships-of-the-line

# Rocks and Shoals

or Holmes with the troop transports from New York. In either case, Durell's chickens were about to come home to roost.

\*\*\*

It was Saunders with eight of the line, three bomb vessels and some supply ships carrying ammunition. He had headed for the rendezvous at Louisbourg but found the harbour still beset by ice. With no sign of Durell's squadron, which should be patrolling the Gulf by now, Saunders sailed to Halifax to meet Admiral Holmes and the troop transports from New York. *Neptune's* bowsprit had hardly come into view when two signal flags soared up her foreyard.

'Flagship's signalling for Admiral Durell to report aboard, sir,' Wishart reported.

Carlisle made no acknowledgement. If there were any truth in Moxon's story about Durell's orders, then it would be a sticky half-hour for the rear admiral. It was quite dangerous enough to discuss the admiral's orders with his first lieutenant privately; it was a step too far to engage in any kind of discussion on the quarterdeck. And yet there certainly was discussion. It appeared that Moxon wasn't the only one of his officers who had heard rumours.

Moxon caught Carlisle's eye.

'Mister Wishart,' Moxon said firmly, 'I'll thank you for attending to your business and not indulge in idle chatter on deck. Your duty can be performed from the masthead if that's what you would prefer.'

The chatter died down as the inhabitants of the quarterdeck each found urgent business that needed their attention. Wishart adopted a rigid attitude, staring hard at the two flagships, determined to be the first to report any movement or new signals.

'Admiral's barge putting off from *Princess Amelia*,' said Wishart, removing his hat to report to Carlisle, 'heading towards *Neptune*.'

Carlisle could see that for himself. *Neptune* was still moving slowly towards her anchor berth, and she wouldn't yet have rigged her entry port. Nevertheless, Durell was putting himself to the inconvenience of waiting off her quarter until the flagship hailed his barge alongside. A guilty conscience would goad even a rear admiral of the red to cast his dignity aside.

It took all the rest of the day for the three Halifax pilots to bring in Admiral Saunders' squadron. Long before they had filled up the harbour, Durell's barge was speeding back to *Princess Amelia*. Wishart had been at sea long enough to anticipate the next signal.

He wasn't the only one. Carlisle had changed into his best frock coat and sword, while Souter had mustered the captain's boat crew in the waist. The longboat had been hauled alongside, and the watch on deck was urgently scrubbing it. The boat's crew watched from the waist, keeping their best clothes clean for what they all knew was an important call on the admiral commanding their division.

'*Princess Amelia's* signalling for all captains,' he said.

With a nod from Souter, the boat's crew scrambled down the side.

'Mister Moxon. In my absence, prepare to weigh anchor and to tow out of the harbour. It may not be necessary, but if it is, there'll be not a moment to lose.'

The bosun's mates were already in position, their pipes in their hands, and to the long, solemn triple tone of their calls, Carlisle climbed the short distance down into the boat.

\*\*\*

Philip Durell was trying hard to avoid looking like a man who had just had an unpleasant interview. He almost succeeded, but it was the nervous fluttering of the hands and the twitch at the side of his mouth that gave him away.

'...and so, gentlemen, you are all to hasten your preparations for sea. A battalion of soldiers will be distributed among the ships-of-the-line, one company each to supplement your crews and to provide a landing force. *Princess Amelia* will carry the headquarters element in addition to her quota of soldiers. I want no tardiness,' he said, as though his captains had not all been anxious to get to sea these last two months. 'We'll sail as soon as you've all completed your stores and I expect that to be tomorrow, no later. You may return to your ships. Captain Carlisle, I need to speak to you separately.'

In the background Carlisle heard the pipes as the captains left the flagship. He thought he knew what was coming next.

'Take a seat, Captain,' said Durell. He still looked nervous. 'How soon can you get *Medina* to sea?'

'I'm stored for three months, sir, and my wood and water are complete. I can weigh immediately but with this wind,' he glanced out of the stern windows, 'I'll need to tow out of the harbour, and there are only four hours of light left.'

'That's what concerns me. If this wind persists, my ships-of-the-line can't get out, but you can. I need you to sail immediately, Captain.'

'May I suggest, sir, that you hang out a signal for a pilot for *Medina* and for her to weigh anchor and proceed to sea? My first lieutenant will know what's afoot and all my people are on board.'

'Then you expected these orders?' asked Durell, suspiciously.

Carlisle prevaricated; it was best to conceal the fact that he had a good idea of his admiral's secret orders.

'I thought it wise to be prepared for any eventuality, sir,' he replied and hurried on, 'and If I may borrow your longboat, I'll be clear at sea an hour earlier.'

'Very well,' Durell replied, eyeing Carlisle sharply. He gestured to his flag lieutenant who hurried away to give the orders.

'Now, here is what I want you to do...'

\*\*\*

# CHAPTER SIX

## Prizes in the Ice

*Monday, Seventh of May 1759.*
*Medina, at Sea. Cape Gaspé southwest 7 leagues.*

The southerly wind made for heavy work in towing *Medina* down the channel, but it blew from the perfect quarter to make a fast passage to the Gulf of Saint Lawrence. It had been a hard winter in Nova Scotia; a hard winter and a long one and only now a belated spring had starting to break up the ice. As *Medina* ran past Louisbourg Carlisle could see that the harbour was still encumbered, although it was evident that the next few days would see it clear. The Gulf, however, was free of ice, with just the coasts still cluttered with floes that fragmented a little more with each tide. Carlisle had expected that the passage between Anticosti Island and Cape Gaspé, the point at which the river met the Gulf, would be blocked, but even here there was a clear passage. He came on deck as the faintest loom of the rising sun started to illuminate the water. A mist was lying over the sea, not thick enough to be called fog but dense enough to reduce the visibility to perhaps a mile.

'Good morning, sir,' said Hosking, touching his hat. It was clear that the master had been on deck for some time already.

'Good morning, Mister Hosking, where are we?' he asked, looking around at the featureless blanket of grey-white.

'Cape Gaspé is seven leagues to windward,' he replied, waving his arm to larboard, 'and Point Southwest on the big island is about the same to leeward. The wind's steady from the south-southwest, and we can see about a mile, although I expect the sun to burn that mist away as soon as it's a hand's breadth above the horizon.'

'What's the sounding here?' he asked, looking at the

traverse board and seeing no evidence that the lead-line had been used.

'It's reputed to be around five hundred fathoms, sir.'

Carlisle nodded. Even their longest deep-sea lead only plumbed two hundred fathoms.

'What about this wind?'

Hosking moved his head in a peculiar motion, four points either side of the tops'l breeze that came over the larboard quarter.

'It's here for the rest of the day for sure, sir.'

There was no point in asking Hosking how he'd come to that conclusion; he probably didn't know himself. It was just a feeling bred of decades at sea. Carlisle had always suspected a measure of bluff in the master's forecasts. He noticed that he rarely gave an opinion when the weather looked changeable.

'Then Mister Durell is probably still in Halifax,' he replied.

'Aye, they won't have towed those damned great two-deckers down the channel in this.'

A scraping and bumping sound prompted Carlisle to look over the side. There was ice there still, broken pieces of the solid river ice that had locked Canada in its frigid grip since December. It would pay to be cautious as they made their way upstream. But the shameful truth was starting to dawn; there was nothing to have prevented the French from getting a supply convoy up to Quebec in the past few weeks, and the full extent of Durell's folly was exposed. He exchanged a knowing glance with Moxon.

'Sail ho! Sail right ahead. The masthead is just showing above the mist.'

'What's her heading, Whittle?' shouted Carlisle.

'I can't quite see, sir,' came the reply, 'All I can see are two bare mastheads.'

'Quarters, Mister Moxon, clear for action. No drums, no pipes. She may not have seen us.'

The boys were sent at the rush to rouse the watch below,

and the sounds of hurrying feet and stifled orders filled the frigate.

'I can see her better now, sir, she's on the opposite tack. She looks like a brig under tops'ls. Now she's wearing, sir.'

Ah, she's seen us, thought Carlisle, she's turning to run back upstream.

'What's the tide doing, Master?'

'Ebbing, sir, a good four knots.'

Then they would be barely making two knots over the ground.

'T'gallants, Mister Hosking.'

'I can see her now, sir,' said Wishart, 'a point on the starboard bow. She's a brig all right and no man o' war.'

'I want that brig, Mister Moxon, and I want her intact. Put a shot across her bows when we're close enough, but don't you harm a plank of her.'

\*\*\*

The brig had the advantage of knowing these waters, but in the end, it was no contest at all. She was heavily loaded, and in any case, she wasn't built for speed; she had no answer to *Medina's* weatherliness and pace. By four bells in the forenoon watch, she was lying meekly under *Medina's* guns without damage to person or property. When Moxon brought the brig's master back to *Medina*, Carlisle heard that he was three days out of Quebec and bound for La Rochelle with a full cargo of furs and deal planks. It was a valuable cargo with beaver and fox pelts fetching a high price in London. Timber, particularly if like this it was cut to a standard measurement, was always in demand for building.

The brig's master had spent three years in a Portsmouth prison hulk in the last war and was keen to avoid the same fate for himself and his crew, one of whom was his nephew, his wife's sister's son. He didn't relish meeting his wife and his sister-in-law after having condemned the youngster to years of incarceration. When Carlisle offered to put the whole crew ashore at the Seven Islands in exchange for information, it opened the floodgates, and it was all that his clerk could do to keep up with the flow of intelligence.

They were too late, that much became apparent as the brig's master told them of the four frigates, four privateers and fourteen storeships that had loitered in the Gulf until the ice broke. Just a few days ago they had made the passage up to Quebec, and he'd spoken to them as they passed in the river. They'd be adding powder, arms, provisions and five hundred army recruits to the defences of Quebec, and all without any interference from the British navy.

'The Comte de Bougainville was on board the commander's frigate,' said the master.

Carlisle looked blank; the name meant nothing to him.

'He's the aide-de-camp to the Marquis de Montcalm,' the master added, 'the military commander in New France. Monsieur de Bougainville was sent to France last year to plead for more support for the colony, it was all the talk over the winter. Now he's back with his fourteen supply ships and who-knows-what assurances. He should have had seventeen,' he continued, 'but he lost contact with three of them in the fog. I'm supposed to be looking out for them. Monsieur de Bougainville hopes that another convoy will be close behind, but the master of the privateer didn't think so, he shook his head at me when the *comte* wasn't watching.'

Carlisle heard something else too. The frigates wouldn't make the return voyage until the end of the year. They were to stay in the Basin below the city, and if there was any danger, they'd move upstream perhaps as far as Trois Rivières, seventy miles beyond Quebec and halfway to Montreal. From there they could quickly descend to threaten any invasion force that didn't have the protection of ships-of-the-line.

This was important information that should reach Durell or Saunders as soon as possible. It would undoubtedly influence the way that Saunders decided to approach the monstrously tricky problem of bringing Wolfe's army to Quebec, and of protecting and supplying it through the campaign season. Durell would be embarrassed by the evidence that he hadn't properly carried out his duties to blockade the river, but Carlisle couldn't help that. One thing was sure; the information must be sent to the admirals as quickly as possible. Carlisle came to a snap decision.

'Mister Wishart, do you believe you can find Halifax on your own?' he asked.

It wasn't a serious question, of course, but Wishart answered enthusiastically. He knew where it was leading.

'Aye-aye sir,' he replied with a grin spreading over his face. 'I believe I can.'

'Just keep the land to starboard,' muttered Hosking, 'and you'll be fine.'

'Then you'll have written orders and dispatches in thirty minutes. The bosun will give you a crew, and I want you underway as soon as the Frenchmen have brought their possessions out of the brig.'

Wishart's grin broadened. Not only was this an opportunity for a few weeks of independence, but it would look good in the journals that he must soon present to a lieutenant's board.

'You're to proceed to Halifax, keeping a close lookout for Admiral Durell's squadron. You must make every effort to find the admiral, and to that end, you are to lie-to overnight to reduce the chance of missing him in the dark. Otherwise, you're to make best speed. There'll be a letter for Admiral Durell. It will inform him that the ice has cleared and that the French have got a convoy up the river already. If you take my advice, you'll say nothing about the ice and the French convoy unless you're pressed. Let my letter be the bearer of bad news. I imagine Mister Durell will detain you while he writes his own letters to Admiral Saunders. However, if you don't meet Mister Durell on the way, and if he isn't at Halifax, then deliver the dispatches to Admiral Saunders. Again, I advise you to let my letter do the talking; there's no honour in bearing bad tidings.'

Wishart looked thoughtful. This wasn't his first prize command, and while he was comfortable with his

## Rocks and Shoals

navigation and seamanship, he was terrified at the thought of explaining himself to an admiral. He resolved to curb his natural loquaciousness.

'I'll give you our position and a course for North Cape and then to weather East Point,' added Hosking. 'From there, keep close inshore to avoid the banks. If the wind doesn't shift, you'll have a hard beat from Louisbourg to Halifax.'

Carlisle paused a moment before retiring to his cabin. The longboat was already taking the French master back to his brig to collect his crew and private belongings. Swinton, the bosun, was telling off a prize crew and they were hurrying away to pack their kitbags for this unexpected jaunt. It was a popular duty, and he could see some disappointed men wrangling with Swinton over his choice. There was no need to interfere. Swinton knew the men better than he did, and he could be relied upon to gather a competent crew. Satisfied that everything was moving as fast as he desired, Carlisle moved onto the next step, the drafting of the dispatches. He needed to be careful about how he phrased the news for Admiral Durell. It was bad enough being the bearer of evil news, but any hint of gloating could only sour their relationship.

'Pass the word for my secretary, Mister Hosking. I'll be in my cabin.'

\*\*\*

The last of the ebb and the swift flow of the Saint Lawrence carried the brig rapidly away down the Gulf. Carlisle could see Wishart standing proudly at the taffrail, looking back at *Medina* occasionally in case of any last signals. By the time the hands were piped to a late dinner, the brig had disappeared in the eastern haze, and the frigate was alone again. *Medina* set a course for the Seven Islands. With a fair wind broad on the larboard beam, they could expect to be there at dawn the following day, and it would be a matter of only a few hours to put the Frenchmen ashore.

Carlisle was pacing the windward side of the deck. The Frenchmen were lounging around the fo'c'sle, but he'd allowed the master the freedom of the quarterdeck and he was chatting happily to Hosking, who understood perhaps one word in ten. They were a philosophical lot. They had no financial interest in the brig or its cargo, and now they were free of the concern of finding their way home in the teeth of the British navy. There'd be no anxious days trying to avoid the blockading squadron off Rochefort, and they could enjoy the Canadian spring in idleness. Who knew, the war could be over soon, and they'd be able to return home unhindered.

Carlisle should have been happy. The brig was a fine prize, and its cargo would fetch a good price in Boston or New York. It may not even get that far. Admiral Saunders had extensive powers as commander-in-chief, and he might condemn it out-if-hand and buy it into the service. He could use the deals for the fast-developing navy yard. The furs could be sent south at leisure, and the brig would be a useful addition to the fleet of transports that by now were crowding Halifax bay.

He had also gained some valuable intelligence. The cargoes from fourteen supply ships would mean the end of any hopes of starving the city into submission, at least for this year. And because of the presence of those four frigates, a superior British force would need to be sent all the way up the treacherous rocks and shoals of the Saint Lawrence at least as far as the Basin below Quebec.

\*\*\*

'There's the channel, sir,' said the French master, 'between the two islands on the bow, Île du Corossol and La Petite Basque. There are two miles of deep water between them, leading to Domaine Royale.' He pointed out the two islands that guarded the entrance to the bay. With their humped, wooded appearance they looked for all the world like gigantic green beavers in a startlingly translucent blue sea.

# Rocks and Shoals

Hosking nodded his agreement. This Frenchman was eager to be ashore, and it wasn't in his interest to put *Medina* aground. Nevertheless, it did no harm to check the facts and, after all, he was a merchant master, not a pilot.

'There's ice on both sides, and the bay is probably full of it,' said Hosking. 'I can see a clear channel about a mile wide. It'll be no problem for the longboat.'

'How big is the town?' Carlisle asked.

'Hardly a town, sir,' the Frenchman replied with a laugh. 'It's more like a village, and a small village at that. There's nowhere for a ship to come alongside and only a handful of houses. But it's the best place for the trappers to bring their furs from the whole of that territory that stretches to the north of Quebec City until you come to the British lands at Hudson Bay.'

He waved an arm carelessly towards the forested shore.

'Your people destroyed it entirely sixty years ago, and it's only recently become a useful port again. That's where we picked up our furs. Your furs now, of course, sir,' he added without rancour. 'We took them to Quebec before the winter, but nobody would buy them; they're all afraid that you English will come before they can profit from the trade. I had to sit in that cold hell-hole of a city from September through to the ice breaking. Then all I could do was to ship them to La Rochelle with my deals, but it's all the owner's loss now, or rather the insurer.'

'And that insurer is probably in London,' Carlisle said, smiling at this friendly Frenchman. By one of the stranger quirks of international commerce, much of the French maritime trade was insured by companies in the capital of their adversary.

Carlisle was coming to like the brig's master. Once he had bargained the best treatment for himself and his crew, he'd put aside any animosity that he felt for his captor.

'Will the people respect a flag of truce?' he asked.

The Frenchman stroked his chin.

'I doubt they'd know what it means,' he replied. 'If you

can land me near the entrance to the bay on the east side then we'll make our own way to the village. It's only about three miles from the point, just where the little river comes in from the hills. It will be free of ice; that eastern channel thaws before the main channel.'

The Frenchman wanted a simple, clean delivery to the shore. Complications with the locals were not of interest to him.

'Mister Hosking. You may bring-to when the tip of Corossol bears west at two miles.'

Moxon touched his hat.

'The longboat's ready, sir. With the wind holding in the southwest, it will be a reach both ways, perhaps an hour in and an hour out. Allow three hours for dodging the ice.'

'Very well. Make sure your men have warm clothes and pistols and cutlasses but keep them out of reach of the Frenchman.'

'Aye-aye sir. I'll stow the frogs for'rard, there should be space for them.'

Carlisle frowned. He didn't approve of wholesale denigration of a nation such as the French, it led to underestimating their capabilities, and he knew that could prove fatal. He'd been at the battle of Minorca after all. However, he could hardly stop his second-in-command using a time-honoured epithet for England's oldest adversary.

'When you've landed the *Frenchmen*,' he said with emphasis, 'if it all looks quiet and there's not too much ice, just poke your nose into the bay and see what's there. This talk of nothing more than a village may be true – I expect it is – but there may be another ship loading furs, and we'd be foolish to leave it there.'

The longboat was about to push off when Carlisle remembered a question that he had meant to ask the French master.

'Monsieur,' he shouted down into the boat, 'how many pilots at Bic?'

## Rocks and Shoals

'Forty or more, but half of them went up with the convoy. The rest are drinking themselves to death for want of business. No vessel is allowed past Bic without a pilot, and nobody in his right mind would try it. The Traverse, you know. It's claimed more lives and ships than the whole of the river. Don't try it, captain, I beg you.'

Carlisle heard Hoskins' snort of derision from his right shoulder. The master had no faith in any English pilots, and French pilots would necessarily be even less reliable.

\*\*\*

The longboat was lost in the haze at five miles. There was a holiday feeling in the frigate; the captain had retired to his cabin, the first lieutenant was away, and the master was absorbed with Enrico in sketching a profile of the shore. The much-anticipated Admiralty order that masters should keep a *remark book* was expected any time now, and Hosking had realised that it would be used as a means of determining the zeal and competence of the whole corps of sailing masters. Rocks, shoals, sea marks, soundings, bays and harbours, times of high water and setting of tides, directions for sailing into ports and roads and for avoiding dangers; all these were to be recorded. And Hosking had an advantage over most of his fellows: Enrico Angelini had real talent as an artist and could make illustrations of the shore that would enhance the master's remarks.

The spring sunshine was warming the hands as they busied themselves in the endless tasks that the bosun found for them. Blocks were re-stropped, and cringles of sails were replaced while the watch on deck pretended to be busy with swabbers and brooms.

'Sail ho!' shouted the lookout. 'Sail to leeward. She's another brig, sir.'

Carlisle hurried on deck. It could, just conceivably, be Durell's squadron, but it was a couple of days earlier than he'd expected and this was too far north for them. Most likely it was a French man-o'-war or a merchant ship that had come through the Straits of Belle-Isle and was taking the northern side of the Gulf to make the Saint Lawrence before the door was irrevocably shut. Or perhaps one of the three lost ships of the French convoy.

'Under correction, your honour. She's a snow. She's close-hauled under coarses and tops'ls,' shouted Whittle as Carlisle made the quarterdeck, 'jib and stays'ls, she's not carrying t'gallants.'

Any man-o'-war would be making her best speed to get through the Gulf. Furthermore, after a North Atlantic passage in the spring, most merchantmen would be incapable of setting t'gallants, even if they carried such lofty sails. That settled it, a French merchantman for sure.

'Can you see the longboat?' Carlisle shouted up to the masthead.

'No sir, nothing in sight up the channel.'

'I can see the chase now,' said Hosking. 'Ah, she's going about, I think she's running, sir.'

'Beat to quarters, Mister Angelini, clear for action,' said Carlisle with the telescope to his eye.

'She's hard on the wind, tacking inshore,' said Carlisle, 'she's not running at all. I think she's making for that eastern channel into the bay. Her master must know this coast well.'

'But will it be free of ice?' asked Hosking.

'The brig's master said so,' replied Carlisle. 'We'll run down to pin her against the land. If the longboat's still there, then she's ours!'

Carlisle and Hosking watched the chase intently. She still had the option to wear and run back down the Gulf, but that would be a most unattractive course if the Seven Isles was her destination. It would mean days of beating back up the Gulf, and in any case, they couldn't expect to out-run a frigate.

'She's furling her foresail,' said Hosking. 'Ah, she's backing her fore tops'l, just for a moment to take the way off, I believe.'

'They'd be concerned about ice, I'm sure,' Carlisle replied.

## Rocks and Shoals

Grosse Boule was alongside to larboard now. Carlisle was taking *Medina* outside the islands to block the snow's escape to leeward. There was little chance of her beating up between Petite Basque and Gross Boule; he could ignore that channel.

The minutes passed, and the snow continued towards the east passage. She was moving slowly now, backing and filling as though unsure whether the passage was clear.

'If they make it through the channel then they're home,' said Carlisle. 'I won't be sending a cutting-out party, not into an ice-bound bay.'

'She's hauled her wind,' said Hosking.

'Deck there. I can see another sail near the snow. I think it's our longboat, sir.'

\*\*\*

'We dropped off the Frenchmen at the southeastern point and then had a quick look inside,' said Moxon, his cheeks red with cold. 'The whole of the north and west of the bay is full of ice. As that Frenchman said, there's a trading post with a dozen houses where a stream flows into the bay. Then we reached back down towards the channel. That's when we saw the snow, sir, backing and filling just beyond the eastern passage. I reckoned you must be bottling him up, so we ran alongside and made a noise about boarding; you may have heard a pistol or two.'

Carlisle shook his head. They'd heard nothing. The snow and longboat must have been at least five miles from the frigate.

'Anyway, he struck his colours without any fuss whatsoever. I took the liberty of putting the crew ashore where we landed the others; I hope that was the right thing to do.' He looked momentarily anxious.

'Yes, it was. Well done, Mister Moxon, very well done,' Carlisle replied.

It *was* well done. Now they would waste no more time in sending the longboat back into the bay, into a situation where the locals would already be aware of the presence of the enemy and may take it upon themselves to fire on the longboat.

'All the papers are intact, sir. She was part of the convoy that came through a few days ago, but she lost contact with them in a gale off North Cape. She's loaded with military stores for the garrison at Quebec. Powder, muskets, swords, uniforms, a pair of six-pounder field guns and limbers, all varieties of shot and shell. There's also a lot of crated furniture consigned to a merchant in Montreal which isn't documented at all; it's probably on the master's own account.'

Then the snow hadn't come through the Straits of Belle-Isle. The master must have been very lost in the fog to have been that far north. Carlisle briefly considered burning the vessel. Giving it a prize crew and sending it back to Halifax would deplete *Medina's* complement and could bring down upon his head the wrath of Admiral Durell when he arrived. On the other hand, it was a valuable prize, and the admiral would have his eighth. He may, therefore, be inclined to look favourably on the decision.

'I'll put Mister Atwater in command,' Carlisle said after a moment's thought. 'He won't be going far; I'll keep him with us so that the admiral has a spare dispatch vessel as soon as he arrives.'

Admirals were always in need of vessels to send away with dispatches, and if Saunders was delayed in Halifax, a sloop-of-war would otherwise have to be spared for the task.

Moxon beamed his agreement. His share of a brig and a snow, both loaded with valuable cargoes, would make a big impression on his bank balance. Then another thought occurred to him; he could expect Carlisle to mention his name in his dispatches after this neat little capture.

\*\*\*

# CHAPTER SEVEN

## The Surveyor

*Wednesday, Ninth of May 1759.*
*Medina, at Sea. Cape Gaspé southwest 5 leagues.*

The wind had veered into the northwest, bringing an abrupt end to the spring-like weather of the previous few days. It wasn't just cold; the wind had a malevolent quality about it, searching out every gap in the men's clothing and bringing a knife-like chill where it penetrated. It would be worse to the north of the island, Carlisle decided. In the northern channel, the wind would be coming straight down from the frozen arctic. With only one frigate on station, this southern channel was the best place to blockade the Gulf, but it left the whole of the northern passage open.

It was only by good fortune that *Medina* had been at Seven Islands yesterday to intercept the second brig. If the little merchant snow had any pretence to a warlike character he'd have sent Atwater to the north, but the snow's sides weren't even pierced for guns. She was the natural prey of the oceans, not a predator, and she was staying within sight of mother.

'If Durell hasn't rounded East Point we'll not see him for a week,' Hosking commented from behind his enormous woollen comforter.

'How would you shape your course in that case, Mister Hosking, if you were the flagship's master?'

Hosking paused for a moment and stared into the wind. He seemed by some mystical means to gain inspiration from the feel of the wind chilling the flesh off his cheeks.

'I'd stand right out to the east, past Sable Island, until I could weather North Cape on one tack. Aye, and I'd be generous about it, I'd stand on well past the island.'

'You wouldn't take short tacks along the coast in case the wind should back again and leave you to leeward?'

Hosking stared to windward again. At that moment it came to Carlisle. The master wasn't engaged in some metaphysical wrestling with the elements, he was gaining thinking time. As a rule, when asked a question by his captain, a master was expected to make an immediate reply. Hosking had developed this mannerism to give him a few moments without appearing disrespectful. Carlisle almost smiled, but that also would have been disrespectful.

'We've got this wind for a few days at least,' he replied, 'nor'westerly or westerly, and that's just what you'd expect this time of year. It's just too dangerous inside the banks with that unwieldy mass of two-deckers. With the wind in the southwest, yes most certainly, otherwise I'd want sea-room and plenty of it.'

Carlisle nodded. He was sure the master was right. If Durell hadn't already rounded East Point at the end of the Île Royale, he'd be standing far out into the Atlantic, watching the weather and estimating his longitude before tacking the squadron.

'Captain, sir,' Enrico interrupted their conversation with a formal doffing of his hat. 'The snow's hung out the signal for sail in sight to leeward.'

Carlisle had stationed Atwater to leeward of *Medina*, close to the island. He would see anything coming from the east before the frigate could hope to do so.

'Bear away two points, if you please, Mister Hosking. Let's go down and see who this is.'

'The snow's signalling a fleet now, sir,' Enrico reported.

'Sail ho!' That was the man at the masthead. 'Sail right on the bow, sir, there are two or three of them… more,' shouted the excited lookout, not knowing that the snow had already reported them.

'Mister Angelini. Signal for the snow to heave to.'

Hosking looked questioningly at his captain.

'Mister Durell must have completed his stores faster than we'd expected,' said Carlisle. 'Otherwise, that's a French fleet, and in that case, we have nowhere to go,' he added, gesturing to the west where the river led only to Quebec. 'However, I'd stake a great deal on that being Durell's squadron. If I signal the snow to join us, the admiral will think she's running and give chase. He'll be rightly annoyed by that when he finds that she's our prize. On the hand, if Atwater holds his course, he'll have to explain his presence to the admiral before we can come down to him.'

\*\*\*

Compared with Carlisle's little sixth-rate frigate, *Princess Amelia* was massive; an eighty-gun third-rate with high sides and two long, long rows of gunports. She'd briefly backed her tops'ls to allow *Medina's* longboat to come alongside, but her entry port was closed, and Carlisle had a dangerous and challenging climb, even with the man ropes rigged. Durell hadn't even waited until he was on deck before filling his tops'ls, and the heel of the ship to leeward had negated the benefit of her tumble-home.

'My apologies, sir,' said the stout figure that met him at the waist. 'The carpenter's working on the entry port to try to free it, but it may need a bit of brute force to get it open. It appears that the winter didn't agree with our timbers. The admiral's in a tearing hurry, and he won't waste a minute.'

John Bray had succeeded Philip Durell as the captain of *Princess Amelia* when Durell was given his flag. The personal cross that he had to bear was having the previous commanding officer hoist his flag as a rear admiral in his old ship within a few months of leaving. The deficiency of the entry-port was Bray's responsibility, and he felt it acutely. His discomfort was compounded by the knowledge that although he commanded a majestic third-rate, this frigate captain was three years his senior on the captain's list. It was quite usual to give a newly-posted captain command of a flagship where he could be under the eye of an experienced admiral. Still, Bray probably hoped for a frigate next, to have a measure of independence and, of course, a better chance of prize money.

'The admiral's in his cabin,' Bray said as they walked aft.

The great cabin was flooded with light from the wide stern windows, illuminating the silvery wig of the admiral seated at a desk.

'You've taken a prize, I see,' he said by way of introduction.

He didn't look unhappy about it. Carlisle didn't know how Saunders and Durell had agreed to split the one-eighth share of prize money due to the commanding admiral, but however much was due to the rear admiral, it was money for doing nothing more than issuing a few orders. Every admiral was delighted when his frigates took prizes.

'Yes, sir. I've taken two. I sent the first to find you with the intelligence that I gleaned from its master.'

A furrow appeared between Durell's eyes. He could guess at the destination of those dispatches if the brig didn't find the squadron. He had reason to wish that he could personally manage the flow of information to Saunders, and it appeared that he was already compromised.

'The first was a brig, outward bound from Quebec. I sent her with a master's mate and orders to report to the commander-in-chief if he missed you.'

Durell fiddled nervously with a pair of dividers on his desk.

'I trust he had orders to search for me diligently, Captain Carlisle. I would be annoyed if I thought he'd slipped past me without a second glance.'

'He did sir. He had orders to take the inshore passage and lie-to overnight to avoid missing you.'

Durell could hardly argue with that. It wasn't practical to give orders for a merchant brig to scour the oceans in search of an admiral, and it was easy enough for them to have missed each other.

'We came outside the banks in case the wind veered,' the admiral replied.

'I have a copy of the letter here, sir,' said Carlisle.

'Just tell me the heads of it, I can read it later.'

Carlisle almost pitied Durell. It was evident that the

admiral had guessed at least some of the content of the letter. If it contained nothing sensitive, then Carlisle wouldn't be so careful in his delivery. He told the whole story, ignoring Durell's growing uneasiness.

'If I may summarise, Captain. A relief fleet passed here just three days ago, a bare twenty-four hours before you reached your station, and it is now on its way up to Quebec.'

'From the information that I've received, that's correct, sir.'

'And you believe this is reliable?'

Carlisle related the stories of the two Frenchmen, the masters of the brig and the snow. Durell could only nod in agreement; it was unlikely that they had made it up.

Durell stood and stared out of the stern window. He knew that within a day, the full extent of his failure to blockade the Gulf would be known by his superior. And there was nothing that he could do the soften the delivery.

'If I may suggest, sir...' said Carlisle tentatively.

Durell wheeled about and stared at Carlisle with something like hatred.

'The snow is loaded with supplies for the army: powder, muskets, uniforms, shot, a pair of field guns. General Wolf would have a good use for its cargo if it can be delivered before he leaves Halifax. You could send her away now with your own dispatches, and it wouldn't weaken your force.'

'Who's commanding the brig?'

'One of my master's mates, sir. Mister Atwater by name.'

'You've already sent one away in the brig. I'll give you a lieutenant from the flagship to take command of the prize, and you can have Mister Atwater back. The wind has veered, so he may not be too far behind the brig if your master's mate lay-to overnight. Wait here, Carlisle, while I write my dispatches.'

At a shout from the admiral, his secretary came hurrying into the cabin clutching his writing implements.

'Now, tell me the main points again, Carlisle.'

*Medina's* longboat took the startled lieutenant and his

scratch crew to the snow. Atwater was disappointed, but the whole transfer was made at such pace, with a visibly agitated admiral watching impatiently from the flagship's quarterdeck, that he had no time to do anything other than to grab his kitbag and tumble down into the boat. With unseemly haste, the snow tacked and reached down the Gulf under all the sail that she could set. Before she was out of sight, her harassed crew had even managed to set her tiny t'gallants, and she made a bold display in the bitter breeze.

***

The wind moderated in the evening and Durell's squadron lay under the lee of the northwest tip of Anticosti. They were all moving steadily eastward under the combined weight of the ebbing tide and the flow of the great river. Durell didn't appear too concerned at this situation, even though in a river estuary it was analogous to losing ground to leeward in the open ocean. No admiral would do that willingly, so Durell must have another motive.

'Gentlemen,' he said to the assembled captains of his squadron, 'I've called you all away from your ships because I've received new information that has somewhat altered my plans.'

Carlisle realised that earlier that day he'd seen Durell at his worst, acutely conscious that he'd been found wanting in his first duty and aware that the narrative had been taken out of his hands by the brig that he'd missed, presumably in the night. This was almost a different person. He'd had time to think through the implications of the news that he'd received and to make appropriate plans. And in fairness, Durell didn't appear to be blaming the messenger.

'For those of you who haven't heard, Captain Carlisle took a brig and a snow and wrung some reliable information from their masters.'

The admiral paused and smiled at Carlisle, a friendly gesture of acknowledgement.

'It appears that a French supply squadron passed up the river only three days ago. Eight frigates and privateers and fourteen supply ships, carrying food and military stores and five hundred army recruits.'

He paused again to allow the information to sink in. It was useless to attempt to hide his failure, Durell knew, and as all these men were guilty by association, they should know the worst of it.

'Also, the squadron was carrying Montcalm's emissary to the French court, the Comte de Bougainville, who will undoubtedly have information for the French leaders in Montreal and Quebec. Now, we know that we can't catch the squadron; they'll be at Bic by now embarking pilots for the Traverse. But at least the situation is clear. With eight frigates and privateers on their way up the river and God knows how many others already there, Admiral Saunders will have to take a substantial force up to Quebec.'

Durell glanced around the room, testing the mood of his captains.

'That being the case, this squadron will push on up the river as far and as fast as it can go.'

The captain's exchanged glances. They knew the stories of the dangerous passage, particularly the Traverse below Orleans Island. There the channel crossed from the northern to the southern bank, negotiating hazardous shoals and rapids in the centre of the river. No French ships-of-the-line had ever attempted it. They also understood their admiral's motivation. He'd made a poor decision to delay his departure from Halifax and now was anxious to make amends.

Durell went on to detail the ships that would stay behind to guard the channel either side of Anticosti Island, to look for the remaining two lost French merchantmen, and to have a fighting reserve in case a French squadron arrived. *Nightingale* of twenty-two guns would provide the early warning far down the Gulf between North Cape and Cape Ray. *Lizard* of twenty-eight guns would guard the main passage between Anticosti Island and the southern shore.

'We have some information on the river,' the admiral

continued, 'unroll that chart, would you?'

It was a large chart, some three feet wide and two feet high, filled with detailed drawings and views of the shoreline. The Saint Lawrence River dominated, running from the bottom left at Quebec to the top right at Anticosti Island. The continuation upstream to Montreal and Lake Ontario was inset at the upper left of the chart and, of far greater interest, the fabled Traverse was inserted at the lower centre. Carlisle couldn't see the details, but it was clear that the north side of the river between Quebec and the Gulf had been surveyed – he could see densely-packed soundings all along the northern shore – while the southern side was mostly empty.

'Admiral Saunders brought it out from England and it's the latest information that we have. The north side of the river, the side of most interest to us, comes from the surveys of the royal cartographer in New France, Jean Deshayes, but he died some fifty years ago. There have been some more recent additions, but frankly, I'm not happy with it. It's one thing to take two dozen merchantmen up the river with pilots who've lived here all their lives, but we'll be bringing a much greater fleet and heavier ships up to Quebec. Nevertheless, it's the best that we have, and I'm having copies made for all of you gentlemen,'

He looked around at his captains. They all appeared sceptical; they had no faith in an old French chart.

'The squadron, except for *Lizard* and *Nightingale*, will move upriver with me, but with caution. Mister Carlisle, you will go ahead to survey the route.'

Carlisle almost jumped in his seat. He hadn't expected this. In fact, he thought he wasn't in the admiral's favour after bringing him the worst possible news.

'Have you met Mister Cook?' Durell asked, indicating a tall man in the plain blue coat of a sailing master who was sitting unobtrusively at the back of the cabin. Nobody could resist the urge to look behind, yet Cook sat impassively under the concentrated gaze of a dozen post-captains.

'I have had that honour, sir,' Carlisle replied, smiling at the man in blue.

Cook rose and bowed in acknowledgement. Evidently, he was unconcerned at being the focus of attention is such a senior gathering. Yes, Carlisle had met James Cook in Halifax. He was the sailing master of the third-rate *Pembroke* and was fast gaining a reputation as a surveyor and draftsman.

'Mister Cook favoured me with a copy of his excellent chart of Halifax,' Carlisle added.

'That's good because Mister Cook will join you in *Medina* to survey the channel. You'll have the orders for the transfer before you leave this ship. Oh, and Captain Carlisle, if you should happen upon any river pilots, don't let them slip through your fingers!'

***

# CHAPTER EIGHT

## The Wilderness

*Wednesday, Ninth of May 1759.*
*Medina, at Sea. Cape Gaspé southwest 5 leagues.*

Carlisle had expected sparks to fly. Hosking was a proficient surveyor himself and at least twenty years the senior of the two men. Cook had only held his master's warrant for two years, and before then, most of his experience had been in the coastal trade. Hosking could be justified in resenting Cook's presence on board. However, as it turned out, Hosking and Cook agreed very well. They'd met in Halifax and Hosking had soon recognised the younger man's skill. They quickly formed an effective team with Hosking concentrating on keeping *Medina* safe, leaving Cook free to survey the channels.

The Saint Lawrence, for most of its length, was still a remote and desolate place, despite the French two-hundred-year tenure. When they heard of Upper Canada, people in England assumed that one approached from the south and that the weather was necessarily less severe at the mouth of the river. It was a common mistake born of the convention that maps and charts were orientated with north at the top and that upper usually referred to the north. However, the mouth of the Saint Lawrence, where Anticosti Island divided it into two, was many, many leagues to the north of Quebec, which in turn was far north of Montreal and even further north of Lake Ontario. Only the hardiest of Europeans spent the winter north of Quebec, and they were predominantly fur trappers and traders. The few fixed habitations were mostly abandoned in November and their owners only returned when the river became free of ice.

The weather was bitterly cold, the river was still full of ice, and howling gales often came surging down from the northeast with squalls that could dismast an unwary ship in an instant. Yet the sixty leagues from Anticosti island to Bic must be surveyed. The work had to be of a standard to safeguard not only Durell's squadron but also Saunders' and Holmes' squadrons that would follow, and then the great mass of transports and storeships that carried Wolfe's army. It was exacting work, and most of it would have to be carried out in open boats.

***

'We'll work on the assumption that the squadrons and the transports and storeships will follow the French advice and stay to the north side of the river until the Traverse,' said Carlisle with his copy of the French chart spread out before him on the dining table.

'I'm sure that's correct,' Hosking replied. 'We don't have the leisure to survey the whole river, not if we're to be off Quebec this season. Even so, it's a monumental task.'

Carlisle and Hosking stared helplessly at the chart; it was difficult to know where to start.

'I beg your pardon, sir,' Cook interjected. 'I've had the advantage of a copy of this chart since last year when Louisbourg fell. Well, not this chart exactly, but a copy of the French original.'

Carlisle looked at Cook with interest.

'May I ask how you came by it?' he asked.

'It was plundered from one of the ships that we took when Louisbourg fell. Nobody else seemed interested in it, and the soldier who acquired it sold it to me for a guinea.'

'A guinea! The key to New France for a single gold coin!' Carlisle shook his head in wonder.

It was easy to imagine how it had happened. In the turmoil of the fall of Louisbourg, there had been so much to do with prisoners to transport, and the defences and barracks made suitable for the winter, that the finer points often were forgotten. Nobody would have paid any attention to a soldier carrying away an apparently worthless roll of paper.

'I believe there's a reason that it's only the north side

that has been surveyed, or two reasons really.' Cook smoothed the chart out, and his long, slim fingers pointed to the western tip of Anticosti Island.

'The passage up the river will always be difficult. The wind comes mainly from the west and south all through the year, dead foul for ships ascending the river. Then, of course, the river is tidal until well past Quebec, and the combination of the wind, current and the tidal stream make a passage in the centre of the river impossible on the ebb. Now, with any other river, we could perhaps ride the flood in its centre and then retreat to one of the shores to ride out the ebb, but this river is just too wide until past Bic, and then it starts to shoal.'

Cook pointed to the small Isle of Bic on the southern shore, two-thirds of the way to Quebec.

'The French saw no value in wasting effort surveying the centre, and in any case, it would take a deep-sea lead and an extraordinary amount of effort.'

Carlisle studied the chart as Cook waited respectfully.

'Then why did they survey the northern and not the southern side?' he asked.

'Because the French own the northern bank and they're protected by the river itself, sir.' Cook replied simply.

Carlisle studied the chart again. The whole southern shore from Lake Saint Francis, past Quebec, to the sea was claimed as British territory. Carlisle knew that it was only nominal sovereignty, that it was disputed continuously, but Cook had a good point. The French would naturally feel more secure on the northern shore, where no Englishman had yet been.

'So, at least as far as the Green Island,' he pointed to a long, slim island thirty miles above Bic, 'it's likely that the south shore is as navigable as the north, it just hasn't been surveyed.'

'Well, we certainly don't have time to sound three hundred miles of channel,' Carlisle said, still studying the chart. 'We must keep to the north as far as the Traverse.'

'We should concentrate on the anchorages, sir,' said Hosking. 'That's where we can do the greatest good. Mister Saunders will have around a hundred and eighty ships that'll need to ride out the ebb twice a day. My guess is those sounding around the anchorages anticipated no more than twenty merchantmen.'

'Mister Cook, what's your opinion?' asked Carlisle. There was something about James Cook's ability to remain quiet and expressionless that eventually, through sheer moral force, broke into a conversation.

'In the six hours of the flood, which will necessarily be weaker than the ebb reinforced by the current, and with the probability of foul winds, the fleet can hardly move further than ten leagues upstream. That's ten leagues a day, sir, and only if we use the extra hour of slack water at each side of the ebb,' he added. 'Being so close into shore the admiral won't want to move at night. Thirty miles a day. I believe we can work on that. I submit, sir, that our task is to mark anchorages at those intervals, large enough for the whole fleet to lie over the night tide.'

Carlisle was pleased to see that Cook was always respectful in his opinions. Having been sent to *Medina* by the admiral he could have taken a high hand, but he was careful only to talk when invited to do so. Nevertheless, it was clear that Cook had spent many hours poring over his French chart and thinking through the problems of bringing a vast fleet up the Saint Lawrence to Quebec. Carlisle needed his ideas because, at this point, they were more valuable than either Hosking's or his own.

'Go on, Mister Cook, I'm interested to hear what you have to say.'

Hosking nodded imperceptibly.

Cook bowed slightly. He took up the dividers and set their points to a league – three nautical miles – against the scale on the chart.

'The French must have had the same opinion, sir. You can see that they've marked anchorages at intervals of less than five leagues.' He stepped off the distances between a few of them to illustrate his point.

'Assume for planning that the fleet can make the Seven Islands without having to lie at anchor over the tide, do you think that's reasonable?'

'I do, sir. I can see why the Seven Islands have been so important to the French. They offer the last properly sheltered anchorage – unless the wind is in the south – before the river narrows at Bald Mountains Point and the tidal problems start. You've been there, I understand.'

'We have,' Carlisle replied. 'There's a large enough road to anchor any number of fleets, without having to enter the bay. Then let's take that as our starting point.'

Cook stepped off the distance from the Seven Islands to the next marked anchorage, La Caouy to the north of the Egg Islands, and then to the next, west of Bald Mountains Point.

'The first leg looks about right, but the second is more like fifteen leagues, and we'll need to stand off the Egg Islands. That's where Admiral Walker lost his ships fifty years ago.'

It was a cautionary tale. During that earlier attempt on Quebec in 1711, the British fleet was set well to the north of the centre of the channel in an easterly wind; they'd become embayed among the islands in the fog and dark. They'd lost seven transports and a supply ship along with some seven hundred soldiers and a hundred and fifty sailors. The expedition had returned to England in disgrace.

They stared in silent fascination at the chart. It was one thing to talk about navigational disasters in the warmth and safety of an inn or around the table in a man-o'-war with many leagues of sea-room under its lee, but this was real. They were in the Saint Lawrence River at the tail end of a late winter season. They could expect fog and ice, aye and east winds, and the Egg Islands were no better known to them than they had been to Admiral Walker half a century before.

'When may I expect to see your plan, Mister Cook?' asked Carlisle breaking their reverie. 'The admiral has told me to start from Bald Mountains Point, while he works the squadron up through the Seven Islands.

Cook glanced at Hosking. Probably they had already formulated a plan for the survey, Carlisle thought.

'At eight bells, sir, at the end of the dogs.'

\*\*\*

It was one of the most strained and perilous fortnights of Carlisle's life. Each day *Medina* would anchor off the wild north shore of the Saint Lawrence in one of the places that the French cartographer had marked with his peculiar upside-down anchor. Over slack water James Cook took the longboat and sounded the anchorage, allowing enough space for the enormous fleet to lie over a tide. There was ice coming down the river still and the occasional fog, but the work had to go on as Admiral Durell was hard on their heels, no more than a day or two behind them. And it was exacting work; the safety of the fleet depended upon them. The bosun was busy making buoys and painting them in bright colours so that each anchorage should be conspicuously marked. Then, when the boatwork was done for the day, when the soundings and the bearings had been taken and the shoreline roughly sketched, Cook, Hosking and Enrico laboured through the night to render their discoveries on paper.

Wishart returned in the first week, a passenger in an armed cutter, with the cheerful news that Saunders had bought the prize brig into the service, that the navy yard had purchased the cargo of deals and that the furs were on their way to New York where they would fetch a better price.

They saw no sign of the French, either on the shore or on the water. If there were any ships bound for Quebec, they were being snapped up by *Lizard* and *Nightingale*, and the few Europeans that visited the north shore in the late spring and summer had not yet started to arrive. It was as though they had found a land unknown to civilisation. Not perhaps Hamlet's *undiscovered country*, but it was something very much like the ends of the earth. The soundless forest looked as though it would be the death of any traveller, and in its sublime horror, it reinforced all the European dread of the frozen wilderness.

'Show me that chart again, would you Mister Hosking?' asked Carlisle.

*Medina* was lying in Laval Bay, the last of the marked anchorages before they came alongside the Isle of Bic. Carlisle knew that they could expect to see French activity once they were past Bic, and they couldn't slip past unseen. Bic was the pilot station for the Saint Lawrence, and here the river narrowed to only fifteen miles between the island and the north shore. The master of the captured brig – was it only two weeks before? – had described how a cutter or sometimes two were always stationed off the island. They placed a pilot onboard every ship that planned to navigate the river beyond that point. Indeed, it was illegal to go past Bic without taking a pilot. Carlisle was nervous about taking *Medina* upriver and only a hundred miles further they would come to the dreaded Traverse. Given time, he was confident that Cook and Hosking could find a way through, but with the season advancing, time was in short supply. There was something else that the brig's master had told him; the pilots were confident that no British fleet would attempt the river past Bald Mountains Point, and de Bougainville had assured them that no French battle fleet was likely at Bic.

'Do we know anything of the soundings off Bic?' Carlisle asked as he studied the scant details on the chart.

'Only what is shown on the chart, sir,' Hosking replied, 'and the few words that I had with the brig's master. There's deep water to the north of the island and eight fathoms between the island and the southern shore. The pilot cutters anchor off the northern shore under this headland here,' he pointed to the bluff that jutted south from the Canadian shore, bizarrely named the Point of a Thousand Cows.

'The cutter will be out of sight of its station on the island then.'

'Yes, sir. It usually has two or three pilots on board, but sometimes only one if they're not expecting much trade. If they need more, they send the cutter back to the island where they make a signal.'

'Does the cutter stand off to make the signal?'

'I believe so, sir. It doesn't touch at the island, but there's a system of flag signals that states how many pilots are required. That would be essential because they will hardly ever be able to see the ships against the northern shore. They're very willing, with the pilotage rates being so high and their master being so particular.'

Carlisle raised a questioning eyebrow,

'It's a royal monopoly, sir. If they signal for ten pilots, then ten pilots tumble into the spare cutters, and they head across the channel without waiting for any by-your-leave.'

'He told me that there would be twenty or so pilots at the station, did you hear the same?'

'Yes, sir, he gave me the same story.'

Carlisle looked thoughtful, staring abstractedly at the chart.

'Is there anything else?' he asked.

'No, sir, I believe that's all that he told me. He'd only been up the river two or three times, but the pilots appeared to work to the same routine come hell or high water.'

\*\*\*

Carlisle heard the longboat hooking on to the main chains, and the sounds of Cook and Enrico and the other midshipman coming back on board. He opened the cabin door a few inches and saw the marine sentry stiffen to attention.

'Pass the word for the first lieutenant.'

They should be weighing anchor now, and quite likely the bosun had already started rousing out the watch below. Let them wait, Carlisle thought, he had other plans.

'Good afternoon, Mister Moxon.'

'Good afternoon, sir. Weigh anchor?' he asked.

'Not just yet, I want to test a plan against you. I need you to be critical; I'd rather see all the problems before we're committed.'

Moxon contrived to look both mystified and expectant. The chart was still spread on the table, held down by various paperweights.

'Now, I want to recruit some French pilots…'

\*\*\*

# CHAPTER NINE

## The Pilots of Bic

*Tuesday, Twenty-Second of May 1759.*
*Medina, Underway. Laval Bay, Saint Lawrence River.*

The sailmaker had thought it was a trick question; he'd harboured a notion that the first lieutenant was having fun at his expense.

'Can you make a French ensign?' Moxon had asked. 'In fact, can you also make a French commissioning pennant?'

The French naval ensign was, of course, plain white, the colour of the ruling Bourbon dynasty, as was the commissioning pennant. The sailmaker, a known wag, thought fast.

'I could, sir, if I may have the tablecloths from the great cabin. Do you think the captain would mind? If not, perhaps the young gentlemen's small-clothes…'

'Very amusing,' Moxon replied. He could afford to take a certain amount of facetiousness from a valuable, skilled warrant officer, 'I was hoping you'd have some suitable sailcloth.'

'Oh, you're in earnest, sir, my apologies,' he said, playing out his innocent role for as long as he could. 'Yes, I have some white bunting, probably enough to make a very creditable ensign. What sort of size would it be?

'The same size as our best ensign, and the pennant the same as our pennant.'

'That'll be four cloths then, laid horizontally. I have some worn old stuff; we don't want the ensign to look like we just made it. It'll leave me short though.'

'You can unmake it after this caper. I can't imagine we'll need it again. But you'll need to get moving; they're both wanted before the morning watch. Now, who's the best tailor onboard? The captain and I need red lapels, cuffs and collars for our coats. Red baize will do, the stuff you use for the manropes. And pass the word for the bosun if you please.'

'Aye-aye sir,' the sailmaker replied, knuckling his forehead as he strode away to his store, shouting for his mates as he went.

'Ah, Mister Swinton,' Moxon called as he saw the bosun hurrying towards him. 'Now, I want your help. What is it about *Medina* that makes her look British rather than French?'

Swinton grinned. 'I suppose the captain is planning a little foolery,' he said, tapping his forefinger against the side of his nose.

Moxon nodded. 'Yes, we need to pass ourselves off as a French frigate tomorrow. Only for a few minutes. We need to trick a pilot cutter until it's alongside.'

Swinton scratched his head and gazed abstractedly up at the rigging, then aft to the taffrail.

'You'll have arranged for the name to be painted over, I imagine, sir.'

'Not yet, the painter was the next on my list.'

'I was looking at that the other day It needs to be refreshed in any case, what with the wind and the frost peeling it away, so it'll be no loss to just slap some black paint over it. If you want a French name that will be more difficult.'

'No, that won't be necessary.'

'Then I can't think of anything else, sir. The French rigging is so like ours that it makes no difference, and any frigate will look a little worn after an Atlantic crossing at this time of year.'

\*\*\*

A provident wind from west-by-north and a flooding tide carried *Medina* towards the pilot cutter's anchorage under tops'ls and jib. The vast white flag fluttered from the ensign staff, and the white commissioning pennant flew gaily from the main t'gallant head. The deck was deathly quiet. The guns were run in, and the ports closed, but behind every port was a gun crew. *Medina's* people were at quarters, the frigate was cleared for action.

'You know the part you have to play, Mister Angelini?'

'Yes, sir,' he replied nervously.

Enrico was wearing his plain blue coat, exactly like the everyday working dress in the French navy.

Carlisle spoke good French, but his accent marked him as a closet English-speaker with his first sentence. Enrico Angelini, of course, spoke the language fluently, and if his accent sounded a little too Italian, at least it could be imagined to be French, perhaps from the French side of the border near Cannes. It was so close to Nice, and the territory had changed hands so often that the accents were indistinguishable. Nice was, in fact, Enrico's home.

Luckily, the uniforms worn by the French officers weren't so different from the British, and in neither navy did the common sailors wear any kind of uniform. Carlisle and Moxon were resplendent in their blue uniforms with temporary red facings, and there was nothing on the deck of *Medina* to suggest that she wasn't a French frigate on passage to Quebec. The only point that made Carlisle nervous was the lack of voices on the deck. In every French ship that he had ever been close to there had been a constant babble of orders, disagreements, and just chatter. There was none of the stoical calm that distinguished the deck of a British frigate. He couldn't replicate that, but he hoped that by the time the cutter was close enough to become suspicious, the longboat would have cut off her escape.

Carlisle looked over the taffrail; the longboat was following close behind. There was nothing unusual about that, and there were a dozen innocent reasons why a frigate's longboat may be following under sail in the Saint Lawrence River. In this case, however, Wishart had orders to board the pilot cutter at the first sign that they'd seen anything suspicious.

'There she is,' said Hosking pointing to a small decked-in lugger that came into sight as they opened up the bay.

'Come right up to them before you back the tops'ls, Mister Hosking. I don't want to give them too much time to inspect us.'

*Medina* stood into the bay in silence.

'Bring to.'

All the sheets and braces were handled from the deck. There was no need for topmen laying out along the yards with all the shouting that entailed. That was one less opportunity for the pilot to become suspicious.

Carlisle brought the telescope to his eye. He could see the activity on the deck of the pilot cutter. The lugger – she was only a cutter by courtesy – was about the size of the longboat with two masts. The forward part was decked over, and probably there was sleeping accommodation below. She was secured to a buoy, so there was no fuss with weighing anchor. The two lugsails climbed up the masts and in a surprisingly short time, she was running down towards *Medina*, the picture of unwary innocence.

Closer and closer she came, still apparently suspecting nothing. There was a man with a boathook ready to hold onto the main chains, and the pilot, bundled into a woollen coat, was preparing to climb *Medina's* side. It was a well-practiced operation, and that very sense of routine would play into Carlisle's hands. He walked back to the taffrail and waved to Wishart, the signal for the longboat to move around the frigate's stern.

The pilot made a trumpet of his hands and shouted up to the quarterdeck.

'*Quel vaisseau?*'

'*À destination du Québec,*' Enrico answered, evading the question and stating the obvious. It was too risky to invent a ship's name; the pilot may know that the chosen ship couldn't be in the Saint Lawrence on this day.

The man in the bows of the lugger stretched out his boathook to grab the chains.

'*Quel vaisseau, Capitaine?*'

Now there was a note of suspicion in the pilot's voice.

## Rocks and Shoals

He turned around to shout something at the man at the tiller, but it was too late. Two grapnels shot out from the waist and caught in the lugger's rigging. She was hauled bodily alongside, her gunwale awash as the pull of the grapnels dragged her sideways. Then the longboat came crashing into her outboard side, and Wishart leapt onto her deck, pistol in hand. There was no resistance.

\*\*\*

'Now then, *Monsieur*, you must be old enough to have served in the last war,' said Carlisle pleasantly as he poured a glass of rum for the pilot.

The pilot dumbly nodded his head, unwilling to commit himself to anything. He looked suspiciously at Carlisle's secretary who was sitting to one side, his pen ready to write.

'You may leave us, Mister Simmonds,' Carlisle said, hoping the Frenchman wouldn't recognise this as a piece of prepared theatre, to put him at ease.

'Your name, sir?' asked Carlisle.

'Jacques Vacher,' the pilot replied sulkily.

'Well, Monsieur Vacher, if you are not yourself familiar with the prison hulks in Portsmouth, you surely know someone who is. You need not answer that if you would prefer.'

He watched the pilot's face. That mention of the prison hulks had made an impact.

'However, I have a proposition to put to you.'

The pilot looked unresponsive, blank-faced, but there was no question; Carlisle had his interest. The prison hulks were notorious. Moored at the head of Portsmouth harbour in two long rows, they offered to the prisoners-of-war a life of stultifying boredom and discomfort that could only be relieved by the ending of the war or death from one of the many diseases that ravaged the hulks. The chances of being exchanged were slim, as Britain always had a far greater number of imprisoned French sailors than the French had English sailors.

'I wish to enlist your services as a pilot for the passage

to Quebec. You should find that convenient; after all, it is your profession. I will pay you in gold coinage at British Admiralty pilot rates. I'm sure it will be a refreshing change from the promissory notes that you must have accumulated over the past few years.'

The pilot said nothing but sipped his rum nervously. That was better than an outright refusal.

'Of course, there would be no question of a prison hulk after you had served as a pilot. You would be sent home as a passenger as soon as this season is over.'

One step at a time thought Carlisle.

'Well, now it's your turn to speak. I really would rather not discuss the prison hulks, and I hope there will be no need.'

The pilot licked his lips and glanced around the cabin as though he was looking for a way of escape. Or perhaps he was confirming that there were no witnesses.

'Will you enter into a regular contract for pilotage, for as long as I am onboard?' he asked, looking at a point above Carlisle's left shoulder.

Got him! Carlisle kept the triumph from his face. Probably the Bic pilots could look forward to a week's pilotage followed by a month of unpaid idleness, and the shaft about useless promissory notes had gone home. There had been no coinage to spare in the whole of French Canada since Louisbourg fell. There would be no more French ships this year, despite de Bougainville's hopes; the presence of a British frigate guaranteed it. If he accepted, he could count on at least a few months of paid work, rewarded by the fabled British gold. He could worry about how his actions would be perceived in France later, but the chance of his disloyalty – treason even – ever being discovered was slim.

'Of course. I can call my secretary back in and write up a standard pilotage form. However, there is one more service that I must ask of you before we commit our agreement to paper.'

The pilot's face fell. He could square his conscience with

acting as a pilot for his country's enemies, but this sounded like it could be a step too far.

'I require the services of all the remaining pilots at Bic. How many are there?'

Carlisle watched the range of emotions on the man's face. This was more than just committing himself. But in a way, he was doing his friends a favour, a contract for steady employment in reward for British gold. And they would all be complicit in this crime against France, they would find a way out of it together.

'Twenty-two,' the pilot replied weakly. 'The others went up to Quebec with a convoy two weeks ago. There has been nothing since, neither up nor down.'

'Nor will there be this year,' Carlisle added, 'and if you wish to remain a pilot for this river, you'll be piloting British ships from now on. I propose to offer your colleagues the same opportunity to make money in their chosen profession as I have offered you…'

'But Capitaine, some may agree, and some may refuse. It will compromise us all,' he interrupted with a look of despair on his face. He could see his agreement going up in smoke just as he had started to understand how advantageous it was. 'There is a road on the south shore to Cape Levi, and some will take that, I'm sure.'

'They won't have a choice, Monsieur. What is the flag signal to demand the services of twenty-two pilots, if you please? It should come as no surprise after the last convoy went through and after Monsieur de Bougainville's news of a second convoy.'

The pilot looked doubtful, then he started to see how this may be achieved. He too had heard of the rumoured second convoy. He smiled.

\*\*\*

The lugger, with Moxon at the helm, led *Medina* across the river towards Bic. Carlisle had no intention of getting close enough for critical eyes to determine that she was a British frigate, just close enough so that she could be seen from the pilot station, corroboration for the demand for all the pilots. He could only see the details of the pilot station through his telescope. It was a stone structure with clapperboard outbuildings and a tall flagpole. Three luggers were lying in the lee of the island.

'Heave to, Mister Hosking. This is close enough.'

He watched as their own commandeered lugger continued towards the island. The flags were a simple numerical code. A blue-and-white flag to designate a need for pilots over two identical red swallowtails to indicate the number required. This was a nervous moment. He wasn't concerned for the safety of Moxon and the half dozen sailors below decks, but he desperately wanted those twenty-two pilots. Every one of them would be worth a hundred times the gold that they would cost. How many pilot cutters would they use? Probably all of them. The longboat and the yawl were both manned and ready, and as soon as the pilot cutters were close to *Medina*, he would send them out to cut off the Frenchmen's retreat. Three boats against three, and Carlisle's were armed and ready. It should be easy – it should be…

'They're flying a flag on the island now, sir,' Hosking said, 'I can't make it out.'

'A single yellow flag is the acknowledgement signal,' Carlisle said, still looking intently at the island.

'It could be yellow,' said Hosking, 'I'm not sure.'

Carlisle could see as well as Hosking, and he couldn't tell what colour the flag was. He was almost sure that it *was* a flag, but with these wisps of mist cutting across his vision that was all he could tell.

Moxon's lugger was only a mile or so from the station now.

'They're hauling in the luggers, sir,' said Hosking.

So they were. The luggers were moored on a long line from the shore so that they could be quickly brought in and manned. So far, the plan was working.

Moxon's lugger came about. The rendezvous in the bay

on the north shore was dead to windward of Bic, and he could see the lugsails hardened in. He'd factored that into his plan. It would explain why Moxon's lugger didn't want to get too close to the pilot station, too far to leeward of where the supposed convoy was waiting.

'They're setting their sails, sir, all three of them.'

It was a pretty sight; the three long, low luggers heeling hard over to the wind as they tacked across the river.

'Mister Wishart, Mister Angelini,' Carlisle called down to the boats that were still hidden to windward of the frigate. 'Stand by for my word. There are three luggers, so you two and Mister Moxon can take one each. Remember, no violence unless it looks like they're getting away.'

Moxon's lugger hooked on to *Medina's* leeward main chains. The pilot had been quizzed about the regular routines, and Carlisle aimed to make it all look as normal as possible, just another day's business at Bic. As far as the other three pilot cutters were concerned, their friend had brought the escorting frigate across the river while he signalled for all the pilots for the expected convoy that would still be out of sight on the northern shore. The duty pilot was aboard the frigate. Soon his lugger would run down to join the others and take a share of the twenty-two to speed up the transfer to the merchant ships. This was all to be expected.

Carlisle was acutely aware that he was under the stern gaze of twenty-two pairs of experienced eyes. These pilots had seen the French navy come and go for years, and while he was able to fool a single pilot this morning, the odds on his deception being discovered were increasing all the time. They were two miles away now. He had to allow for the difficulty and discomfort in looking to windward, but even so, he would soon be pushing his luck.

'Mister Moxon. You may proceed. As soon as you can place yourself to leeward of those three.'

Moxon's lugger pushed off from *Medina's* side. The brails on the lugsails were loosed, and the boat moved quickly to leeward.

'They've hauled their wind, sir,' said Hosking, 'it looks like they're shouting to each other.'

Carlisle leaned over the rail.

'Now! Longboat and yawl. As fast as you can!'

Moxon's lugger was within hailing distance of the French pilots now. He was manoeuvering to get to leeward of them. As though with one will, all three swung off the wind. They were running for home; they'd realised they were being duped.

'Run down to them, Mister Hosking.'

It was a race now. Carlisle watched Moxon's boat come heavily alongside the lugger that had been first to turn off the wind. There was a brief scuffle on the deck. Moxon hardly had an overwhelming force against seven or eight pilots and a lugger's crew of three, but his men were armed, and they were prepared to fight. The sails came down with a rush as someone cut the halyards. That was the first of the three luggers in the bag.

The other two were to leeward now and running fast for Bic. Moxon left the crippled lugger and set his sails in pursuit. Now three boats were chasing two, and the two were a quarter-mile ahead.

'Mister Atwater. Take the gig and four men, you'll need cutlasses. Take possession of that lugger and follow me. Be careful; there are ten or so Frenchmen on board. I'll stay close until I see that you have them under control.'

The gig was already in the water and Atwater hurried off to find his crew.

***

Half a mile ahead a drama was unfolding as the two French luggers, the longboat, the yawl and the captured lugger raced towards the pilot station. It was going to be close, and Carlisle knew that once ashore, the pilots would be lost to him.

'Mister Gordon, run out the larboard battery. When your guns bear, I want single shots, all aimed by you. Pitch them well ahead of the boats. Don't drop any shot among them. Those are our people, and I hope the Frenchmen will be too.'

'Aye-aye sir,' the gunner replied. He was happy to be out of his magazine among the guns that he loved. There was little chance of him needing to make up fresh charges today.

*Medina* ran on, closing the gap with every minute. The frigate, with its big square sails, could easily run faster than any lug-rigged boat or navy ship's boat.

'What do you think, Mister Gordon?' he shouted.

The gunner ran up to the fo'c'sle and looked briefly at the four boats ahead. They were fast closing on the shore, and the luggers were still in the lead.

'It's now or never, Mister Gordon. Can you do it?'

'Aye sir, I can.' Gordon shouted back and ran to his guns.

'Bring her to, Mister Hosking. Put her beam-on to the boats.'

*Medina* swung gracefully to starboard as the tacks were passed, the braces hauled around, and the sheets heaved in.

'Brail up the main and fore courses,' said Carlisle still watching the boats.

They had just enough men left to do that at the same time as providing crews for a battery of guns.

Bang! Number one gun fired. Carlisle gulped as the ball fell close to the yawl. That must have soaked Enrico. An image flashed across his mind of telling Chiara that a shot from his own ship had killed her cousin. Not a pleasant picture.

Gordon waved to show that he acknowledged his fault. Perhaps he had failed to compensate for the frigate's heel becoming less as the leverage of the lower sails was lost. All along the line of guns, the captains were knocking out the quoins to increase the elevation.

Bang! That was number three gun. It had pitched ahead of the lead lugger and nicely in line. That should show them what would happen if the persisted in running for the shore.

Carlisle had a moment to ponder what he would do if the luggers didn't heave-to. Would he sink them? He certainly could at this range. He could sink them and consign all those Frenchman to the depths. Few of them would survive a minute immersed in these temperatures; they must know that.

Bang! That was number five gun. It produced a high spout only yards in front of the lugger.

'Fire by divisions, Mister Gordon.' Carlisle could see the race being lost for want of the application of force.

Four guns had a far different weight to a single gun, and *Medina* shuddered under the recoil. Carlisle couldn't see where each of the shot fell, but they were all close to the two luggers.

'By divisions again, Mister Gordon.'

'We've got them, sir,' shouted Hosking. 'They're brailing up.'

'Cease Firing…'

But it was too late, another division fired, and another four spouts appeared among the boats, miraculously missing all four but certainly holding their attention. Moxon, Wishart and Enrico's boats were quickly alongside the last two luggers.

\*\*\*

Carlisle had allowed his first pilot to speak to the others, to put the business proposition to them. He'd already signed his contract, he was committed, and now he was the best person to persuade the others. It took an hour or so, but eventually they all agreed. Perhaps it was when Sergeant Wilson – possibly the most terrifying person that Carlisle had ever met – was introduced as being responsible for the custody of prisoners-of-war that the last few holdouts capitulated.

'I want to make these gentlemen feel welcome, Mister Moxon. Would you invite them into your mess until we meet the squadron? It will only be for a day or two, and I'm sure you can arrange staggered mealtimes. They can sling their hammocks at the aft end of the gundeck.'

'Aye-aye sir.' That was the only response that Moxon could make. It was easy for Carlisle to make light of the problem, but it would be most uncomfortable for the frigate's officers.

'Mister Cook, I'm sure, would like to question them about the Traverse. I think we can free Mister Angelini from watches to translate for him.'

The truth was that Enrico hadn't been a regular watchkeeper for the past two weeks. He'd been fully employed making sketches for James Cook. The young man had a rare talent, and it would be a shame to waste it.

*Medina* made a curious sight as she ran back down the river to find the squadron. In addition to her usual complement of boats, she had four luggers towing in a long string behind, like ducklings following their mother.

***

Chris Durbin

# CHAPTER TEN

## The Coudres Channel

*Wednesday, Sixth of June 1759.*
*Medina, at Anchor. Goose Cape, Saint Lawrence River.*

The ebb tide, the westerly wind and the natural flow of the river had stretched the catenary out of *Medina's* anchor cable; it was bar-taut, as straight as a rod from the hawse to the water. The frigate was lying in fourteen fathoms in good holding ground just a few hundred yards off Goose Cape with sixty fathoms of cable veered. The bitts groaned under the strain, and the bosun kept his boot on the cable, feeling for the first sign of the anchor dragging. The ice had cleared, and with it, the fog. The air was crystal clear. All along the banks of the river the deciduous trees – aspen, maple, birch and red oak – were in full leaf while the evergreens, higher up the mountains, had lost their capping of snow. Spring had come and gone in just a few weeks, and now Canada was on the cusp of a glorious summer.

'Well, here we are, Mister Cook.'

Carlisle was in a talkative mood. He'd presented his charts for the passage from Seven Islands to Isle Aux Coudres, and Admiral Durell appeared impressed. With those charts and the twenty-two French pilots that Carlisle had delivered more than two weeks before, the ascent of the Saint Lawrence appeared more feasible each day. Those same pilots were distributed among the ships of the squadron, except for Jacques Vacher, the first pilot they'd taken. He'd formed an attachment to *Medina* and had been kept in the frigate. The pilots would be a welcome gift for Saunders and Wolf when the main body of the fleet arrived, and they would go some way to rehabilitating Durell's reputation, and that of the rest of his squadron as well. Pilots or no pilots, Carlisle felt that he could navigate the north shore of the Saint Lawrence with confidence, at least as far the Isle Aux Coudres.

By contrast, Cook was not a complacent man. While Carlisle could take a few moments to bask in the early summer sun and in the knowledge of a job well done, James Cook's restless mind was already plotting the next moves in the survey of this watery highway into New France. Carlisle was marvelling at nature's cycle of death and rebirth while Cook's mind was on the rocks and headlands, soundings and leading marks.

'It's the one thing every seaman knows about the Saint Lawrence, sir,' Cook said, gazing to the southwest.

'Eh, what's that?' asked Carlisle, taken unaware.

'The Traverse, sir. More ships have met their end there than anywhere on this coast. To get there we must pass the Isle Aux Coudres, and that's our first real test. The lower Saint Lawrence was simple by comparison.'

Carlisle found himself forced back into the here-and-now. He'd returned from the admiral only an hour before and was enjoying this very brief pause. He hadn't yet had a chance to tell his officers what the admiral wanted next, although it should be obvious to even the least thoughtful. He took a last look at the sublime beauty of the Canadian wilderness and reluctantly turned back to the business of war.

'Would you join me in the cabin and ask Mister Moxon and Mister Hosking also?' he asked, stifling a sigh.

\*\*\*

'The Coudres Channel, gentlemen,' Carlisle said theatrically. 'That's the next task, then the Traverse. Mister Durell expects the main body in about two weeks and by that time we are to have surveyed the Traverse and buoyed it right up to the point where it becomes the South Channel, past Isle Madam. Spread out that chart if you please Mister Hosking.'

They were all familiar with the chart by now. They had anxiously consulted it as *Medina* had moved up the river, marking down every headland and shoal, every anchorage and channel. From the Gulf all the way to the Isle Aux Coudres their charts were now better than the French ones – more accurate and more richly detailed. Nevertheless, beyond the eastern point of the island it was an unknown land, no British navigator had penetrated as far into New France for decades.

'We'll worry about the Traverse after we've conquered the Coudres Channel. The admiral has placed *Pembroke* under my command. We have the four French luggers, and I can call on the boats of the squadron and any officers that we may need. *Pembroke* will join us tomorrow, but I intend to weigh anchor at the first of the flood. Mister Cook, would you be so kind as to summarise what we know of the channel?'

Cook had studied the chart more diligently than anyone else. He'd also spent hours with Jacques Vacher learning all he could about that dangerous stretch of water. He adjusted the chart and cleared his throat.

'It's just six miles from here to the Isle Aux Coudres, and you can see the channel between the island and the north shore.'

He pointed on the chart to the island that lay to the southwest of them. From the deck, it looked uninhabited, a green Eden with virgin forest running down to the water. However, their pilot had told them that all but the eastern tip was inhabited and farmed, the first real civilisation that they had encountered thus far on the Saint Lawrence.

'How wide is the channel?' asked Carlisle.

'A little over a mile at its narrowest,' Cook replied. 'Monsieur Vacher thought that we might meet some resistance from the militia on the island. Just muskets, they don't have anything heavier, but they'll be a hindrance when we're sounding in the boats.'

'The chart mentions a whirlpool in the channel, did Vacher have anything to say about that?' Carlisle asked.

'He did, sir. The whirlpool certainly exists, and as the chart suggests, it can throw a ship onto the island at the flood, and onto the mainland on the ebb. However, in a well-found ship with a fair wind, it's no real danger. It does mean that the squadrons can only pass through with the wind between north and southeast. The pilots always anchor here, off Goose Cape while they wait for the wind.'

'Is the channel to the south of Coudres impassable?'

'For all but small craft, yes, sir. The chart shows a least depth of eight fathoms, but the pilot says it's not that much. There's a possible channel right over on the southern bank, but it's never been surveyed, and Vacher doesn't trust it.'

Carlisle studied the chart. If there were musketeers on the island, then it would be dangerous work in the boats. They would have to take soundings right up to the shore of the island, and the Canadian militiamen and the even the farmers and trappers were notoriously good marksmen.

'Once we're through the Coudres Channel, it's an easy passage to the Traverse,' Cook added.

'Can we anchor nearer the island than this Goose Cape?'

'Yes, sir, in the right conditions. Vacher says there's good holding ground on the ebb just off the northeast point of the island. If the wind stays in the west, it's safe on the flood too, but if the wind shifts to the east, it's too dangerous. That's why the pilots don't generally use it.'

Carlisle looked at the chart again. The detail was woeful, but it looked as though the tide and the current had deposited a long shelf of silt at the end of the island, and it was entirely feasible that it would provide a good anchorage.

'Then that's the first task, Mister Cook. As soon as the flood starts, you may survey that anchorage. Take the longboat, and Mister Wishart can follow you in one of the luggers. A file of marines in each and a swivel in the longboat. If it's suitable, I'll bring up *Medina* and *Pembroke* to lie there while the boats survey the Coudres Channel.'

It was late in the evening when the longboat and lugger returned. They hadn't been molested from the shore, but they'd seen movement and what looked like a militia patrol. Perhaps it had taken time for the locals to the west to be aware of the boats; in any case, they probably wouldn't yet be sure that they were British.

The survey had shown a good anchorage in twelve fathoms, dropping off to twenty, for two or three ships, but no more. It was satisfactory for Carlisle's needs while the channel was being surveyed, but the squadron would have to anchor off Goose Cape while waiting for a leading wind.

\*\*\*

*Medina* and *Pembroke* were anchored peacefully in the lee of the Isle Aux Coudres. The tide was starting to turn, and the gaggle of boats attached painter-to-painter to the ships was already swinging upstream. *Pembroke* was a sixty-gun fourth-rate ship, far bigger and more powerful than *Medina*, but her captain John Wheelock had been posted in December '57. He was a full two years behind Carlisle on the post-captain's list and would forever be subordinate. That two years of seniority made Carlisle the commander of this small force, the tip of the spear that Admiral Saunders was thrusting into the heart of New France.

It was a beautiful day. The wind was in the northwest, and the high clouds drifted lazily across the endless, light-blue sky. Winter clothes had been discarded, and the boat crews were all in shirts and waistcoats. There was a holiday atmosphere in the six boats that were taking part. Moxon was commanding from *Medina's* longboat with Cook directing the survey from the larger of the luggers. There was a master's mate or older midshipman in each of the four luggers and *Pembroke's* longboat. The flotilla was to move southwest through the passage, the longboats protecting the luggers, two of which were to sound each side of the channel. Probably the channel wouldn't need to be buoyed, as it looked quite deep right up to either shore. That was to be confirmed by the soundings.

Moxon's longboat pulled steadily away from *Medina* with the five other boats following. He had two files of marines and a swivel gun in each longboat today. They'd seen a militia patrol on the island, and that suggested that there may be similar patrols on the mainland shore on the opposite side of the channel. With a wave of his arm he sent *Pembroke's* longboat away to cover that side.

'Pull easy,' said Moxon.

The captain's coxswain, Souter, was sat beside him in the stern-sheets, the tiller grasped loosely in his capable hands. The longboat was far faster under oars than the luggers and Moxon wanted to keep his force close. He'd agreed that Cook would direct the two luggers on this side while Wishart did the same on the other.

It all looked very peaceful; only Lieutenant Hook, *Medina's* officer commanding marines, looked apprehensive. He scanned the wooded shore and kept glancing at his marines, ensuring that they were vigilant. As the northeast end of the island came abeam to larboard, Cook's luggers started their work. A sounding was taken with a lead-line, and at the same time, the bearings of some distinguishing feature were recorded from the boat compass. A little cape on the northern shore and the left-hand edge of the wooded island were the most suitable marks, as was the right-hand edge of Goose Cape. However, they would have to use fresh marks as they moved up the channel.

The longboat was no more than half a cable off the shore, and there was still no sign of any resistance.

'It looks like they've taken Falstaff's advice and decided that discretion is the better part of valour,' Moxon said. 'Perhaps your swivel and the marines won't be needed after all.'

Hook didn't reply but kept watching the line of trees above the brownish-grey shoreline.

'I see some movement on the shore, sir,' said one of the marines.

'Where? Point to it, man,' Hook replied.

'In that thin patch of trees to the right of the great rock. I thought I saw something.'

They all looked anxiously where the marine was pointing. There was nothing. Not even a bird was stirring in the virgin forest that reached down to the river.

'You just be sure before you make a report,' said the corporal savagely.

The marines were on edge. It was the wilderness of the northern forests that so affected them. They'd all heard tales of the savages that lived there, the scalping and the burning. With the tall, silent trees so close, and no sign of life, it all seemed too real.

The longboat had turned to face downstream and was stemming the flood tide, an occasional pull on the oars keeping her in her place alongside the tall rock. The luggers were moving slowly along the channel, taking their soundings and bearings. After the marine's false alarm, it all appeared quiet.

'Sir…,' It was the same marine, the one who thought he'd seen movement. He pointed dumbly at the shore.

There was a group of men, perhaps a dozen, dressed in the brown of farmers, kneeling or standing and pointing muskets at the longboat. A volley crashed out, and one of the marines gasped and dropped his musket, clutching his chest where blood was seeping out and staining his white pipe-clayed cross-belt.

'Return fire, Mister Hook,' Moxon ordered.

He looked again at the clearing, but all that he could see was a pall of powder smoke hanging over the place from where the volley came. The smoke drifted slowly away down the river, leaving the eerie feeling that they'd imagined it, but the marine's blood testified otherwise.

Hook looked questioningly at Moxon. 'I'll reserve my powder if you don't mind, sir.'

The wounded marine had slumped into the bottom of the boat. Moxon could see that he was severely injured, probably fatally. He'd seen chest wounds before, and there was rarely anything that could be done. He tried to remember the marine's name. Jones. That was it, Jones. A Welshman, a shepherd before he enlisted, from somewhere in the Cambrian mountains. It was odds-on that he'd never see his home again.

Crash! Another volley from the woods. This time there was nothing to be seen except the powder smoke. The musketeers had fired from the deep cover of the woods. That was an intelligent commander; he wouldn't risk exposing his men after the first surprise volley.

'Aim at the smoke,' said Hook calmly. 'Corporal look at that man's musket; it's pointing too low,' he snapped. 'At my word… Fire!'

Nothing. It was as though five muskets had discharged into the air. Not a leaf moved. The smoke was gone; there was nothing to show where their tormentors had been.

Moxon looked at the two luggers nearest to him. They'd suspended their surveying. At only a hundred yards from the woods, it would be foolish to persist. He studied the shore. There was no indication of where the enemy would fire from next. The boats were sitting targets, and his men had no cover except for the gunwales.

Crash! Another volley and this time a flying splinter from the gunwale hit an oarsman in the face. At least the stout oak had saved him from the ball which would surely have killed him otherwise. The fragment was protruding from his cheek, and it had penetrated right into his mouth. He turned to his mate who probed inside his mouth and grasped the long sliver of wood, pulling it out in the direction that it had entered with barely a murmur from the injured man. He pocketed the splinter – a souvenir to prove the tales he would tell around the mess table – and spat a great gobbet of blood over the side before turning back to his task. Moxon shivered. He hoped he'd manage to display the same *sang froid* if he were ever wounded.

'Let's get out of range, Souter. Pull for the northern shore.'

Moxon stood up and waved for the luggers to follow him. It was a retreat, but there was no glory in staying to be target practice for these French Canadians hiding in the trees.

\*\*\*

Admiral Durell frowned. This was the first check that he'd experienced in his ascent of the river, and he wasn't happy or impressed.

'Was there nothing more that you could do, Captain? Between *Medina* and *Pembroke*, you could muster a half company of marines, couldn't they clear out those Frenchmen? How many were there, a dozen or so?'

'My pilot assures me that there are at least two hundred militiamen on the island, sir, as well as the farmers who all have muskets.'

Carlisle was holding his ground. He knew that he was right; the Coudres Channel couldn't be sounded under fire, and he didn't have the means in his two ships to secure the island. Surveying was a precise science that required concentration and a static platform; no sailors could be expected to sit quietly on their thwarts under accurate fire without any protection or any hope of replying. He knew that the admiral had six hundred soldiers scattered throughout his ships-of-the-line and the three transports attached to his squadron. He'd heard that Durell hoped to reserve them to be put ashore on Orleans Island as a grand gesture to show that this time he had exceeded the expectations of his superior.

Durell gave Carlisle a long, hard stare.

'Very well. Then we'll raise the stakes. I'll have Colonel Carleton in here if you please,' he called to his secretary.

In the few minutes that it took to locate Carleton, Durell quizzed Carlisle on the condition of the island. He wasn't really listening to the answers, as Carlisle could see, but he was fidgeting with the inkwell and gazing out of the window, as though looking for inspiration. In one respect, Carlisle could see why Durell wanted to reserve those soldiers. It would make a powerful statement if he were able to present the whole of the route to Quebec in British hands, along with the tactically important ground of Orleans Island. From the island, the army could dominate the vast anchorage in the Basin and the South Channel; they could observe Quebec City and the Beauport shore. However, if they left Coudres in enemy hands, it would be a constant threat to their supply lines. It was the first bottleneck on the ascent, and it should be a vital objective for Durell's advance force. It would be much better to offer Saunders and Wolfe a secure line of supply and leave it to Wolfe's army to occupy Orleans Island, the last obstacle before the fleet could reach Quebec. Carlisle doubted whether a single battalion would be enough to subdue Orleans Island in any case, while they could surely clear the militia and farmers from Coudres.

***

# CHAPTER ELEVEN

## The Quartermaster-General

*Thursday, Seventh of June 1759.*
*Medina, at Anchor. Isle Aux Coudres, Saint Lawrence River.*

Carleton was an energetic man in his mid-thirties, about the same age as Carlisle. He wore his own hair which marked him as an individual in an army in which, for officers, the wearing of wigs was almost universal. He was Wolfe's quartermaster-general, but in the free and easy way in which the general moved his people around, he'd been given command of this mixed bag of infantry under Durell, with the orders to *cooperate with Admiral Durell in any service that may be thought practicable*. From Carlisle's perspective, there could be no better use of those six hundred men than to seize and garrison the Isle Aux Coudres.

Durell made the introductions. Carlisle was already notable in the squadron as the only post-captain who hailed from the American colonies, and Carleton was charmed to meet him. Carlisle knew him by reputation only; he was said to be a man who was eager, if not desperate, to make his mark. He'd been with the Duke of Cumberland in Hanover, part of the Army of Observation, and was tainted by association with that disastrous expedition. As a result, the King had refused to endorse an appointment as Wolfe's aide de camp for the attack on Louisbourg the previous year, and he'd had to accept another post in Germany on Duke Frederick's staff. It had taken Wolfe's dogged insistence and some powerful intervention to persuade the King to allow his present appointment.

'How long will you need to secure the Isle Aux Coudres, Colonel Carleton,' asked Durell without any sort of preamble.

There was a profound silence for a space of ten seconds. Carlisle feared the worst. Either Carleton had never heard of the island, or he felt that it was impractical with the forces under his command.

'Must I describe the island for you, Colonel?' asked Durell, tapping his fingers irritably on his desk.

There was another short silence. Carlisle was starting to be disappointed in Carleton.

'Coudres is five miles by two-and-a-half, I believe, sir,' Carleton asked looking sidelong at Carlisle for confirmation.

Carlisle nodded warily.

'My understanding from talking to our pilot is that the western three-quarters is all farmland and a few small patches of woodland, what we'd call thickets, although they're not managed for timber. The eastern quarter is forested, mostly oak and maple. There's a strong and active militia on the island. I understand you've already met them, Captain Carlisle,' he said bowing slightly.

Carlisle relaxed. Carleton's hesitation was nothing more than a pause to collect his thoughts, it appeared.

'There are no fortifications, or there were none a month ago when the pilot last passed that way. However, the farmers are well-armed. It will be no walkover, sir. How many boats may I have?'

'You may have all the boats in the squadron except those from *Medina* and *Pembroke*. I want Coudres subdued and secured as quickly as possible.'

'Then I'll put an assault company ashore at first light tomorrow. They can seize a landing area for the main body. Do you have a suggestion for the landing site, Captain?'

It was Carlisle's turn to pause for thinking time.

'From what I have seen, and my officers have reported, most of the island has a rocky shoreline. The eastern point is possible; there's some silt build-up there.'

Carleton considered again. He was not a man to be rushed when vital decisions were to be made.

'That would mean having to march six hundred men through a mile or two of thick forest. The irregulars would have the advantage, and it could take days.'

'I don't have days,' Durell snapped.

'The alternative is halfway along the northern side of the island,' Carlisle continued. 'That seems to be where the boats leave for the mainland, and it's the least rock-bound part of the island.'

Carlisle knew where he would land if he commanded this force, but he was letting Carleton come to that conclusion.

'It's also the main concentration of houses. It'll be the hardest place for the grenadiers to secure. They'll have to fight their way ashore,' Carleton responded. He appeared to be considering whether his force could achieve an opposed landing. He studied the admiral's chart. It offered little enough inspiration, merely showing the island as an oval obstruction in the stately flow of the Saint Lawrence.

'Nevertheless, that's where I will land, sir,' Carleton said firmly. 'If I can use all the squadron's boats, I can put my two hundred grenadiers ashore in the first wave. They'll be able to subdue any resistance around the landing area. Then the second wave can bring in the next two hundred. They'll all be ashore in three lifts, sir. Can you bring the transports into the channel?'

Carleton's way of speaking left Carlisle breathless. The whole plan was fully formed in the few minutes that he'd been allowed. The admiral was looking closely at the chart, and Carlisle looked at Carleton who winked at him. No, the man didn't have demonic powers, he'd planned for this landing since he'd first embarked with Durell. He had no confidence in this idea of saving his force for Orleans Island. It was quite clear to the quartermaster-general – the man in charge of Wolfe's logistics – that Coudres must be in British hands to secure his supply route. Carlisle smiled in return. A man after his own heart.

Durell also looked stunned by the barrage of positives.

'Captain Carlisle, when can you bring three transports into the channel?' Durell was throwing the ball back at him.

'Slack water at six, or thereabouts, sir, just after dawn. The ebb will be too strong to hold a position by eight.'

It was Carlisle's turn to think fast, and he hadn't prepared the answer as Carleton had.

'I'll take them up on the flood, sir, and lie-to about two miles into the channel. We'll be to the east of Charybdis…'

Durell was looking at him quizzically.

'My apologies, sir. There's a whirlpool between the island and the north shore. Mister Cook christened it after the one that Odysseus encountered in the straights of Messina.'

'This is no time to be quoting Homer at me, Mister Carlisle, let's keep to the facts, shall we?'

Carlisle attempted to look contrite but couldn't quite stifle a smile.

'If the grenadiers go ashore at five, then we should have all the soldiers ashore by eight and the transports can drop back downstream on the ebb. If necessary, they can anchor off the eastern end of the island; there's a good holding ground there for a few ships. May I have a pilot for each transport, sir?'

'You may. And Mister Carlisle, you will command the expedition until Colonel Carleton's force is established ashore. Understand this; I expect you to be in the lead boat. I want no cock-ups, Captain!'

\*\*\*

It was still dark as Carlisle stepped down into his longboat. He'd agreed to keep *Medina's* boats out of the landing so they could be ready for surveying, but he wanted the reassurance of his own coxswain, Souter, and his own boat's crew, and that meant *Medina's* longboat.

*Medina* and the three transports were lying-to in the centre of the stream, just occasionally letting their tops'ls fill so that they stemmed the fading tide. The wind had veered a few points into the northwest, but Carlisle had planned for that. It seemed to be the rule that the westerly breeze veered just before dawn.

He felt the boat tilt as Carleton dropped into the stern-sheets. There had been some competition between the majors as to which should have the honour of commanding the first wave of the assault, but Carleton had disappointed them all by declaring that he would command.

Carlisle had three files of his own marines in the boat under lieutenant Hook's command. While the grenadiers would secure a perimeter around the landing site, *Medina's* marines would guard the longboat. That way Carlisle had personal control of a nucleus of fighting men. They may not be many in comparison to two hundred grenadiers, but he knew how important even a tiny reserve like that could be.

The plan was to keep *Medina* and the transports out of sight of the landing-place until the grenadiers were ashore. Then they could move in closer, disgorge the four hundred musketeers, then drop back with the ebb.

\*\*\*

The first hint of the approaching dawn showed over the dense woodland of the eastern end of the island. Carlisle had little hope that they would be able to affect a complete surprise. From Moxon's reports, the militia seemed to be a competent body of men, and with British ships so close, they would probably have placed sentries at lookout points around the island. Yet even though surprise was unlikely, they may be able to persuade the militia that the landing would be on the southern side of the island. He'd sent two of his luggers with boat guns to make a noise and create uncertainty until there was enough light for boats to be seen from the shore.

Carlisle nodded at Souter.

'Give way,' Souter growled. There was little need for elaborate orders for crew. They all knew what to do, and most of them had rowed for Carlisle for a few years now.

Dimly, in the grey dawn, Carlisle could see other boats putting off from the transports. There seemed to be a vast number of them, and all were packed with grenadiers. This was to be an infantry affair. There was no cavalry in the whole of Wolfe's army, and no guns were to be put ashore on Coudres.

'The luggers have opened fire, sir,' said Hook, cupping his ear to the southwest.

'Then stretch out, Souter, stretch out for all you're worth.'

The day was coming fast, and the other boats were no longer grey shapes on a black sea. Now Carlisle could see the red coats of the grenadiers and the many-coloured facings – green, yellow, buff, blue – the colours of the regiments from which they'd been drawn. Fifteen or twenty grenadiers in each boat, fourteen boats in all.

He could clearly hear the luggers, and so would anyone not in a deep sleep on the island. They were firing as fast as they could load, not concerning themselves with aiming, and they were making a fine noise. In the faint light of the morning, it would take a very steady commander to decide where the blow was to be struck. At the least, he would have to divide his force to cover both the north and south sides. Unless the whole militia had been stood-to overnight, it was unlikely that Carleton would be opposed by a great enough force to prevent the grenadiers landing. All they had to do then was to hold a perimeter until the rest of the troops joined them. An hour should see the job done, then a day to clear the northern side of the island so that the survey could continue. The southern side could be mopped up at leisure.

The longboat was moving fast now, and the tide was slacking by the minute. The tree-clad shore sped past to larboard. Nobody had yet seen the landing site, and it was for Carlisle and Carleton to decide exactly where to land and to mark the spot by the simple expedient of running the longboat ashore.

\*\*\*

'You see that jetty and the wharf area around it?'

'Yes, that will do,' replied Carleton. 'If you can place me just past the jetty, then we'll command the whole of that cleared area around it. No militia, and certainly no irregulars will stand against grenadiers in the open.'

Carlisle could see what he meant. There was a wide area, something like an expansive village square, with a few barns and houses dotted around. It was coming up fast. Souter had heard the conversation and needed no further instructions.

'There's a column coming up from the south, sir,' said Hook. 'It looks like about fifty men with muskets.'

Yes, Carlisle had already seen them. It was a race now because whoever first made it to the landing site would have the advantage. Fifty muskets could hardly stop the landing, not against the picked men who made up the grenadier companies, but they could inflict heavy losses on the close-packed men in the boats.

'Here! said Carleton eagerly. 'Land here, then we can be ashore before they are on us.'

'Hard to larboard, Souter,' said Carlisle calmly. This was no time to unsettle the men, but he could see what Carleton meant. This may not be the optimum place for a landing, and there was no wharf, but the silt beach looked hard, and the grenadiers in the boats close behind them could be on dry land before that column reached them. But they wouldn't be first ashore, that honour would go to *Medina's* marines.

'Steady boys,' said Hook as the longboat arrowed towards the shore. He pointed towards the advancing column. 'Sergeant Wilson, you'll take up a position ten paces from the boat and form a line.'

Wilson shifted his halberd into his left hand.

'These are the boys who did for Jones,' he said quietly to his marines. 'Let's serve 'em proper.'

Jones had bled to death in the night. He'd been a popular man in the ship, and not only among the marines. There was an answering snarl from the oarsmen.

Carlisle had already given Souter his orders. The oarsmen were all armed with pistol and cutlass, and they were to form an inner cordon behind the marines. If a marine fell, a sailor was to take his place. They looked a piratical crew, with their pigtails and with their weapons stuffed into belts and sashes.

Crunch! Carlisle swayed forward as the longboat ran up the unyielding grey shore. The first of the marines were over the side before he'd recovered, and they were already moving forward towards the advancing column as Carlisle swung his leg over the gunwale.

'Form a line,' shouted Wilson, pushing the marines into their places with the butt of his halberd.

Carleton was out of the boat before Carlisle, waving the following boats into the shore. It looked chaotic as boat after boat surged forward, jostling for a place to land.

Carlisle heard the first shots. A ragged volley from the French militia, but they were winded having run God-knows how far from the place where they had mustered. A single marine staggered back and supported himself on his musket, his left arm hanging limply in his sleeve.

'Cock your muskets… Present your muskets…'

Wilson used the halberd to knock one musket barrel up a little. The enemy was no more than forty yards away; the marines couldn't miss.

'Fire!' shouted Hook.

A volley from eleven muskets is nothing in the grand scheme of land battles. Nevertheless, eleven musket balls smashing into a compact and disorganized group of fifty men in the half-light before dawn had an enormous impact. At least half a dozen men fell immediately, and more had been wounded but were still standing. It was a creditable performance by Hook's marines.

Over to his right, the grenadiers were forming a line that was growing and deepening as each boat came crashing onto the beach. There was Carleton waving his sword, and then the whole line started marching forward. There was no wild charge, just an inexorable line of bayonets moving through and past the line of marines. Carlisle saw them halt. He heard the words of command then a truly devastating volley hit the French ranks. They were brave men to have stood before the line of grenadiers, brave but foolish. Fully half of them fell and then the grenadiers charged. The line of bayonets surged over the unfortunate Frenchmen, and when it passed, none were left standing. The only remnants of that gallant force that had tried to protect their homes and farms were fleeing west away from the landing area.

\*\*\*

Carleton was wrong. It didn't take all day to secure Coudres; the job was done by noon. Many of the French escaped in boats from the western end of the island, and those who remained threw down their weapons. If any among them had harboured romantic ideas of carrying on an irregular war from the forests, they quickly realised their error. Coudres just didn't have enough wild spaces for warrior bands to hide.

By the dog watches James Cook was able to continue his survey of the channel. Now it was easy. With a friendly force on the island there was no threat from that side. Having heard from the fleeing survivors of Coudres, the militia of the north shore wisely chose to do nothing more than loose off the occasional musket from deep in the woods, hurting nobody. After the first few times, when the men in the boats realised they were in no danger, the random shots didn't interfere with the survey work in any way.

'We'll be finished tomorrow, sir.'

'That quickly, Mister Cook?'

'Yes, sir. The channel is deep and regular, we've found, and all I need to do is determine that there are no obstructions beyond a cable from the shore. That still leaves nearly a mile of the channel, and can you feel the wind?'

Carlisle could indeed. It was dropping fast, nearly a dead calm now.

'Vacher says that it will come from the east tomorrow and stay there at least a few days. We should be able to get the whole squadron through on Saturday. And as I've got the measure of Charybdis now, we can slip past easily enough with an easterly wind.'

Carlisle gazed out of the window. This was happening faster than he had hoped.

'Then I'll tell the admiral that we'll push on to the Traverse on Sunday. That should please him even if he needs to leave all his soldiers behind on Coudres.'

\*\*\*

# CHAPTER TWELVE

## Hogsheads and Luggers

*Saturday, Ninth of June 1759.*
*Medina, Underway. Cape Torment, Saint Lawrence River.*

The easterly breeze filled *Medina's* tops'ls and raised a satisfying chuckling sound from her forefoot in this calm water underneath Cape Torment. They were approaching the Traverse of dread reputation, yet here under the Cape, the river was serene and welcoming. Nevertheless, there were leadsmen in the fore chains, both anchors were acockbill, and Moxon was on the fo'c'sle ready to let go at the first sign that the frigate was straying from the safe channel. They were stemming the first of the ebbing tide and making no more than a knot over the ground.

Under the pilot's directions, they had crept upriver from Isle Aux Coudres, staying close to the northern shore and sounding as they went. The channel should have been buoyed, but it looked as though some enterprising Frenchman had removed them all, perhaps when the British fleet was first sighted, dashing all hopes of a second relief convoy.

It was easy to see why ships had to wait off Goose Cape for a leading wind before attempting this part of the passage. There was no room to tack and no good holding ground. From fifteen miles west of Isle Aux Coudres a ship was committed. It could do nothing but go forward until the tide or wind changed.

'You see the Butt now, sir,' said Vacher the pilot, pointing to the smaller hill to the west of the Cape.

'Yes,' Carlisle replied, studying the northern shore. The Butt was an obvious landmark, like a monstrous lump of proving bread dough deposited in the meadows below the Cape.

The pilot was speaking French. He had a little English,

but it was safer for Carlisle and Hosking to translate the French than to rely on the pilot's translations to English.

'Now sir, if you observe between the Cape and the Butt, there are four mountains in the distance, decreasing in height from right to left.'

The mountains were clearly visible to the northwest. There were smaller mountains in sight, but it was clear which ones Vacher was referring to.

'When the furthest left of them has passed over the left-hand edge of the Butt, you should come to larboard to enter the channel.'

The furthest west of the mountains was still a hand's breadth clear of the Butt. That probably meant about a mile to go before the turn, Carlisle decided.

'By the mark, thirteen,' called the larboard leadsman.

'Deep fourteen,' the starboard leadsman added.

'We appear to be right in the channel, sir,' said Hosking.

The Traverse was the Scylla to Coudres' Charybdis, the second of the twin obstacles on the passage to Quebec. Yet the six-headed monster of the Traverse held a higher rank than the whirlpool in the bestiary of the river's hazards. It was the terror that the Bic pilots used to justify their high fees and profitable monopoly. Hosking was privately sceptical. He would judge this Traverse on its merits.

The smaller of the mountains slipped steadily towards the Butt.

'Half a mile now, sir,' said the pilot.

'And a half, fifteen.'

Plenty of water here, but the pilot had warned of the channel's constriction. There were shallows and jagged rocks between *Medina* and the centre of the river, and fully seven-eighths of the width was unnavigable here above Isle Aux Coudres.

Now they could see Orleans as a distinct island, rather than a continuation of the northern shore. This is where an unwary ship without a good chart or the services of a pilot would come to grief. There was a tempting channel to the north of the island, just like at Coudres, but the chart showed no soundings. It was narrow, winding and treacherous with unmarked shoals and dangerous rocks that were awash only at low tide. The true channel was to the south, but to the uninitiated that wasn't clear at all.

'In five minutes, sir, you should come three points to larboard.'

The pilot wasn't watching the river ahead; he was staring over the starboard quarter at the Butt and the mountain beyond. The peak had just crossed the left-hand edge of the butt.

Hosking was also watching the transit, but he was sparing half his attention for the water on his larboard bow. There was nothing to indicate a channel, no disturbance in the water to mark the shallows that they would evade.

'Coloured water on the bow,' shouted Wishart from the fore masthead.

Wishart had been stationed there as a check on the pilot. After all, the man was French, an enemy, and he could have been plotting to wreck a British frigate while posing as a man who was happy to avoid the prison hulks and secure his future employment.

'How does it look two points to larboard?' Hosking shouted back.

That was the route that the pilot was advising; two points on the bow now would be the track of the ship if it made a three-point turn in a couple of minutes.

'Clear water on the larboard bow, sir.'

The conditions were ideal, a sunny day with an easterly wind and an ebbing tide. It couldn't have been better.

'Now, sir,' said the pilot, 'three points to larboard, if you please.' He sounded like the professional pilot that he was, not a coerced prisoner.

Carlisle nodded at Hoskins.

'Larboard your wheel quartermaster, make your course sou'west by south.'

'Deep twelve,' called the starboard leadsman.

'Bring up the sheets a touch, Bosun.' Hosking was swinging the stern off the wind; they'd be on a broad reach now.

'You can see the coloured water now on our starboard quarter,' Vacher said. 'Those are the *Battures*, the shoals you say in English, that's why our helm-over point is so critical. They're not visible when coming up the river, except at low water. You can only see them when you're past.'

With the wind on her larboard quarter and only her tops'ls and jib showing, *Medina* made slow progress against the ebb tide. Carlisle was happy with that. At one or two knots over the ground and with two leadsmen in the fore chains, it was unlikely that they'd run aground between casts of the lead.

*Medina* was close to the shore of Orleans Island. Less than half a mile to starboard he could see a hilly land with low cliffs in some places and a rocky shore everywhere. There was cultivated land, farmhouses and barns. The uninhabited little islands of Rots and Madam slipped by to larboard.

'When the first Frenchmen came here, they found wild vines, and now the islanders make their own wine,' said Vacher.

It was hard to reconcile this pleasant, civilised land with the wilderness of the Lower Saint Lawrence. It was warm here, and the people clearly made a good living. Of course, they'd been here over two hundred years and had been industriously improving the land ever since. This was no frontier outpost.

'That's Saint Francis village coming up now, sir.'

Carlisle studied the village through his telescope. A cluster of houses and agricultural buildings, a church with a short, pointed bell-tower.

'There's an anchorage over to larboard between the two islands, sir,' Vacher said. 'We only use it in emergencies, but it's quite safe, ten or twelve fathoms and good holding ground.'

'How far is that from the Orleans shore?'

Vacher gave a Gallic shrug. He'd never thought of the distances in those terms before, but Carlisle knew that they were knocking on the door of Quebec's outer defences now, and they could expect opposition. An anchorage out of range of artillery on the island could be valuable.

'Mark ten.' That was the starboard leadsman.

'Just a little off the centre of the channel, sir,' said Vacher. 'Bear away a point if you please.'

'Clear water ahead,' shouted Wishart from the fore topmast. 'The channel looks to be about five cables wide; then there's coloured water on both sides.'

'There's a little stream that runs off the island just ahead, sir. Before we reach it, we'll be at the narrowest part of the channel, there's less than half a league from Orleans Island to Isle Madam,'

'It's called the Delphine River on the chart,' Hosking remarked.

There was a sudden whirring sound overhead. A waterspout appeared off the larboard beam, accompanied by the barely-heard sharp crack of a light field gun.

'We're under fire,' said Hosking, quite unnecessarily.

'I expected nothing less,' said Carlisle. 'Can anyone see the guns?'

They all turned to the Orleans shore, scouring the bluffs and low cliffs with their telescopes.

'There's just a faint wisp of smoke two points abaft the beam, sir,' said Enrico, pointing to a barely discernible column of smoke rising from the trees a few hundred yards inland.

'That's from one of those farmhouses we passed. You should be looking for a wider spread of smoke. It'll disperse quickly in this breeze.'

Crack! There it was again, and a waterspout leapt up close on *Medina's* starboard quarter.

'I saw it that time, sir, but it's gone now. Just to the right of the stream, maybe three hundred yards.'

# Rocks and Shoals

An unusual site for artillery, thought Carlisle, but if the gunners hadn't prepared a firing position, it would be difficult to find a suitable place among the close-packed trees. The flat space at the estuary would probably be much better, and most likely there was a road going down to the shore for fishing boats.

Crash! A hit this time and judging by the speed of firing there were at least two guns. Three-pounders most likely, the smaller field pieces of the French Royal Artillery.

'I see the guns now, sir. They're firing from behind some rocks on the northern shore of the stream.'

That was good news. *Medina* would only have to endure this harassing fire for ten minutes or so, and then they'd be out of range. The guns would be unable to ford the stream quickly enough to keep up with the frigate as it continued down the channel. They'd done well to score a hit, even if the French gun crews hadn't seen it.

'You may fire broadsides, Mister Moxon.'

The first broadside caught Carlisle by surprise. He should have known that Moxon's gun crews would already be pointing their guns at the enemy. *Medina* tilted alarmingly as the entire battery of guns fired nearly simultaneously. There was no need to tell Moxon where the balls landed. He could see as well as Carlisle that his elevation was too great.

'You'll only get three or four more broadsides before we're out of range,' Carlisle shouted.

Moxon waved his hat in reply. It was amazing how the activity on *Medina's* deck had changed with the firing of the guns. A minute ago, Carlisle could issue orders in a conversational voice, but now the rumbling of the gun trucks on the deck, the shattering sound of the broadsides and the shouted orders and reports from the crews had brought the deck to something approaching bedlam.

'Mister Hosking, send a midshipman to relay the soundings, we mustn't miss any.'

The French gunners were firing more wildly now with *Medina's* broadsides falling about their ears. The field guns could no longer be heard, and the waterspouts were all astern. It was a commonplace that field gunners failed to train their guns fast enough to keep pace with a ship even when it was making only two knots over the ground. However, they'd chosen a good site, and *Medina's* balls that fell short were absorbed by the mud of the estuary instead of skipping over the ground to skim above the gunners or fall right among them. It would have been a lucky shot that scored a direct hit, and nothing else would harm the Frenchmen.

After four broadsides the French field guns were too far astern, and there was no question of *Medina* yawing in this narrow channel.

'Beg pardon, sir.'

That was the carpenter reporting the damage from that single hit.

'The ball's still stuck in the timbers, sir, just below number four gun. I'll get one of my mates over the side to pry it out when we're next at anchor.'

Carlisle refrained from demanding that it be done immediately. Someone would pay a few coins for the ball as a souvenir, and there was a risk of it falling over the side if they tried to shift it while the ship was underway. That was the carpenter's perk, the only one left to him when he couldn't illegally sell lengths of the King's timber in the yards.

\*\*\*

Cook looked tired as he walked into the cabin. He'd spent the last three days sounding the Traverse and laying buoys. They'd used hogsheads, four-and-a-half feet high, quarter filled with sand and with the bung and the chime well sealed with hot pitch. The coopers and their mates from *Medina* and *Pembroke* had worked around the clock to produce those buoys. Then the carpenters fixed a six-foot mast to each buoy, a complex task when there could be no question of a nail penetrating the staves or the head. The sailmakers fastened a square red flag to each buoy, and then

## Rocks and Shoals

the bosuns rigged a rope cradle that encompassed the hogshead and secured the cable and its anchor. It was all highly skilled work taking up the time of busy warrant officers and consuming the stores that they'd jealously hoarded over many months away from a yard.

Each buoy had been carefully laid in six fathoms at low water. That required fifteen fathoms of mooring bridle to allow for the tidal range and to give some scope for swinging. All the grapnels that the two ships possessed had been consumed as anchors, each backed up with six nine-pound shot, for which a further rope cradle had to be fashioned. And all that prodigious outpouring of the ships' resources had produced only twelve buoys, moored at one-mile intervals on both sides of the channel.

'It's done, sir, but it's not enough. Those flags can only be seen at a mile if the conditions are perfect. Anything more than a mile and they won't be visible at all, and we can be sure that at least one in four of them will sink within a week.'

Carlisle had never seen Cook look despondent. He was always the man to see his way around problems, to offer solutions rather than despair.

'Ideally, we'd have ten times that number, sir, one every cable.'

Cook smoothed out his own chart. It bore little resemblance to the chart that they'd started with. Now it was full of supplementary soundings, clearing bearings and transits, all the arcane language of pilotage. Cook spent hours at a desk collating the information that he brought back to *Medina* each day, then Enrico took over and amended the old charts and drew up new ones as fast as the data came from Cook.

They'd discussed this before. They'd done all that two ships could do, and now they needed help. Durell had stayed at Coudres, and with this easterly wind, it would take a day to get back to him.

'Well, we've surveyed the channel and marked it. I

believe that Mister Durell won't attempt the Traverse until Admiral Saunders brings the main body up, and he won't be here for two weeks. I'm going to send you back to Admiral Durell tomorrow, after you've had a good night's sleep, with a letter that I'll write this evening. At least we have time now, and the intelligent work has already been done.'

Cook bowed in acknowledgement of this clear endorsement of his labours.

'I'll ask for a boat from each ship of the squadron, nothing smaller than a yawl, because I'll require men to live onboard for days at a time. We already have the four luggers from Bic, with eight more yawls we can anchor a boat between every two buoys. I'll have a crew of four and a petty officer in each, with muskets and cutlasses. They'll be able to see off any small boat that comes out to interfere, and I'll also ask for two longboats to patrol the channel. The masts will give enough height for a flag to be seen at well over a mile and they can rig lanterns at night.'

'At night, sir?' Cook asked. 'Admiral Durell was certain that no ship could pass the Traverse in the dark.'

'And is that your opinion now, Mister Cook, with your new-found knowledge of the dangers?'

Carlisle was looking amused. He knew that Cook had been too bound up in the surveying and buoy-laying to be able to stand back and see the bigger picture.

'Well, now you ask, I find I must revise my opinion. With the channel marked by boats with lanterns, and in the absence of fog, yes, any self-respecting master could safely pass the Traverse.'

'It's my opinion, Mister Cook, that the French pilots have made too much of the danger. It's been in their interests to do so; they have a profitable royal monopoly to be maintained. If the passage of the Lower Saint Lawrence, as far as Quebec, ever becomes a routine, they'll be out of their feather-bedded positions.'

Cook could manage a smile at that.

'The Saint Lawrence above Bic will always be pilotage

waters, in my opinion, sir. However, you're right, they make too much of it, and I'm sure they do so to preserve their monopoly. There's no reason why the pilotage can't be opened to competing companies. When we've taken all New France, and the Saint Lawrence is ours, perhaps their Lordships will invite Trinity House to give an opinion.'

Carlisle stood and walked to the window. *Medina* was anchored between Rots and Madam islands, snubbing gently to a long cable. *Pembroke* was back at Cape Torment. Between them, they dominated the Traverse, and there had been no more field artillery on the Orleans shore.

'Then I'll write a letter and lay out our plan. I can't believe that Mister Durell will choose to modify it greatly. I'll give you a copy so that you can argue the points if you need to.'

'I'd like to take the latest soundings with me, sir, but they need to be properly laid down.'

'I'll have Mister Angelini work through the night. He's young and willing, and he can sleep through the day tomorrow.'

They both grinned at that. The thought of anyone sleeping through the day in the rowdy chaos of the midshipman's berth was truly laughable.

\*\*\*

Carlisle and Simmonds worked on the letter late into the night, making the strongest case that they could. Cook joined them at four bells in the middle watch. Apparently, he didn't sleep for longer than four hours at a time; he'd been a sailor before the mast for too many years. Between them, they completed the plan that would be laid before Admiral Durrell. The boats, the men, the weapons, the provisions, the lanterns, the tarpaulins for shelter – all the myriad of items that would be needed to sustain five men in each boat anchored in the river for perhaps four days at a time. Carlisle was determined on that point. No man should be required to spend more than three or four days in an open boat, even in these halcyon days of early summer. At last, the letter was complete.

'I expect to see you tomorrow with eight boats, manned and equipped, Mister Cook.'

'Aye-aye sir,' he replied. 'I believe the admiral will listen to me, and I'm sure he's mindful of the advantages of providing a buoyed channel for Admiral Saunders when he arrives.'

That was the first time that either of the two men had acknowledged the cloud that hung over Durell. His reputation would probably never recover, but this feat – and both knew that it was a substantial accomplishment – of surveying and marking the Traverse would go a long way towards appeasing Saunders and Wolf.

\*\*\*

# CHAPTER THIRTEEN
## The Great Traverse

*Monday, Twenty-Fifth of June 1759.*
*Medina, at Anchor. Cape Torment, Saint Lawrence River.*

Carlisle knew the Traverse intimately by now, probably better than the plantation in Jamestown where he was raised. No, certainly better than that antediluvian enterprise that was kept afloat by the sweat of enslaved labour. He shivered and shrugged off the evil memory of his last visit. For over two weeks his sole focus had been on learning the secrets of the twelve tortuous miles that carried the main upstream channel of the Saint Lawrence from the north bank to the south bank, from Cape Torment to the South Channel. And he'd done it, he and James Cook. They'd sounded it, surveyed it, buoyed it and drawn up the charts. Now all was ready for the invasion force to make its way through this last barrier on the way to Quebec.

Standing on his quarterdeck in the half-light, facing the easterly breeze, Carlisle's view down the river offered a truly breathtaking spectacle. The invasion fleet was coming slowly up the channel from Coudres to Cape Torment under single tops'ls, keeping close to the northern shore. Durell's squadron had remained east of Isle Aux Coudres as a covering force in case a French battle squadron should arrive, yet there were still over a hundred-and-sixty ships underway towards Quebec. Carlisle was privileged to witness this spectacle because *Medina* and *Pembroke* had been detached from Durell's squadron to see the fleet safely through the Traverse. *Pembroke* was anchored halfway down the Traverse, between the islands of Rots and Madam while *Medina* lay at the south-western end of the anchorage under Cape Torment, the point of departure for the Traverse.

'I'll take my leave now, sir, if I may,' said Cook, touching his hat.

'Yes, certainly Mister Cook.'

Carlisle was distracted, watching the great armada stemming the ebbing tide with the easterly wind on their quarters. They'd waited a week for this wind, and now they had it they must move quickly to get the whole invasion force and Saunders' and Holmes' squadrons through the Traverse and into the relatively open waters of the South Channel before the wind changed. They must move fast, but it was still a desperately dangerous stretch of water. So far – and Carlisle unconsciously touched the wood of the quarterdeck rail – so far, not a ship had been lost in the whole passage up the river. It was important to maintain that record of success, and that meant constant vigilance until the fleet was through. There was one thing that he must do though, and it was best done in the hearing of his officers on the quarterdeck.

'I must thank you, Mister Cook,' he said in a formal voice, 'for your exemplary efforts in surveying and buoying the channel. This,' he waved a hand at the advancing ships, 'is largely your achievement.'

Cook was the most self-confident of people, but even he looked a little embarrassed at this public commendation. He was aware that the officers of *Medina* were watching him with interest.

'I couldn't have done it without your people, sir,' he said. 'Mister Hosking, Mister Angelini, and the boat crews.'

'Yet it's your triumph Mister Cook, and you are justified in taking pride in it. I trust that we'll meet again, but until then, I wish you the best of good fortune.'

Cook went down the side into the waiting yawl without any kind of ceremony. He was a warrant officer, after all, and naval ceremonial was reserved for commission officers. *Medina's* yawl spread her lugsail and ran down to the sloop *Zephyr*, from where Cook would navigate the way through the Traverse.

Carlisle turned back to the job at hand. *Medina* was to act as the marshalling point for the transit of the Traverse, and his deck was crowded with French pilots waiting to be rowed out to the men-o'-war, transports and storeships.

\*\*\*

Three days, that's how long Vacher claimed the east wind would hold. So that was the span of time that Carlisle had to work with. Three days, but Hosking was sceptical. He'd looked back at the log. It was plain that these easterly winds in the Saint Lawrence could turn westerly after just one day and often did so after two. It would be a disaster to have half the force safely through the Traverse, while the other half was swinging from their anchors under Cape Torment waiting for a favourable wind. Carlisle planned to get the whole fleet through in two days, and even that length of time made him nervous. It was a full twelve miles from the Cape Torment anchorage to Saint John Point and the start of the South Channel. That was half a day at the cautious pace that the pilots felt was safe. The plan that Carlisle had given to Saunders split his fleet into ten divisions of sixteen ships each. The first division would be all men-o'-war to move swiftly up to the Basin and suppress any opposition. Each following division would be a mix of men-o'-war and transports until the final two divisions which would have all the supply ships, with the last few men-o'-war bringing up the rear. He aimed to get them all through in daylight, but the anchored boats that marked the channel would light their lanterns to guide any stragglers. In midsummer, at this latitude, the daylight lasted from the six o'clock until ten o'clock. The first division could start at six, and the last must be underway at the end of the afternoon watch. That meant a division must start the passage of the Traverse every two hours. It would be tight. Getting a mixed bag of sixteen ships-of-the-line, frigates and transports to weigh anchor, receive their pilots and be underway within a two-hour window was asking a lot. And the pilots, once embarked, couldn't get back to Cape Torment until the next day. Even the swiftest and most weatherly lug-rigged boats would have a long beat back down the Traverse against the easterly wind. Four pilots for each division. Only every fourth ship would have a pilot, far less than the one-ship, one-pilot that the station at Bic had insisted upon for their countrymen in peacetime.

It was Carlisle's responsibility to allocate the pilots and get the divisions moving. It was the captain of the lead ship of each division who would enforce the sailing discipline and ensure that his division was clear of the anchorage within two hours of his start time. That left little room for error, just a few extra hours at the end of each day to take up any straggling divisions or individual ships, and the possibility – no more than that – of an extra day of the easterly wind.

\*\*\*

The marine turned the glass, and the messenger struck four bells. The sun was still below the hills in the southwest, but its pre-dawn glow had lit up the anchorage, and the ships were suddenly visible as more than indistinguishable grey shapes. Carlisle took a deep breath.

'Make the signal for the first division, Mister Wishart. A gun to windward if you please, Mister Moxon.'

Carlisle watched the signal flags soar up the mainmast. He jumped as the gun fired. He always jumped, even though he had ordered the gun only a minute before. In that minute, he had quite forgotten his previous directive and his mind had rushed forward to consider his next moves. He privately blessed the efficient crew that allowed him to think ahead rather than having to monitor their performance of his orders.

*Zephyr* made the acknowledgement almost before the sound of *Medina's* gun had stopped echoing back from the Cape. Greenwood was a steady officer. In his late thirties, he was rather old for a sloop, but many officers had languished for a decade or more as lieutenants before this providential war propelled them to the rank of commander. With Cook piloting and Saunders' flag in sight to exert its massive dignity over them, Carlisle had few fears for the lead division. It was those that followed that concerned him. He didn't know the quality of one in ten of the captains and masters who commanded them, and their ability to handle the French pilots was completely unknown.

'*Zephyr* has weighed, sir,' said Hosking. 'She's casting up-channel under tops'ls, jib and driver.'

The snow backed and filled as *Lowestoffe* moved up astern of her. Saunders had shifted his flag into the handy frigate for the Traverse; he was determined to be among the first to reach the Basin. Carlisle had moved Vacher into the temporary flagship. He'd spent weeks cultivating the goodwill of the French pilot, and now he was to be let loose on the commander-in-Chief, who Carlisle knew spoke excellent French. With Cook in *Zephyr* and Vacher in *Lowestoffe*, the lead division was in good hands. The two fourth-rates weighed their anchors and fell into line, then the transports and another frigate brought up the rear.

The whole of the first division was soon moving serenely up the channel with no more than two cables between each ship, as Carlisle had recommended, and Saunders had ordered. The division took up three miles, and the rearmost ship was clear of the anchorage before seven bells had been struck. A very encouraging performance, but Carlisle knew that it wasn't likely to continue. It would only take one of the unwieldy transports to fall across another's hawse to bring confusion where now there was order. The admiral's instructions were explicit; if any ship failed to join its division, it was to anchor clear of all other ships and wait until Carlisle could allocate it to a later division.

\*\*\*

The day wore on. It was the fourth division that caused the problem. As he'd feared, one of the transports missed stays as she was waiting to take her station and she drifted across the bows of a two-decker that was still winning her anchor. The angry bosun of the two-decker fended her off, but the transport then fell across two others. With the tide now flooding and the wind firmly in the east, there was no hope of the division holding its position while the damage was repaired. There was nothing for it but for the three ships to anchor again at the very southwest end of the holding ground. They would just have to wait until the fifth division had left the anchorage, then they would form their own, smaller division – the division of shame – in the last of the daylight. It was exactly what Carlisle wanted to avoid, but it was just what he had envisioned when he had built in the spare two hours at the end of the day.

***

'Well, I hope I'll see you before the morning watch, Mister Moxon,' said Carlisle. 'In any case, you know what to do. If the wind holds' – he touched the quarterdeck rail again – 'you must start the divisions moving at dawn. You have the admiral's authority to insist that they keep to the order of sailing.'

'Aye-aye sir,' Moxon replied. They'd already discussed this in detail. Carlisle had always intended to go up the Traverse with the last ships of the day and come back down in one of the boats. When they'd planned it, he'd hoped to be leaving two hours earlier and in one of the men-o'-war. Now it would have to be a transport, and there were only two pilots left at this end of the Traverse, and one was already in the damaged ship. He would embark in the *Good-Will* – the last transport left to run the Traverse on this day – taking the final pilot with him, a man whom he didn't know. Souter would follow in the longboat so that there was no delay in finding a boat to bring him back to *Medina* at the end of the day. Only the frigate *Richmond* was left to bring up the rear, bringing the twilight with her to close the Traverse for that day.

***

'Ye'll be sailing with us then, sir,' declared the master of the *Good-Will* as Carlisle heaved himself over the gunwale.

He was a short, stout man dressed in ordinary brown working clothes, but his enormous whiskers, his extraordinarily bandy-legged gait and his mahogany skin all

# Rocks and Shoals

declared his profession as a seaman.

'And this will be the pilot,' he added, as the Frenchman followed Carlisle onto the deck. 'You're both very welcome, but I'll thank you, Monsieur Pilot, to rest your buttocks by the taffrail and speak only when you're spoken to. I need no advice to get me past these few rocks and sandbars.'

The pilot knew enough English to understand that his advice was to be disregarded. Carlisle was in an awkward situation. He had no authority to direct the working of this transport and had no desire to enter an argument with this gruff person on board his own ship.

'Then we shall be lost,' said the pilot in his broken English. 'No ship can pass the Traverse without the direction of a pilot; it is unheard of, impossible. I wash my hands of you,' and he made a theatrical motion of scrubbing his hands in the air. Then he snapped his fingers under the master's nose and retreated to sulk at the taffrail.

'You just take the helm, John,' said the master to a man who appeared to be the first mate of the transport. 'I'll con from the fo'c'sle, listen for my orders.' With that. he took up the speaking trumpet and waddled forward, smiling and jesting with the men on deck as he went as though he didn't have a care in the world.

'There's no hope of changing his mind, sir,' said a voice from behind Carlisle, 'he's taken this attitude since we sailed from Halifax.'

Carlisle turned to find a soldier facing him, a major by the look of his uniform.

'We've suffered this for seven weeks now. Montgomery, sir, forty-third of foot,' he said saluting. 'There appears to be nothing that I can do to influence him and to be fair, we've had an uneventful voyage so far.'

Carlisle thought for a moment. He had no authority either, not in the handling of the ship. If the master had proposed to remain at anchor or ignore the orders sent down to him, then Carlisle could intervene, but it was any master's right to ignore the advice of a pilot if he wished.

The *Good-Will* was moving steadily into the Traverse. Carlisle braced himself to act – he didn't yet know in what way – if it looked like the truculent master was putting the transport in danger. He knew that Saunders would back him up if he relieved the master of his command, but he wasn't at all sure that the crew would follow him. All the indications suggested that they were loyal to the master. Carlisle realised that he didn't know the man's name. He nodded grimly at the soldier.

'He's taking the ship in the right direction, at least,' Carlisle replied.

There was a steady flow of helm instructions coming back now, and the mate looked confident.

'I'll join the master on the fo'c'sle,' said Carlisle to Montgomery. 'Would you send one of your officers forward with me? In case I need to send a message.'

'Lieutenant Knox!' Montgomery shouted, and a younger officer turned around from where he'd been watching the green shores of Orleans island.

'This is Mister Knox, sir,' Montgomery said. 'You may consider him your ADC for the time that you are on board.'

Knox grinned, he appeared to be enjoying the situation.

'Follow me, if you please, Mister Knox.'

Carlisle and Knox worked their way for'rard through the ship's crew who were manning the sheets and braces. The soldiers, about a hundred-and-twenty of them, had been confined below for this passage, but there was a handful of officers of the forty-third disposed along the gunwales.

The Master was still smiling as Carlisle and Knox came onto the fo'c'sle.

'You see, Captain, this is not so difficult at all. I'll not have that Frenchman believe that I need his help. Damn me, if there are not a thousand places in the Thames River fifty times more hazardous than this.'

The master kept up a running tirade against the Frenchman and all pilots in general, interspersed with shouted orders back to his mate. He clearly knew his

## Rocks and Shoals

business, and he pointed out the changing colour of the water and the ripples and eddies that showed where hidden dangers lurked. Carlisle had been through the Traverse a dozen times now, and as far as he could see the *Good-Will* was as squarely in the centre of the channel as she could be. The anchored boats with their coloured flags slipped past them at regular intervals, and the master shouted across to each, a joke, a laugh, a word about the weather and the tide.

'Captain Carlisle!'

That was Hankerson's voice, *Richmond's* captain. Carlisle hurried back to the quarterdeck. Hankerson was six months senior to him, and he couldn't be ignored, even though they were coming to the most difficult part of the Traverse.

''I see your fellow isn't using the pilot and you know that I must follow you as I have none. Does he know the way?'

'He appears to, sir,' Carlisle replied.

*Richmond* had closed the distance to the *Good-Will* and conversation between Carlisle on the transport's quarterdeck and Hankerson on the frigate's fo'c'sle hardly needed the two men to shout.

The French pilot was talking excitedly and so rapidly that nobody could understand him. However, his meaning was clear; without his guidance, they were all doomed. Since Samuel de Champlain had sailed up the river a hundred and fifty years ago, nobody had ever survived the Traverse without a pilot. He held no responsibility for the consequences, and he damned all foreigners, and Englishmen particularly, for all eternity. He was properly ignored.

'What's his name? My sailing-master is asking.'

Carlisle was just about to admit that he didn't know when the man himself answered from the fo'c'sle, using the speaking trumpet, although with his stentorian bellow it was hardly necessary.

'It's Old Killick,' he shouted. 'Tell your master that's all he needs to know!'

Hankerson turned to see his sailing master waving in

reassurance from the frigate's quarterdeck.

'Well, if it's good enough for the master, it's good enough for me,' said Hankerson. 'You'll keep an eye on him, Carlisle, I'm sure.'

The mate grinned as he spun the wheel a few spokes to starboard in response to Old Killick's next shout. The hands at the braces shifted the yards until they were nearly athwartships. The transport followed the channel to starboard and *Richmond* obediently followed in her wake.

The frigate dropped back a cable into her proper station, and Carlisle returned to the fo'c'sle. He briefly wondered whether Killick was really the master's name, or whether he'd been nicknamed after an archaic anchor as some sort of recognition of his nautical prowess.

'May I ask, sir,' asked Knox, 'does this Old Killick know his business?'

'Yes, I believe he does, Mister Knox, I believe he does.'

'Well, we've all become used to him. He'll accept no interference, but he's kept us safe so far.'

The day's final division of ships was sailing right into the path of the setting sun. There was still enough light to pass Saint John in the daylight and reach the anchorage beyond, and Carlisle was starting to relax. The steady stream of orders still came from the fo'c'sle and the French pilot, discouraged beyond words to find that the ship still floated, had fallen asleep on a spare tops'l that had been left under the taffrail.

*Good-Will* anchored at last to the west of Saint John Point. *Medina's* longboat came alongside, and Carlisle made his farewells to Montgomery and Knox. While the transport had been anchoring Souter had gathered up a dozen pilots for the night-time beat back down the Traverse. It would be a tedious passage, but at least the tide was turning, and they would have the full force of the ebb behind them.

'You see,' shouted Old Killick as they left the transport's side, 'there was nothing for an Englishman to be concerned about. But we'll mark it up in the log as a damned difficult passage if you like, otherwise we'll get no credit at home.'

His laughter followed the longboat as it slipped away into the gathering gloom, bound for Cape Torment, and soon even that enormous voice was lost astern. Only the French pilot kept up his monologue to his fellows, no doubt describing how close they had come to disaster as his advice was ignored.

'Silence in the boat,' ordered Souter. The pilot started to argue the point, then Davis, a big, ill-favoured brute pulling number three oar turned and faced him, tapping his hard oak stretcher against the palm of his hand. Quiet at last.

\*\*\*

## CHAPTER FOURTEEN

### Infernal Engines

*Thursday, Twenty-Eighth of June 1759.*
*Medina, at Anchor. The South Channel, Saint Lawrence River.*

Perched on the top of cliffs overlooking the swift Saint Lawrence, Quebec sat at the point of a peninsula formed by the confluence of the Saint Lawrence and Saint Charles rivers. To the north and west beyond the city's strong fortifications lay the Plains of Abraham, a high plateau dotted with farms that merged into the forests to the west. Occupying the plain would merely lead to a long siege and with only three or four months left before the fleet must leave to avoid being trapped by the ice, that didn't seem a very sure way of reducing the city. Across the Saint Charles, the Beauport shore looked promising at first sight, but it was guarded by shallows that prevented the men-o'-war from getting close enough to support a landing, and Wolfe would still have to force a crossing of the Saint Charles to approach Quebec. In any case, the Beauport Shore was where Montcalm waited with his own army.

It had been a remarkable feat of surveying, navigation and fleet management that had brought a battle squadron and an army, with all its logistic tail, up the Saint Lawrence. That had been Admiral Saunders' job; now, the focus shifted to General Wolfe. How would he address the reduction of this powerful fortress? His energy was impressive. By the end of the day on the twenty-seventh of June, he had put his army ashore on Orleans Island.

Carlisle pondered all this as *Medina* lay at anchor, his thoughts paralleling those of Wolfe and Saunders. There had been no sign of the French frigates that had brought the last convoy up the river. The deserters said that they'd moved the seventy miles past Quebec to Trois Rivières. They would be a constant worry. They couldn't hope to fight Saunders' fleet of ships-of-the-line, but they could disrupt a landing above Quebec, and with the guns of the Citadel commanding the passage, it wasn't clear that any British ships would be able to pass upstream to get at them.

\*\*\*

After the previous night's storm that had wrecked two transports and a host of flatboats – the first casualties of the expedition – the wind had moderated to a tops'l breeze blowing from the west. *Medina* lay at anchor off Orleans Point at the far western end of the island. Carlisle could see the lights of the city three miles away to the southwest. To the east lay the ships of the battle squadron, and beyond them, the transports and storeships were anchored in the South Channel. Only their riding lights were visible now that the slim crescent moon had set.

'Well, here we are, Mister Moxon,' said Carlisle as he stood beside his first lieutenant at the taffrail. The lantern at the stern illuminated the two men, giving their faces an unearthly pallor.

'Yes, sir,' Moxon replied, 'here we are, and I'm not sorry to be quietly at anchor for a while. It's the soldiers' turn now, but the good Lord only knows how they'll tackle that,' and he nodded towards the city perched on the cliffs.

From the river it looked impregnable, a high city looking down over the narrow passage, the gateway to Upper Canada.

The light from the lantern only enhanced the haggard look of the lieutenant. He'd been fresh-faced only a few months ago, but the passage of the Saint Lawrence had etched its mark on those previously smooth features. He appeared to have aged ten years since they spent Christmas in Virginia, and it was hardly surprising. Carlisle had shouldered all the weight of surveying the Saint Lawrence, leaving the running of the ship to Moxon. He'd been doing two men's work since the end of April.

'I expect the general will attack over the Beauport shore. That's the easiest landing place. If they can get a toe-hold on dry land, then it will force Montcalm to fight.'

Moxon nodded and continued gazing at the city. There were lights enough there, but at three miles they were dim and didn't give a real idea of the city's outline. However, it was clear that there was an upper and a lower part, the main city at the top of the cliffs and a lower, more commercial town at the foot.

Suddenly Moxon stiffened.

'Sir, do you see some extra lights?'

Carlisle was looking past *Medina's* stern lantern, but the glow was affecting his vision. He moved around to the other side.

'There, sir,' said Moxon pointing. 'Just to the left of the city and low down. Right on the water.'

At first, Carlisle could see nothing. Then he saw them, a cluster of dim lights right down on the river's surface, as Moxon had said. They had a slightly reddish tinge, not like lanterns at all. One of the lights brightened, and then faded, as though a shield had momentarily dropped.

'Fireships!' exclaimed Carlisle, 'and they're close!'

'Ring the bell and keep ringing it,' Moxon shouted at the marine sentry. That was the universal warning at night. It would alert the other frigates, and in the dead of night, they'd quickly guess that French fireships had been spotted.

'Away all boats!' shouted Carlisle above the din.

The bosun came rushing on deck, wakened by the bell.

'Bosun, get the crews into the boats. Mister Moxon, take the yawl, I'll take the longboat. Mister Hosking, you're in charge, get the spare yards ready to bear off anything that comes too close.'

Carlisle hadn't stopped to think before committing himself to the longboat. A captain's place was in his own ship when fireships were threatening, but in this case, he could see that the wind and tide would take them to the south of *Medina* – his ship was safe. If he were quick, he could tow some of them away before they reached the rest of the fleet.

# Rocks and Shoals

In only five minutes, the boats were manned and pulling fast towards the advancing horror. It was amazing how much closer the lights were, and now he could see that the fires were being lit.

'The pickets have most of them, sir,' shouted Moxon from thirty yards away.

It had been expected that the French would try fireships, but it looked as though the combustibles had been lit too soon. The crews would naturally have made their escape as soon as the fireships were well alight. Now the infernal engines were at the mercy of the wind and tide, and of the British picket boats stationed between the fleet and the city for just that purpose.

The ebbing tide was sweeping them inexorably down the South Channel towards the British fleet; it looked as though they would all pass to the south of the frigate.

'How many do you think, Souter?'

The coxswain stared hard for a moment.

'Maybe six or seven, sir. Look, there's one of them that has passed through the pickets.'

'Then take us to it,' said Carlisle.

'Aye-aye sir,' Souter replied. 'I'll get ready to jump if you can take the tiller for a moment.'

'You manage the boat, just get me close enough so that I can put a line over something.'

Carlisle could see Moxon making for the same fireship. He looked over his shoulder; there was a veritable flotilla of boats putting off from the frigates and further up the channel he could see the ships-of-the-line doing the same. It seemed that the fireships would be outnumbered ten-to-one, no, fifty-to-one. However, they were still a potent menace. It only took one to get through and set a two-decker alight for the French to have won this sordid little battle. Once a ship took fire, it was horribly difficult to put it out. Dry wood, pitch, paint, and canvas burned readily, and then there were the tons and tons of black powder stored way down in the bowels of the ship. It took time for a fire to penetrate that far, but once it had taken hold, there was nothing to stop it. And a magazine exploding in that crowded anchorage didn't bear thinking about.

The fireship was awfully close now, and Carlisle was looking for something to throw a rope over so that they could tow it clear. To his horror, he realised that there was nothing. She'd been well-prepared; there were no vertical projections to take the bight of a rope, the decks had been swept clear except for the combustible materials.

'I'll jump,' said Souter, preparing to relinquish the tiller.

Carlisle pushed him back into his place. He'd already taken off his coat, now he kicked off his shoes and elbowed his way to the bows. He took the longboat's painter in his hand.

'Run the inboard end aft as soon as I've made fast,' he shouted to the bow oar.

'Stand by, sir, almost there.'

Souter was standing to get a better view over the heads of the oarsmen. Carlisle had a moment to see that they all looked apprehensive, as well they might when their every effort was directed towards moving closer to that floating inferno.

The flames had really taken hold on the fireship. The sails had gone, but the masts were still whole, and the fire was concentrated in the bows.

'I'll take a turn around the mast,' Carlisle shouted, then he jumped.

It was only a matter of a yard or so, but it seemed more. He landed in his stockinged feet on the low gunwale at the stern. Even here, far from the seat of the blaze, it was hot, and he felt foolish in so quickly discarding his shoes. Still, it shouldn't take long. He looked back to see Souter moving the longboat along the blazing brig's side, keeping pace as he ran to the mast. A quick turn then back to the longboat grasping the painter. There was the bowman leaning out to take the end of the painter. Carlisle thrust it into his hand then gathered himself for the leap.

Rocks and Shoals

At that moment, a gust of wind, perhaps an eddy caused by the nearby Cape Levi, blew the flames back and Carlisle overbalanced as the intense heat swirled around him. In another moment he was in the water. It was wonderfully cool, but he plunged deep, and it was a few seconds before he surfaced spluttering and gasping for air. In the unpredictable way of tidal currents, he saw that he was astern of the longboat, perhaps ten or twelve feet, and he caught a glimpse of Souter looking in the wrong direction, staring at the point where he had slipped into the water. The wind was pushing the fireship and the longboat fast towards the east. It was the wind that was the problem, of course; the boats were affected by it while he was so low in the water that only the tide influenced where he drifted. He tried to shout, but the water slopped into his mouth each time. He saw with despair that Souter was still looking in the wrong direction. They had the fireship in tow but were drifting, still looking for him. At that moment Carlisle wished with all his heart that they'd release the fireship. Forget about it; let it blow up the flagship with the admiral and general, damn them all, just come back to find him.

\*\*\*

The blow almost stunned Carlisle, he wasn't to know that it was a boathook fishing for him in the darkness. It felt as though his skull had split in two. His head went under again, and this time his breathing was out of sequence. He took an involuntary gulp of cold, brackish water deep into his lungs. Time seemed to stop as he struggled, coughing and drawing more water with every convulsion. Then he felt a tug at his neck. Something was drawing him along, though whether it was up towards life or down to his death, he had no way of telling.

His head broke through the surface again. He tried to take a breath of air, but it just brought on a violent coughing fit as his lungs tried to expel the water. He knew that he couldn't keep afloat and tried once more to draw in air. More coughing. Then he realised that he wasn't sinking.

Something was miraculously keeping him afloat.

'Hold onto him!'

That was Moxon's voice.

'Boat your oars, larboard side. Hand him back. No, Jefferson, take a grip of his collar and walk him aft.'

He felt himself being hauled along the rough side of a boat. His mind was working surprisingly well, although he could feel it starting to slip. If only he could take a breath.

'Don't let go Jefferson. Now, Taylor, get a grip under his arm.'

Carlisle felt a muscular arm under each shoulder, and then he was being hauled into the boat. He should have felt the pain of being dragged over the gunwale, but the agony in his lungs blocked out all other sensations.

'Now, lay him on his front. Move over there, Jefferson, make space. Is he on the thwart? Then push hard on his back in time with your own breathing.'

All this Carlisle heard, but it was as though they were talking about a different person. He felt the huge, rhythmic pressure on his back, but it wasn't painful. Another cough, then he spewed up a flood of water followed by the remains of his supper. Now he could breathe again, a blessing in disguise as he quickly discovered when the pain returned. This was real suffering. The bruises and cuts that he'd received from the boathook and the unceremonious entry into *Medina's* yawl were bearable, as was the continued pummeling on his back. It was the raw pain in his lungs that caused him to gasp.

'Belay that, Jefferson, sit him up.'

Carlisle looked around. He could see the bright flames of the fireships a mile or so away, and he could see one of them much closer, just a cable or so. That must be the one that he had slipped from. It seemed an eternity since he fell into the river.

'How do you feel now, sir?' asked Moxon.

Carlisle could only nod. Speech was impossible.

'They're all being towed clear, sir. Some are already

Rocks and Shoals

beached on the point of the island and some under Cape Levi. Only yours got through the pickets, as far as I can tell, and Souter has towed it clear.'

A dull boom came down to them on the wind. That would be one of the fireships on Cape Levi. The fire must have reached the powder casks on the deck, completing the destruction.

Carlisle knew that he should be concerned about Souter. He must take the fireship on a long, long tow, tying all his painters end-to-end, so that the longboat would survive an explosion. But really, he couldn't raise the energy. He fell back, comforting himself with the thought that his coxswain knew very well what he was doing.

\*\*\*

Carlisle took the best part of a day to be back on his feet. The surgeon prescribed laudanum; it must have been in heroic quantities, he realised later, because he remembered no dreams during that drug-induced sleep that lasted until four bells in the afternoon watch. He did remember, most vividly, the sensation of peacefully drifting as the tincture took its effect, but he couldn't recall any of the delirium that he had understood was commonly experienced. The main sensation on waking was the burning in his lungs, accompanied by hoarse, uncontrollable coughing and an aching in his limbs and chest.

'You'll be on your back for at least another day,' said the surgeon, 'and even then, you must be careful. The ingestion of such a body of water – and remember, it's partly river water, which is deadly – often leads to infection in the lungs. I've made up some pneumonics for you,' he said, holding up a brown bottle. 'You should take a dose now, and I'll be back every turn of the watch.'

His next visitor was Moxon, trying hard to look grave and failing to suppress a smile.

'Admiral Saunders sends his congratulations, sir, and his wishes for your speedy recovery.'

Carlisle could barely raise his head, and his look of

confusion was comical.

'How…?'

'They watched it all from the flagship, sir. They saw the pickets take each fireship in tow and they saw one get through, steering directly for *Stirling Castle* with the wind and tide at its stern. You can imagine their distress until they saw our two boats gather it up. I told Souter to deal with the fireship while I searched for you. Apparently, we were silhouetted against the glow, and by all accounts, it was a gallant scene! The admiral sent for you. He wanted to thank you in person, but you were already fathoms deep under the doctor's laudanum. I went instead, and I hope I was right to do so, sir, and leave *Medina* to Mister Hosking.'

Carlisle nodded and smiled. With the frigate at anchor and the fireships all dealt with, it was perfectly normal to leave the sailing master in command.

'Did he speak to…'

A fit of coughing cut off his question.

'He did indeed, sir,' Moxon replied, no hint of concern left in his face, it was one big smile. 'He congratulated me, sir, and said he'd remember my name. His secretary even wrote it down! I spelt it out for him to avoid confusion, there's a *Moxton* in the fleet you know.'

The first lieutenant's beaming face filled the whole of Carlisle's vision.

'Oh, and he wishes you a speedy restoration to duty, sir,' he continued almost as an afterthought, 'and he sent you a case of burgundy, to aid your recovery.'

Carlisle would have laughed if it wasn't so painful even to breathe. And yet it was a significant moment for Moxon. Saunders was not only the commander of the naval element of this expedition, he was also the commander-in-chief of the King's ships in North America. He had the power to award acting promotions, and with the war showing no sign of ending, and the reduction of Quebec quite likely, acting promotions to master-and-commander would almost certainly be confirmed by their Lordships. Yes, Moxon had good cause to smile.

***

# CHAPTER FIFTEEN

## Running the Gauntlet

*Wednesday, Eighteenth of July 1759.*
*Medina, at Anchor. Cape Levi, Saint Lawrence River.*

They were to sail on the first night tide with a fair wind, the admiral had ordered, and as though he spoke directly with the weather gods, the next day the wind turned easterly with the flooding tide. The moon wouldn't rise until after midnight, and it was a waning moon, in its third quarter, and would shed little light. With nautical twilight ending at nine o'clock, there was time enough – three hours or so – for a few bold ships to accomplish their clandestine purpose.

'*Sutherland's* underway, sir,' said Hosking in a whisper, looking at the dim shape on the larboard bow.

The nearest enemy was over a mile to leeward and silence was absurd, but Carlisle had often enough seen that reaction to a secret nighttime expedition. He looked at his watch in the glow of the binnacle light. Nine-thirty, and as if in confirmation the marine sentry struck three bells.

'That will be the last bell, Mister Hosking, tell the quartermaster if you please.'

'Aye-aye sir. I'll have the clapper brought aft, just to be doubly sure.'

One by one the ships won their anchors and cast their bows to the southwest, grey shapes moving against a black background with muted orders and no bells or pipes.

'*Diana's* underway.'

There was the big thirty-two gun twelve-pounder frigate moving past their starboard side.

'Good evening, sir, it's a fine night for a cruise.'

Carlisle jumped, then he relaxed. That was Alexander Schomberg, *Diana's* captain, passing the time of day. He sounded as though he was right beside Carlisle on *Medina's* quarterdeck when in fact, he was a good half cable to windward. *Diana* was close, but not close enough to cause concern.

'Good evening to you, Schomberg,' Carlisle replied. He was two years senior to *Diana's* captain. Each encounter of this kind reminded Carlisle that his time in frigates was coming to an end. He expected to have to bid his farewell to *Medina* when this affair was over, when the weather made it necessary to withdraw from the Saint Lawrence and return to Portsmouth or perhaps Halifax. That started another current of thought. He'd been lucky so far in being able to see his wife and child in Williamsburg, but it couldn't last. In a frigate, there was always a chance of running convoys up the coast from the West Indies to New York, but in a fourth-rate? Or a third-rate? It was hardly likely. With Chiara seemingly delighted with her lodgings in Virginia's colonial capital, and talking of buying a house in the city, and with this war appearing to have no end, it could be years before he again saw her and his son.

'*Diana* has passed us now, sir.'

That was Hosking's polite way of waking up his captain. He recognised the signs that Carlisle was becoming abstracted and he had a shrewd idea of the cause.

'Thank you, Mister Hosking,' Carlisle replied, trying to look as though this was exactly the moment that he had intended to issue his next order.

'Weigh anchor, Mister Moxon.'

*Medina's* anchor was at short stay, just gently holding the frigate in place against the flooding tide and the wind.

'Anchor's aweigh,' shouted Moxon from the fo'c'sle, seconds later.

'Set sail and follow *Diana*, Mister Hosking.'

Their little squadron had gathered to the east of the fleet between Cape Levi and Orleans Island. Since the incident with the fireships, Wolfe had ordered that Brigadier-General Monckton should occupy Cape Levi and place heavy batteries on the heights to bombard the city and dominate the Basin. With a brigade and batteries on Cape

Levi, another brigade below the falls of Montmorency, and the main body of the army on Orleans Island, the city of Quebec was being steadily surrounded. The batteries on Cape Levi had allowed Saunders to move his ships out of the South Channel into the safer waters of the wider river. Now it was time to strangle the French supply line and to prove to the enemy that British naval power didn't end at the narrows under Quebec City. That in fact, it had no limits on the Saint Lawrence.

\*\*\*

It was the blackest of nights, and each ship was darkened except for a lantern at the taffrail, and that was masked so that it could be seen only within three points of the stern. *Medina*, her tops'ls just giving her steerage way, slowly followed Schomberg's frigate towards the southwest. Far in front of them were the ships that formed the principal purpose of this expedition, three cats: tough, capacious supply ships designed and built as Whitby colliers. In fact, many of the fleet's cats had previously been in the North Sea coal trade and had been sold or leased to the Navy Board by owners who saw an opportunity for profit. James Cook would know all about them. The sailing master – now a noted surveyor – had found his sea-legs on Whitby colliers, running the precious black rock to the energy-hungry homes and industries of London.

Now Cook was piloting *Zephyr*, leading the first British ships ever to pass Quebec and doing it at night with no moon. *Zephyr* was followed by John Rous, commanding the squadron in his fourth-rate *Sutherland*. The three cats came next, then the sloop *Hunter* and three frigates: *Squirrel*, *Diana* and *Medina*. It was a useful little squadron, and *Medina* was bringing up the rear to take in tow any casualties.

The cats carried a month's allowance of supplies for the thousand men who were crammed into them: three companies of grenadiers and a battalion of Royal Americans under Colonel Carleton. The squadron could sustain itself above Quebec and with a fourth-rate, three frigates and two sloops they were more than a match for the French frigates and privateers that were known to be still in the river. For Montcalm hadn't unloaded the convoy that had eluded Durell. He had sent them upriver, passing the rapids at Richelieu to be out of reach of the British, he hoped. Out of reach of the population of the city, too, when hunger started to bite, and civic discipline became strained.

'Tops'ls and jib, Mister Hosking. Keep the mizzen brailed; we may need it if we're seen.'

*Medina* backed and filled, manoeuvering to take her station on *Diana*.

Rous had made a great play on the need to maintain the distance between ships. It was unnecessary and irritating. They were all seasoned captains and understood the need. But perhaps, Carlisle thought, he wasn't making enough allowance for the strain that Rous must be suffering. This was an important, possibly vital, part of the plan for squeezing Quebec and forcing Montcalm to come out and fight. Rous was an up-and-coming captain; he must have watched with envy the rise of his contemporaries such as Richard Howe who commanded a squadron for the raids on France the previous year. He too could be plucked out of the middle of the post-captain's list to hoist his broad pennant and command a battle squadron. This was perhaps the critical test.

Carlisle could just hear Schomberg's voice calling to *Squirrel* ahead of him, but that was the last shouted command that he heard. At that moment, exactly as ordered, Monckton's batteries on Cape Levi opened a diversionary fire. He checked his watch; ten o'clock. On their larboard bow the blackness was split by the red and orange tongues of flame that shot out from the Cape. After the quiet of the night, the roar of the guns was tremendous and overwhelming, stultifying the senses.

Perhaps Montcalm had thought the city was out of range from Cape Levi. It was difficult, otherwise, to understand why he hadn't fortified it to prevent just what was now happening. Those were heavy guns. Naval thirty-two pounders had been hauled ashore with enormous effort and dragged up to the high ground by the concerted efforts of commandeered oxen and horses, and the disciplined power of two hundred sailors. Monstrous great mortars added their deeper, softer tones to the cacophony. The noise, even down here on the river and a mile from the narrows, was deafening. It was hard to imagine the terror of Quebec's citizens as the awful reality dawned upon them, and they realised that Wolfe had it in his power to bring their city down in ruins.

'Are the yards manned, Mister Hosking?' Carlisle had to bellow to be heard.

'Aye sir, we're all ready for your word.'

'Then carry on and follow *Diana* at two cables.'

\*\*\*

The nine ships ghosted up the river with the wind and tide behind them. The guns on the point were too high and too far ahead for their flashes to silhouette the squadron, and it was some time before the French gunners realised what was happening. However, the guns of Quebec's fortress were well-sited, and the artillerymen had spent years practising for exactly this event. They knew the range to the yard.

'They've opened fire, sir,' said Moxon.

Were they firing at Monckton's batteries, or had they seen the nine ships furtively running upstream with the tide? It felt unreal to be sailing between the two headlands only a mile apart with a deadly artillery duel raging over their heads.

Rous was steering tight to the southern shore, close under Cape Levi and as far as possible from the batteries in the city. The leadsmen were busy in all the ships. God help us if any ship loses steerage, thought Carlisle, there's no room for error in this narrow channel.

The flashes from the French side were clearly visible, but so far there was no indication of the fall of shot. The darkness hid the evidence.

## Rocks and Shoals

'There, sir,' said Moxon pointing at the starboard bow.

A waterspout was briefly illuminated by the flash of the guns above their heads. Unless the French gunners had lost their pre-set elevations already, that shot wasn't aimed at Cape Levi. They must have seen the ships that were penetrating the heart of New France under their very noses.

The next salvo from the French dispelled any ideas that the squadron hadn't been seen. There was a crash overhead, and a shower of fragments of wood and cordage rained down on the quarterdeck. At the same time, a near miss raised a waterspout that wetted the waist. The splinter nets had caught the larger, dangerous pieces of wood and metal, but still, there was damage aloft.

'Get your men up there, Mister Swinton, and let me know the damage. Where's the carpenter?'

There was no question of *Medina* returning the fire. Her guns wouldn't reach the lofty French batteries, and the flash would only provide a better aiming mark.

'Get your crews down behind the gunwale, Mister Moxon. They can stand to at my order, but I doubt they'll be needed.'

*Medina* staggered from a blow to her hull.

'Twenty-four pounders, sir,' shouted Hosking above the roar of Monckton's guns.

'Just keep us in our station, master, and let me worry about the French guns. I fancy you're a little astern.'

Hosking gave Carlisle a covert glance. It wasn't like his captain to show signs of nerves. Normally he was the steadiest of leaders under fire.

Crash! A shot hit the belfry. Not a sound came from the clapperless bell as the stout oak framework sagged forward and the bell came to rest on the fo'c'sle. By the occasional flash, a huddle of men could be seen carrying a shrouded shape back to the main hatch. One casualty at least. It was ominous that no cry of pain had come back to the quarterdeck; that usually meant that the man had been killed instantly or at least rendered unconscious.

*Medina* stood on, faithfully following *Diana*. The cats ahead were doing an admirable job of keeping station. Of course, the cats' masters had been sailing in convoy since December, and even the most obdurate merchant master would have picked up the navy's ways in that time.

'*Diana's* foretopmast has gone, sir.' Enrico shouted, gesturing ahead.

Carlisle couldn't see past his own masts and sails and their spider's web of standing and running rigging. He ran over to the starboard side and leaned out over the mizzen chains. No sign of the frigate. He ran back to larboard, cursing himself for a fool. If *Diana* had lost her foretopmast, she would tend to turn uncontrollably to windward, and the wind was coming over the larboard quarter. He reached the larboard side just in time to see Schomberg's frigate swinging wildly towards the shore. He watched in fascination as the big frigate struck the rocky beach below the cliffs of Cape Levi. The darkness hid the worst of the disaster, but he dimly saw her main topmast follow the fore topmast over the side.

Carlisle had no more than a few seconds to decide. If he did nothing, they'd be past *Diana* in five minutes, and then there was no going back; the wind and tide would see to that. Rous would have lost one frigate from his squadron, and probably she'd be battered into a wreck by daylight. The loss of a frigate from Saunders' fleet hardly mattered, but to leave its broken carcass under the gaze of the citizens of Quebec would only give heart to the defence of the city. *Medina* had been placed in the rear principally to take a cat in tow if needed. It was the cats that were essential to the mission, not the frigates. Nevertheless, *Diana* was in mortal danger. In this darkness, the French were almost firing blind, but the moon would rise in an hour and then she'd be a sitting duck. Carlisle could help *Diana*, perhaps tow her back downstream on the ebb, in which case Rous would have lost two frigates. Did that matter? He still had a fourth rate, a frigate and two sloops; that should be enough force to deal with the French if they should offer battle.

Then the thinking was over. He couldn't possibly leave *Diana* to her fate; his personal reputation wouldn't stand such a blow. Always lurking in the back of his mind was the fact that he was a colonial, and he suspected that his fellows sought some evidence for their prejudice against officers who hadn't been born in Britain. Saunders could always send *Medina* upstream again the following night. It would be dangerous with the French garrison alerted to the possibility, but it could be done.

'Put the ship about, Mister Hosking. Mister Moxon, stand by to anchor.'

He mustn't lose another yard of ground upstream.

'Forty fathoms here, sir, more-or-less' said Hosking.

Too deep. They must move in closer.

'*Diana's* right ahead of us, sir, and she's aground.'

*Medina* was heading directly for the shore.

'I know that, damn you. Now carry out my orders. Keep her full and by.'

'Only doing my duty, sir.'

The last thing Carlisle needed was Hosking making fatuous reports.

'A cast of the lead,' Carlisle snapped.

He looked closely at a mark on the shore. There was a pointed rock just visible; its seabird-fouled peak gleaming white in the darkness. He couldn't find a transit so that would have to do. As far as he could see they weren't moving west; if anything, they were making a tiny amount of ground to the east, downstream.

'Mister Angelini, take a bearing of that rock and let me know if it changes and in which direction.'

The compass had already been set on top of the binnacle, and Enrico bent over to take the bearing.

'What time's slack water, Mister Hosking?'

'East by south, half east,' Enrico reported in a calm voice.

Good reporting. He didn't wait for Hosking to make his

report, Enrico's was more important.

'Thirty minutes, sir.' That was Hosking. 'There's just about half a knot setting us upriver now.'

That was one of the good things about Hosking; he didn't sulk. After the way Carlisle snapped at him, many sailing masters would have moved to the other side of the quarterdeck and made themselves unavailable for a period.

'The Rock's bearing is steady, sir,' said Enrico. It was interesting that his Italian accent wasn't noticeable at all when he made reports – something to ponder another time.

'By the deep, nineteen,' called the leadsman in a voice that could still a gale. He was in the main chains and didn't want his report to be missed.

Nineteen fathoms. Still too deep.

'Starboard a point, Quartermaster.'

'Mister Moxon. I'm going to edge down on *Diana* until I get a sounding of ten fathoms, or thereabouts. Be ready to anchor at my command.'

They were moving crabwise across the river, their forward movement balanced between the wind and the last of the flood tide.

'Anchor's a cock-bill, sir,' Moxon replied. He could let go in seconds when Carlisle gave the word.

'Mark seventeen,' shouted the leadsman.

'Bearing's drawing left.' Enrico had dropped the *sir*. It was understandable in the circumstances; they were starting to drift upstream, and that was more important.

Carlisle gritted his teeth and watched the dim shore. He felt the wind on his cheek and tried to imagine how the tide was running under the frigate's keel. Thirty seconds passed.

'East by south, sir, drawing left.'

Steady…

'Deep fourteen.'

That would have to do. Moxon would have heard that report from the leadsman as well as he had. He'd have preferred ten fathoms in this stream, but if he waited until they had moved that close, they'd be too far upstream of the stranded frigate.

'Let go!' Carlisle shouted at the top of his lungs.

Hosking was already giving the orders to furl all the sails, and the gun crews were racing up the shrouds to hand the courses and tops'ls.

Now Carlisle had a moment to look around. *Diana* was just fifty yards on the starboard bow and heeling noticeably. My God, were they that close? The swift river had carved a channel here where it narrowed between the two great buttresses either side. Strictly speaking, there was no holding ground at all, just the deep channel and then the rocks. But for a few hours, this would have to do.

'Away longboat and yawl.'

The bosun's call echoed back from the rocks of Cape Levi. Overhead the cannonade continued, and the occasional shot fell close to the two frigates. Otherwise, it appeared that the French hadn't seen the unfolding drama at the base of the Point. With Monckton's thirty-two pounders hammering away just a hundred feet above them it was hardly surprising, everything at the base of the Cape must be in deep shadow.

'Tide's slackening, sir,' said Hosking looking over the side. 'The ebb will be noticeable in half an hour. Wind's steady in the east.'

Here, under the cliffs, a local calm held sway. The tide was slack, and the wind had dropped to a whisper with the occasional williwaw that could be expected in such a place.

'Bearing's steady, sir.'

Then they weren't dragging. Good.

'Mister Moxon. Have the longboat pull a messenger over to *Diana*. You know what to do,'

The heavy second cable had already been dragged aft in anticipation of *Medina* having to tow a cat up the channel. It just needed a lighter line – a messenger – to be taken over so that the cable could be hauled across. It would be back-breaking work, and it must be completed as soon as possible.

'How long to moonrise, Mister Hosking?'

'It's been over the horizon this half-glass, sir, but there's a low bank of cloud in the way.' He pointed to the northeast from where they'd come. 'Ah, there it is.'

The quarter moon at last rose above the clouds, half a point to the left of the edge of the Cape, casting its baleful silvery light over the scene. After the blackness, it looked unnaturally bright and picked out the two helpless frigates in awful detail.

'For what we are about to receive…' Hosking intoned in his best church-going voice.

Carlisle had a realistic view of the accuracy of a twenty-four pounder firing at the extremity of its range. It would be an uncomfortable couple of hours for *Medina* and for Alexander Schomberg, but unless *Diana* was bilged, *Medina* should be able to pull the frigate clear, and the ebbing tide would be stronger than this easterly wind. Hopefully, the commander of the Cape Levi battery would have enough sense to keep up the counter-battery fire rather than embark upon the reduction of the town that Wolfe had ordered. The effectiveness of the French batteries would be halved – no, quartered – if they were kept under fire.

Carlisle watched as the longboat carried the messenger across. It was a heavy rope; it needed to be to take the weight of the cable that was to follow. Then came the massive cable, dragged across foot-by-foot.

'The tow is secured, sir,' said Moxon looking dishevelled and dirty. He'd been in the longboat and had come back with a report of the situation. 'Captain Schomberg's compliments. He believes they'll be afloat momentarily, and his hull is sound. And he says thank you, sir.' Moxon grinned in the moonlight. 'He suggests that our longboat and yawl help to pull him off.'

'Very well, Mister Moxon. Go in the longboat yourself. You know the situation; we must be off without delay.'

As if to emphasise the point there was a crash forward as a French twenty-four pounder found its mark below the fo'c'sle.

Twice more *Medina* was hit in her rigging, but no more balls hit her hull. In twenty minutes, they were underway with the crippled *Diana* in tow. In thirty minutes, they were out of range of the French batteries. Behind them, Monckton's guns were still bellowing with unabated fury, but so were the French guns, even though they could hardly reach Cape Levi even at their best elevation. How long before the French realised that they needed heavier artillery at the fortress? And did they have anything larger than twenty-four pounders? Probably not, it was only by taking guns from the second and third rate ships-of-the-line that Saunders was able to offer such decisive firepower to Wolfe. And the French had nothing larger than frigates in the whole of their dominions in Canada.

Carlisle looked over the frigate's larboard quarter. Yes, the French guns were certainly still firing. He knew that Monckton's artillery would continue through the night, to give the French citizenry a taste of things to come, but the French appeared to be wasting powder and shot on a target that was beyond the range of their lighter guns.

***

# CHAPTER SIXTEEN

## The Admiral's List

*Saturday, Twenty-Eighth of July 1759.*
*Medina, at Anchor. The Basin, Saint Lawrence River.*

Ten days had passed since Carlisle had towed the frigate *Diana* from under the French guns of the citadel. She'd gone now. Her damage was too extensive for anything but a quick fix, enough to get her downstream and south to Boston convoying a couple of dozen American supply ships. There she'd be made safe for a transatlantic passage and so home to England with the season's mast ships. The Portsmouth yard would no doubt declare that nothing short of a great refit was needed. *Diana's* people had cheered as they sailed away. With a bit of luck, the frigate would be paid off in Portsmouth, and if they weren't turned over to another ship, and if they could evade the press, they could see their homes again. Even if they were drafted directly into another ship, there was a good chance of a week or two of leave. There were many envious sailors in the squadron who didn't return the cheer but watched stony-faced as the convoy sailed away down the South Channel.

It had been largely a time of waiting as General Wolfe's army considered its options. *Medina's* damage had been repaired by her own carpenter and his crew. The shot holes in the hull had been fixed with scarfed-in planks, and all the seams had been caulked. The frigate was watertight, and the pumps were only in use for ten minutes in each watch. Ten minutes was no hardship for *Medina's* crew, it was more of a pleasurable burst of exercise to blow the cobwebs away after their off-watch sleep. Nevertheless, Carlisle was becoming concerned about the state of his command. It was many months since she'd had the services of a King's yard and her last careening was at Hampton Roads in December.

'Take your seats, gentlemen,' he said as the carpenter, the

bosun and the gunner filed into the great cabin. Moxon and Hosking were already there, and the subject of the meeting had set a sombre tone.

'You first, Chips.'

'Well sir,' the carpenter scratched his head. He always scratched his head before offering any kind of opinion. 'As you may have guessed, it's not such a rosy picture.'

He described the state of the ship's structure in depressing detail. *Medina* had been out of the builder's yard only three years, but in that time she'd suffered as much damage in battle as most ships would see in a long lifetime. Until now, none of it had been severe enough to warrant a refit, but it was the repair on top of repair that was weakening her. There were butt ends where there should be continuous planking and scarfs that rested upon fractured knees. The spirketing, often ignored in any structural survey, had suffered badly and was by the carpenter's own admission a bodged job in many places.

'My fear, sir, is that a butt-end will spring at a time when we can't get to it, or one of the scarfs will fail. Then we'll be in trouble.'

Chips looked worried, but then Chips always looked worried. In fact, every carpenter Carlisle had ever known had a permanently anxious look, and with good reason. They were responsible for keeping a wooden structure afloat for months on end in all weathers and often many leagues from any kind of help. Then, to round off their problems, from time-to-time the enemy lobbed great iron balls at their precious ships, without so much as a by-your-leave.

'Thank you, Chips. Bosun, what do you have to tell us?'

Swinton's report was more encouraging. With supply ships within easy reach, carrying all manner of naval stores, he could keep on top of his problems in his running rigging, and his sails were relatively new.

'I'd like a complete overhaul of the standing rigging, sir. The main shrouds are stretched so far that the deadeyes are nearly chock-a-block. We need a good week or so for that, and I gather we won't have that leisure until this is all over.'

'I'm afraid that's so. Can't you replace them one shroud at a time? We should be safe enough as long as we're in the river.'

'Aye, sir, I can. We'll look a little odd for a while, with our lanyards more like a Brixham lugger's than a King's ship's, but if you can abide that, then I'll get the work underway.'

'Mister Gordon, how are the guns?'

'All well, sir. There's some honeycombing in number five, but we can't exchange that until we get back to Halifax, if they have any nine-pounders. It'll hold for perhaps fifty shots, sir. Now, if you would just fire the guns more, it would save me turning over the powder in the magazine…'

Carlisle smiled at that. *Medina* had spent a fair amount of her time cruising or escorting far away from the eyes and ears of admirals, and the gunner had been able to fire his guns as often as he liked, within the bounds of their allowance. Now that they were firmly part of a squadron, and in the enclosed waters of the Saint Lawrence, they could only practice firing when they were told to do so, and that had not been often enough for the master gunner.

Carlisle fingered the written reports that each of his warrant officers had provided. There had been no need for a report from the purser; he could draw on the supply ships for all that he needed, and there were opportunities aplenty to take in wood and water. He made a weekly report to the flagship, but that was a statistical summary. It wasn't a suitable time to reveal the finer detail that these reports showed, particularly the carpenter's. Should he tell the admiral? That was the question. Possibly it would irritate Saunders – if he ever saw it. More likely it would be buried by his staff who had greater matters to concern them than the spirketing on a sixth-rate.

'It seems we are safe enough in the river, gentlemen. Go ahead with your shrouds, Bosun, I'm not concerned about our looks at present. However, there's no immediate remedy for your troubles, Chips, until we return to Halifax. When the time comes to leave the river for the winter, then I'll tell the admiral that we need the services of a yard. For now, keep her tight Chips, keep her tight.'

\*\*\*

'From the admiral, sir,' said Simmonds as he laid a folded note on the desk. Carlisle had been looking over the carpenter's report in more detail and depressing himself with every new item. It appeared that *Medina* was due for a great refit and that could only be in England. Either he'd be relieved of command – which seemed most likely – or he'd have to spend months in England fretting himself into a fever over his wife and child in Virginia. Neither sounded attractive.

Carlisle picked up the note. Simmonds had broken the wafer that bound the fold, but he could see that there was no seal. His immediate thought was that it couldn't be of any great consequence; these weren't formal orders which would have been covered and sealed correctly. Simmonds would certainly have already read it; he'd be less than human if he hadn't. He folded the note flat on his desk.

> *Sir Charles Saunders has directed me to inform you that you are hereby to report immediately to General Wolfe at his headquarters below Montmorency and there to receive orders for the furtherance of the King's service against the city of Quebec. A blue flag at the main masthead will serve as an acknowledgement that you have received this note.*

'Call away the longboat, Mister Simmonds. Where's my servant? Best frock coat and sword, I want to be underway in five minutes. Pass the word for Mister Moxon and tell the officer of the watch to hoist a blue flag at the main masthead. He's to keep it there until the flagship also hoists one then dips it.'

That was the usual form for flags; it was a tried and trusted way of ensuring that the message had been received and that the recipient knew that his acknowledgement had been seen. And orders – even in the shape of an informal note – from a vice-admiral sending a post-captain to report to a major-general demanded instant action.

\*\*\*

'Stretch out, Souter,' said Enrico softly as the longboat shot away from the frigate's side. This was important business; the captain's boat had a coxswain *and* a midshipman when either could easily have managed alone. Not for the first time Carlisle noticed that there was a rapport between Midshipman Angelini and Souter. They managed with the minimum of orders and without the showy overbearing attitude that many of his young gentlemen believed was necessary when under the eye of their captain. It was a curious pairing, the scion of a noble Sardinian house and the tough, rootless petty officer. And yet they were in many ways similar. Carlisle would have been hard-pressed to say which had the most innate intelligence, and Souter was even more literate than most of the lower deck, at a time when many sailors could at least read, even if they found writing a challenge. Souter, he knew, could read and he could write in a fair hand, not like the crabbed scribblings of some of those who strode the quarterdeck.

Wolfe had shifted his headquarters frequently since the fleet had sailed into the South Channel a month ago. To what extent, Carlisle wondered, did his peregrinations track the general's changing view of where his blow against Montcalm should be struck? He'd toyed with the idea of an amphibious assault above the city, with a crossing of the Montmorency River and with an assault on the Beauport shore where the New Englanders had tried to land in the last war. His indecision was starting to look like procrastination and all the time, day-by-day, the season was wearing on. Soon there wouldn't be enough time to both roll over Montcalm's army and to conduct a regular siege of the city. Then this great fleet would have to turn ignominiously around and sail for home, leaving a battered but undefeated city in its wake. England would surely not stand for that. Wolfe was only a major-general by courtesy; his rank was effective in the Americas and nowhere else. When he returned to England, he'd automatically revert to his substantive rank of colonel, and that couldn't be an attractive future for such an ambitious man.

This was the first time that Carlisle had seen the Falls of Montmorency at close quarters. They were set back half a mile from the shore with dense forest on either side that hid them from the Basin and the anchorage in the South Channel. Approaching from upstream along the North Channel they were entirely invisible, and it was only when the Montmorency River Estuary opened to larboard that the magnificent vista was revealed. Framed by the green and grey of the forest and the cliffs, the wide tributary of the Saint Lawrence tumbled over a high ledge and plunged nearly three hundred feet into a lagoon that the force of the water had scoured out over millennia. Carlisle had an academic understanding of the concept of the sublime, that mixture of grandeur and danger that the literary folk rated so highly, but it was only now that the full force of the idea was brought home to him. There was something hypnotic in the way that nature had provided such a beautiful and yet perilous spectacle. He could imagine walking as if in a trance into the swift-flowing waters at the top of the falls, to be swept away to a magnificent and glorious death. It was fortunate that Enrico was there to direct Souter to the makeshift jetty, because Carlisle was lost in wonder and awe and a sense of his own insignificance, as the longboat swept through the clear, blue-tinged water that the Montmorency offered as a tribute to the murkier Saint Lawrence.

The jetty was crowded with boats of all kinds from ship's longboats and yawls to the ubiquitous American bateaux and the French pilot luggers that Carlisle had taken at Bic. Ranged on the shore were twenty or so of the stout flatboats that Saunders had brought from England. They'd been tested the year before on the French coast – Pitt's *descents* that were supposed to ease the pressure on Germany – and were now the defining item of equipment for amphibious operations. There was one boat that caught Carlisle's eye at the same time as Enrico pointed it out; the admiral's barge was there with its crew in their best rig. That meant admiral Saunders must also be at Wolfe's headquarters.

\*\*\*

'Would you wait here a moment, sir?' said the flag lieutenant. 'Admiral Saunders would like a word before you meet the general.'

He'd intercepted Carlisle outside the largest of the complex of tents that made up Wolfe's headquarters and had evidently been waiting there for that purpose.

Carlisle had always known that a land commander's headquarters operated at a quite different scale to a sea commander's. A vice-admiral's staff numbered perhaps a dozen, twenty at the most and he could at a pinch embark in any size of vessel and operate with little more than a flag captain, a flag lieutenant and a secretary. By contrast, a general's staff was a magnitude greater. There were teams of staff officers with responsibilities for artillery, engineering and logistics. There were brigade majors running in and out and a plethora of messengers as well as numbers of officers just standing around and talking. It was bewildering, and Carlisle was grateful when he was conducted to a small tent where the admiral was dictating a letter to his secretary.

'Ah, Carlisle,' he said, stopping his dictation in mid-sentence, 'it's good of you to come so promptly. You've seen my note? Excellent. I sent it before I realised that I would be here when you arrived. But it's all to the good because I can tell you what to expect in person.'

Carlisle was ushered into the only other seat in the tent. The secretary opened a bound volume that was evidently his day-book and flattened down a new page. The flag

## Rocks and Shoals

lieutenant stood beside the tent flap, for all the world as though he was ready to prevent Carlisle from escaping.

'You're probably wondering what this mysterious summons means. Well – and this must remain in confidence – General Wolfe has decided that his blow will fall on the Beauport shore upstream of the Falls.'

He paused and looked at Carlisle with his head tilted to one side.

'You look as though you have a question already.'

'I apologise, sir, but I thought the Beauport shore was determined to be unsuitable. It's too shallow for our ships to get close enough to support the landing…'

'That's where you come in, Carlisle. No, I'm not sending *Medina* in there, not least because your nine-pounders are too light for the task. You are to take two of the empty cats. What are their names, Flags?'

'*Russell* and *Three Sisters*, Sir Charles. Both five hundred tons and they're anchored in the South Channel.'

'They're Whitby ships and almost flat bottomed,' Saunders continued, 'so they'll take the ground well. I had imagined that all cats came from Whitby, but apparently, it's a term used for any of that type of craft now, and not all cats are created equal. It's the Whitby ones that we need for this job. Incidentally, why are they called cats, Flags?'

The flag lieutenant looked puzzled; the secretary shrugged his shoulders.

'Mister Cook gave me a reason, sir,' said Carlisle, 'and he spent nine years in the trade. The Whitby ships are built to carry coal from Newcastle to London, and when that business is slack in peacetime, they carry timber from the Baltic. They became known as *Coal and Timber Ships* – cats.'

Saunders gave Carlisle a sharp look.

'You believe that?'

It was Carlisle's turn to shrug.

'Who knows, Sir Charles, it's as good a story as any.'

'Well said, Carlisle. Never let the truth get in the way of a good yarn, I say. And you may be relying on Mister

Cook's word very soon. It was he who surveyed the North Channel, and he assures me that your cats can get close enough to do their business. Flags will give you copies of the charts. Now, if those cats aren't empty, then you're to clear their holds into other cats. You have two days to fit them out as floating batteries to take twenty-four pounders, as many as you can stuff into them but fourteen each sounds about right, leaving space for crews to work them. They'll need gunports and eye-bolts, and their decks may need strengthening, but I'll leave all that to you, you'll have everything you need. By this evening you'll have a list of which of the ships-of-the-line will provide guns, ball and powder, which will provide the crews, and which will provide the carpenters. The cat's masters will stay with their ships to help you work them into position and you'll have a lieutenant for each one. When the general decides to move, you'll run your cats aground as far up the shore as you can get. You'll be his assault artillery.'

Carlisle was speechless. He tried not to show his surprise, but the task was so novel, so unprecedented, that he could do nothing better than to mutely stare at his admiral with his mouth partly open.

'You're probably wondering why I've chosen you, aren't you?'

Carlisle was wondering nothing of the sort; his thinking processes had come to a standstill as he tried to assimilate this change in his fate.

'General Wolfe asked for you by name.'

Now Carlisle really was amazed. He'd met Wolfe, certainly, but he didn't know that the general was aware of his existence.

'Apparently you covered his landing at Louisbourg last year. Cormorant Cove, wasn't it? He attributes his success to you. You're his lucky charm, Carlisle.'

Now it was becoming clearer. Carlisle had a momentary dislocation as he remembered that desperate hour when Wolfe – then a mere brigade commander – had come close

## Rocks and Shoals

to abandoning his assault on the French positions to the west of Louisbourg. His had been the main effort; the other landings had been feints to stop the French reinforcing Cormorant Cove. Wolfe had been repulsed from his chosen landing site, and his boats were in retreat. It was *Medina's* guns that had indicated where three of Wolfe's boats had found a tiny, lightly defended beach to the right of the main objective. Wolfe had swiftly turned his boats around and sped for the beach as *Medina* bombarded the French defences. At that instant, the battle had turned. Carlisle hadn't imagined for one moment that Wolfe attributed his success on that day to *Medina*. He nodded and smiled. This was an onerous duty, without doubt, but the admiral had coated the bitter pill with just the right amount of sugar.

'I'm honoured, Sir Charles.'

'Good. Can your first lieutenant manage in your absence? Honestly now, Carlisle.'

This was a question that it was easy to answer candidly. He had every confidence in Moxon, now. However, he didn't get a chance to express it. The secretary spoke.

'You'll remember, sir, that *Medina's* first lieutenant towed away the fireship that eluded the pickets last month.'

Saunders looked puzzled for a moment as he thought back to that wild night.

'Yes, of course. Morgan, wasn't it? Something like that. He did very well. I have his name on my list.'

'Moxon sir,' said the secretary, 'Moxon with an x, and indeed he is on your list, sir,' he said, holding his thumb in the page while he consulted some secret entries at the back of the book.

'Then I have no doubts at all. Your frigate will be in good hands, Carlisle, don't you think?'

'Indeed, sir, it will.'

He didn't like to point out that it was Souter who had towed away the fireship while Moxon rescued his drowning captain. But what was that list? Carlisle thought he could guess, but he hardly dared to hope…

\*\*\*

The admiral was as good as his word, and Carlisle was showered with all the specialist help and all the materials that he needed. The work of cutting the gunports and reinforcing the deck went on into the night with his small army of carpenters in two watches. Carlisle made one addition: he had both ships prepared for destruction in case they had to be abandoned to the enemy. Fuses were laid to the magazines, combustible packets were prepared, and the lieutenants and masters were warned of the possibility of having to set fire to the ships.

At midnight there was an outbreak of firing in the Basin to the west. It was different in quality to the thirty-two pounders and mortars that rained down their destruction from Cape Levi day and night. These were lighter guns, twelve and nine-pounders from frigates. Carlisle stared earnestly up the channel, and then he saw it. First, it was a general red and orange glow; then he saw more distinct flames. Another attempt by fireships, he decided, but this time there was something different. Rather than half a dozen individual ships, it looked like a wide, low mass of flames. Rafts perhaps, but if they were rafts, then there must be hundreds of them lashed together.

*Medina* was out there at the forefront of this deadly battle, but he could do nothing, it was three or four miles away, and he had the two cats to look after. He called the crew on deck, those who hadn't already been roused by their mates, and had spars made ready and buckets filled, but there was little else that he could do. He watched as the flames grew and he heard the explosions, quite distinct from the sharper report of a cannon, as the barrels of powder ignited. Then, gradually the flames subsided and disappeared around Orleans Point. It looked as though this attempt had fared no better than the previous one. The picket boats had towed the rafts aside just far enough for the wind and tide to sweep them away down the North Channel.

'Ha!' said the carpenter who was still sawing away at the projecting end of a massive knighthead, 'that's shot their bolt, sir. Maybe now they'll come out and fight our soldiers like men.'

Carlisle smiled in reply. Privately he thought that Montcalm was playing a losing hand to perfection. His army may outnumber Wolfe's, but there was no question of that mixed assortment of regulars, militia and *troupes de terre* outfighting the magnificently trained British infantry. He needed to keep his army intact and hold Wolfe at arm's length until the weather forced a retreat. Then New France would live to fight another year.

***

# CHAPTER SEVENTEEN

## The Whitby Cats

*Tuesday, Thirty-First of July 1759.*
*Cat Russell, the North Channel, Saint Lawrence River.*

*Russell* rounded Orleans Point, and the westerly wind caught her tops'ls and wafted her up the North Channel. What must this look like to Montcalm? Carlisle pondered. So far, the only activity he would have seen would be this tiny flotilla: *Centurion* of sixty guns in the lead with the two innocent-looking cats, *Russel* and *Three Sisters* following obediently behind. Probably it looked like a resupply for the camp on the eastern side of the Montmorency River. What they couldn't see was the mass of flatboats and other small craft gathering out of sight in the South Channel, three hundred in all. They were filled with soldiers; grenadiers from all the regiments forming a composite brigade and followed by the musketeers of the line regiments. On the other side of the Falls, further battalions were waiting to cross the river.

'I'll force him to come out and fight,' said Wolfe as he leaned eagerly across the quarterdeck railing and studied the advancing shore.

Wolfe's staff – the few who had joined him on the cat – were keeping their distance. There was a definite tension in the air; it wasn't the sort of atmosphere that bred co-operation, nor an efficient planning and fighting command. Wolfe was easier with Carlisle, and he could be a charming companion when he wasn't distracted and undecided.

'You see the lines there, Carlisle? That's the Chevalier Levis' main defence on the high ground, well above the tidal mark.'

He pointed to the long line of earthworks that stretched unbroken from the Montmorency Falls all the way west to the Charles River that guarded Quebec's eastern flank. That

# Rocks and Shoals

was the Beauport Shore where the British expedition against Quebec had been thrown back in the last war.

'Montcalm needs Levis to hold that line while the main body of his army waits behind. Today we'll break through those earthworks and force Montcalm to come down and fight. Then we'll have him, and the city will be ours for the taking.'

Wolfe looked excited, and he scanned the length of the earthworks with the huge telescope that one of his aides carried.

'There! Do you see the two redoubts on the foreshore? One's more obvious than the other. That's his weak point. The shore there isn't covered by fire from his lines – that's why they're there – but neither are the redoubts covered. He can't see his redoubts; he's made the simplest of errors. When we take them, we have a foothold in his territory. We can launch a regular assault at any time, this very day, I hope.'

Carlisle studied the redoubts with his own telescope. They were small, less than six guns each, he thought, and they were sited purely to cover the shore, as Wolfe had said. They couldn't stop ships using the North Channel freely, the range was too great.

'You have all afternoon to reduce those redoubts, Carlisle. I cannot launch the attack across the flats under the Falls until low water.'

The Falls were high, but the volume of water that came over them didn't match their grandeur, and at low tide it was possible to wade across the sand where the Montmorency ran into the Saint Lawrence. That would still put an attacking force below Levis' defended lines, but if they could join up with a strong amphibious assault at the redoubts, they'd have a fair chance of breaking through the lines.

And yet surely the general was wrong. Carlisle studied the defences more closely. The lines were on high ground, and the approach to them was a steep grassy bluff. It looked very much as though the redoubts *were* covered by the lines. That would change everything. Winning the redoubts would be meaningless if Levis' artillery could play on them from higher ground. They would be untenable, and the lines would be no more vulnerable than they would have been to a regular assault from the river.

Carlisle stole a glance at Wolfe. Yes, he'd realised the mistake, and by the expressions of his staff officers, they had also seen it. Perhaps they had cautioned against this plan. That would account for the fracture that Carlisle had observed between the general and his staff officers.

Wolfe was chewing on a fingernail, still staring at the redoubts now drawing closer and closer. This was the time to abandon the plan; before the boats moved out of the South Channel and before the magnitude of the failure was displayed to the world. To persevere ran the risk of a repulse that would give heart to the enemy, quite apart from the waste of men and ammunition that would surely result.

Now Wolfe was conferring with his staff. Carlisle kept his distance; this was an army matter.

'What's afoot?' asked Larkin, the ship's master. He was a man of middling years, perhaps a little older than Carlisle, and he'd volunteered to stay with his ship even though he knew it was going into danger far beyond anything his contract had anticipated.

Carlisle pointed out the problem and Larkin nodded sagely.

'He'll not turn back, sir,' he declared. 'Look at him, he's stubborn, and he's not listening to those other officers. Mark my words, this attack will go ahead.'

Carlisle liked the master, although he'd felt there was some reserve about him, something that he wasn't saying.

'It'll be a bad business,' Carlisle replied, 'but on the whole, I'm with Wolfe. I've seen these army staffs; they view a battle as an academic exercise where the odds can be neatly calculated, and the result is predictable. They take too little account of morale. We've been here for a month now, and

## Rocks and Shoals

most of the soldiers left England and the colonies in January or even in December. I think even a bloody repulse may be better than a tame withdrawal, and I believe that's Wolfe's view,' he said nodding to where the general was still conferring with his staff.

'We sailors have to leave a lot more to chance when we fight,' said Larkin with a sidelong look at Carlisle.

He should have known. This master was old enough to have served in the navy in the last war. In fact, as they were discussing odds, the chances were better than fifty-fifty that he had.

'I was master's mate in *Centurion*, sir,' he said nodding towards the two-decker ahead of them. 'I missed Anson's cruise and joined after the refit in '47. I was at Cape Finisterre and the action with La Motte in the Bay. When the old girl paid off, I bought a share in a collier – this collier – with my prize money from La Motte's convoy, and here I am today. I don't want my ship to be lost, but if she is, I won't lose financially,' he said patting the binnacle. 'I'm guaranteed compensation.'

'Then you chose to name her *Russell*?'

'My grandfather was at Barfleur and La Hogue, he was just a boy really, rated captain's servant, and he never saw a penny of the allowance. Yet he was desperately proud of those battles, and I named the cat *Russell*, after the admiral, to please him. He was old by then, and he died a few months later, but I'm glad I did it. He died happily, I think.'

\*\*\*

Carlisle and the master were right, Wolfe had no intention of calling off the attack. The general strode purposefully away from his officers, his resolve stiffened by their resistance.

'You know what to do, Carlisle.'

'Yes, sir.'

Carlisle looked at his watch. Eleven o'clock.

'High water in thirty minutes, sir.'

Wolfe nodded without commenting.

'Take her in then, Mister Larkin.'

Carlisle turned to wave to *Three Sisters* astern. There was a lieutenant from *Vanguard* onboard the second cat, and he waved his hat in acknowledgement.

'Helm a-lee,' said the master. 'Furl the fore tops'l and the mizzen, harden in the jib and main tops'l sheets.'

The cat came onto the wind and headed directly for the easterly of the two redoubts. The tide was in the last stages of the flood and was already losing the battle against the strong flow of the river and the first stirrings of the ebb.

*Centurion* was moving up to her position opposite the Montmorency river from where she could cover the assault across the tidal flats and contribute to the coming battle with the redoubts.

'Mark thirteen,' shouted the leadsman.

'We'll draw just a touch less than two fathoms with all the cargo gone,' said Larkin.

'Deep eleven.'

It was shoaling fast. Carlisle referred to Cook's chart that he had folded into his pocket. That was about right, but now they were starting to get closer to the shore where Cook's soundings stopped. That was understandable because they'd be in range of random shot from the redoubt soon. No surveying operation could be carried out under that threat.

A spout of water leapt into life a cable ahead of them. That was the smaller of the redoubts, the one further to the west, but it was a warning of things to come.

'What do you think, Mister Fulling,' Carlisle asked the lieutenant that had been assigned to *Russell*.

'The range is too long, sir, I'd rather wait until we're anchored,' he replied, touching his hat.

'Very well, anchored or aground, whichever comes first.'

It was a poor attempt at a jest, and in the tense mood of the cat's deck, it fell flat. The guns were all manned, and their crews were talking among themselves, easing their nervousness as the cat sailed boldly into range of heavy guns in fixed emplacements. The fourteen guns of the cat had

## Rocks and Shoals

been arranged in the usual way with seven to each side in the waist. That was an insurance policy so that they could fight either side regardless of the vagaries of the wind and tide. Nevertheless, when the cat was in position, whether anchored or on the bottom, she'd only have one side facing the redoubt. For that reason, Carlisle had an extra three gunports cut on each side so that the broadside could be increased to ten guns once they knew which side would be engaged. There'd be some heavy work before those extra three guns could be brought to bear.

'Mark seven,' called the leadsman, 'shoaling, sir,' he added unnecessarily.

Carlisle and the master exchanged glances. At the top of high tide, there should be more water here.

'Deep six.'

'It's still too far, sir,' said Fulling as another waterspout appeared on their larboard bow.

Carlisle and the Larkin had discussed this eventuality. If the guessed-at depths proved false, they'd abandon the idea of anchoring and sail straight in and put the cat aground. If necessary, they would tow the stern around to open their arcs for the battery.

'Away longboat,' shouted the master.

The crew tumbled down into the boat. They knew what to do.

'Deep four.'

'Furl the jib,' shouted Larkin, 'stand by to furl the main tops'l.'

They had to slow down the cat at the same time as keeping enough steerage way to turn her as soon as they felt her forefoot take the ground. Too fast and she'd run up with her bows pointing at the enemy and may lose her main topmast into the bargain. Too slow and there was no knowing how she would come to rest. Either way, it was the end of the cat, in all probability. They'd be grounding at the top of the tide, and they'd be high and dry at low water with the enemy's cannon punching holes in her hull below the waterline.

'Mark three.'

There was an edge in the leadsman's voice. Carlisle looked over the side and could see the tips of the water weeds standing straight in the slack water. Any moment now.

When it came, the grounding was the gentlest imaginable. Only Larkin noticed it at first.

'Helm to larboard,' he bellowed.

The timing was perfect. As *Russell's* bows sliced into the soft mud, the stern swung to larboard under the influence of the rudder, and the boat lent its extra weight to haul the cat beam-on to the shore. They came to rest with the easterly redoubt a point-and-a-half for'rard of the beam.

'You may commence firing, Mister Fulling,' said Carlisle. 'You'll have the boat crew back on deck when they've laid out the anchors.'

\*\*\*

'Well done, Captain Carlisle, that was fine work. I'd hoped to be closer, but I see this is the best that's achievable,' said Wolfe. 'Now where are those boats?'

*Three Sisters* had grounded a hundred yards west of *Russell*. She hadn't made quite such a good job of it; her redoubt lay on her larboard quarter and Carlisle could see a man swinging a great axe to cut away the after edge of the for'rard gunport. It would do.

Onboard *Russell*, the guns had started to fire, and the three extras from the starboard battery were being moved across. Already there was no hope of getting her off until the next high tide, the glistening stretches of mud were extending towards the stranded cat every minute, and she was easing down with no more than a five-degree list to starboard.

'Here they come, sir,' shouted a staff officer, and all eyes turned to the south to see the great armada of boats moving around Orleans Point and heading towards the cats.

## Rocks and Shoals

The sound of the firing was intense, but so far, the cat was unscathed. The range was long for the French artillery, and they appeared to have only twelve pounders. Still, the cats would be soon smashed to pieces if many of the shot hit. But Carlisle could see that their own fire was sweeping the embrasures of the redoubts, and now there were ten guns on *Russell's* larboard side, all hammering away at what looked like only five on the French side.

\*\*\*

'So far, so good, hey Carlisle,' said Wolfe, rubbing his hands. And it *had* gone well, so far. The cats were both engaging their respective redoubts, *Centurion* was adding the fire from her twenty-four pounders, and the artillery battery on the heights on the east side of the falls was adding to the din. Yet still, Carlisle was uneasy. The cats had grounded perhaps two cables further out than he'd hoped, and if the soundings were so different to their expectations, how would the flatboats, let alone the longboats, yawls and bateaux, get close enough to disgorge their first wave of grenadiers?

It was a brave sight as three hundred boats pulled hard down the North Channel with the wind and the strengthening ebb behind them. Many of the boats were flying regimental and company colours that shone in the bright summer sunshine. On and on they came, heading for the space between the two cats. Three of them, seemingly empty, were steering directly for *Russell*. Those were the boats that would take Wolfe and his staff ashore immediately behind the assault wave of grenadiers.

Carlisle turned to check that the guns were all firing. They were into a hearty rhythm now, with guns being sponged and reloaded at a steady pace. There was a deadly pattern to it all, the loud report, the thunder, flame and smoke, the recoil, the worm, the sponge, the powder canister, the ball, the wad, the priming, the run-out. 'Stand back!' An enormous explosion, the gun flung back against its breeching. 'Stop your vents!' and the whole macabre dance started again. *Russell* hadn't been hit yet, and the men were grinning like idiots.

'Why have they stopped Carlisle? Why are the boats just milling about over there?'

Wolfe was a phlegmatic sort of man, but he was almost dancing with frustration now.

Carlisle ran over to the starboard side. Sure enough, the first wave of boats was holding some two hundred yards away. He looked more closely. Two of them were using boathooks as sounding poles. There was Chads of *Vesuvius* standing in the stern-sheets looking up and downstream. The appalling truth dawned upon Carlisle. They were two hours past high tide now, and the cats were almost high-and-dry. There must be a reef or a sandbank out there that *Russell* and *Three Sisters* had narrowly scraped over but with this lower tide was stopping the flatboats joining them.

'They've hit upon a shallow patch, sir. The tide's fallen ten feet since we grounded, they're trying to find a way through.'

Further up the channel, the following waves of boats were trying to hold their positions and let the first wave go in, but it was proving impossible, and the tide was falling every minute.

They watched in exasperation as the boats tried and failed to make their way over the obstruction. Slowly the problem became evident as the receding tide showed the ledge of rock, bare and smooth, that protruded from the mud. And that was how, eventually, after hours of frustration, Chads found a way to get the boats up to the cats. As the water slipped away, it revealed a channel that at first sight merely wandered off to the west, towards Beauport and Quebec, but was soon revealed to dog-leg back to the cats. Four hours after the cats had first taken the ground, four hours of hard service with enemy shot whistling over the naval gunners' heads, and the first flatboat grounded fifty yards from *Russell*. That was the closest it could get until the tide turned and the flood

# Rocks and Shoals

covered the foreshore.

\*\*\*

# CHAPTER EIGHTEEN

## A Bloody Repulse

*Tuesday, Thirty-First of July 1759.*
*Cat Russell, aground, the North Channel, Saint Lawrence River.*

Wolfe looked dubiously over the cat's side. The foreshore was an undulating plain of hard-packed sand with wide stretches of mud, and over it all was a mat of green stuff, lying flat now that it was deprived of the buoyancy of the water.

'It looks hard enough, what do you think, Carlisle?'

The grenadiers were already swarming off the flatboats and making their way to the shore. Soon they'd become attractive targets for the guns in the redoubts, but for now it was the cats that were still in the greatest danger. *Russell* had taken a few hits, and there were some superficial wounds. *Three Sisters* had a damaged mizzen, and the yard was shot through, hanging by its halyard with the peak pointing disconsolately downwards. The destruction had happened in the first hour. As the redoubt's guns had heated up the windage between the bore and the balls had increased, and some of the force of the powder was lost. Only the occasional twelve-pounder could reach the cats; most fell short. However, the cats' twenty-four pounders were still reaching the redoubt, and great holes were being torn in the walls. Only three guns were still in action from the larger redoubt.

'It'll bear your weight, sir, but it looks like sticky going. I can't offer a boat until the flood reaches us in another three or four hours,' Carlisle replied, 'and even then, it can only go back into the river, not the shore.'

Wolfe looked longingly at his grenadiers swarming ashore. He desperately wanted to be close to them, but the opportunity was slipping away. Already the first of his men were reaching the dry ground and gathering for a rush at the

## Rocks and Shoals

redoubts. He kicked at the rope ladder which hung from the quarter, testing its strength.

'Very well, I'll go. I'll be in time to direct the assault on the lines in any case, even if they've taken the redoubts before I get there.'

And with that Wolfe threw his leg over the quarterdeck rail and gingerly descended the ladder, followed by his staff. He was a fighting man; Carlisle knew that already. Despite his frail appearance, Wolfe would always want to be in the forefront of a battle. Nevertheless, he'd be hard-pressed to influence the storming of the redoubts.

The guns in the redoubt had shifted their aim now, and they were hurling balls into the waves of grenadiers advancing across the foreshore. They were doing little damage though; the soft sand and mud absorbed the balls rather than allowing them to ricochet across the battleground. That was how solid shot usually had its greatest effect on infantry, by bouncing along the ground at knee-height. Many a recruit had lost a leg or a foot by believing that he could stop a spent ball as he would a rolling football. The grenadiers were hardly inconvenienced, and they looked strangely innocent in their waistcoats or in some cases, merely their shirtsleeves. The bright reds, yellows, blues and greens of their regimentals had been left behind at their camps; this was their preferred rig for an assault.

Carlisle blew his whistle.

'Cease firing,' he shouted. 'Mister Fulling, reload and stand by. The grenadiers are about to charge.'

Carlisle looked over at *Three Sisters*. A waved acknowledgement showed that they'd heard the whistle and seen the situation. He could leave the management of the guns to Fulling; now he had the time to watch the unfolding drama of the redoubts.

These were true redoubts, not mere lunettes or batteries. The earthworks surrounded them on all sides, making them forts in miniature. Nevertheless, it was clear that they couldn't hold out long against the waves of grenadiers now rushing towards them. There didn't appear to be much order in the charge, but it was effective, and before Wolfe had started his trek across the mud and slime of the foreshore, he could see the white waistcoats and shirts pouring through the embrasures and over the parapets. The French artillerymen evidently had few illusions about the strength of their position once determined infantry were ashore, and they were running fast up the slope to Levis' lines.

\*\*\*

'That was neatly done,' said Carlisle, 'but they won't be able to hold that position long. Look, the French are already firing into the redoubts.'

'Heavier guns and closer range,' Larking replied, 'it appears we had the better part of the bargain.'

All along the lines, the guns were firing. French eighteen-pounders by the sound of them and they were tearing great holes in the rear faces of the two redoubts. Wolfe was still no more than halfway to the greater of the two fortifications.

'Look, sir,' said Larkin, pointing to the west.

This part of Quebec was notorious for its summer storms, and it looked like one was on its way now. The clouds to the west were grey and menacing and the wind, veering into the north, was starting to whip up little waves on the river. They'd both seen this before.

'Thirty minutes, do you think, Mister Larkin?'

'We'll be lucky if we have that long, sir. Twenty at most, I'd say.'

Carlisle's attention was taken by a sudden increase in the firing from the shore. It was difficult to see with the powder smoke rolling down from the defended lines towards the redoubts, but certainly something was happening. He wiped his eyes and a gust of wind, cooler than before, blew a hole in the smoke. The grenadiers were charging the lines!

Down on the foreshore, the musketeers were starting to leave their boats, but the grenadiers, after months of inaction and frustration, were taking the battle into their own hands. Wolfe hadn't even reached the firm ground, and he'd already lost control of the battle. Carlisle gasped in horror as the white-shirted figures charged at the green slope.

It was a formidable position designed by the inheritors of two hundred years of French dominance in military engineering. The lines themselves were high earthworks punctuated by redans that carried guns that could pour an enfilading fire upon attackers. The grenadiers were attacking with reckless courage, each unit racing its neighbour for the honour of being the first to break through. Wolfe was waving his sword, trying to call them back, but he was still too far away, and anyway it seemed unlikely that he could halt that wild rush.

Carlisle watched impotently as little groups of grenadiers were scythed down by grapeshot from the French guns. Then the leading grenadiers were at the slope, and now the French muskets started to take their toll. The wild rush began to lose its momentum, and all along the green slope, he could see groups of white figures slowing and hesitating. One group, bolder and less sensible of their own safety was at the earthworks now, and a few hardly souls had scaled them. Perhaps it would work. Perhaps this undisciplined mob, by sheer bravery and brute force, would make a breach in the lines.

Then the rain came. A few tentative drops at first, then a hard downpour that felt bitterly cold after the heat of the day. It beat down upon the grenadiers, soaking the priming in their muskets and turning the grassy bank into a slippery precipice that offered no grip for leather boots. One by one the companies and platoons started to withdraw, then they started to run and soon it was a race to the dubious safety of the redoubt.

The attack on the lines was over before the commanding general was able to influence it. It was doubtful whether he could have restrained his excited men, but at least he could have brought some order to the assault. If they had waited until the storm was past, they would have had a better chance, for while it lasted the redoubt was safe from the French artillery which could no more keep its priming dry than the grenadiers could. But the moment was lost. The storm lasted an hour, and by that time there was no question of renewing the attack with men soaked to the skin and hardly a musket that would fire. If the cats had managed to get closer it might have been possible, but Carlisle's guns would barely reach the redoubts, and his shot fell far short of Levis' lines. The redoubts themselves were untenable under the baleful mouths of the guns on the lines, that much was obvious.

As the rain stopped, Wolfe's army started to withdraw to the boats. Most of the men had found their proper units, and they trudged back across the sand and mud in some sort of order, but they were beaten; Carlisle could see that. He could also see that Wolfe and his staff together with some of the musketeer companies were striking east to ford the Montmorency river below the falls.

'It's all over, I believe,' said Larkin, lowering his telescope. 'We must shift for ourselves; it seems.'

'I regret that we'll have to burn your ship, Mister Larkin,' said Carlisle.

The master didn't look at all disturbed at that news. *Russell* wasn't insured; ships taken up from trade were covered by the generous compensation that the Admiralty provided. Carlisle guessed that he'd be richer if *Russell* never left the Saint Lawrence.

'Mister Fulling. Prepare to burn the ship. Set a fuse on the magazine and spike the guns.'

Now that the firing had largely ceased, he could communicate with *Three Sisters* by shouting. The lieutenant and the master shouted back. They'd heard the order and knew what to do.

'I'm going to get us some boats,' said Carlisle and with that, he ran down the ladder and started his laborious walk

## Rocks and Shoals

to the boats that were still a hundred yards away from the cats. He blessed his decision to wear long leather boots rather than half-boots or stockings and shoes. It wasn't bad on the hard sand, even though the green weed lay a foot deep in places, but the bands of mud, narrow though they were, slowed him amazingly.

***

'Mister Chads, Mister Chads,' shouted Carlisle, waving his hands as he ploughed his way towards the water. Most of the ship's boats, the bateaux and the luggers had already left, taking the line infantry back to their camps. The grenadiers were still pouring across the foreshore, carrying their wounded with them.

Chads was hurrying the soldiers into the flatboats casting nervous glances to the shore where it was clear that the French were preparing to sortie. This should have been Wolfe's moment; he could have taken the sortie in the flank, but it was too late. He was far to the east, wading the ford below the falls, and the retreating grenadiers were in no condition to fight. They were merely a retreating rabble, no better than the Canadian militia that they so despised.

'Mister Chads, blast you!' Carlisle shouted again.

He realised that he couldn't be seen among the retreating soldiers. He'd left his blue coat in the cat, and at fifty yards his white breeches and waistcoat looked little different to the Grenadiers. In desperation, he drew his sword and placed his hat on top of it.

'Mister Chads!' he roared.

This time Chads looked right at him.

'Captain Carlisle, sir,' he said in a mixture of astonishment and guilt.

'I'll thank you for keeping four of these flatboats back…' Carlisle said breathlessly.

Chads looked around him, there were just eight flatboats at hand and five hundred soldiers jostling to get on board.

'…and keep back a company of grenadiers as a rearguard. Two boats for the cats' crews and two for the rearguard.'

Chads was a good officer, and he'd been plucked out of his command of the fireship *Vesuvius* to command the boats for the assault. A good officer, but he wasn't thinking fast enough.

'Hey, Captain,' Carlisle bellowed at a soldier at the head of about thirty grenadiers. 'Yes, you, sir, Mister Montgomery.'

He'd recognised the soldier from the transport that he'd taken through the Traverse a month before.

'Gather together a hundred men who still have some fighting spirit and form a line thirty paces from the boats. You'll go in the last two flatboats, but the French may be upon us before then.'

Montgomery looked over his shoulder and saw the truth of what this sea-officer said. Privately, Carlisle doubted whether he'd be able to hold back a hundred of these beaten soldiers. Then he saw a man stop in his tracks. A private soldier by the look of him, but he also looked behind. There were the crews of the cats struggling across the foreshore, and there was the French sortie pouring over the ramparts and down the grassy bank.

'Fellows!' the soldier shouted in a broad Irish accent. 'Will ye show them your knapsacks, the damned French! Will ye turn your backs and leave these brave lads to be taken? Who'll stay with me? Hooray for Mister Montgomery, who'll stay with him?'

One by one, soldier by soldier, they hesitated, then shouldering their muskets they ran to Montgomery, taking no account of regiment or battalion or company. They ran to the captain and formed a line as they had done a thousand times in training. Three ranks, with the first rank standing, as General Wolfe had ordered.

'Those who need to, load your muskets. Fresh priming for every musket,' shouted a sergeant major who a moment before had been at the head of the rush to the boats. There were more than a hundred men there, perhaps a hundred and thirty, but the flatboats could take that overload at a pinch.

'Mister Knox take the left flank,' said Montgomery in an even tone, 'that's where they'll try to turn us.'

He was steady now. It didn't take much to reassert the ingrained discipline of a line regiment. All along the triple ranks the grenadiers were reloading, drawing damp powder and blowing on priming pans to remove the moisture.

'The company is ready, sir,' reported the sergeant-major when he saw that each man had a loaded musket.

'Fix bayonets,' ordered Montgomery.

There were grim smiles from the grenadiers now as they went through the steps of fixing their long, wicked bayonets to the muzzles of their muskets.

'Front rank, take your aim.'

The sailors were just yards away now, and they threaded through the two lanes that the grenadiers had left in their ranks. The last sailor passed through and, at an order, the grenadiers closed their ranks. Now they presented a solid wall to the advancing French.

Carlisle grabbed Fulling's shoulder as he came through.

'Make sure the boat guns are ready,' he said, 'this will be tight.'

Boom! Carlisle jumped in surprise. Then he saw the plume of smoke and the planks and barrel staves that was all that could be seen of the gallant little cat *Russell*.

Boom! That was *Three Sisters* following her. The lieutenants had done well. It took a cool hand to set fire to a slow match outside a magazine. They'd leave nothing for the French to convert into a fireship or a block for the narrow channels. The cats had come a long way from Whitby, but they'd carry no more coals from Newcastle, nor deals and masts from the Baltic ports.

'Here, put this on, sir,' said Larkin, offering Carlisle his coat. Carlisle was infinitely touched that this merchant master had bothered to encumber himself with his coat when he was fleeing for his life from French infantry.

The sun was sinking on their left over Cape Levi, and the shadows were lengthening.

Carlisle stood beside Montgomery as the last of the sailors scrambled into the two flatboats that had been left for them. He saw the boats back their oars to pull astern off the mud; then they waited there with their guns facing the shore and a determined-looking gunner testing the sighting.

'I'll let them get close,' said Montgomery, 'they look blown.'

The enemy approached in a ragged line, not the usual column that they preferred for the attack. They were looking a little more cautious now, and there were officers trying to make some order out of chaos. Here and there small groups stopped and formed ranks, but the bulk of them, perhaps two hundred, came on, their bayonets levelled and a killing light in their eyes.

Carlisle could see the obvious danger that the French line would envelop the grenadiers on the left, just as Montgomery had foretold, but he could see that Knox was bending the line a little to catch the enemy in their own flank if they should charge past.

There was something very comforting about having three ranks of grenadiers between you and the enemy, Carlisle thought, but he knew how quickly it could disintegrate. A brief mental image flashed across his mind, of his friend Holbrooke being shot and nearly bayoneted as he withdrew to the boats on a French beach a year before. Where was Holbrooke now? Probably somewhere in the forested wilderness a few hundred leagues to the south and west.

'Front rank fire!'

Carlisle jumped. One day, one day, he would get used to that first sound of gunfire.

It was hard to see through the close-packed ranks in front of him, but they had clearly delivered a crippling volley, even though a good number of muskets had misfired. There were Frenchmen flat on the ground,

## Rocks and Shoals

Frenchmen kneeling and clutching their wounds, but many, far too many still standing.

'Centre rank, fire!'

That was a good volley too, but now the French were much closer, the bolder among them pushing forward with their bayonets.

'Rear rank, fire!'

That volley was delivered right in the face of the blue-and-white uniformed enemy, but now the front rank of grenadiers was fighting at bayonet-point. There was no chance to reload. Carlisle drew his sword.

'Company will advance!' Montgomery shouted with lungs of brass. Somehow a drummer had appeared at his side, and he was beating a steady rhythm. Not the charge, but a more orderly call for the whole body to move forward to meet the enemy. To Carlisle it appeared impossible, but somehow, at the point of the bayonet, the grim grenadiers pushed forward. Now the training and discipline started to tell. Half of the French were militia or *troupes de terre*, and they were no match for Wolfe's men. Steadily, yard by yard, the enemy was pushed back. Then suddenly there was clear ground between the opposing sides.

'They're regrouping,' said Montgomery quietly, 'now's our chance.'

'Rear rank to the boats, Sergeant Major,'

The men knew what to do. They had to keep the enemy guessing for as long as possible, so they crouched as they ran. They leapt into the two boats and scrambled forward.

'Centre rank, Sergeant Major.'

That left just a thin line facing the enemy.

'Mister Knox. To the boats with your wing.'

Now there was no hiding it from the French; only thirty men were left facing them.

'The company will retire.'

The Sergeants stood at either end of the line and kept them in order. They backed towards the boats with their bayonets to the enemy.

Carlisle looked over his shoulder. The grenadiers in the boats were frantically reloading.

'Now men. To the boats!'

It was every man for himself, and Carlisle was caught up in a rush. The enemy was close behind, although still cautious. Only the most reckless were pushing forward. He saw a grenadier fall beside him, struck in the back by a musket ball, and he heard the reports of the muskets from ahead and behind.

With a convulsive heave, he was over the gunwale and pitched headfirst into the bottom boards. Trying frantically to free himself as more men piled on top of him, he heard the coxswains' orders to back water the oars. He hauled himself through the struggling mass of bodies just in time to be a witness to the final act. It had grown suddenly dark. The boats had backed away from the shore, and all around him grenadiers were aiming and firing into the hordes of Frenchmen. The few of their fellows left on the strand were being summarily bayonetted by the enemy. The naval gunners were sighting along the barrels of the two-pounder boat guns.

'Fire!' shouted a voice from the stern of the flatboat.

A tongue of flame spat out from the gun, the sound of the discharge so close beside him making Carlisle's head ring. It had been loaded with canister, of course, and the package of musket balls cut a bloody swathe through their attackers.

'Back water larboard, pull hard, starboard,' shouted the coxswain and the flatboat span around in its own length much faster than a longboat would have done without a deep keel to bite into the water.

'Steady. Pull together.'

The four flatboats drew quickly away from the shore, and in seconds they were out of musket range. The day was almost done, and they pulled back towards Orleans Point in the gathering gloom with the flooding tide beneath them. Only the twin pyres of the two gallant Whitby cats illuminated the scene as the flames consumed what the explosions had left.

***

# CHAPTER NINETEEN

## Bilged and Stranded

*Wednesday, Twenty-Ninth of August 1759.*
*Medina, at Anchor. The Basin, Saint Lawrence River.*

It had been a good supper, all things considered, and now Carlisle and his guests, James Chads and Moxon were enjoying the cigars that Chads had generously provided. Rations weren't scarce in the fleet, but they had been reduced to the plainest of fare, and luxuries such as cigars were jealously hoarded. There were still two bottles of Carlisle's best Madeira, however, but when he'd drunk those, he'd have none left. He'd been in half a mind to serve a poor sherry that had lain in his store for two years, overlooked in favour of its more sumptuous cousin. That, of course, would have been a shabby trick, even if Chads never knew about it, because it was Chads who had plucked Carlisle off that muddy strand underneath the French lines. He probably owed his life to James Chads. The three men sipped the Madeira gratefully as they smoked their cigars and watched the half-moon dip below the cliffs of Cape Levi.

'He had not thought it proper to persevere,' said Carlisle. 'That was what Wolfe said in his letter to Pitt, or so the admiral's flag lieutenant told me.'

Carlisle recognised the change that had come over him during this long and frustrating campaign. A few months ago, he wouldn't have dreamed of commenting on the commanding general's decision in front of two junior officers, but the whole mood had changed. It had been four weeks since the debacle at the Falls of Montmorency, and in that time no coherent plan had emerged, Wolfe was ill with a fever and his brigadiers, by all accounts, had lost confidence in him. There appeared no way out of the stalemate; Montcalm held the northern shore, and even when his supply line upstream had been threatened, he had proved obdurate. He knew that the heavy ships would have to withdraw soon, and Wolfe's army could hardly sustain themselves in their makeshift camps over a Canadian winter. All he had to do was to hold on, to resist the temptation to be drawn out of his defensive positions and to wait for the first frosts. If Amherst's army had marched faster from Crown Point, he would have been forced to act, but the latest news suggested that the ever-cautious general was consolidating his position for the winter and leaving the advance on Montreal and Quebec for the next year.

Chads nodded but made no comment. He was about the same age as Carlisle, but he'd spent the years of peace as a half-pay lieutenant and had been promoted to commander less than a year ago. It wasn't a question that Carlisle could possibly ask, but there had to be something in Chads' past that had irked their Lordships. Otherwise, he'd have been made a commander two years earlier in the first mad rush of promotions for this new war. Chads' position was much more precarious than Carlisle's; he couldn't risk the faintest possibility that his words would come back to haunt him.

'Wolfe lays the blame on everyone and everything. James Cook is culpable for his charts of the North Channel. *Centurion* he deems to have anchored too far east. The cats didn't lie directly opposite the redoubts. But he forgets that the plan was predicated on the French guns not being able to cover the redoubts. As soon as the grenadiers realised they couldn't stay in the redoubts, they must advance or retreat; they chose the bolder course and attacked. They might have accomplished it too if that storm hadn't arrived at that moment.'

Perhaps it was the Madeira, perhaps it was a sense of foreboding about the task that they were soon to attempt, but Carlisle knew even as he spoke that it was unwise to do so. And more than that, he was compromising his own principles. Moxon broke the awkward silence.

'You said, sir, that there are no guns in the batteries of

the lower town. Is that a certainty? We'll be awfully close.'

Carlisle considered for a moment. He'd almost forgotten the task at hand, the convoy that he must take past Quebec to join Admiral Holmes above the city. Moxon had raised an important point. In fact, it was the key assumption that lay behind this plan, not unlike Wolfe's assumption about the redoubts on the Beauport Shore. The heavy guns on the citadel, high above the river, had proved a menace to all the ships that had made the passage between Quebec and Cape Levi. It was only practicable at night, and that made the navigation of the south side of the channel particularly difficult. They all knew the consequences. *Diana* had almost been lost to those guns; she was so severely damaged that she'd been sent back to New York. However, those guns on the citadel couldn't depress far enough to threaten traffic on the north side of the channel. That was covered by the batteries in the lower town, mounting twelve-pounders and a few twenty-fours. If they were absent, then it might be possible to pass unchallenged right under the noses of the French artillery by staying close to the north shore.

'The whole of the lower town was swept by fire a few days ago. It's deserted now and as far as can be seen the batteries have been abandoned.'

'It's thought that the guns and the gunners have been sent back up to the frigates above the Richelieu rapids,' said Chads, glad to be able to contribute to a safe conversation. 'It makes sense, those frigates are being wasted lying there with skeleton crews. If they sailed, they could threaten Holmes' ships in the upper river. It would at least provide a diversion.'

'Well, we'll find out soon enough. I regret that we'll have to break up this gathering, gentlemen. The flood starts in an hour, and we must profit from this easterly wind, after all these days.'

\*\*\*

The convoy weighed anchor in silence and with the turn of the tide reached to the north across the Basin.

# Rocks and Shoals

*Vesuvius* was leading three cats and a transport with *Medina* bringing up the rear. The night was pitch-dark, with no moon and an overcast sky. Only the dim lights on the taffrails of the ships ahead could be seen. Carlisle had stationed *Medina* in the rear for two reasons: first, so that he could take any ships of the convoy in tow if they received damage, and second, in case the guns of the lower town *were* in place and *were* manned. If that were the case, there was still a hope that the French gunners would be caught unawares, and that the leading ships may slip through without being engaged. The rear of the convoy would take the worst punishment, and of all his squadron, *Medina* was the most capable of surviving damage. He remembered that previous passage through the narrows. Was it really six weeks ago?

'Mister Chads is doing well, sir,' Hosking remarked. 'We're well over to the north but clear of the shore.'

It had been an important point in the decision to give up the head of the convoy to a little eight-gun sloop. Chads had proved his steadiness at Montmorency, and Carlisle had faith in his ability to keep a clear head in the darkness. There was nothing, absolutely nothing, that Carlisle could now do to influence the track that the convoy would take. He could neither see *Vesuvius* nor communicate with Chads. On him and his master rested the responsibility for navigation.

\*\*\*

Carlisle looked at his watch in the faint glow from the binnacle. Eleven-thirty. It was a small point, but if the French changed the watch at midnight – and he'd been assured by the pilots that they kept the same time as the British – then at eleven-forty-five their vigilance would be at its lowest. Sentries would be thinking of their reliefs and surreptitiously edging towards the path leading to the barracks. And in fifteen minutes *Vesuvius* should be just passing under the citadel.

Carlisle shivered even in the heat of a warm summer

evening. It wasn't just the darkness; it was the stillness that was playing on his nerves. The guns on Cape Levi and the Citadel were silent and with the wind just a point off the starboard quarter there was little noise in the rigging. The ships weren't making the usual sounds of a wooden hull forcing its way through the sea's waves; in this river, with this wind, there wasn't even a ripple to splash against the forefoot. The quietness of the grave.

Suddenly the darkness was ripped apart by a double flash from starboard, closely followed by the sound of the cannon and the crash of the balls striking ship's timbers. They seemed so close at hand that Carlisle could have reached across and touched them. And he hadn't even jumped! Was he expecting the guns, deep down?

He heard a cry from forward; someone had been hit in one of the cats. It was too close to be *Vesuvius* and too far away to be the transport immediately ahead of *Medina*.

'Mister Moxon. Commence firing; you can see your target.'

Now that the convoy had been discovered it was important that the French should be lured away from the valuable cats and the transport full of soldiers. He could rely on Chads to hold his fire, and in any case, he must be past the batteries by now. *Medina* was deliberately making herself into a target.

The first broadside pushed the frigate bodily to larboard. The flash from the guns momentarily lit up the deck and showed a scene that could have come straight from Dante's Inferno. The nine-pounders were caught in the act of recoiling. The shirtless crews were leaning back from the roaring beasts, holding their rammers and sponges, their linstocks and cartridges as though they were the very instruments of torture. The shore was slipping past quickly, and the ship's lantern ahead was forging forward through the darkness.

*Medina's* second broadside was more ragged. Moxon must have allowed the gun captains to fire as fast as they could reload. That was good; they were experienced gunners and could be relied upon to make every ball count. But the real reason for opening fire was to distract the French batteries – the batteries that had no right to be there – and attract all the fire to *Medina*.

Crash! It was working; the first balls came smashing through the frigate's fragile bulwarks. It was a strange thing to be under fire and be glad that your plan was working.

In the brief instants of the flashes, Carlisle could see the outline of the lower town, nestled under the cliffs. Ten or twelve minutes, he decided, that was how long it would take to run far enough upstream to be safely past the guns. Then there would be another five minutes when the guns further west could reach them. Then they would be clear. He resisted the temptation to look at his watch.

Men were falling now. He could see a seaman lying where he'd been shoved aside to clear the gun's recoil. He couldn't see who it was; the dead man had no name, yet.

All his guns were still firing. The transport ahead of him must be nearly clear by now. He blew his whistle, a sharp sound that cut through the thunder of the guns.

There was no need to continue to attract the enemy's fire, not with the convoy past the danger zone.

*Medina* reeled from another hit, somewhere under Carlisle's feet, then another forward.

'Foretopmast's going, sir,' shouted Hosking.

A shot must have smashed the starboard forechains. The wind wasn't strong, but without that lateral support, there was no saving the foretopmast. With a great lurch and a dismal creaking, it tottered and fell slowly to leeward taking the jib and fore staysail with it.

'Helm to windward,' Hosking shouted at the quartermaster, 'hold your course!'

Without the leverage forward to keep the bows off the wind, the frigate would luff violently, and the hostile shore was waiting to windward, with its jagged rocks and French guns. Carlisle watched the ship's head intently as Moxon led a charge to cut away the shrouds and stays holding the fore topmast alongside. *Medina* was moving to starboard!

'Helm's not answering,' the quartermaster reported, and the steersman spun the unresisting wheel between his hands.

There were relieving tackles rigged below the deck to assist in heavy weather or to steer the ship when the wheel tackles had been shot through. A steady petty officer and four hands were already stationed there, and the skylight had been opened. All these precautions were detailed in Carlisle's standing orders. He'd never had to use the relieving tackles in battle, but now they were essential.

Hosking shouted down the skylight.

'Helm hard a-starboard,'

The orders had to be given in reverse, because down below they were moving the tiller, not a wheel. There was a dreadful pause as *Medina's* bow continued to turn to starboard, towards the shore.

'Rudder's not answering, sir,' Carlisle heard faintly, 'I can't shift it, it feels jammed.'

And still, the bows swung to starboard.

'Brail the mizzen,' Hosking called to the bosun.

That was the last resort; it may be just enough to balance the rig and give time to get the frigate back under control.

Carlisle looked over the side to see how the frigate's course was being affected by the trailing foretopmast. Moxon's men were still hacking at the mess of standing rigging that was holding it alongside.

'Belay that Mister Moxon,' shouted Carlisle, 'leave the fore topmast as it is.'

It was dragging over the larboard bow with the effect of a sea-anchor. It would be more effective if it were trailing off the ship's quarter, but even for'rard it would help.

That was better, but *Medina* wasn't under control. She was moving at the whim of the wind and tide, and she was

## Rocks and Shoals

moving fast, the dimly-seen shore was rushing past at perhaps six knots as the flooding tide and the wind had her in their grip.

There were no more guns now. They were past the lower town and too close to the shore for the higher batteries.

'By the mark, five,' called the leadsman.

Five fathoms! Good God, they must be almost aground!

'Get the sails off her Mister Hosking.'

There was still a hope that the tide and wind would carry them downstream without hitting a rock or being cast ashore.

Carlisle felt rather than saw the topmen running aloft to furl the main tops'l. It was an act of pure heroism with the upper masts in such a precarious state.

Then he felt the frigate's hull scraping against something solid. It broke free, then another scrape followed by a shuddering halt as *Medina* was brought up with a lurch. There was an awful splintering sound as the main topmast leaned forward and then fell onto the wreckage of the foremast, just before the topmen had reached the yard. Their lives were saved by seconds.

Carlisle looked over the side; they must have hit a rock as the shoreline was still thirty yards away. The enemy shore! They were aground just a pistol-shot from French-held territory. At all costs he must get the frigate away to the south side if the river.

'Damage report, Mister Moxon. Bosun man the pumps.'

He was fighting hard to keep his voice steady. They could expect no help from *Vesuvius*; she was upstream with no hope of getting back against wind and tide. Carlisle's mission had been accomplished, now he had to save his ship.

'Four foot in the hold, sir. The pumps are just keeping pace, but I can see the boulder showing through the side, just under the fore chains.'

'What will happen if I haul her off, Chips?

For the first time ever, the carpenter didn't scratch his head.

'We'll fill and founder, sir,' he said with an appalling certainty.

'How quickly,'

Now the carpenter did scratch his head.

'Maybe half an hour, sir, maybe more if we're lucky, but if it rips away any more planks…'

He didn't need to say any more.

'Mister Moxon, get as many men on the pumps as you can. You can take anyone from the gun crews that you want; we won't need them. Chips, get your whole crew below with all the timber you need, take anyone else. When we're off the rock, you know what will happen.'

'Aye-aye sir,' the carpenter replied. He hurried away, shouting instructions at his mates.

'Bosun, get the longboat in the water and be ready to haul us off.'

'Tide's still rising, sir,' said Hosking.

'Yes, I know that. We can't wait here even if the tide would let us. When we're free, we'll make for the southern shore and put her aground. Now, let's get that rudder moving.'

It was the hardest two hours of Carlisle's life. The rising tide and the desperate efforts of the longboat crew got her off the rock after an hour and a half. By then they'd got the rudder working with the relieving tackles. With the courses drawing and thirty men on the pumps it was a mad dash for the friendly shore.

The carpenter saved the day. With his crew and a dozen others, he lashed hammocks into a cargo net and stuffed the whole mass into the gaping hole as the frigate was hauled away from the rock. The water still poured into the hold in torrents, but the pumps drew it onto the deck and over the side almost as fast as it came in. Almost.

Then the French artillery on the heights found their range, but the balls that ploughed into the hull went almost unnoticed.

It was a relief when *Medina* took the ground under the cliffs to the south of Point Aux Peres, even though it opened another hole on her larboard side. But they were safe, on a friendly shore and out of range of the enemy's guns. Carlisle's ship was cast ashore a scant mile from the very spot that *Diana* grounded, but there was no following frigate to help *Medina*.

\*\*\*

# CHAPTER TWENTY

## Flotsam

*Friday, Thirty-First of August 1759.*
*Stirling Castle, at Anchor. The Basin, Saint Lawrence River.*

Carlisle was piped aboard the flagship with all the honours due to a post-captain, but nevertheless, he felt like a fraud. His ship, his beloved *Medina*, was aground under the cliffs to the west of Point Aux Peres. She was out of range of the French guns, but she was bilged both larboard and starboard, and if she ever sailed again it would be to limp down the river as far as Louisbourg, then on to Halifax for whatever repairs that embryonic shipyard could provide. She may be able to be patched up sufficiently to take a convoy home to England, but only if she left before the winter storms started. Otherwise – and more likely – *Medina* would spend the winter in Halifax. He was a captain with a ship that couldn't float, and he felt useless and dejected.

The flag lieutenant called him in with hardly five minute's delay. Saunders at least had some empathy for a captain whose ship had just been mauled, and he strode around his desk to shake Carlisle's hand.

'That was one of the finest actions this campaign, Carlisle, I'm honoured to shake your hand.'

Carlisle was so startled that he was momentarily unable to respond. For the past day-and-a-half he'd been turning over in his mind all the possible ways in which the admiral would greet him, but this fulsome accolade hadn't been one of them.

'Thank you, Sir Charles,' was all he could say when he recovered the power of speech.

'Monckton himself told me that there were no guns in the lower town, and I must say that he apologised most handsomely. I'm sure he'll have a word for you when you meet.'

## Rocks and Shoals

*When we meet?* Was the admiral referring to more than a casual possibility?

'The important thing was that the cats and the transport should get up the river. Every convoy I've sent has been delayed, and it was starting to look as though we weren't trying. I'm sorry for *Medina*, but the brutal fact is that you won a small but important victory, Carlisle, and I don't mean merely against the French.'

Saunders looked meaningfully at Carlisle.

'I think you understand me.'

The admiral was, indeed, being as clear as he could. This delay in taking decisive action against the city was starting to open the cracks in navy and army cooperation. The accord between the two commands would always look good when things were going well, but the temptation to blame the other service when they went badly was difficult to resist. The expedition had been menacing Quebec for over two months and yet had achieved nothing. The city appeared impregnable, and Montcalm was sticking to his defensive strategy in a way that few would have thought possible, and the short Canadian autumn was approaching. His action of the night before last had not only delivered the supplies and reinforcements that Brigadier Murray needed, it had also demonstrated that the navy was prepared to take risks – and to take casualties – in support of this great endeavour.

'*Medina* was a small price to pay, and I hope you'll forgive me for saying that. Oh, we'll get her home, I'm sure, but her usefulness here is over. I'll be taking the guns out of her and redistributing your men. I don't doubt that you'll miss her, but she's not a post ship anymore.'

Carlisle tried in vain to keep his profound shock from showing on his face. He'd assumed that he'd remain in command until the frigate was repaired. He'd already started planning what minimum work would suffice to enable him to reach Louisbourg.

'I'll come to you in a moment, Carlisle, there's a valuable

service that you can do for the cause…'

A valuable service? That didn't have the sound of a ship, and how could it? All the post-captains were distressingly healthy, and there was no two-decker; no, nor even the smallest frigate, without a captain.

'…but before that, we've discussed your first lieutenant previously; do you still consider him a worthy and deserving officer? I have a mind to make him a commander and send him home in *Medina*.'

Now he was on surer ground; this was a question he could answer easily.

'Most certainly, sir. I've known few officers more worthy of promotion than Mister Moxon.'

'Good, then my secretary will write out his commission now, and you may be the bearer of the glad tidings. I assume he'll be happy.'

This, of course, was a rhetorical question, a small jest on the great man's part. It required no answer, and Carlisle merely inclined his head and smiled.

'I'm sure their Lordships will approve the promotion and give him a sloop. The yard won't give up *Medina* for many a month, and she'll have a new captain by then.'

This was a huge compliment to Carlisle, of course. The promotion of a first lieutenant to commander was as much a recognition of his captain's success as it was of the lieutenant's readiness for command. The danger, as Carlisle realised, was that this was the limit of the admiral's largess, that Moxon would benefit at Carlisle's expense.

'Now, as for you, Carlisle. I can't offer you another ship immediately, of course, but I'll keep you in mind.'

He gave Carlisle another of his penetrating stares.

'In a way,' he continued, 'this loss of *Medina* is fortuitous. I need to send a captain to General Wolfe's staff, and he thinks highly of you. You even came out of that affair with the cats off Montmorency with your reputation intact. In fact, it's the only part of the affair that we haven't squabbled over.'

## Rocks and Shoals

Carlisle resisted the temptation to interrupt with the obvious question about his responsibilities on the staff. Saunders was too professional to send a post-captain away without a defined role.

'As I mentioned, this delay in the army getting to grips with the enemy is causing friction. You'll be my man on the general's staff. He's agreed that you'll attend all meetings, be privy to all discussions and correspondence. Carleton has fulfilled that function for me, on-and-off, but now I'm to have a permanent addition to my staff, another colonel. You see it cuts both ways and the objective is to ensure that Wolfe and I march forward – if I may use that expression – in step.'

There was another pause while Carlisle digested this unexpected turn of events. He knew very well that he'd be in a prime position to be the scapegoat if the expedition should fail in its main objective, and that he'd be unnoticed in the general euphoria in the event of success. With three admirals out of four, he'd suspect that he was being set up as a mark, but there was something about Saunders. He had an air of sincerity and appeared to scorn self-promotion. He'd been as good as his word – or his hints – in promoting Moxon. In any case, there was no question of refusing the appointment, not while he was on active service. Saunders would be within his rights to convene a court-martial, which would break him – at best – or he'd be swinging from a yardarm before the week was out.

'Well, Carlisle, what do you say?'

There was that in the admiral's eye which acknowledged the lack of attractive choices; acknowledged it and in his own way sympathised. Nevertheless, he had to provide a captain for Wolfe, and it would look odd indeed if he didn't choose to send Carlisle, if he plucked another captain out of his ship while he had a ship-less captain kicking his heels.

Carlisle took a breath.

'I'm honoured, Sir Charles, and grateful that you've entrusted me with this commission.' If the thing had to be done, it might as well be done with grace.

Saunders smiled and raised an eyebrow.

'Then you'll have your commission at the same time as you have Mister Moxon's. Now, I can't allow you a great number of followers, and certainly no lieutenants, but I'd look favourably at any request for midshipmen and servants, and the general himself suggested that you may want your marine sergeant as your personal protection. I perhaps should have pointed out that General Wolfe has no concept of staff officers who stay back in the headquarters when there's a battle to be won, but I gather you've experienced that already, at Montmorency.'

'I have Sir Charles,' he replied, thinking of Wolfe's staff wading through the mud and slime towards the redoubts on the Beauport Shore.

'Now, you should know that the general is ill, in fact the doctors fear for his life. He's been abed for most of the month since that debacle at Montmorency. He has a fever and consumption – the King's evil – I believe. If the worst should happen, Townshend will succeed him. But meanwhile, he's at loggerheads with all three of his brigadiers over where and when the army should land. There are threats of parliamentary enquires rumbling through the camp, and there are half a dozen competing contingency plans in case nothing has been achieved before the weather forces me to leave. You'll bear that in mind in your dealings with the brigadiers. I'm sending you there to be Wolfe's man as much as mine.'

\*\*\*

It had taken longer than he'd anticipated for the two commissions to be drafted, written in fair copy, signed and sealed. It wasn't a matter to be rushed, certainly not by the admiral's secretary, a man of such deliberation that he would happily make three drafts of an order to reef tops'ls in a squall. He'd found it impossible to refuse an invitation to dinner and by the time that he'd taken a boat to the shore and walked the four miles to where *Medina* lay on her side, the tide had risen just sufficiently to require the use of a boat from the shore to the ship. He was tired and dispirited when he came on board, and it was hard not to think of himself as so much flotsam; goods inadvertently lost overboard when the ship foundered.

The carpenters had been forced by the rising tide to cease their work on the lower hull, but the sound of hammer and maul, adze and saw still rang through the ship as they worked on the damage above the waterline. There was no peace.

'Mister Moxon, would you join me in my cabin?' he said as he acknowledged his first lieutenant's salute. He didn't ask about the repairs; within the hour it would be no business of his, and he must avoid any tendency to cling onto this ship that had been his home for three years.

'The bottle of Madeira, Walker.'

'The last one, sir?' asked his servant, his eyebrows so high that they merged with his sparse hair.

Walker was a man of very few words, almost none under normal circumstances, but his captain so casually demanding the last bottle of his treasured Madeira wrung the unnecessary question out of him.

'Yes, the last one, I regret.'

He turned to Moxon who had just entered after giving a few orders on the deck.

'However, it will go down in a good cause, Mister Moxon.'

He searched Moxon's face for some hint that he knew what was coming. There was enough coming and going between the frigate and the flagship – even though it required a trip overland – for the news to have leaked, but if Moxon knew his face wasn't betraying him.

Carlisle withdrew the sealed letter from his pocket and held it out. Moxon looked at the envelope, then looked up at his captain, then back at the envelope. Carlisle's smile suggested that it could only be good news, and there were only a handful of explanations for a sealed letter addressed to him in person. Then through a mist he saw the magical, unbelievable second line of the address. He didn't move, and his face slowly drained of colour.

'You should take the letter' Carlisle prompted.

*To Patrick Moxon, Esq.*

*Master and Commander*

*His Majesty's Frigate Medina*

Moxon tried to open the seal, but it resisted his trembling fingers.

'Here,' said Carlisle offering the paper-knife from his desk.

Moxon read the first few lines, but he took little in, just the glorious confirmation of his elevation.

'May I be the first to congratulate you, sir,' said Carlisle.

Walker returned at that moment with the bottle and two glasses on a tray, just in time to steady Moxon who was close to collapse and was certainly incoherent.

'But… but what about you, sir…'

Moxon realised that he might have asked a highly indelicate question. Perhaps his captain was in disgrace and was merely putting a brave face on it.

'Oh, don't worry about me. The admiral needed a post-captain to join Wolfe, and I fell right into his lap. He's delighted with our performance in the narrows, can't sing our praises highly enough and thinks *Medina* a small price to pay for passing the convoy upstream and showing the army what we're made of. But *Medina's* service in Canada is over. You're to patch her up and take her to Halifax, then to England, if she can be made seaworthy. You'll probably have a convoy across the Atlantic. Then it's a sloop for you; the admiral doesn't foresee any problems.'

'I…I don't know how to thank you, sir,' Moxon stammered.

'Don't thank me, thank your own zeal and diligence. You've been an exemplary first lieutenant, and you'll make an excellent commander. To tell you the truth, I don't exactly envy you taking this shattered hull back across the Atlantic, and I'd advise that you make best speed to Halifax, before the weather turns. But I don't have to tell you that.'

'Who will you be taking with you, sir?'

'Mister Angelini, of course, and Wishart, Walker and three of his mates. I can't really leave Whittle behind, much as I may wish to,' he added with a smile. 'Oh, and Sergeant Wilson and Souter as my personal protection. Apparently, I may need them.'

Moxon's brain was starting to function again after the shock of his promotion. It was a very modest following that Carlisle was taking with him, no warrant officers and only one master's mate and one midshipman. Sergeant Wilson would be missed, but they'd manage. He'd have to promote two of the volunteers and find a new coxswain, but that wouldn't be difficult with such a seasoned crew.

'I fear you'll lose most of your guns to the army and some men to make up the complements in other ships, but I made the point that you have a hard voyage ahead of you and can't do it on a skeleton crew.'

There was little to discuss. Moxon knew *Medina* inside-out, and this was not the time to be giving him advice. Moxon would have to form his own leadership style, make his own mistakes and prove himself fit for command of a man-o'-war.

'Well, shall we muster the men?' asked Carlisle.

That was the last order that he would give as commanding officer of *Medina*. If fate were unkind to him – and there were a hundred, no, a thousand slips along the way – it could be the last order he'd give onboard a ship. If Quebec didn't fall, their Lordships would be ill-disposed to the captains who had failed so badly. Those with commands were probably safe, for a while at least, but it would be a difficult time to be asking for a ship. For that matter, confirmation of Moxon's commission may not be as forthcoming as Saunders seemed to assume.

Moxon's answer was forestalled by a knock on the door. It was Hosking.

'Begging your pardon, sir, but we've heard the news and the other officers are asking. May they come and say their farewells?'

Carlisle hadn't thought of that. The long-established protocol insisted that after the new captain had been read in, the old captain must leave the ship immediately. He hadn't thought of farewells.

'Can you wait for a half-hour or so to be read in?' he asked Moxon. It really was his decision; any delay in the transfer of command could only be sanctioned by the new man.

'Of course, sir,' he replied hastily drawing his hand from his breast pocket where he was covertly caressing the thick paper of his commission. 'It will give the men time to clean for the muster, in any case. Shall we say an hour from now, at eight bells?'

The warrant officers filed in looking strangely shy in front of this person whom they knew so well, who was shortly to leave them. It was like a bereavement. Even the carpenter had left his work, and the marine sentry had laid aside his musket to brush the sawdust from Chip's coat before he entered the cabin. The standing officers – the bosun, the carpenter, the purser, the gunner – were used to changes of command, although this was the first in *Medina*. They stayed with a ship even when it was laid-up in ordinary. *Medina* was really their ship, and only loaned to passing captains. Yet even they recognised the gravity of this moment, and each wanted to express his best wishes for the future. Carlisle found it embarrassing, and when the bell struck eight, the end of the first dog watch, and the master-at-arms reported the people mustered in the waist, he was grateful to end what was becoming a mawkish gathering.

\*\*\*

Carlisle walked behind Moxon across the sloping deck. Nothing could so vividly illustrate the plight of the frigate as that sickening list and the lack of the healthy motion of a ship subject to the tide, the wind and the waves. She was still aground, still unable to float freely.

Moxon stepped up to the lectern and unfolded the letter that he had kept close to his heart.

> *'By Sir Charles Saunders, Vice-Admiral of the Blue*
> *and Commander-in-Chief of His Majesty's Ships*
> *and Vessels in North America, to Patrick Moxon,*
> *Esquire.'*

His voice was close to cracking with emotion and he paused to clear his throat.

> *'Whereas Captain Edward Carlisle of His Majesty's*
> *Frigate Medina is removed to the staff of Major-*
> *General James Wolfe, you are hereby required and*
> *directed to take upon you the Command of His*
> *Majesty's Frigate Medina in the rank of Master and*
> *Commander…'*

He came to the end where he again read out the name and title of the commander-in-chief, and then it was done. He was legally responsible for this frigate and all the people in her.

'Your boat is waiting, sir,' said the bosun. He, at least, had kept his wits and knew the protocol. Carlisle raised his hat to the new captain of *Medina* and then walked down into the waist.

'Man the yards,' shouted the bosun, and a stream of men – sailors that Carlisle had known for what seemed like an eternity, ran up what was left of the rigging and cheered and cheered as the boat pulled him slowly to the shore.

\*\*\*

## CHAPTER TWENTY-ONE

### The Deserter's Tale

*Monday, Tenth of September 1759.*
*Sutherland, at Anchor, Cap Rouge, Saint Lawrence River.*

At last, Wolfe was showing signs of his old strength. The fever had come close to killing him, and his doctor had let so much blood that his weakened frame was in no fit state to fight off the consumption that had dogged him for years. Yet he continued to give orders, to dispose his brigades and to cast in every direction for a way of forcing Montcalm to leave his defences and come out to fight. For Wolfe's only certainty was that while his adversary had a great number of bad soldiers, he had a small number of good ones, and a pitched battle on open ground would reveal the fatal weakness of Montcalm's army.

By the third of September, Wolfe had concluded that nothing could be achieved on the Beauport shore. Weakened though he was by his illness, he gave orders for the regiments that were still at the Montmorency camp to be moved to the south shore. The next day all the flatboats were sent up the river along with Townshend and Monckton, and Admiral Holmes transferred his flag to *Sutherland*. Now Wolfe's army was concentrated on the south shore with two-thirds of it embarked in ships or in temporary camps above Quebec.

On the eighth, Carlisle was swept up in the furious activity for what looked like a decisive landing at Pointe Aux Tremble – Aspen Point – some seven leagues above the city. It would have threatened Montcalm's overland communications with Montreal and perhaps forced him to come out and fight. Holmes' squadron had moved up, and the flatboats were manned with expectant soldiers. Then, as if the very gods mocked their endeavours, the heavens opened, and a torrential downpour caused the landings to be abandoned. It was like the battle at the Montmorency Falls all over again.

The army was in the depths of despair as the first chills of autumn warned them that the Canadian campaign season would soon be over, and Wolfe appeared no nearer deciding where he would land the decisive blow.

\*\*\*

'What's going on, Carlisle,' asked Admiral Holmes. 'It appears that you have the general's ear; God knows I don't and nor do his brigadiers. Does he know that he has perhaps three weeks left? Less if the weather breaks before then. Three weeks and then he'll be explaining to King and parliament why this huge enterprise came to naught. None of us can afford to be caught up in the acrimony – the witch-hunt – that'll be generated. There'll be a scramble of senior officers volunteering to overwinter in Halifax just to keep clear of London.'

Carlisle was learning to deal with Holmes. He knew all about the rear admiral of course. It was the same Holmes who, as a commodore, had arrived at Emden the previous year just in time to carry away his friend Holbrooke's laurels from the capture of that strategic German city.

'I believe, sir, that he has determined that his attack will be above the city…'

'My yeoman of the sheets could have told me that,' Holmes exploded, 'why else did he abandon Montmorency and move into my ship? It is evident – clear to the simplest mind – that he intends a strike above Cape Levi. But is it to be at Pointe Aux Trembles, at Cap Rouge or somewhere nearer the city? You're Saunders' eyes and ears on his staff, Carlisle, I expect you to find out.'

Holmes was hampered in fully expressing himself by the knowledge that Wolfe was only a deck below him, and in a fifty-gun fourth-rate – the largest ship that it was deemed could manoeuvre upstream from the city – any raised voices would certainly be heard by at least one of the soldiers on his staff.

'Yes, sir. However, it's my belief that the general is keeping his options open and waiting for some intelligence that will reveal a gap in Montcalm's defences. I don't believe he'll attempt a direct assault upon the city; he's frequently told me that it would be far too bloody a business and it would offer all the advantage to Montcalm.'

Holmes' efforts to keep his temper were showing on his face. There was a nervous tick in the left corner of his mouth, a sign that Carlisle had learned to look out for.

'Well, something must be done, and very soon. What is it?' he shouted at his unfortunate secretary who chose that moment to knock at the door.

'Your pardon sir. The guard boat picked up a deserter an hour ago, sir, and I thought I should tell you before…'

'What's so special about this one? We pick up half a dozen of the wretches every day. I'd hang the lot of them as an example to any of ours who may be thinking of skulking over to the French. Send him to that provost-marshal person that Wolfe has in his baggage.'

'It appears, sir, that he has some special knowledge and I thought you might want to speak to him first.'

Holmes stared hard at his secretary until the unfortunate man could no longer meet his eyes. Satisfied, he turned back to Carlisle.

'You'd better have a look at him, Carlisle. Your French is better than most of my officers, and if he tells us anything of value, you can bring it to Wolfe as a gift from me.'

\*\*\*

The Frenchman was brought before Carlisle in his cabin. It was a tiny space with nothing more than a cot, a desk, a washbasin, and Carlisle's trunk. Some unfortunate lieutenant had been evicted to make way for him, but he didn't lose any sleep over it; no lieutenants or warrant officers had managed to retain their cabins when first Holmes and then Wolfe swept aboard with all their followers. The deserter had been given into the custody of Sergeant Wilson which may have partly accounted for his evident uneasiness, that and being at such close quarters with a gold-braided Englishman.

There was no spare space in the cabin with Enrico sat at the desk, quill and inkpot in hand, and Carlisle perched on his trunk.

'*Votre nom?*' Carlisle asked in French. The man's face was no more than two feet away from him, and he could smell the sweat and the odour of clothes too long on the body. He wore a blue uniform that had lost its badges and insignia.

'Corporal Deschambles, your honour,' he replied nervously in an accent that sounded as though it came from Paris, or somewhere close by, but had been modified by long years in Canada.

'And your regiment?'

'*Troupes de la marine*. My company is from Montreal, but it was sent here to Quebec.'

That would account for the blue uniform and could offer a reason for his dissatisfaction. The *troupes de la marine* were the colonial soldiers of France and most had married and settled in their new homes. If he'd been sent far downriver from his home, and faced another winter of separation, he could well have decided to throw his lot in with his country's enemies. Carlisle could see no reason to question him on this point; if he were a spy, then he'd have a plausible story. It was far better to gain a general impression.

'Very well, and how did you come here, Corporal?'

He licked his lips and looked around the little cabin.

'Has he been searched, Sergeant Wilson?'

'He has, sir. He had nothing except the normal soldier's gear.'

That was good enough for Carlisle. A man who'd been searched by the stalwart sergeant would certainly not be concealing a weapon.

'Then be so good as to fetch him a cup of water, he looks ready to expire.'

Carlisle watched the Frenchman carefully to see whether

he understood English, but either he was an expert actor, or he had no understanding of the language at all.

'I repeat, corporal, how did you come here?' he said again in French.

The water arrived quickly, and the man took a great gulp.

'My company is stationed two miles beyond the city walls towards Saint Foy and Sillery, on the Plains of Abraham, your honour, on the cliffs above *L'Anse au Foulon*. We kept a small boat at the foot of the cliffs, and I took it in the night and rowed out to your guard boat.'

Carlisle looked at him impassively. So far, the man had said nothing worth wasting the time of a post-captain. Deschambles recognised the signs. He didn't want to be summarily dismissed, and he set his face as though coming to a decision.

'There's a path up the cliff. I can show you.'

Carlisle held his non-committal expression. He nodded at Wishart, who was waiting outside the door, as there wasn't enough room in the cabin. Wishart took the gesture at its right meaning and hurried off to consult James Cook, who had charge of the charts. If there were such a bay, a path into the heart of Montcalm's defences, then surely it would be known, and Wolfe would already have considered it. There must be some flaw in this intelligence.

'How many men guard this *Anse au Foulon*?' Carlisle asked, to keep the conversation going until Wishart returned.

'A company, your honour, my company, but it is short of men; there are only forty-five there.'

'Are there any guns? Any artillery?'

'Oh no, sir, no artillery. My company is only infantry.'

Carlisle was watching the man's face as he answered. He could swear that he was telling the truth, as much as he knew of it. Nobody could fake that terror mingled with shame.

'And you say there is a path up the cliff from the bay?'

'Yes, sir. It's a small path, and we have blocked it with abatis, just tree branches, some of them staked down but some loose. The path is hard to see from the river, but it's there, and I have been up and down many times.'

He looked furtive.

'Nobody expects a landing in the bay, monsieur, it is impossible for an army, but a few men may climb up the path, a raiding party, no more.'

This wretched man was selling his comrades for the deserter's bounty. He wasn't offering information that could be used to land the army, just enough for a party of men to destroy his company. He must have some strong motivation, but Carlisle still didn't ask. He knew that all he'd get would be lies contrived to paint the corporal as the victim.

'Describe this path. How long is it, how wide, how steep? Are there steps? Apart from the abatis, are there any other obstacles?'

The Frenchman was singing now, spilling everything he knew. He'd burned his boats ten minutes ago, and there was no going back. He knew the penalty that a deserter would suffer for misleading his captors, even if he was a genuine deserter and not a spy placed by the French command. He knew, and he clearly didn't relish the prospect of being hanged for his troubles.

Carlisle heard of a path that, if it were true, was suitable only for a handful of men to climb in the dark – it could only be at night – and they would have to be fit, determined men. A raid then, and possibly a profitable one with the prospect of taking an officer who would certainly know more than this corporal. And yet... and yet. The general was desperate for a way to land his army. If a few men could scale the cliff and claim a foothold on the Plains of Abraham, then maybe – just maybe – an army could follow. If Montcalm were faced unexpectedly with Wolfe's army in fighting formation a mile-and-a-half from the city walls, he'd have to march out of his lines at Beauport and either reinforce the walls or give battle on the Plain. It was an idea, nothing more. A desperate grasping at a straw fit only for desperate times.

'Sir,' said Wishart squeezing into the cabin. 'Here's Mister Cook's best chart with some elevations of the cliffs. He thinks the bay is just here.'

Wishart jabbed his finger at the shore just opposite and half a mile downstream from where the Etchemin River flowed into the Saint Lawrence. There was nothing to suggest a bay and the elevations showed no break in the cliffs.

'Is this the place?' Carlisle asked the corporal.

The man looked as though he was about to burst into tears. He gave a Gallic shrug that ended in a dejected stoop of the shoulders.

'I cannot read a map, your honour, I'm only a corporal. Maps are for officers.'

Carlisle tried not to show his frustration.

'You must know the distance from the Citadel to Sillery. Is this bay halfway, or is it nearer to one place?'

The corporal thought for a moment. He could make judgements of distance; he was an infantryman and deeply interested in how far he would need to march from one post to another.

'Halfway, your honour, exactly halfway.'

'And what lies between your company position and the walls of the city?'

The corporal shrugged again, but this was a different gesture, not one of ignorance but one indicating that the question, to his mind, was irrelevant.

'Just farmland, your honour. Fields, one or two barns and a few houses, but nothing at all close to the city. The ground has been cleared for artillery.'

He meant that the field of fire for the guns at the citadel and the city had been kept clear. Probably there were no buildings within a mile of the walls.

Carlisle studied the deserter again. If his story was true, then it was quite likely that General Wolfe would be interested. However, he knew that the relationship between the general and his brigadiers had degenerated to a new low since the failed landings of two days before. If he had any plans, Wolfe was keeping them to himself; not even his staff knew what was in his mind. Yes, he must tell the general of this opportunity, slender though it was, and he must do that when the general was alone, to give him the chance to evaluate it without pressure from his subordinates.

'Sergeant Wilson.'

'Sir!'

'Keep this man in custody in this cabin. He is not to leave your sight for any reason. Mister Wishart will find him some food and a glass of wine – one glass, mark you – and will keep any other officers from seeing him. Keep him safe until I return. Mister Angelini, you have a transcript of this interrogation?'

'Yes, sir,' Enrico replied, showing Carlisle the sheets of paper on which he'd written the questions and answers. Carlisle was surprised at first to see that it was all in French, but then realised the wisdom of recording the words in the language in which they were spoken. Enrico was fluent in French, much better than Carlisle. Wolfe also spoke and read French with the proficiency you'd expect of a man of his background and education.

'Then follow me.'

Wolfe was using Captain Rous' great cabin as his headquarters. Carlisle entered to see that it was almost empty except for Wolfe, his ADC, and his servants.

'Ah, Captain Carlisle, you wish to speak to me,' said Wolfe. He evidently liked Carlisle and managed a smile, the first that had been seen for days. 'And you have Mister Angelini with you, how pleasant.'

Wolfe was one of the politest soldiers that Carlisle had ever met, and he wasn't above noticing a mere midshipman. Then, of course, Enrico's family connections – the noblest of the Sardinian nobility – would commend him to any officer who hadn't entirely abandoned any idea of returning to society after this campaign.

'I have something to tell you, sir, that is best said in the strictest privacy. Mister Angelini is necessary, but it would be helpful if we were otherwise alone.'

He glanced meaningfully at the ADC and the servants.

Wolfe gave Carlisle a sharp look. He noticed the report that Enrico held and saw that it was written in French. Intrigued, he nodded at his ADC who, with a questioning look at Carlisle and Enrico, left the room, snapping his fingers at the servants to follow him.

'Now, Captain. What's all this…'

\*\*\*

'You believe this deserter, Carlisle?'

Wolfe had listened in silence to Carlisle's explanation, and now he was running a finger over Enrico's report.

'I do, sir. He must know that his head is in a noose if he betrays us. Normally deserters can only tell us about their regiment's position, how strong it is and so on, and that's not dangerous information. For whatever reason – and we'll never know for sure – this man has given us true gold. He's no hero, sir. He's just a venal man who's backing the side that he believes will be the winner. He's no spy.'

'I could never bring him here without my staff and my brigadiers knowing; you know the situation that I'm in, I believe, Carlisle. I'll have to rely on your judgement. Now, as for this *Anse au Foulon*, I agree with you. If we can get a company up that cliff path quickly, then it can be held while the army comes up. Montcalm will have to come out and fight then!'

Wolfe strode restlessly around the cabin, his mind buzzing with all the preparations that he'd have to make.

'We can approach from our anchorage here?'

'Yes, sir. The flatboats have all come up, and we can take seventeen-hundred men in the first wave.'

'Good. But can we approach without being seen?'

Carlisle had been rehearsing what he knew of the tides and moon ever since he'd decided to bring this news to the general.

# Rocks and Shoals

'We need an ebbing tide at night, sir, and a moon that allows the flatboats to see the cliffs but keeps them hidden from the sentries.'

Wolfe looked surprised.

'Not a dark night, then?'

'No, sir, there's too much chance of the boats going astray. They'll have to cover five miles at night and in silence. That's a lot to ask of all the boats if they can't see the shore. Two nights from now the moon will rise at around nine o'clock in the evening. At two o'clock in the morning, it will be a little south of east and forty degrees or so above the horizon. By four o'clock it will have moved to the southeast and risen to sixty degrees. From the city they'll see nothing of the boats; the moon won't illuminate the southern side of the river, but the boats will see the northern shore clearly.'

'Two nights? Won't tonight or tomorrow serve, Carlisle?'

'No, sir,' said Carlisle firmly. 'The moon will rise earlier and will be more in the south, and the tide will start to flood too soon. I'll get the exact times from Mister Cook, but the figures I've given you are close enough for now. Any day before the night of the twelfth risks a longer passage for the boats and a greater chance of being seen. After the twelfth, the conditions will get less favourable every day.'

'Then I'll see those calculations when you have them, but for now, we can work on the boats setting off at two o'clock on the morning of the thirteenth, and if God is with us, my army will be marching on Quebec at dawn!'

\*\*\*

# CHAPTER TWENTY-TWO

## Anse au Foulon

*Wednesday, Twelfth of September 1759.*
*Sutherland, at Anchor. Cap Rouge, The Saint Lawrence River.*

Wolfe carefully observed his brigadiers' reactions. He was evidently enjoying their surprise and consternation.
'Then you all know what you must do, gentlemen?' he asked.

'May I ask sir, from where this information came? This *Anse au Foulon* is unknown to me, and I've spent more hours than I care to remember studying the shore.' Monckton was unhappy that this plan had been dumped on him fully formed.

'No sir, you may not. And furthermore, there is to be no gawping through telescopes before sunset. That is why I have kept this from you until now. Secrecy is of the utmost importance. In just twelve hours the flatboats will start downstream, and I have no intention of letting Monsieur Montcalm guess our plans before he hears of the army's arrival on his doorstep. Admiral Saunders will keep Montcalm occupied on the Beauport Shore; he has enough marines to make a credible display, and his sloops can get close enough to bombard the lines. Admiral Holmes – he nodded in a friendly manner at Holmes – will similarly feint towards Point Aux Tremble. Bougainville has worn out his shoe leather following the squadron up and down the river, and I'm confident he will do so again tonight. Anywhere between Cap Rouge and Pointe Aux Tremble will keep him clear until the army's ashore.'

'Are you then so certain that this path exists, that it can be climbed, that it is defended by no more than a company of *troupes de la marine*?'

'I am. And for your information, Captain Carlisle has seen it with his own eyes on a reconnaissance.'

Three sets of eyes swivelled and came to rest on Carlisle.

## Rocks and Shoals

He knew this would happen, and he was ready for it. He nodded gravely at the brigadiers.

'You see, gentlemen, if I had sent you to look at the bay and path, Montcalm would immediately know what was in my mind. A sea-officer passing by in a longboat is such a familiar sight to them that they suspected nothing. It's a Godsend! With Montcalm fixed to the east, Bougainville drawn away to the west and the centre left open, we have our chance. Everything has been prepared. This is the moment, perhaps the last possible moment this season. Let us seize it.'

'I protest, sir,' said Monckton. 'This risks a battle before the whole army is in place. If Montcalm guesses the plan, or if this is a trap, then he can march his army from Beauport long before four thousand men can scale the cliffs. We should land further west where we can establish the army unhindered. We can brush Bougainville aside and cut off communication between Quebec and Montreal. If we hold both sides of the river, there'll be no more supplies from those ships upstream. We can march on Quebec at our leisure.'

'At our leisure?' Wolfe exploded. 'At our leisure? Good God, man, it's nearly mid-September, and you talk of leisure? Saunders will have to take his ships-of-the-line away before the weather breaks. When will that be Carlisle, tell them!' He spat.

Carlisle held Monckton's hard stare.

'No more than two weeks, sir,' he said. 'It's not just the icing of the river; it's the chance of storms in the Atlantic. We're a long way from home here, and Admiral Saunders has been entrusted with a large proportion of the King's navy. There's an invasion fleet mustering in France, and an army to match. This is no time to hazard the battle squadrons.'

Did they know that this was a prepared speech? Carlisle was parroting the words of Saunders himself, the line that he was to take if questioned on this matter by these very people.

'If the army stays here after the end of the month it will have only frigates and sloops in the river, and a few months after that they'll be in ice, and then they'll be a liability to the army rather than an asset.'

Monckton looked as though he would say something more, something uncomplimentary about the navy, but he closed his mouth with a snap.

This was the consequence of a summer of dither and procrastination, thought Carlisle. He knew that his understanding of military affairs was no match for these brigadiers, but he did understand morale and momentum and enterprise. And he'd seen all these principles squandered since the fleet had first anchored in the South Channel. In this, he agreed with Wolfe; it was now or never, and he prayed that they weren't putting too much faith in the word of a disaffected French corporal.

\*\*\*

Supper was an intimate affair in *Sutherland's* great cabin. Wolfe had invited Admiral Holmes, Carlisle and Rous, as well as his senior staff. The brigadiers were all with their fighting formations making the final preparations. Wolfe wasn't at all concerned that his army had scant notice of this operation. He knew the mettle of his men. He knew the frustrations that had built up over the summer, and he knew that they'd rise to the occasion. His problem was not in motivating his soldiers, but in holding them back from mad impetuosity. An hour to prepare or a week, it made no difference.

'Now,' said Wolfe, carefully folding his napkin, 'if you'll indulge me a moment, Admiral, gentlemen, I have a few lines of verse that I would like to share with you. My fiancé gave me this when I was in London.' He produced a slim, leather-bound volume. It was much handled and looked as though it had a permanent home in his coat pocket. It was clearly a treasured possession. Carlisle had no idea what was coming next.

'There's a certain sadness to it, pathos even, and I hesitated before offering this on the eve of battle. However, it's the tragedy of a lost French empire in America, to which I dedicate these lines, as I hope tomorrow will prove.'

Wolfe stared thoughtfully at the page for a breathless moment, with his finger poised on the top line. Then he started reading in a quiet voice.

*The curfew tolls the knell of parting day,*

*The lowing herd wind slowly o'er the lea,*

*The ploughman homeward plods his weary way,*

*And leaves the world to darkness and to me.*

It came like a punch in the stomach to Carlisle. Those lines, that poem, would forever remind him of that silent pull up Archer's Hope Creek towards his home in Williamsburg, just a year ago. That very verse had been going through his mind at exactly the time – unbeknown to him – that his son was taking his first breaths in this new world. Only an hour later, with all the leagues of the barren sea from Louisbourg to Hampton Roads behind him and with uncanny timing, he'd seen his newborn son for the first time.

*Now fades the glimm'ring landscape on the sight,*

*And all the air a solemn stillness holds,*

*Save where the beetle wheels his droning flight,*

*And drowsy tinklings lull the distant folds;*

It was the most emotional moment that Carlisle could remember since he said goodbye to his small family and came away to war. His heart went out to Wolfe. Already he seemed a tragic figure, the witting subject of Thomas Gray's death-knell, however much he may dedicate it to his adversary.

\*\*\*

The bell on *Sutherland's* deck struck twice, then twice again; two o'clock on a chill September night. Carlisle looked up to the masthead where a pair of white lanterns signalled the flatboats to start their journey downriver. Was that an omen? Was this day to end with two… what? Two deaths? Wolfe and Carlisle? He shook off the grim thought.

'Give her a good shove,' Souter said in a low voice to the bow oarsman.

The flatboat left *Sutherland's* side. At first, it appeared to be hardly moving, but then the strong ebb and the westerly wind caught it. The two-decker suddenly merged into the night and became a remote, distant object. Only the two lanterns showed its position.

'Lay on your oars until they've all caught up,' said Carlisle.

There were thirty-four flatboats in this first wave. Most were the larger sort that took fifty soldiers – half a company – but some were designed to take only thirty. Large or small, they were all crowded with as many soldiers as they could take. The first eight boats held the light infantry and the boat immediately behind Carlisle's carried Colonel William Howe who would lead them. They would be the first up the cliffs, and their job was to overwhelm the guards and chase away the under-strength company of *troupes de la marine*. The remainder would land nearly half the army and four field guns. Carlisle could imagine the confusion, the noise, if he lost control of the landing, or if the boats became separated and landed piecemeal.

Did William Howe know that it was his brother, Commodore Richard Howe, who had first used these flatboats in the raids on northern France the previous year? On a night for omens, that was a good one.

The quarter moon was bright on their starboard bow. It

gave the impression that they were exposed, easily visible from the shore. And yet that wasn't so. As Carlisle had calculated, the moon shone over the high land on the southern shore, not down the length of the river, and the boats were as good as invisible to the French sentries.

Montcalm's army was being held on the Beauport shore by a demonstration of boats from Saunders' ships. Earlier they had laid buoys with lanterns to persuade Montcalm that an attempt would be made at the very place that Wolfe had always planned to land, until the French defences and the tidal flats proved it impossible. Now they were energetically manoeuvering in the dark while the sloops and armed cats bombarded the lines. Bougainville was away to the west, perhaps as far as James Quartier's River, thirty miles distant. With any luck Montcalm's whole attention would be focused on the Beauport shore, allowing Wolfe to slip between Bougainville and the city which, if the intelligence proved correct, was guarded by only a few companies of militia.

'Move over to the northern shore, Souter,' Carlisle whispered.

He looked astern. He could sense rather than clearly see the great mass of boats following him down the river. The first eight boats were in a tight gaggle and immediately behind them was Wolfe, then Monckton and then Townshend. Murray would follow in the second wave.

'Are you ready, Mister Angelini?'

Enrico was squeezed between Carlisle and the gunwale; he had an important duty to perform, one that could hold the key to the success of the operation. He cleared his throat, whether through nervousness or a sensible preparation for his vital role, Carlisle couldn't tell.

The cliffs on their left side grew higher and sped past as the flotilla rushed down the river. Five knots, perhaps six, and the oarsmen were hardly pulling at all. They'd be early at this rate.

*'Qui va là?'*

Someone shouted a challenge from a post below the cliffs, on the shore. That would be Sillery, and above the sentry was a strong battery of guns. Carlisle laid his hand on Enrico's shoulder to restrain him.

'Let him shout again,' he whispered.

*'Qui va là?'*

More insistent this time and the shout was echoed by a second voice.

'Now,' whispered Carlisle.

Enrico stood up in the boat.

'Fournitures pour le Québec,' he shouted back. Supplies for the city.

There was a confused shouting from the post. It could have been a demand for a password.

*'La France,'* Enrico shouted. *'Vive le Roi!'*

For a few breathless seconds, there was no response, and all the time the flatboat was drawing away from the sentry post. Wolfe's boat would be almost abeam now, and the general himself would soon be adding to the sentry's confusion.

Then there was another shout from the shore, well abaft the beam now.

*'Vive le Roi. Bonne chance!'*

They'd passed! Wolfe knew that the French were running boat convoys from the ships that were anchored safely up the river. It was a consequence of Montcalm's determination to keep the valuable food out of reach of the population of the city. Whether a supply convoy was expected that night hardly mattered, they only needed a few minutes of uncertainty for the initial wave of boats to get past these first watchers. The password hardly mattered either. The chances were slim that a French boatman coming from forty miles upstream would both know and use the correct password. The sentries would be aware of that and so would their officers, and the time-honoured French battle cry would do as well as any other.

*'Vive le Roi…Vive le Roi!'*

Wolfe's boats joined in the call as they sped past the sentry.

***

Now the moon proved itself a real blessing. It hid the flatboats but illuminated the rising cliffs on the north shore. Carlisle had carefully noted all the features that he'd pass before reaching the little bay. A conical rock, a pine tree, a runnel of water tumbling down the cliff, he mentally tallied them all as they passed.

'There, Souter, you see the moonlight on the gravel beach?' he said, pointing to a spot on their bow.

The coxswain nodded wordlessly and edged the tiller to starboard. Carlisle looked astern to see that the next flatboat no further than twenty yards behind was easing into their wake.

'The current's strong here,' said Souter as he pushed the tiller further to starboard, 'we're being swept past, sir.'

Carlisle swore. There was another cove just a hundred yards downstream, but it had no path up the cliff or none that Carlisle was aware of. However, at this state of the tide there was a strip of shingle joining the two coves. Carlisle stood up and waved to make sure that the boats knew they must land upstream from him. He'd underestimated the combined force of the river and the ebbing tide, and he was ashamed of himself. Would anyone notice? Probably not, he thought. It would just look as though he'd chosen the downstream end to allow the other boats enough space below the cliff path. Nevertheless, it was a nuisance, and his light infantrymen would have to run back to Anse au Foulon before they could start their climb.

'Here will do, Souter, put her ashore.'

There was no alarm from the beach, no ripple of gunfire from the cliffs nearly two hundred feet above. It was easy to see why this place would be lightly defended; it didn't look at all suitable for an army to disembark. Yet Carlisle had seen the path through his telescope, or at least he'd seen the line that he imagined the path took. It started beside a small stream that trickled down from the heights and angled upwards and to the right across the face of the cliff.

The sound of the flatboat running up the gravel was obscenely loud, audible surely from the top of the cliffs. Even if it were guarded only by an under-strength company, someone would be awake and listening. Yet there was no alarm, no shot.

The light infantry tumbled ashore; all along the cove the boats crunched onto the beach. The path was better than Carlisle had expected, at least at this lower end it was wide enough for the cannon that he'd brought from the ships to be manhandled up.

'Good luck,' said Carlisle as Howe led his light infantrymen up the cliffs.

It was starting to get congested on the beach now, but Wishart at least was keeping his head and clearing the western side for the boats carrying the guns. Naval six-pounders, plundered from the sloops and mounted on campaign carriages, were lashed onto platforms where the soldiers' benches would normally be fitted, and stout ramps were provided to get them ashore. A flatboat could only carry two guns, and only two of the boats were thus fitted. Four guns. It didn't sound like much, but in the essentially infantry encounter that Wolfe envisioned, it may be enough. If they had to lay siege to the city, the heavy guns could follow once the Plains of Abraham were in British hands.

The sounds of the light infantry scrambling up the cliff path could be clearly heard but the men were silent. They must have reached the part where the abatis blocked their way, but that was no real obstacle to infantry unless it was covered by fire, and so far, not a shot had been heard.

'Get those guns ready to go, Mister Wishart. Where's the hauling team?' he whispered.

It was difficult to count in the dark, but it looked as though a thousand men were already packed onto the beach. The dim shapes of boats lurked on the edge of visibility, pulling hard to avoid being swept downstream as they nosed into the gaps. He could hear some confused shouting from the cliffs, but still no shots. Carlisle looked at his watch by the moonlight; he had to press his face close to the glass to see the hands. Four-fifteen. They were a little ahead of schedule, but that didn't matter.

There was a tap on his shoulder. Wolfe, looking fresh and eager, with no sign of the fever or consumption that only a few days before had him abed.

'I'm going up now, Carlisle,' he said.

At that moment there was a spattering of musketry from high above them. Wolfe cocked his head and waited. A few more shots, then silence. There was a rushing crash as something fell from the heights. It was a tangled mass of tree branches lashed together; part of the obstructions that should have stopped the path being used by invaders.

'That's Howe clearing 'em away,' he said. 'I'm off. God go with you Carlisle and get those guns up before daylight.'

There was a steady stream of men climbing the path now, and they were moving faster now that the obstructions had been moved bodily aside. There was no need for secrecy; it was a race to get Wolfe's army up to the heights before Montcalm realised that he's been duped and brought his own men across the Saint Charles River.

A flash from upriver split the night, followed almost instantly by the boom of cannon fire. That would be the battery at Sillery over to the west. Then Carlisle saw an answering flash and boom, also to the west but closer, that would be the Samos battery joining in. The French must be thoroughly awake now. How long would it be before Montcalm realised that the blow was being struck at his centre rather than either flank?

It looked like chaos, but the boats were arriving in regular order, and each of the brigadiers led their men up into the darkness. At last, the beach started to clear. The last of the first wave of infantry was clambering from boat to boat and reaching the shore more slowly than those before them were disappearing up the path.

Here was Lieutenant Fulling. Like Carlisle, he'd been selected for this task largely because of his steady performance at Montmorency. Fulling had charge of the four six-pounders that were to be brought up the cliff immediately behind the infantry and before the boxes and boxes of entrenching tools that would be needed for a siege. It was Fulling's job to get the guns up the cliff path quickly enough to be used in the battle that Wolfe hoped would start long before the heavy guns could be brought up.

'My men are ashore now, sir,' he said, removing his hat to Carlisle, 'and two of the guns are ready to be moved, the other two are following.'

Carlisle looked again at the boats. They were empty, and a last company of highlanders was filing towards the path.

'As soon as those soldiers are clear, you can start dragging them up. Take the two to start with; you can take the other two up if the second wave of infantry isn't here soon.'

Infantry first and guns second, that was Wolfe's order. He knew that it was the musket and bayonet that would win the day, useful though artillery was.

Here was the fruit of careful planning and detailed orders. Two hundred seamen had left the boats and were gathered at the western end of the cove. Forty men could manhandle a six-pounder up that path, but it would take another thirty to carry up enough cartridges and ammunition for each gun. Already the ropes had been attached to the axles. The seamen were testing the weight, pulling in the slack and shifting the guns a few feet at a time.

'I'll leave you to it then,' said Carlisle. 'Mister Wishart, you stay on the beach to bring in the second wave.'

Dimly he could see the bulks of the ships that were dropping down with the tide to reduce the distance that the boats had to row. The second wave was probably only minutes away.

It was a long climb up the cliff path, and he and Enrico helped drag each other over the more difficult parts. He could see where the brushwood and, in some places, whole trees had been pulled aside to clear the way. Yes, the guns could be brought up there, and already he could hear the cheers and oaths as the heavy brutes started their journey. He quickened his pace to be certain of reaching the top before he was overtaken.

Halfway up the cliff and the transition from darkness to light was swift as the upper rim of the sun peeped over Cape Levi. Up on the heights, it was already daylight with the slanting rays revealing a glorious yet ominous spectacle.

\*\*\*

# CHAPTER TWENTY-THREE
## A Shattering Volley

*Thursday, Thirteenth of September 1759.*
*The Plains of Abraham.*

The high Plains of Abraham hadn't yet been seen by the attacking force. The information from deserters and the recollections of those few among the British who'd been there before were all that Wolfe had to work with and all that Carlisle knew. As he reached the top of the path, he saw the plain before him. It was a narrow finger of flat land, a mile or so wide between the Saint Lawrence and the bluffs above the Saint Charles and perhaps three miles long between the villages of Sillery and Saint Foy and the walls of the city. To the north he could see woodland stretching to the bluffs, to the southwest he could see the houses and barns of the villages. To the northeast the spires and towers of Quebec stood tall, catching the low morning sunshine. Across the plain in front of him, the companies and battalions of Wolfe's army were forming a line facing the city.

'Ah Carlisle,' Wolfe greeted him with a huge grin, 'the guns are moving, I trust.'

'They are sir. The first was close on my heels. I expect two of them to be up on the plain with their powder and shot within the hour.'

'Good. Hold them close to the path for the time being. You see that it all looks peaceful, but at any moment I expect Montcalm to cross the Saint Charles. I wouldn't be surprised to see Bougainville come upon us from the west, although I see no sign of him yet. I've sent the light infantry over towards Saint Foy to warn me. I'll be able to see Montcalm with my own two eyes. Stay close Carlisle, then I'll be able to tell you where to place the guns.'

Wolfe scanned the ground carefully. From the river over

## Rocks and Shoals

his left shoulder, right across the plain to the walls of Quebec, nothing stirred except a few farmers hurrying to clear the field of battle. Over to the north, a horseman galloped westwards. A messenger for Bougainville, no doubt, whose brigade had been holding the northern shore to the west of the city, and who was in danger of missing the battle.

'Why no counter-attack?' Wolfe wondered aloud. He was showing at least some caution by not rushing wildly onto the plain. With his back to the river, he still had a chance of withdrawing the way he'd come.

He stood for a long time, surveying the eerily quiet scene. His army stood in their ranks waiting with the patience of old campaigners while the men of the second wave came up the cliff path in an unbroken stream. Now there was some movement. He could see what looked like militia units and Indians moving in column to the north, taking up positions from where they could fire from cover at the British. In a few minutes, the puffs of smoke and the humming of musket balls showed where they had already started firing.

Wolfe snapped shut his telescope.

'Townshend. Take the two battalions of Royal Americans and push those skirmishers back. You'll guard the left flank when we're in line.'

The brigadier hurried off to gather his men.

'Murray, you'll take the left wing and Monckton the right. The line is to stretch right across the plain. What do you think? About a thousand yards? We won't have enough men for three ranks, so we'll form a line two-deep. I'll want flank guards on the right in case they try to get between us and the river. The centre of the line will be on that road, the Grande Allée.'

Wolfe pointed to all the prominent features of the ground. His line would be just over a mile from the walls of the city. If this didn't force Montcalm to leave the Beauport shore, then nothing would.

'Then what are you waiting for?' he said in irritation. 'Deploy your battalions, gentlemen. Ah, look over there,' he said, pointing.

A group of horsemen were hurrying up the bluffs from the Saint Charles River. The uniforms and the mounts could only belong to Montcalm and his staff.

\*\*\*

A rattling and bumping sound heralded the arrival of the first of the guns. The two six-pounders had been hauled by brute force up the path by the bands of sailors. Two more were following. They'd be late for the battle if they arrived at all before it was over, but Wolfe didn't look concerned; his beloved infantry was all on the plain now.

Carlisle had gathered a hundred twenty-four pounders from the fleet, and he had readied the army's mortars, but they hadn't moved from the ships yet. They'd be brought ashore in case Montcalm should decline battle and reinforce the town instead. Wolfe would need all those guns for a siege, but they were too heavy for the rough-and-ready way that the six-pounders had been brought up. Tackles and miles and miles of rope would have to be rigged; they'd be brought up in stages, and it would take several days. For today's battle, the six-pounders would have to be enough, and even two of them were better than nothing.

Wolfe studied Montcalm again. The Frenchman was giving orders now, pointing towards where the British were forming their line and sweeping his arms from right to left.

'I do believe he is coming out to fight us at last! Then the day will be ours; you can count on it, Carlisle. His only hope was to avoid coming out from his defences, to decline battle, and now he's throwing that hope away. What do you think, Mister Angelini? A squadron of Sardinian cavalry would sweep away that left flank, eh?'

Wolfe didn't wait for an answer; his delight was plain to see. If the French had refused to fight in the open, then the defences of the city could hold out for perhaps weeks. A regular siege with de Bougainville in the rear could be a protracted and chancy affair, and all the time General Winter was waiting in the wings.

'Send one of your guns to the centre and the other to the right,' said Wolfe. 'Tell James Murray that he should place his gun on the road. Monckton will tell you where he wants his. Then you come back here if you please. I want you beside me.'

Carlisle had planned to keep his guns together as a single battery. It was axiomatic in his kind of warfare – sea battles – that guns should be used *en masse*. It was the shock effect of heavy broadsides that won the day, not the bee stings of individual shots. However, he conceded that he knew little of land warfare and had never seen an engagement between armies, and there was an edge to Wolfe's manner that wouldn't brook any argument. Besides, he liked Wolfe and knew that he had enough dissent from his brigadiers without Carlisle adding his own opinions on the use of artillery in a situation that was utterly new to him.

'Mister Fulling! Run your gun over to Brigadier Monckton, you can see him on the right of the line. General Wolfe's compliments and the gun is at his disposal. Where is Mister Wishart?'

'Here, sir,' came a breathless voice behind him. Wishart's gun was the second to reach the plain; he'd raced to reach Carlisle before the battle started.

'I ordered all the cartridges and ammunition to come up next, sir. I'm afraid the other two guns will be some time. When I last saw them, they hadn't come off the boats yet.'

Carlisle nodded; it was as he expected. There was no use having four guns on the heights and no ammunition; better to have two well-supplied guns.

'You're for the centre, Mister Wishart. Come with me you fellows,' he shouted at the gun's crew.

Carlisle ran alongside the gun as it jogged over the plain. Wolfe had a core of Royal Artillery gunners available, but they were with the heavy guns and the mortars. Today the crews were made up of sailors taken from the ships with a quarter gunner to each weapon. They were in high spirits at the thought of this novel way of engaging the enemy, and they hauled the gun at a furious pace across the flat ground. Carlisle found Brigadier Murray standing in the centre of the Grande Allée, studying his enemy.

'Your gun, sir,' said Carlisle. 'General Wolfe wishes you to position it on the road.'

Murray was flanked by Fraser's Highlanders on his left and the Forty-Seventh Foot on his right. Like Wolfe, he was watching Montcalm through a telescope that rested on the back of an obliging aide. He was nearer to the French than Wolfe and he could see the first two columns of infantry starting to hurry out of the gates of Saint-Louis and Saint-Jean. Such was their haste that they were in no regular formation as they raced to take up their positions to face the British.

'Just one?' said Murray. 'Well, I expect it will be enough. You have ball and grape?'

'Yes, sir, and canister. Mister Wishart will take your orders; I'll be with the general.'

Murray made no reply but continued to study Montcalm's movements through the telescope.

A band of sailors brought cartridges in canvas buckets, then more canvas containers filled with ball and grape. They were Carlisle's innovation. He'd foreseen how difficult it would be to carry heavy, awkward objects up the cliff path and had given a design to the sailmakers for bags of a size that could be managed by one man or two, with straps that could be looped over the shoulders. The rammer, sponge, worm, and handspike followed. The hoary old quarter gunner applied flint to steel, and a minute later, the linstock was glowing and a thin trail of smoke drifted away on the lazy breeze.

It was well done. In less than fifteen minutes after the first muzzle had appeared over the rim, Wolfe's guns were ready for action. Carlisle doubted whether horse artillery could have done better. Admittedly there were only two, but well-handled artillery could influence a battle out of proportion to the weight of shot. The six-pounders looked small to the naval eye, but he knew that they were the standard size for field guns in both armies. Twelve pounders were starting to be used in the European theatre, but here in the colonies the six-pounder was still the queen of the battlefield.

The battalions were taking their positions. Each company marched into its place as the sergeants placed the flank markers to ensure that they took up their allotted space, no more and no less. It was easy to forget the precision with which companies and battalions had to take their places in the line. If they took up too much space their flanking units would be squeezed; too little, then gaps would emerge, gaps that an enemy could exploit.

The contrast between the rigid discipline of the British line and that of the French was stark. Montcalm's army was a mixture of regular infantry in the centre and militia on the flanks. Their drills were different, and their arms were different, and not all the months spent in static positions behind the Beauport lines had made them into a coherent fighting force. And they were tired. They'd been under arms for most of the previous night, with constant alarms as Saunders' sloops and boats manoeuvred in the North Channel, threatening a landing at the very point where Montcalm had always expected it.

\*\*\*

'They pause, you see, Carlisle. Monsieur Montcalm is waiting to see whether Bougainville can arrive in time.'

Wolfe looked over his shoulder. Away to the west, his light infantry was holding the road to Cap Rouge.

'What Montcalm doesn't know, and I have just heard, is that Bougainville is far away, nearly at Cap Rouge. If he comes, then the light infantry will give me warning and hold him for a while. I can wait, but for Montcalm time is running out. Now he cannot even withdraw to the city walls because he knows that I'll advance if he does and engage him before he can reach safety. No general relishes a fighting retreat. Sooner or later he'll realise that Bougainville is too far away to help him and then he has no alternative but to attack.'

'They're advancing, sir,' said a major.

'Yes, they're moving their line to that ridge,' Wolfe replied. 'Let's see what they do when they reach it.'

Crack! Wishart's gun started firing ball on the left; the range was too great for grape or canister. Then Fulling's gun on the right joined in. It was long range even for ball, but Frenchmen were falling as they formed their lines on the ridge. British soldiers were falling too, from the Canadians and Indians firing from the high corn on the left of the British line. Now the French artillery joined in. They had hardly any more guns than Wolfe, but here and there their cannonballs found targets along the British line.

'Have your men lie down, colonel,' Wolfe said. 'The other battalions will soon follow when they see what you're doing. No need to offer targets for those Canadians; they're good enough marksmen without our help.'

Cannonballs were skipping across the battlefield now. Wolfe's army was suffering steady attrition, and only his two six-pounders were replying.

'Here come the other guns, sir,' said Carlisle.

A gang of sailors appeared at the top of the path in the army's rear, dragging the two guns. At the same time, a company of red-coated soldiers streamed up onto the plain from a boat that had missed the landing place and had spent a hard hour rowing back against the ebb.

'Ah. He's seen that,' said Wolfe. 'It must look like a third wave of landings. That will make him think. Now Monsieur, advance or retreat, what's it to be?'

A drum rolled from the French side, followed by others until all along the French line the drums were beating their thrilling tattoo.

'Here they come,' said the major.

'Get the men on their feet.'

## Rocks and Shoals

The sky was cloudy now, and it threatened to rain. Yet the colours of the British line stood out against the browns, greens and golds of the farmland. Four thousand regular British soldiers were now facing an equal number of French who were advancing at a walking pace.

'Here it comes,' said Wolfe who was standing tall, an easy target for a marksman, 'too soon, Monsieur, too soon.'

Crash! It was an irregular volley and fired at too great a range. Here and there a British soldier fell. The major who stood beside Wolfe dropped noiselessly to the ground.

The French Regulars stood to reload while the militia and the Canadians on the flanks dropped to the ground to perform the difficult task from a prone position, as though they were fighting a woodland skirmish. The regulars reloaded fastest and immediately started forward again while the others were still struggling with their ramrods. The French line was fast disintegrating as the better-drilled line regiments advanced faster than their fellows.

Crash! This volley was even more ragged than the first, and although fired at closer range this time, there were fewer casualties in the British line.

'Steady, boys, hold your fire, hold the line.' Officers and sergeants were restraining the men, tapping muskets barrels up and down with their pikes and halberds. There were always a few for whom aiming was the last thing on their minds, and the easiest item to forget entirely in their excitement.

'Now!' shouted Wolfe.

A trumpet sounded behind the general and almost as one the British line fired. The French were close, awfully close, and they appeared to sway backwards as the hail of lead bullets whistled through them. Like a sudden gust of wind through a wheat field, Carlisle thought.

Crash! Another volley. They were firing by companies to Wolfe's improved plan, which meant that there was no long gap between volleys. To the French, it must have felt as though they were under near-continuous fire.

Now parts of the French line were withdrawing, backing away from the awful savagery of the British muskets. A third volley just as disciplined as the first two, and now the enemy was in general retreat, leaving their dead and wounded on the field. Carlisle looked at his watch, less than ten minutes from the first volley to the retreat.

Over in the centre, the highlanders had drawn their claymores and were charging forward at the French. Everywhere officers were trying to control their men. There was still a chance that Bougainville could appear in their rear, or that Montcalm's reserves could come pouring across the Saint Charles River. Let the French run; the victory had already been won.

The spectacle fascinated Carlisle, and he was surprised that he'd felt no fear in this his first taste of a land battle. He'd lost contact with Wolfe as the general had strode from place to place giving orders and encouraging his men. Now he was nowhere to be seen, but a cluster of his staff officers twenty yards away brought Carlisle running. His fears were confirmed, Wolfe was lying on the ground, evidently gravely wounded. One of the colonels looked back at Carlisle and shook his head; there was no hope.

***

# CHAPTER TWENTY-FOUR

## A Ship of the Line

*Wednesday, Nineteenth of September 1759.*
*The Upper Town, Quebec.*

'We have a ship!'

The door flung open and Carlisle strode in, catching Wishart and Enrico in the very act of rolling dice for who would have the bed and who would have the cold stone floor. Wishart was an incorrigible gambler, and he knew that his captain disapproved. Nevertheless, he was never parted from his dice, even when he had to face the French guns in the open. For the last week they'd rested unused in his pocket as they'd dug the siege artillery into the good earth of the Plains of Abraham, expecting a hard fight to take the city. Then the French, leaderless when Montcalm died after the battle, had capitulated. It was all over.

Without a ship to call their own, they'd been making the best of their situation in the gatehouse of the Ursuline convent. A room for the captain, a room for the two officers and a room for Sergeant Wilson and Souter and the others. They'd scrawled a sign in chalk to keep the soldiers away; *Naval Headquarters Quebec – No entry.*

'We have a ship!' Carlisle repeated to their astonished faces. 'You can clear all this away, I want to read myself in before eight bells,' he said sweeping his arm around the accumulated spoils that cluttered the rooms. 'There are two boats waiting at the customs wharf in the lower town. I'm off to pay my respects to General Townshend. Mister Angelini, you'll come with me. We'll meet you at the wharf in an hour Mister Wishart. There are berths for Sergeant Wilson and the rest of my people. You'd better take what you most want of this stuff; there's not the slightest chance of seeing it again if you leave it with the army.'

He turned to go then paused on the threshold. He spared

a disparaging glance for the ornate sword that Enrico had tucked into his belt; its original owner presumably had kept the scabbard when he fled the field of battle a week ago.

'You'd better leave that with Mister Wishart,' he said.

'By the way, Mister Wishart, you're to have an acting commission, you'll be third.'

And with that he was gone, leaving an astonished Wishart to stare dumbly at the door swinging loosely on its ruined hinges.

'My congratulations, sir,' said Enrico quickly but with all the formality that he could muster for his berth-mate of the last two years, 'but what ship?' he whispered, his eyes wide with wonder, and then he too was gone.

Wishart was overcome with emotion, rooted to the spot. He'd been a volunteer, a midshipman and master's mate under Carlisle since before the war. He'd been waiting a year for the opportunity to take his lieutenant's examination, but *Medina* hadn't been back to England in all that time. At this stage of the war when the balance between the number of ships and the number of sea officers had settled down into equilibrium, there had been no hope of a board meeting anywhere other than the Navy Board offices in Seething Lane. Now his promotion was gifted to him. He'd still have to take the examination, eventually, but there was no hurry anymore, their Lordships were unlikely to overturn acting promotions made by a commander-in-chief at the end of a successful campaign. But what ship did Carlisle have? Clearly a fifth-rate at least if it had three lieutenants or more, but could it be a fourth-rate or a third? That was an important point – nay, a vital point. It had been clear for a year that Carlisle's time in frigates was ending. If he'd been given a frigate – even a big fifth-rate frigate – as a temporary command to take home, then Wishart would likely be looking for another ship in a few months. But if it was a ship-of-the-line…

'What ship indeed?' he muttered to himself. 'But one thing's for certain, I'd better get shifting. I must tell Sergeant

## Rocks and Shoals

Wilson sharpish and get all this clutter down the hill.'

There had been spoils of war aplenty left on the battlefield. Anything larger than a pistol was the property of King George, but Wishart and Enrico had collected swords, pistols, hats and halberds, all of which were classed as personal plunder. Now they had to get them down to the lower town along with their own meagre possessions. Yet not all the cares in the world could spoil Wishart's day. He was a lieutenant! He didn't yet have a commission in his pocket, but his captain had said he was promoted, and that was enough for him. He didn't even have to deal with the envy of his friend. Enrico couldn't take the oath that went with King George's commission; he was a naval anomaly and served by the grace and favour of Edward Carlisle, his cousin's husband.

***

Sergeant Wilson saved the day with a hand-cart that he'd commandeered. Nevertheless, it was a steep road from the upper to the lower city, and the cart tended to run away if they didn't restrain it. The little band was hot a flustered by the time they reached the customs wharf.

Wishart pulled off his hat and fanned his face. There were perhaps a hundred boats drawn up to the wharf, longboats and yawls, jolly boats and luggers, bateaux and flatboats with, at the far western end, a gaggle of cats and transports. He started to feel foolish; he had no idea which boats he was looking for. He didn't even know which ship to ask for.

'We could try…'

Wishart's sentence was drowned out by a stentorian bellow from Sergeant Wilson.

'Boat for Captain Carlisle! Boat for Captain Carlisle! Sing out there! Which boats are for Captain Carlisle?'

He stared around in the stunned silence that had descended over the wharf.

'Would that be Captain Carlisle of *Dartmouth*?' asked an extremely small person dressed in the fashion of a midshipman, removing his hat as a precaution, just in case this man in naval uniform standing beside the large marine was his new third lieutenant.

*Dartmouth*! A fifty-gun fourth-rate. Wishart's heart skipped a beat. He was just quick enough to forestall Sergeant Wilson.

'It is, and he'll be here momentarily, Mister…'

'Horace Young, Midshipman…'

'You call me sir,' said Wishart firmly, 'or are manners different in *Dartmouth*? Now have all this put in the boats before Captain Carlisle arrives.'

Wishart almost regretted his brusqueness. There were important things that Young could have told him about his new ship, things that he now could hardly ask. But it was better to start by establishing the immeasurable chasm between a midshipman and a lieutenant, even if only an acting one. He could always mellow his tone later. In any case, midshipmen expected little else of new lieutenants. He strode along the wharf waiting for Carlisle and Enrico while the captain's followers settled into the yawl and Sergeant Wilson and Souter stood officiously beside the longboat, daring any other ship's boat to block its way out into the river.

The wharf was a hive of activity. When the terms of the capitulation had been agreed, the army had quickly taken possession of the upper town while the navy had taken the lower town. The campaign for Quebec was over, but the war wasn't yet won, and the British army would have to survive a winter in the devastated city while Vaudreuil's still-considerable army threatened them from upstream in Montreal. It was a race against the seasons to get enough stores ashore before Saunders and the bulk of the storeships and transports would have to leave the river. Only a few frigates were to remain to counter the French men-o'-war further up the river, but food and other supplies for four thousand men must be landed quickly. Wishart nodded to acquaintances from other ships, each one of them employed in getting the stores ashore. They thought him a master's mate without a ship, a nobody without even a patron, Carlisle being also without a ship as far as they were aware. None of them yet knew of his elevation. None knew that he was the third lieutenant of a fourth-rate, and he hugged the knowledge to himself like a warm blanket. And now that he came to think of it, *Dartmouth* was a fine ship. From what he could remember she'd been commissioned between the wars, with twenty-four pounders on her lower deck and twelves on her upper. She had a proper poop-deck, too. At fifty guns she was too small for the line of battle, but that was perhaps a good thing, as the fourth-rates were used where a battle fleet wasn't needed, like a frigate only vastly more powerful. He'd have the upper gun deck, he imagined; twenty-two guns, all his own.

\*\*\*

'Lieutenant Wishart!'

Carlisle's call broke into his reverie. He was heading a small procession down the last slope from the upper town and onto the wharf. He and Enrico were unencumbered, but the soldiers behind him carried or dragged bundles and boxes, bales and casks.

'Get these into the boats, Mister Wishart. Who's this? Midshipman Young? Then make space for General Murray's goods.'

Sergeant Wilson took charge. The soldiers passed the goods across into the boats, which sank deeper and deeper under the burden.

'We'll have to get it all in,' Carlisle said, 'We sail with the morning ebb, and these are the items that the general wishes to be taken to England. He'll be wintering in Quebec.'

It was fortunate that the day was fine with only the lightest of westerly winds, otherwise those sorely overburdened boats would surely not have reached the ship. Wishart was burning with a hundred questions, but all Carlisle would say was that *Dartmouth's* previous captain was removed into Commodore Colville's flagship to spend the winter in Halifax, and her first lieutenant had been given an armed sloop to remain in the river. It seemed that Colville had been granted a broad pennant and a post-captain under him, which was a long-overdue compliment to his years on the American station.

It was a long pull to the eastern end of the Basin. The boats didn't dare take advantage of the fair wind to set a sail; their freeboard was dangerously low even for steady, careful pulling and a sail would have been foolhardy. They rowed past ship after ship; grand third-rates and fourth-rates, frigates, cats, storeships and sloops. Far over on the northern shore, they could see the burned remains of *Russell*. There was no sign of *Three Sisters*, she'd been burned to the bilge. At this state of the tide, the waters covered her nakedness.

Now, at last, *Dartmouth* came into view. It was something of a shock for Carlisle to see a ship looking so pristine, so untouched by war and weather. He'd left *Russell* a burned and dismasted hulk and *Medina* a bilged wreck. While the frigates and sloops and cats had braved the fire of the enemy, the ships-of-the-line for the most part had stayed safely at anchor, unable to bring their firepower to bear on an enemy that wouldn't stir from his defences. Yet they hadn't been idle, and every ship had provided men and guns for Wolfe's final effort. Even now, those twenty-four pounders that weren't needed to defend the walls through the winter and into the next spring were being brought down from heights to be replaced in the ships before they sailed.

A figure on the poop deck raised his speaking trumpet.

'Boat ahoy!' he shouted as if he didn't know exactly who his longboat would be carrying.

'*Dartmouth*!' replied the coxswain, and he steered for the larboard side.

Third-rates had an entry-port, but these new fourth-rates had a similar arrangement to frigates; one entered the ship on the waist, through a removable section of the gunwale.

# Rocks and Shoals

It was a longer climb up the side than he was used to, but the far greater tumble-home helped him once he was past the lower tier of guns.

The pipes squealed, the side-boys stood ready to help Carlisle over the last few feet of the climb, and the ship's officers were all gathered ready to receive him. There were so many of them! More lieutenants than he was used to and a great line of midshipmen and volunteers that stretched across the waist to the starboard side.

'Lieutenant Gresham, sir,' said a short, powerful figure who stepped forward to meet him, 'First Lieutenant, at your service. May I introduce the officers?'

'Yes please, Mister Gresham, just the commission officers and the standing officers. I'll meet the others later.'

He tried his best to concentrate on the names, but after John Halsey, second lieutenant and Arthur Beazley, sailing master, he lost his focus. It didn't matter, none of them expected him to remember and the introductions would be repeated later.

'Thank you, Mister Gresham. This is Lieutenant Wishart, the new third, and Mister Angelini.'

He didn't elaborate on Enrico's status.

'Now, as Captain Downey has already departed, if you'll call the people together, I'll read myself in.'

They were waiting, of course, gathered on the lower gun deck and eager for the first glimpse of their new captain, the man who above all others would be the master of their fates for the coming months and years.

'The hands are mustered, sir,' said Gresham, removing his hat and bowing.

Carlisle took his commission from his pocket and smoothed it onto the lectern that had been placed at the quarterdeck rail. It was already growing dark, and he had difficulty reading the words, but he said enough of them in the right order:

*'By Sir Charles Saunders, Vice-Admiral of the Blue and Commander-in-Chief of His Majesty's Ships and Vessels in North America, to Captain Edward Carlisle Esquire…'*

\*\*\*

# CHAPTER TWENTY-FIVE

## Stolen Moments

*Monday, Fifteenth of October 1759.*
*Dexter's Print Shop, Williamsburg, Virginia.*

'And then the captain of the port, bless him, winked at me and asked if I'd fancy a quick convoy to Hampton Roads before I headed back to Portsmouth! I'd given up hope of seeing you for many, many months until he spoke. Of course, a ship-of-the-line is entirely the wrong beast to be sending with a coasting convoy, but he at least had the excuse that he didn't have a sloop to hand at that moment, nor even a frigate. There's always the potential for a French privateer to be lurking off Sandy Hook or Cape Henry, you know. In any case, his need and my desire coincided, and here I am with two whole days before I must sail.'

Carlisle was finding that his speech was running away with him. A nervous reaction, he thought, that went with the relentless guilt of not being with his family. Chiara was her usual serene self, her equanimity hardly affected by this sudden appearance of her husband, washed in, apparently, on the morning's sea-breeze.

'Which captain are you referring to now, Edward? I must say there is a plethora of naval gentlemen in your story and I'm finding it hard to keep up.'

'Oh, my apologies. It was Captain Griffiths who's looking after New York; he was kind enough to give me the convoy to Hampton Roads. Admiral Saunders – you remember me speaking of him, from Quebec? He sent me to New York with the transports and supply ships. I would have been straight to Spithead from there were it not for Griffiths.'

'Well, in any case, here you are.'

They were interrupted by a tentative knock on the door. The whole household seemed to be walking on eggshells since Carlisle's arrival on the doorstep an hour before. They were doing their best to leave him and Chiara alone together as much as possible. However, little Joshua Carlisle had been washed and brushed and clothed for his father's inspection, and the transformation wouldn't last long. A one-year-old who had just started walking could be relied upon to cover himself in nameless secretions in a matter of minutes, and Susan, Chiara's maid, knew that there was not a moment to lose.

'Is this my little man!' Carlisle cried out in wonder. 'He was a babe in arms nine months ago, now look at him!'

Susan held Joshua carefully as he caught his balance, then she tentatively released her grip. He sagged, she caught him up again. Then, when he looked as though he could toddle the few yards to his father, she let go again. One step, two steps and he lurched forward onto his knees. Nothing daunted, he rushed forward on all fours towards his father. Then he looked up. A puzzled expression crossed his face. He looked again and sped forward, swerving to the right and straight to his mother who knelt to pick him up.

'Never mind, dear,' she said, holding her son protectively. 'I'm sure he'll soon become used to you. Perhaps I should show him your miniature from time to time.'

Carlisle opened his mouth to say something then thought better of it. He was only home – if these apartments at the back of his cousin's shop could be called home – for two days, and the last thing he wanted was a misunderstanding with his wife. He held out his hands and Chiara passed his child to him. Joshua looked over his shoulder for the reassurance of his mother and Susan and he tried to push himself away. Carlisle had never had much to do with children, and he was unprepared for this apparent rejection.

'I'll take him and sit beside you, Edward,' said Chiara, 'then perhaps he will learn come to you.'

Susan curtsied and left the room. They sat in

companionable silence on the chaise lounge while Carlisle offered his fingers as playthings for Joshua.

'He looks so like you, don't you think,' said Chiara, searching for the most amenable thing she could say after her unfortunate comment about the miniature.

She really loved her husband, but she resented the way he had disappeared for nine months, leaving her in a foreign country with a new baby. Certainly, she'd been made very welcome by Carlisle's cousin, and Edward's father had been trying as best he could to make up for the chill of their first meeting. She really had not meant to be shrewish, but what had started as a harmless joke had misfired.

Carlisle was not a man without empathy, and in his own way, he had a misty understanding of his wife's thought processes. He'd learned to hold his tongue the hard way, in the midshipman's berth of a variety of King's ships, and he'd learned to make the most of a stolen moment. He'd be off in just two days and who knew when he'd be back?

'That was the nicest thing you could have said to me,' he looked at his wife and again at his son, 'and look, I do believe he wants to come to me.'

Sure enough, young Joshua was holding out his chubby arms to Carlisle. Chiara smiled.

***

'Now, that is the house I was telling you about,' said Chiara, pointing down Governor's Green. 'There, on the left, next-but-one after Elizabeth Wythe's home.'

They'd had a trying time walking through the city. News of the fall of Quebec had preceded him, and everyone wanted to hear the story and meet one of the captains who had sailed up the fabled Saint Lawrence. It was the most welcome news, better even than the capture of Louisbourg the previous year. The English colonists in America were largely disinterested in the war in Europe or the East Indies, but the news that the French were but one campaign away from being evicted from North America stirred them as little else could. They gave no thought to the difficulty of maintaining a battle-weary garrison in the wreckage of a beaten city through a Canadian winter. The danger that the Marquis de Vaudreuil may sweep the British garrison away before a relief squadron could ascend the Saint Lawrence in the next spring hadn't even occurred to them. Carlisle knew the fragility of the victory at Quebec. Only a few years ago it looked entirely likely that the French would encircle the thirteen colonies, cutting them off from the vast continent before them and making them forever reliant upon the good offices of their mother, England. He also knew that words of caution were not wanted now, for today the city was ecstatic in its rejoicing.

There was another factor that he had to consider. This victory was won largely – almost exclusively – by the British navy and by regular British soldiers; the colonial militia had played only a very minor part. However, Carlisle was himself a colonist, one of the few to hold a regular commission in either the sea or land forces. He was a tangible bridge between the colonies and England, and the citizens of Williamsburg loved him for it. Carlisle knew that he must decide where to put down his roots. Would it be a rural home in the English counties? Or perhaps a townhouse in London. He could afford both, he knew, having seen the last statement of his affairs from Campbell & Coutts, his London bankers. Then, of course, he could settle here, in Williamsburg. Such a thing had never really occurred to him until Fauquier had spoken to him last winter. When he went to sea at the age of fourteen, he thought he'd shaken the dust of Virginia from his feet. It was sheer chance that had brought him to his hometown at exactly the moment when it became evident that the expectant Chiara should travel no further. Even then, he'd imagined that she'd soon be pressing him to arrange a passage back to England, or even to her native Nice. And yet here she was pointing out a property for sale, a substantial property, and just yards from the Governor's Palace. Well, it would be, wouldn't it, he thought ruefully.

'It really is most convenient, you know. Elizabeth arranged for me to look around it last month. Oh, I said nothing, I gave no hint that I was anything other than merely curious, just another vulgar busybody. But you know, it is such a nice home, and so close to Barbara and Cranmer, and with the most eligible neighbours,' she added nodding towards the Governor's Palace and favouring Carlisle with her most winning smile.

Carlisle had the distinct impression that he was being manoeuvred. Chiara had a heightened sense of her position in society and a dread that she should ever be thought anything less than a Great Lady. She would usually have come no closer to her husband than a light hand on his arm in public, but now she was positively clinging to him.

'Would you like me to arrange for us both to look around the house? We could do that tomorrow. It may be a relief after dinner with the lieutenant-governor this evening.'

'Oh yes, Edward,' said Chiara, moving away slightly as she saw an acquaintance approaching them. 'Mister Wythe is the seller's agent; I'm sure he would be delighted.'

I'm sure he would, Carlisle mused. George Wythe would have a shrewd idea of Carlisle's fortune; he was, after all, a man of business as well as the law. He could probably name all the prizes that Carlisle had taken in this war and would be able to tally the values to within a hair of the truth. Little did Carlisle know of property prices in Williamsburg, but he was confident that they couldn't be greater than London or the home counties. No doubt Elizabeth had already told George of Chiara's interest, and he was probably anticipating a visit from his old school friend.

'Then I'll send a note to Mister Wythe before we go to dinner,' Carlisle said. 'I'm sure he'll be most surprised.'

That earned him a sharp look from Chiara, but she also was trying her best to make these brief few days as pleasant as possible, and it quickly changed to laughter as she hugged his arm tightly.

\*\*\*

'I keep meaning to ask, my dear, how you are getting along with my father. Have you seen much of him?'

Carlisle was wrestling with his silk stock, and he felt as though he was all thumbs and no fingers.

'Here, let me,' said Chiara, and with a few deft twists she tamed the unruly length of silk. 'Have I seen much of him?' she laughed. 'He can hardly be kept away. Truly, he's a changed man from the one that we met last year.'

She paused and stared at the window as they both remembered that dreadful day when they'd paid a dutiful visit to Joshua Carlisle at his Jamestown plantation. The father had been unfriendly but Carlisle's older brother, Charles, had been outright hostile. Neither thought that there was any possible healing for that family rift.

'I couldn't wish for a more pleasant father-in-law.'

'And Charles?' Carlisle continued, 'have you seen much of him?'

Chiara's face darkened, and she bit her lower lip.

'He frightens me, Edward. If there is any danger of seeing him, I take my servant with me. You know that he would die for me, although I hope it won't come to that. You know that it was I who suggested the name Joshua. It's a normal compliment to a grandfather in my country and I felt that your father deserved it. Now I wonder; it seems to have ignited a jealous spark in your brother. He can hardly contain his fury when he sees me.'

Carlisle nodded thoughtfully. He knew that he'd have to confront his brother and he wasn't looking forward to it. It wasn't that he was afraid, not physically at least, but it was a public admission of failure for two brothers to fall out. Perhaps it was already too late. It was likely that all of Williamsburg knew how matters stood.

'But I spoke in haste. Your father's expression when he sees little Joshua is worth any number of furious stares from your brother. I do believe that for two pins he would throw over Charles' inheritance in your favour, or even in Joshua's.'

## Rocks and Shoals

How much did Chiara really know about inheritance law? Carlisle himself knew almost nothing, but he imagined that it was impossible to disinherit an older son, under the law of the colony. But was that correct? He could hazily remember instances where land had been willed not to the eldest son, but to a younger, or to a further distant relative. Had his father written a will? Probably. He would have to ask him. But first, he'd presume on his old friendship with George Wythe to clear up his understanding of the law. He'd never thought of it before, and he knew why. He'd always been the unwanted son, the disregarded second sibling, and only last year it would have been unthinkable that his father would even have acknowledged him in his will and testament. How things had changed!

\*\*\*

The lieutenant-governor's invitation to dinner had been most unwelcome to Carlisle. He yearned to spend time with his son, to have a simple meal with his wife and his cousin and to hear the common gossip of the city. However, an invitation to the palace carried the force – almost – of a royal command and Carlisle could only bow to the inevitable. Chiara, however, was in her element. She'd been bred to the court of King Charles Emmanuel, and she missed the sense of being at the centre of, if not world, then at least regional affairs.

Carlisle was, of course, the focus of attention. Here in the heart of the colonial government, the affairs of the world were given their due consideration. They'd heard the momentous news from Europe. Prince Ferdinand had won an important battle at Minden and Hanover was safe, for now. Boscawen had caught a squadron of the French Mediterranean fleet under de la Clue on its way to reinforce Bompart in the Caribbean. The admiral had breached Portuguese neutrality to destroy de la Clue's squadron in Lagos Bay close under Cape Saint Vincent. However, the Virginia colonists cared nothing for Portugal and its neutrality, just so long as it kept exporting its fortified wines, its Madeira and port. Even the news from the East Indies was encouraging, where it seemed that Admiral Pocock was getting to grips with the French on the Coromandel Coast.

Word of the fall of Fort Niagara in the summer was, of course, welcome and anyone who looked at a map could see how British control of the head of Lake Ontario split Canada from the western French possessions. Amherst's army was wintering at Crown Point on Lake Champlain, just a week's march or a day's sailing with a fair wind from the Richelieu River that flowed into the Saint Lawrence below Montreal.

All those victories were important, and the bells of the parish church had hardly paused in their ringing, but it was Quebec that really stirred their imagination. With Quebec in British hands, there was no communication between Montreal, the capital of New France, and King Louis in Versailles. It would be difficult for even a message to be sent to Governor-General Vaudreuil, while supplies and reinforcements were out of the question. If Murray could hold on to the shattered city until the spring brought fresh reinforcements and supplies flowing up the Saint Lawrence, then the campaign season of 1760 must surely see the end to the long dream of New France.

When the ladies had withdrawn, Carlisle's opinion on these great events was eagerly sought. He had an advantage; the war that had started on the Ohio River had become global, and its conduct was the principal subject of conversation when the captains of Saunders' fleet had met. That and the perennial talk of prospects of promotion, removals to larger – or smaller – ships, whose star was in the ascendant and whose falling; but that was the background hum of naval intercourse. Most of all the governor's guests wanted to know about the campaign for Quebec. How had Wolfe died? and Montcalm? Where was Vaudreuil while his battle was being lost. Could Murray hold out through the winter? What sort of man was he? Cautious? Impetuous? Carlisle could give a considered opinion to each of these questions. His reputation rose as the minutes passed and few men left the table without wondering what part Carlisle would play in a post-war Virginia. For although Carlisle had only heard earlier that day that he was considering buying a house in the capital, it had been well known among the leadership of the colony for at least a month.

\*\*\*

Carlisle had been uncomfortable with the prospect of meeting his father the next morning. He wasn't prepared for the almost fawning way in which the elder Carlisle deferred to him. He was clearly enormously attached to his namesake grandson and missed no opportunity in calling him by name. Carlisle was jealous as well because little Joshua was evidently at ease with his grandfather while he was still wary of his father. Perhaps it was too much to hope that he could mend the absence of nine months in a day, but still, it hurt.

'Oh, he'll scowl, but he'll do nothing,' said Joshua when Carlisle raised the subject of Charles Carlisle. 'He's jealous because you have everything and he has nothing, at least nothing that he now values. The plantation is mine, although he manages it.'

He looked reflective for a moment.

'Aye, he manages it well enough, but it's rooted in the past. There are plantations that produce far more tobacco for each acre under cultivation. I can't do it, I'm too old, and Charles is unwilling.'

He gave Edward a curious, conspiratorial smile.

'We live in separate parts of the house you know. We barely talk except for business. I hardly know what pleases him any longer. It's strange, isn't it? I'm the one growing old, contemplating my mortality as it were and yet I have so much to live for,' he said bouncing little Joshua on his knee, 'so much to live for,' and he smiled down at his grandchild.

Carlisle didn't follow up on the conversation. It was the wrong time, but he could hardly fail to catch the hint that the inheritance may not be as settled a matter as he'd imagined.

\*\*\*

'See how the morning sun floods into the sitting room,' said Chiara, 'and the back of the house will catch the evening sun.'

'It's a beautiful house,' Carlisle agreed. 'Perhaps the coach house is a little inconvenient, but it doesn't matter as we'd only need a coach for the governor's palace and that's so close that it would hardly be worth wheeling it out; we could walk.'

Chiara didn't dignify his remark with either a word or a look. She knew that he was amused by her insistence on using a coach for even the shortest trip when she was in her finery. For the governor's palace, she would use a coach even if she lived next door, and this house *was* almost next door. She was so certain that in this matter her husband was absurdly wrong, that she had stopped rising to this frequently offered fly.

'Well, if you like it and if you are determined to live in Virginia, then certainly there's no financial reason why we shouldn't buy it outright. I know an attorney who will act for us – it's a pity that George is already acting for the seller otherwise I'd have asked him – and I have no doubt that you can handle the affair here in Williamsburg in my absence.'

Chiara maintained a dignified silence in front of the young man who had opened the house for them, but inside her heart leapt. Carlisle wondered what he'd committed himself to and how on earth he could reconcile a home in Virginia with continued service in the navy. But then, he thought, this war wouldn't last forever, and the chances were that he'd be cast ashore on half-pay in a year or two. Suddenly that prospect didn't seem so dreadful.

\*\*\*

# CHAPTER TWENTY-SIX
## The Wide Ocean

*Monday, Fifth of November 1759.*
*Dartmouth, at Sea. Bishops Rock, east by north 500 leagues.*

Arthur Beazley swayed with the rhythmic motion of the Atlantic swell, his feet well apart and his eye fixed on the sight vane of his octant. He held the instrument in his right hand while with deft, minute movements of his left he followed the sun's image as it ascended toward its zenith. He rocked the instrument from right to left as he swept the image of the sun in an arc across the horizon.

Midshipman Young stood behind the master with a slate and chalk, ready to record the altitude. By tiny increments, Beazley pushed the sight arm away from him until, for a few breathless seconds, the sun hung motionless in his view. Then, almost imperceptibly, it required the smallest backward movement of the arm to keep the sun on the horizon. It would rise no further today.

'Noon,' the master declared. He held the index of the octant up to his eye and studied the markings on the inlaid ivory scale.

'Twenty-six degrees, twenty-five minutes, just a hair over.'

Horace Young carefully marked the sun's altitude on the slate.

'Eight bells!' called Lieutenant Gresham to the mate of the watch.

The marine sentry was already at the belfry on the fo'c'sle. He struck the bell eight times in four groups of two: ding-ding, ding-ding, ding-ding, ding-ding.

It was indeed noon, both legally and astronomically. The watch was changed, and the off-going hands jostled down the main hatch to their dinner.

Beazley consulted a copy of the tables that he kept in his

pocket and made a few secretive runes on the slate. He checked his figures then turned towards Carlisle who had been watching the way that the fore-tops'l tended to bag in the foot. He was considering whether the sailmaker should be asked to improve it.

'Noon, sir,' Beazley said, removing his hat. 'Forty-seven degrees, fifty-two minutes north. By dead reckoning, we're forty-six degrees west of Greenwich. A hundred and eighteen nautical miles run, noon-to-noon, sir.'

'Thank you, Mister Beazley.'

'That puts us at the latitude of the Île de Sein, sir, eight leagues south of Ushant. Our course is east-by-north a half east which will bring us to the Chops of the Channel in five hundred leagues or so.'

Carlisle knew all this. But he had no objection to such a thorough noon report. The latitude was certain; no competent sailing master in fair weather with a clear sky could mistake that. However, the longitude, he knew, was speculative at best. They were eighteen days out of Hampton Roads, and although they'd caught the Atlantic Drift within a day of clearing Cape Henry, the wind had proved baffling, and they'd made poor progress. They'd had fog off the Banks and no sight of land.

It was understood that when the master gave an opinion of the longitude, it was little more than a guess based on his estimate of the ship's speed through the water, the strength of the ocean currents and the leeway that the stout two-decker made as the wind tried to push her sideways. They could easily be a hundred miles out in the longitude without the master feeling any shame, and it was only by running down the latitude that they could safely approach the Chops of the Channel in anything other than clear weather and daylight. And with the year grown so old, the chances were good that they'd sight neither the Scillies nor Ushant on their way up the channel.

'I think we'll continue to follow the great circle for now, Mister Beazley, and when we reach the height of Guernsey,

# Rocks and Shoals

we'll run the latitude down.'

'Aye-aye sir,' replied the master, touching his hat. Carlisle had said just what Beazley expected him to say. They'd continue slanting northwards following the shortest distance between the two points on a sphere and then, for safety, follow the line of latitude until they struck soundings with the deep-sea lead. It was a tried and trusted method of navigation. It only needed a sight of the sun every few days to be as safe as any navigation could be, until a solution was found for obtaining longitude at sea.

Carlisle glanced at the traverse board. Then with a word to the second lieutenant who had just relieved Gresham as officer-of-the-watch, he dropped down the quarterdeck ladder and into the great cabin.

\*\*\*

Well, he was behind time, but his conscience was clear, or very nearly so, near enough for naval purposes in any case. He'd overstayed in Hampton Roads by a day so that his attorney could give him a statement of the asking price for the house on Governor's Green. It still caused him to gulp whenever he looked at that enormous figure. It *was* less than a similar house in the home counties, but not by nearly as much as he had thought. He could afford it, certainly, but he was concerned at whether it would hold its value. On the face of it, the war was going well, and when the French threat of encirclement was gone, and the lands of the Virginia colony stretched across the vast continent from the Atlantic to the Pacific, surely the value could only increase. Or would that huge glut of land depress the price on the eastern seaboard? It was the toss of a coin, but Carlisle was nervous about gambling with the fortune that he had amassed. With the war likely to end in the next few years and with his free-roving days in a frigate behind him, he didn't believe that he could make a second fortune quite so readily.

He couldn't keep his mind on one thing. If some sharp-eyed admiralty clerk compared the ship's log to his written orders, the day's discrepancy would be noticed. He'd been careful to write a few words about delays in obtaining wood and water in Hampton Roads, and that would probably cover him. However, the fact remained that if their Lordships wanted to break a captain, they could always find something in his conduct, some misdemeanour brought to light in the log. And then there were his officers. They were all aware of the stolen day, and he didn't yet know them well enough to be sure of their loyalty.

Enough! It was a fruitless line of thought. He was being altogether too careful. And yet…

'Mister Halsey's compliments, sir,' said the nervous midshipman at the door, 'the wind's shifted a point to the west and he believes he can set the fore topmast stuns'l, sir.'

'Have the people finished their dinner?'

'Yes, sir, just five minutes ago.'

Carlisle stared at the youngster. He knew that Lieutenant Halsey was tender with the men's welfare. Probably he'd concluded that the stuns'l could be set soon after Carlisle left the deck, but he'd waited until dinner was over. In principle, he had no objection to his officers thinking of the men's welfare, but when it came to something as important as the speed with which they'd make an ocean passage, the decision should have been his. He'd have to lay down the law to Halsey one of these days.

'The master's on deck, sir,' added the midshipman.

Now he knew he was being managed. Halsey had told the damned midshipman to mention the master if the captain looked as though he was hesitating whether to come on deck. The master's presence was intended to keep him in his cabin.

\*\*\*

Without another word and with a look of thunder, he strode up onto the quarterdeck. The startled officers shrank back from him, hiding their guilty countenances by suddenly becoming busy in some matter that kept their eyes down; the compass, a strand of cordage on the deck, anything.

## Rocks and Shoals

Carlisle went straight to the traverse board. It told the story to one who knew how to read it. At one bell in the afternoon watch, thirty minutes after noon, the wind had veered a point, and since then he could see with his own eyes that it had veered another point. The stuns'l could have been set forty-five minutes ago. It wasn't much, it was the loss of perhaps half a mile, but it was unforgivable.

'Mister Halsey!'

'Sir?'

'Call the hands and set the fore topmast stuns'l. This instant Mister Halsey.'

'Aye-aye sir.'

And Mister Halsey…'

'Sir.'

'The decision to defer the setting or reducing of sail is mine and mine alone. I will decide whether to delay so that the hands can finish their dinner. Is that quite clear?'

Carlisle was standing in the centre of the quarterdeck for full effect. He was heard by all the officers: the quartermaster, the steersmen, the marine sentry and the messenger boy. Another hundred or so observed the drama from the waist and the fo'c'sle but didn't hear the words. They soon would. A ship was like a village in its appetite for gossip, and before long the whole ship's company would know that the second lieutenant had been hauled over the coals.

Carlisle waited to see the stuns'l set, and he deliberately held his pocket watch in his hand to show that he wasn't taking this routine drill for granted. It hadn't needed both watches to be turned out, but he wanted to make the point about authority quite publicly. He was discovering that the command of a two-decker required a quite different leadership style to a sixth-rate frigate. He needed to be more aloof, the person who the lieutenants – and there were three of them rather than the one he was used to – turned to when a situation was beyond their competence. So much was clear, but what was also becoming clear was that the lieutenants needed to understand the limitations of their authority. This would be a salutary lesson.

\*\*\*

The sun was setting over their larboard quarter and, for the first time since Carlisle took command, *Dartmouth* was really showing her paces. Towards the end of the afternoon watch the wind veered another point westerly, and the fore topmast stuns'l had been joined by its counterpart on the mainmast, this time without any delay. Now the ship was bowling along with a bone in her teeth and a broad straight wake stretching far astern. The log showed nine knots, which was a little disappointing but probably all that could be expected of a two-decked fifty-gun ship that hadn't seen a dock for nine months. A British third-rate with her longer waterline and taller masts would eat the wind from her and a Frenchman – well, a French third-rate would sail her under the horizon in little more than a watch.

'Who has the first dog, Mister Halsey?' Carlisle asked.

He could tell that the second lieutenant was still smarting from his admonishment; he walked stiffly, and his habitual smile was absent. Well, it was unfortunate, but an example had to be made, and Halsey had chosen the wrong moment to attempt to manipulate his captain.

'Lieutenant Wishart, sir,' he replied tonelessly.

'Very well. My compliments to Mister Gresham and the master, and I'd be grateful if they would meet me in my cabin.'

'Aye-aye sir,' Halsey replied just as Wishart came onto the quarterdeck. Even he, the sole survivor of Carlisle's little band of followers, couldn't muster a friendly smile for his captain of four years. Almost the sole survivor, because at that moment Able Seaman Whittle came sauntering onto the quarterdeck to take his trick at the wheel. Whittle was impervious to Carlisle's occasional tantrums, as he described them to his messmates.

'Good day, your honour,' he said as he passed. Carlisle forced a smile in return.

## Rocks and Shoals

There were some crosses, Carlisle thought, that were easier to bear than others, and Whittle, for all his subversive good fellowship, could at least bring a smile to his face.

\*\*\*

How magical a smile was, thought Carlisle as he called for sherry for his two officers. If it wasn't for Whittle, he'd be greeting his second-in-command and his sailing master with a grim, forbidding face. But the smile that he forced for the able seaman had lasted all the way down the quarterdeck ladder and into the great cabin. There, the sight of the sunset through the stern windows completed the transformation. Few people were immune to the restorative effect of seeing the sun kiss the horizon through the stern windows of a ship-of-the-line, and certainly not Edward Carlisle. Each and every time it reminded him of the impulses that had driven him to sea, the play of the light through the windows of the chapel in the College of William and Mary, and the feeling that there was a better life outside the schoolroom and the courthouse.

\*\*\*

Matthew Gresham had the physique of a prize-fighter or a travelling strongman of the sort that had occasionally visited Williamsburg in Carlisle's youth. He had a dark complexion, unruly black hair and at some point, his nose had been broken, giving him a dangerous appearance. He'd been Captain Downey's second lieutenant since the ship had been re-commissioned, but in those years, *Dartmouth* had seen little real fighting. She'd mostly been employed in protecting the more important convoys – the East Indiamen and the Smyrna trade – but only down as far as the Line or the Gut. Gresham, for all his seniority as a lieutenant, had never been to the Mediterranean, the West Indies, or the Baltic, let alone the East Indies or the Cape. There was nothing about his career that would suggest to their Lordships that he should be plucked out of the ranks of lieutenants and made a master and commander, no significant actions, no notable family and no spark of exceptional ability. Or almost none. From what Carlisle had seen so far, and from the hints dropped by the warrant officers, Gresham was quite an exceptional seaman. He was one of those rare officers for whom the proverbial dismasting on a lee shore held no terrors and who could give a ship an extra knot merely by judicious adjustment of the sheets and braces. In all other respects, he was a run-of-the-mill lieutenant and probably resigned to end his days at that rank.

That all being true and well known to Gresham himself, he had high hopes of his new captain. Word of Carlisle's fighting ability had preceded him, and he had a reputation as a consummate and fortunate taker of prizes. Where Carlisle went, so the rumour ran, trouble followed, and victory was hard on its heels. For Gresham this opened two opportunities: first, that Carlisle might lead him into a famous fight that would make his name or, failing that, he would become moderately rich from prize money and could snap his fingers at the navy and its nepotistic ways.

So it was that Gresham looked eagerly at Carlisle as he came into the cabin. Zeal was written all over his pugnacious face as his massive paw enveloped the dainty sherry glass.

'Your health, gentlemen,' Carlisle said and raised his glass.

It was a decent sherry, not great, and Carlisle still missed his Madeira, but it had travelled well from its birthplace in the Andalusian hills behind Cadiz and was a suitable drink for the occasion.

'Your best bet now, Mister Beazley, if you please. When will we reach Spithead?'

It was an unfair question as they all knew because not even the best sailing master in the world could command the weather, and the science of forecasting was still three-quarters of a century away. Nevertheless, Beazley was an experienced seafarer and his guesses would be worth listening to.

'Well, sir. We have the best part of five hundred and fifty

leagues to run. We're making nine or ten knots now, and with the state of her bottom she won't go any faster. This soldier's wind won't last. Let's say twelve days, sir, the seventeenth of the month.'

Carlisle was quick at arithmetic. He raised an eyebrow.

'That's just six knots, Master. You don't think we'll benefit from some westerly gales this time of year?'

'We may, sir, but we may also suffer some contrary winds or no wind at all. I'd say the seventeenth.'

'Very well. Now the reason I've asked you here is to get your opinion on the work priority for the yard. I've seen the carpenter's report and the gunner's and the bosun's, and I know what the purser needs.'

He patted a pile of paper reports on his desk. The top one was the bosun's which was written in a neat hand, strangely like that of the purser's. It confirmed his suspicion that the man was almost illiterate and that his friend had written the report for him. It was unusual but not unheard of. Some bosuns were given their warrant in faraway stations where the scrutiny was less rigorous than at Seething Lane.

'Now I want to know your opinion of the priorities.'

This was the kind of detailed discussion that could banish any lingering bad blood from the incident on the quarterdeck. Carlisle could accept the specialist knowledge of these two officers who had served so long in the ship. Docking and standing rigging, futtocks and knees, cables and rudder, all these were aspects of the care of a two-decker that Carlisle needed to be more familiar with and he listened with interest and respect to Gresham and Beazley.

'Then it sounds like the master-attendant will want us in dock for a week and in the basin for perhaps two more, maybe a month in all allowing for other priorities. If we can get back before Saunders and Holmes, and if the Channel Fleet is at sea, we should be greeted with open arms.'

'Do you know anything about our future after that, sir?' Gresham asked.

'No, nothing at all, but my guess would be that we'll be back to convoy work or perhaps the Leeward Islands or Jamaica. These fifty-gun ships don't stand in the line of battle anymore, and if Hawke has the Channel Fleet again, he won't want more than one or two of us. I'm sure none of this will come as a surprise.'

'No, sir, I'd expected it,' said Gresham.

Perhaps he wasn't surprised, thought Carlisle, but he was certainly disappointed.

'Still, one never knows when something will heave over the horizon. There could be a French West Indiaman lumbering along ahead of us at this instant, or we could stumble across a fleet action. Never despair, gentlemen, our future isn't written yet.'

\*\*\*

# CHAPTER TWENTY-SEVEN
## The Channel Fleet

*Saturday, Seventeenth of November 1759.*
*Dartmouth, at Sea. The Chops of the Channel.*

Even the master's estimate of *Dartmouth's* progress proved optimistic, and the wind that should have wafted them towards home turned foul and backed right into the ship's face. Tack upon tack they made, never straying far from the direct path to the Channel for fear that a shift in the wind would leave them even further to leeward of their destination. They saw the Scillies, and Ushant too, in their weary beat to windward as the weather appeared intent on frustrating their every attempt to make soundings.

Carlisle was muffled deep in a huge coat as the cruel east wind searched for any gap in its defences. As it happened, the gales that had plagued them for the past twelve days had just moderated and veered almost four points. *Dartmouth* was hove-to in what the master hoped was the Chops of the Channel.

'Ninety-five fathoms, sir, right on the five-fathom knot,' called the bosun from the main chains.

'Then I'm satisfied, sir,' said the master. 'I had a good noon sun yesterday, and now that we've struck soundings, we can be sure of our position, some thirty miles north of Ushant. We can put her on the starboard tack, sir, full and by.'

'Be sure to make a note in the log, Mister Beazley, and let's get underway.'

The wind sang in the rigging as *Dartmouth* heeled to the breeze. Home was on the bow and the weather was fair. With the breeze blowing from the southeast-by-east they could just about put their head on Saint Catherine's Point at the south end of the Isle of Wight. If the wind held and Beazley proved skilful at working the tides, they could be at anchor on the nineteenth.

'Sail ho!' cried the lookout, 'Sail right on the ship's head.'

'Up you go, Mister Young, and tell me what you see,' called Wishart. He didn't expect the youngster to perceive anything more clearly than the experienced seaman at the fore masthead, but it would do him good to feel important.

'There's more than one, sir,' the lookout shouted, 'and they're coming down fast.'

The first lieutenant was on the deck by now, and he and Carlisle exchanged glances.

'The Channel Fleet, sir?'

'Aye, in all probability,' Carlisle replied, not choosing to commit himself. He'd sighted the channel fleet far fewer times than his first lieutenant.

'I'll take a look myself, sir,' said Gresham, and with surprising agility, he ran up the main shrouds.

Carlisle paced the quarterdeck. If it were the Channel Fleet, then he'd have to pass within hailing distance of the flagship to explain himself and request permission to proceed. It was usually a formality, but he'd heard in Hampton that the French were trying to concentrate their Brest and Rochefort squadrons to embark an invasion army. If Hawke were to the north of Ushant then he must have been forced into one of the channel anchorages by the weather, Plymouth or Torbay or Portland, and he'd be hurrying to round Ushant to re-establish his blockade. *Dartmouth's* manoeuvre must be perfect because he'd get no second chance; Hawke wouldn't hold up the whole fleet to speak to a fourth-rate.

'It's the Channel Fleet, sure enough,' said Gresham as he regained the quarterdeck. 'That's *Royal George* in the van, flying an admiral of the blue's flag.'

Hawke, then. Carlisle eyed the rapidly approaching squadron.

'Up helm, Mister Beazley. Let's get across his track then round-to six points on his starboard bow, at pistol-shot or closer.'

'Aye-aye sir,' said the master, touching his hat. He gauged the wind for a moment, looked for'rard at the fast-approaching squadron and down at the compass in the binnacle. Then he gave his first command.

'Up helm, quartermaster, your course is east-nor'east.'

The hands were already at the tacks and sheets, and Wishart gave the orders to check away until the sails were drawing just so on their new course.

Carlisle watched with approval. He knew that he couldn't do any better than the master and, in any case, he needed to concentrate on how he would answer the inevitable questions from Hawke or his flag captain.

\*\*\*

*Royal George* loomed massively as *Dartmouth's* head came neatly through the wind. The awful moment when she may have missed stays – with potentially catastrophic consequences to the flagship – passed and within minutes she'd dropped back so that her quarterdeck was exactly opposite the vast three-decker's quarterdeck. Despite her foul bottom, *Dartmouth* could easily match *Royal George's* speed. A fleet could only move at the pace of its slowest member, and there were some old, old ships in the three lines that followed Hawke; otherwise *Dartmouth* would have been left behind in seconds.

Carlisle saw that Edward Hawke himself, the grand old sea-warrior, was waiting for his report. There was no need for the traditional *what ship, where bound?* That was reserved for chance meetings with merchantmen. Carlisle opened the exchange. Being to leeward, he would have to work much harder at this conversation than Hawke would.

'*Dartmouth*, Captain Carlisle, last from Hampton Roads, bound for Spithead under Admiral Saunders' orders,' he bellowed through the speaking trumpet.

Hawke turned to speak to someone beside him, his flag captain, presumably. John Campbell, that was his name, Carlisle remembered. He'd been kind to Holbrooke during the raids on the French coast in '58 when he commanded

*Essex*; he'd put in a good word for him with Commodore Howe at a time when his friend had desperately needed it.

'My congratulations for Quebec, Captain Carlisle,' shouted Hawke, he needed no speaking trumpet to be clearly heard from his windward position. 'How long can you stay at sea?'

There was an audible groan from the hands in the waist who were shamelessly eavesdropping. They'd counted on a period in the yard and the probability of leave after so long away from home. That hope was torn into shreds with just a few words from the admiral. It was a cruel, hard service as Carlisle knew, and it showed at its worst at moments like this. However, there was only one answer that Carlisle could give.

'Stores, water and wood for six weeks, sir, three-quarters powder and shot, no serious defects.'

That sealed their fate, Carlisle knew, but there was one more question.

'When were you last docked, Carlisle? Can you keep up with me?'

'January sir.' A shockingly long time ago. 'Her boot-topping was scraped and payed in the Saint Lawrence in July. I can make ten knots sailing large.'

Hawke turned to his other side this time, to a man who looked as though he could be a sailing master. Their conversation was brief. Carlisle was proud to see that *Dartmouth* hadn't dropped a yard astern of the flagship while they had been talking.

'That'll do, Carlisle, you're fast enough; I've ships that can barely match your speed. You're part of the Channel Fleet now, the main division. Take station astern of *Chichester*. When I can, I'll detach you to the independent squadron under Commodore Duff; they're all your ilk there. The Brest Fleet is at sea, Admiral Conflans, and I hope for a meeting with him.'

That stopped the groans. They all desired leave, but there wasn't a man among them who didn't understand the meaning of the Brest Fleet being at sea. Nothing less than an invasion of England would tempt King Louis to risk his greatest naval asset.

'Aye-aye sir,' shouted Carlisle in reply. Hawke was evidently concerned that a ship with such a foul bottom might slow him down. That would hardly balance out the minuscule additional force that *Dartmouth* would bring to this massive fleet. The addition of *Dartmouth*, if she were to retard the fleet's speed, would have a negative effect on its capability. Duff's squadron must be composed entirely of fourth rates, he thought, and briefly wondered where Duff was. Well, he could wonder all he liked, unless he had the chance for a shouted conversation with *Chichester's* captain, he wouldn't know until he was summarily dismissed by Hawke.

With a wave, Hawke was gone from sight. The duties of the commander-in-chief of the Channel Fleet allowed only a few minutes to deal with a lowly fourth-rate.

\*\*\*

'I'll put her about when *Chichester's* abeam, sir,' said Beazley.

Carlisle didn't answer; he was watching *Chichester* through his telescope. It seemed to him that her captain, or someone who looked like the captain, was leaning out of the mizzen chains waving to him. Carlisle knew Bill Willett as a passing acquaintance; he'd been posted seven or eight years earlier than Carlisle and notwithstanding Hawke's clear orders to fall in astern, he couldn't ignore the gesture.

'What do you make of it, Mister Angelini?'

'I do believe he's asking you to come alongside, sir.'

'Hmm,' Carlisle couldn't see him that well, but he didn't care for it to be known that his eyesight wasn't so sharp these days.

'Mister Beazley, you may need to put us alongside *Chichester*.'

'Aye-aye sir,' the master replied. 'I'll just remark that in five minutes we'll be past the point where we can do that.'

Carlisle nodded and said nothing. Beazley was right, of course, and he had only a few minutes to decide.

'I'm certain now, sir. He's waving us alongside.'

'Very well. Mister Beazley, put me alongside *Chichester*.'

The master gave a rapid series of orders, and in response, *Dartmouth* came neatly through the wind onto the larboard tack with *Chichester* comfortably on her quarter.

'Brail up the mains'l,' Beazley shouted.

With the mainsail not drawing the fourth-rate slowed perceptibly and the third-rate came surging up onto her beam. The orderly pattern of the waves was lost between the two massive hulls, and the turbulent water surged back and forward in confusion, causing columns of water as tall as the spouts from a thirty-two pounder.

'Oh, it's you, Carlisle,' Willetts shouted across the narrow gap. 'How do you do? Are you joining us? You had *Medina* last time we met.'

'Very well, thank you, sir, although I had to sacrifice *Medina* at Quebec. I'm to take station next astern of you until we come up with Duff's squadron, then I'm to join him.'

The two ships were so close that conversation was possible without too much strain although Carlisle, as the leeward of the two, still had to use the speaking-trumpet.

'How was Quebec?'

'Splendid. The army's making itself comfortable for the winter and Saunders will be nearly home by now. Wolfe was killed, you know.'

'I'd heard that, and I'm sorry for it. But he had a great victory.'

Willetts paused for a moment.

'I imagine the old man told you almost nothing. We heard yesterday that Conflans is out with twenty-one of the line, probably heading to pick up the transports from Morbihan. Duff's at Quiberon Bay now, bottling up the mouth of the Gulf and if he's not careful, he'll be trapped there by Conflans. He has Rochester, Portland, Falkland, Chatham and four frigates.'

Rocks and Shoals

Four ships just like *Dartmouth*, Carlisle thought. If Conflans caught Duff before he left Quiberon Bay, he'd destroy the small British squadron.

'There's one thing you should know in case you don't have the chance to join Duff. If the conditions are right, Hawke intends to abandon the line of battle. You'll know when he does, he'll hoist a red flag at the main for engage and haul down the flags for the line-of-battle. Then it's a free-for-all, and we're each to take on the ship nearest us.'

'Thank you, sir,' said Carlisle. It really was most obliging of Willetts.

'I don't like the look of this weather,' Willett's added, 'it'll be a hard blow tonight. Well, good day to you, Carlisle, and good luck. You'll need it yardarm-to-yardarm with a seventy-four, ha-ha!'

\*\*\*

The fleet surged south, around Ushant and without so much as a glance at the base of the main French fleet at Brest, sped onwards in search of Conflans.

Carlisle had never sailed in a battle fleet, and he wasn't at all sure that he enjoyed the experience. He had no decisions to make regarding the course he should steer, or what he should do. His sole responsibility was to juggle his sails to hold his position a cable astern of *Chichester*. It had its own challenges; the fleet was sailing at no more than eight knots, and even with her foul bottom *Dartmouth* tended to run up to *Chichester's* stern at the slightest loss of concentration. Beazley never left the quarterdeck.

As they rounded Ushant in the night, the generally southeasterly wind veered further to the south and headed the squadron. Now Hawke had to stand far out into the Atlantic and even at the disregarded rear of the line, Carlisle could feel the admiral's frustration. By sheer chance, Hawke had sailed from Torbay at the same time as Conflans had left Brest, and it gave the French a two-hundred-mile advantage in this race to the south. That Conflans was steering for the Gulf of Morbihan was as near-certain as anything could be. Thirteen infantry regiments were camped around Vannes and the transports to carry them to England were anchored in the Gulf, waiting for the French battle fleet to escort them across the Channel. Thirteen superbly trained French regiments of the line landing in the south of England could nullify all the gains that had been made in the Americas. The squeezing of the French imports from the Caribbean, the loss of Île Royale and the isolation of New France, all would be traded for a French toehold in Hampshire or Dorset, or – unthinkably – London. This was King Louis' roll of the dice to counteract the British victories of 1759, and if Hawke should miss his appointment with Conflans, there was no force of arms that could stop the lilies of France waving over English soil.

\*\*\*

Hubert de Brienne, Comte de Conflans, had a lot on his mind as he sat and pondered in the great cabin of his flagship, the eighty-gun *Soleil Royale*. He'd achieved what everyone thought was impossible by bringing his battle fleet out of Brest without having to face the English fleet. True, he'd had some luck. Hawke had been forced off station by the weather, and the Channel Fleet was at anchor far to leeward in Torbay. That gave him two, perhaps three days in which he'd be free to act. Then, as if the gods were with him, Bompart brought his squadron in from the West Indies on the wings of the westerly gale, and Conflans was able to rob it of experienced seamen to complete his own fleet. On the fourteenth, the wind shifted into the east, and he took his chance, leading his ships through the Passage du Raz and out into the Atlantic. Now all he had to do was sail some thirty-five leagues to Quiberon Bay, chase away – or better still, annihilate – the small British squadron that lay there at anchor and bring out the transports with the Army of England, as it was starting to be known. In his heart, he knew that this was at least a two-stage campaign and if he brought his battle fleet to Quiberon Bay, he'd have achieved the first part of the campaign. At Versailles, they predicted panic in the City of London when they heard that the French navy and army had joined up. The British government was none-too secure, and it could even fall at the news, and a new government might be inclined to sue for peace. It was possible that Conflans would have to do no more than bring his fleet safely into Quiberon Bay to fulfil his mission.

So, one step at a time. He was free of the land, now he had to make the best speed to weather the Penmarks, round Belle Île and the Cardinals and sail into Quiberon Bay. Once anchored in a defensive formation behind the formidable navigational perils that surrounded the bay, not even Hawke would dare to attack him. He could wait for the next westerly gale to blow Hawke back to the Channel. Then, when the inevitable easterly followed, he'd have another window of opportunity to get the combined fleets to sea. If it was required.

But first he had to make his way south and east, and now he found that the same easterly that had allowed him to escape from Brest had become a full gale blowing right into his face. *Gross mers et gros vents*, his flag captain had written in his log. Indeed, high seas and high winds. He knew that neither his ships nor their rusty crews could make ground against such weather and he'd been forced to run out into the Atlantic. Now he was sixty leagues to the west of Belle Île, and he could feel the appalling presence of Hawke closing in on him from the north.

\*\*\*

# CHAPTER TWENTY-EIGHT

## A Rising Gale

*Tuesday, Twentieth of November 1759.*
*Dartmouth, at Sea. Belle Île east 7 leagues.*

'Well, Mister Gresham, what do you think now?'

'I think, sir, that we'll have a famous battle today if we can keep clear of Mister Duff and his squadron. I fear that Hawke may choose not to hazard us fifty-gun fourth-rates against the French. It's said that Conflans has nothing smaller than a third-rate in his line. If we can stay hidden behind our friend *Chichester* here,' he said, waving at the bulk of the third-rate ahead of them, 'then perhaps we'll be forgotten.'

Carlisle grinned. His first lieutenant was showing his true colours as a right fire-eater. It was madness to pit *Dartmouth* against even the smallest third-rate, but war was all about madness. He was rolling his own dice. A successful boarding that led to a Frenchman striking would probably give him his step. A bulldog-like defence when his captain had fallen would do the same. However, neither of these things would happen if they were sent away from the line-of-battle.

'We'll have a westerly gale before the day's out,' said Beazley, 'then we'll see whether there'll be a battle. A fight on a lee shore, forsooth! An act of desperation,' he turned away, shaking his head.

'We'll see indeed,' said Carlisle, 'we'll see…'

\*\*\*

Between his first lieutenant's fighting madness and his sailing master's calculating caution, there was a factor that they were forgetting: Hawke! The admiral was still recovering his reputation from the previous year when he had hauled down his flag and declined to take the Channel Fleet to sea. It was over a squabble – a misunderstanding really – about the leadership of the raids on the French mainland, and Lord Anson had stepped in to command the fleet for the rest of the year. Hawke needed a famous victory, something that would set the church bells ringing in England. He'd been planning for this day for the last six months, ever since it became clear that King Louis was seriously preparing for an invasion of England. No gale, no lee shore, no rocks, no shoals would keep Hawke from a decisive encounter with Conflans.

'Captain, sir,' that was Whittle at the masthead, 'there's a cutter beating up the line. It looks like it's speaking to each ship as it comes by.'

'That'll be news,' said Gresham. 'Good news, I trust.'

It took twenty minutes for the cutter to make its way to *Dartmouth*. Whittle had been right. The cutter's captain was timing his tacks so that he was briefly in irons alongside each ship in the line, and when he passed *Chichester*, they heard the cheering that followed in the little vessel's wake.

Carlisle tried to look as though he was waiting in patience, but even he was eagerly stretching over the hammock cranes as the cutter drew nearer.

'The French have been sighted,' shouted the lieutenant in command of the cutter. 'They're just over the horizon to leeward. They were chasing Duff's squadron, but now they know we're here and they're trying to form a line as they steer for the Cardinals.'

'Where's Duff?' shouted Carlisle, but the cutter had already brought her head off the wind and was filling on the opposite tack to take the word to the other squadrons. The lieutenant shrugged his shoulders and shouted something unintelligible, then he was gone, beyond hailing range, his voice lost in the howling gale.

'Well, that saves him disobeying orders,' said Beazley to the first lieutenant. 'If he doesn't know where Duff is, he can't join him, can he?'

Gresham said nothing, but a fierce smile split his grim features.

\*\*\*

The wind increased from the west throughout the forenoon until Beazley's forecast gale became a screaming, spray-blown reality.

'Sir,' shouted the lookout from the main topmast head, it being too dangerous for him to be higher, 'I can see tops'ls on the starboard bow, sir, they look like British fourth-rates.'

Carlisle recognised Whittle's voice again. There was a danger in taking this report at face value. Most lookouts had no idea what they were looking for, they just reported whatever they saw, but Whittle always spoke to the mate of the watch before going up for his trick at the masthead. He would know that Duff's squadron was in the area and that his captain was keen to know where they were. That could lead to excess eagerness, a desire to report what the captain expected to see rather than what the lookout really saw. Nevertheless, it made sense that Duff should be away to the west. If he'd escaped from Quiberon Bay just ahead of the French fleet, then he could only have sailed south and west, putting him on the starboard bow of Hawke's fleet. He caught a quizzical look from Gresham. Evidently his first lieutenant was wondering what he would do. Carlisle ignored him. Hawke's plan for *Dartmouth* was just that, a plan, and without specific orders, Carlisle would stay in the line.

'Signal from the flag, sir, repeated by *Chichester*,' said Enrico, 'Form line abreast.'

'Make sail, Mister Beazley, all the sail she'll carry. These Channel Fleet ships with their bottoms as smooth as a Portland pebble will walk away from us if we're not careful.'

*Dartmouth* was the last ship in the main squadron; she'd have to move fast to come up alongside *Royal George*.

'Flag's signalling, sir,' said Enrico. 'It's one of the new signals. *Magnanime* and the first seven ships to chase the enemy, sir. *Magnanime's* a seventy-four, Captain Howe,' Enrico added.

'Then Hawke's committed,' said Gresham, pounding the quarterdeck rail with his fist. 'He can't turn back now and leave Howe to face Conflans alone.'

Carlisle could see what Hawke was doing. By sending Howe ahead with seven of the line – and they would be the fastest ships being ahead of the main fleet – he could force Conflans to turn and fight before he got into the bay. Conflans would no more relish a fighting withdrawal into Quiberon Bay than Montcalm did on the Plains of Abraham. Howe would set his teeth into Conflans' rearguard and unless the French admiral was prepared to lose a third of his fleet he'd have to come to their aid. Had Hawke planned this? If so, Richard Howe was a natural choice. He'd been a temporary commodore only a year before, leading a huge squadron to raid the French coast; Howe knew all about command.

'Signal from the flag, sir, repeated by *Chichester*,' said Enrico echoing the structure of his earlier report, 'engage the enemy.'

'I think we know what the next hoist will be Mister Gresham.'

'I trust we do, sir,' the first lieutenant replied, rubbing his hands in anticipation.

'Signal from the flag, sir, repeated by *Chichester*,' said Enrico 'Form line of battle is hauled down.'

'Now, Mister Beazley, if you don't want to miss the battle, you'll crack on like the devil's on your tail.'

'Wind's still rising, sir,' he replied.

'I can see that,' Carlisle snapped. 'Nevertheless, you can shake out the reefs in the tops'ls. She'll bear that for another hour at least.'

\*\*\*

*Dartmouth* was yawing wildly as the westerly wind drove her forward towards Quiberon Bay. The quartermaster gave rapid helm orders while Beazley watched it all with a cold intensity. This was dangerous indeed, not the usual danger of losing a t'gallant or a topmast, but of broaching-to and shipping so much water that the ship lay over on her beam-ends and foundered.

'The lower gunports are closed, Mister Gresham?' he asked the first lieutenant as he came up from below.

'Yes, sir. Closed and secured.'

They both knew the danger. In the centuries since guns were carried as a broadside, many a ship had foundered after taking water through the lower ports. It had happened to Mary Rose two hundred years ago, at Spithead, under the eye of King Henry.

'If I get the choice I'll engage from leeward,' Carlisle said, 'but of course, I may have to take what I'm given. In any case, the lower ports are to be closed after each broadside.'

'That'll slow the rate of fire, sir,' Gresham replied.

Carlisle made no answer; he was watching the sickening behaviour of *Dartmouth* as she was over-pressed with sail. Yes, she was yawing, but the master and the quartermaster appeared to have it under control. The important point was that they were catching up on the van. He could see *Royal George* clearly now, and the massive first-rate was having no easier a time of it. He could see Howe's impromptu squadron closing in on the French rear. It looked like the French were still trying to form a line before passing around the Cardinals, and that was letting Howe get among them.

'Mister Beazley, how well do you know these waters?'

'I've never sailed into the bay, sir,' he responded, not looking at Carlisle but carefully watching the sails, the waves and the helm. 'I've studied the *Neptune Française*, but in truth, I know little more than the main passages in and out.'

'How close can we shave Belle Île and then the Cardinals?'

Beazley paused. Belle Île was clearly visible on the larboard bow, a rock-girt island that rose steeply from fifty fathoms depth. If you could see the southernmost extremity of the island, then you could pass it safely. The Cardinals were a different matter. They lay off Hoedic Island, and the last half mile of jagged rocks was all submerged, a constant menace to any vessel entering the bay through this southern passage. A French pilot may be able to shave it, but without local knowledge, a ship would do well to give the Cardinals a very wide berth indeed.

'A mile, no closer, sir. If we can see 'em, that is, if we can't then…'

Beazley ended with an expressive lift of the hands.

'In which case we can pass inshore of the third-rates, I do believe. Bring the ship onto the larboard flank of Mister Hawke's squadron.'

'I'll not be answerable until I see those rocks clear of the water, sir.'

'Very well, Mister Beazley, you have your orders.'

'Aye-aye sir,' the master replied, looking thoroughly unhappy.

With the wind now dead astern *Dartmouth* yawed and wallowed even more than she had done before but now they were starting to move up onto *Chichester's* beam. The second and third rates were all jostling for position but staying astern of the flag. They passed apparently unnoticed between the squadron and Belle Île and continued to overhaul the van.

'Gunfire,' said Gresham, cupping his ear to leeward and looking quizzically at Halsey.

The second lieutenant leaned eagerly forward, straining for the sound of battle.

'I hear nothing,' he said.

'It's gone now,' said Gresham, 'but I certainly heard it. Perhaps a dozen guns from the van.'

'The battle will be over before we get there,' Halsey grumbled. He caught a firm grip on the hammock crane as *Dartmouth* took a lurch to leeward.

'There'll be plenty of battle left for us, gentlemen,' said Carlisle. 'Perhaps you could look to your duties rather than speculating on the unknown.'

Halsey left the quarterdeck looking like a chastised schoolboy and Gresham became suddenly interested in the set of the main tops'l.

Carlisle took a few turns on the suddenly empty quarterdeck. He knew that he was becoming gruff, perhaps a natural consequence of commanding ships for four years in wartime. He was tired of adjusting to a new set of officers. He pined for Holbrook, and for Moxon and wished with all his heart that he could keep a gang of followers together for more than a single commission.

He didn't want to explain what he was doing; his previous first lieutenants would have known instantly. Duff's squadron had escaped the bay to the southeast, and they were now on the starboard side of the advancing fleet. If he had come within signalling distance, he'd have had no choice but to join them, and he knew in his bones that Hawke intended to keep the fourth-rates and the frigates out of this fight. By moving up the larboard wing of the fleet, he was both cutting the corner to get nearer the front, and he was keeping out of sight of Duff. He could almost be believed if he swore that he hadn't seen Duff's ships far away on the other flank of the fleet; almost. It was a risky plan, and Hawke could be excused for expecting *Dartmouth* to be stretching away to join Duff's squadron, but the other thing that he knew in his bones was that he desperately wanted to be in the action.

'I can see Howe's vanguard now, sir. They're just coming up to the Cardinals, about six miles ahead, maybe seven.'

'I'll be on the poop deck,' said Carlisle taking up his telescope. He wanted to climb into the maintop, but with the ship performing these acrobatics, the poop was the furthest from the quarterdeck that he dared go. From there he could shout instructions down to Beazley and the quartermaster if he needed to.

'Come up two points, master; I need to see ahead.'

He could sense Beazley's reluctance. That would bring them even nearer the Cardinals. Nevertheless, he wasn't concerned. If he followed the mass of ships crowding into the bay, then eventually he'd sight the rocks and steer clear.

Ah, now he could see. Howe was in action. It appeared that the French rearguard had formed a concave V-shape or a crescent, and Howe was steering straight into it. He could dimly see the main body of the French fleet in an untidy column pushing further into the bay. The leading ships at the head of the column had hauled their wind on the larboard tack. They must have passed the Cardinals and be reaching deeper into the bay. Between *Dartmouth* and Howe's vanguard, the ships of Hawke's fleet were elbowing for position as they ran pell-mell towards the sound of the guns.

'Well, we're not quite as sluggish as I thought, Mister Beazley,' shouted Carlisle.

'No, sir, indeed not. There's the flagship not more than a mile on the starboard bow.'

*Royal George* was unmistakable; a massive first-rate with a hundred guns when the French had nothing bigger than an eighty. She was hard-pressed under all plain sail with reefed t'gallants, and still the wind increased with frequent, dangerous gusts. It was no weather for a battle, but it offered a clear advantage to Hawke with his superb crews, their skills honed by years of blockade service in all weathers.

'Do you see the Cardinals, sir, right on the bow at about three miles? We need to be half a mile to the east of them. We should come two points to starboard.'

'Very well, Mister Beazley, make it so.'

*Dartmouth* was a trifle more comfortable now although her lee lurches were still profoundly unsettling. If they became too pressed by the wind, then the only thing to do was to let all fly and turn hard to windward. Then they may perhaps save their masts. It would be untidy, and if it happened now, they'd lose their place in the fleet.

'Deck there! One of our fourth-rates is still in the bay; she's beating up to the north. You can see her just past that island, sir.'

It was Whittle again. He was referring to Hoedic Island, the parent to the Cardinals.

Carlisle trained his telescope on the island then moved it a fraction right. The ship immediately sprang into view. It was a lot closer than he'd imagined and must be almost scraping the weed off the Cardinals. Certainly, she looked like a British fourth-rate, she could be the twin of *Dartmouth*. Carlisle looked closer. There was something wrong. Ah, that was it. Her tops'l yards were too small in proportion to her main yards. It gave the leeches of the tops'ls a distinctly inward-slanting look. Those yards and those sails didn't come from any of King George's yards!

'I do believe she's French, sir,' said Gresham, just beating Carlisle to that conclusion.

'I believe you're right, Mister Gresham. Now she's more our size. Heading for the Gulf of Morbihan by the look of her.'

'Flagship's made our number sir,' said Enrico, 'and the flag for a chase to leeward.'

Beazley and Gresham exchanged uncomprehending glances. They were already chasing to leeward as was the whole fleet.

'There's someone waving from the flagship's poop, sir.'

There was, indeed; it was Campbell, by the look of him. Carlisle raised a hand in acknowledgement.

Campbell raised his arm again then lowered it stiffly to the horizontal, straight at the French fourth-rate. He repeated it twice.

Carlisle waved again. Campbell stood and watched for a moment before he disappeared down to the quarterdeck.

'Signal to Flag, Mister Angelini. Acknowledge.'

Hawke had found a use for him! He could hardly have spent much time worrying about a single small French two-decker that was going to escape him but perhaps Campbell had suggested sending *Dartmouth*. Carlisle's was the only British ship that was too small for this great battle and yet a match for the Frenchman. Nevertheless, it was a forlorn hope. With the safety of the Gulf of Morbihan to leeward, it would be sheer luck if *Dartmouth* caught her. Once through the narrow entrance, she'd be safe among the transports of the invasion force, for there was no doubt that the French would have covered the narrows with batteries.

'Mister Beazley. Come as close to the Cardinals as you dare then follow around and chase that ship.'

Beazley nodded. This would be a dangerous moment as *Dartmouth* came off the wind onto a beat to follow the chase. A squall at the wrong moment could be embarrassing.

*Dartmouth* was really flying now, as though the ship scented the coming fight. The Cardinals were abaft the beam, and the French fleet was on her bow and spread out to starboard. The chase was perhaps three miles ahead and hard on the wind, heading nor'west.

Carlisle stood impassively as Beazley gave the orders to brail the mainsail and foresail to reduce the press of canvas. Then the master looked to windward, judging the right moment. The squalls were unpredictable, coming out of the clear sky that was fast growing dark as the early November sunset drew near.

'Hard a-larboard,' he said in a firm voice to the quartermaster.

*Dartmouth* started to turn. Her head came slowly around, and now the force of the wind was pressing on her beam. She heeled, the waves on her larboard side coming right up to the upper deck gunports. Then it happened. The pitch of the wind in the rigging became shriller, and the force of the gale increased, all in a few seconds.

'Let fly the tops'l sheets!' shouted Carlisle, 'Let fly the headsail sheets. Let her come up, Mister Beazley.'

But Beazley wasn't at his normal station beside the binnacle. A quick glance showed the sailing master struggling in the lee scuppers, and as Carlisle watched, a surge of water from forward broke right over him. Beazley was in no immediate danger, but nor could he contribute to managing the ship.

*Dartmouth* came over almost onto her beam ends. Almost, but not quite. There was a great clattering of blocks and yards as her head sought the wind and then, with the pressure on the sails reduced, she started to come upright again. It was undignified, but a quick glance to larboard showed that three or four of the third-rates had suffered from the same squall.

The master appeared at the binnacle, 'begging your pardon, sir, I was caught unawares,' he said, touching his forehead where his hat should have been. 'It's easing now, sir. I'll get us underway again.'

'Captain, sir,' shouted Enrico excitedly, 'the chase, she's lost her main t'gallant.'

So she had. What had looked like a remote possibility now looked like an even chance. Perhaps, after all, they could catch this Frenchman before he entered the Morbihan.

\*\*\*

# CHAPTER TWENTY-NINE
## Quiberon Bay

*Tuesday, Twentieth of November 1759.*
*Dartmouth, at Sea. Quiberon Bay.*

It was almost dark now, and the scudding clouds flew across the moon, obscuring the last glow of the setting sun as it faded in silver majesty. *Dartmouth* was feeling the full force of the westerly gale as she beat to the north under headsails, courses, tops'ls and double-reefed t'gallants.

She was carrying too much sail for the conditions, of course, but with a chase in sight and with Hawke's fleet to leeward charging into battle in the noblest, most reckless way, there was really no alternative. If he reduced sail the chase would doubtless head for the Gulf of Morbihan and safety, and he could make that on a single tack. By keeping the pressure on, he hoped that the Frenchman would conclude that he'd be caught as he reduced sail for the entrance to the Gulf and make for the open sea through one of the two northerly passage instead.

'What do you know of those northerly passages, Mister Beazley?'

'Not enough to take us through, sir.'

'Fetch your *Neptune François* then. Yes, here on the quarterdeck, we can't go below now.'

Beazley came back on the quarterdeck shielding a large, leather-bound book from the constant spray. Under the shelter of the poop deck and with the solid planking of the ship's side to blunt the wind, he carefully opened it. The French, as always, were ahead of the British navy in the scientific aspects of naval warfare. The Admiralty had only just woken up to the need for the comprehensive and accurate charting of the oceans and the shores, whereas the French navy had been publishing the *Neptune François* for over sixty years. It covered the European coast from

Norway to Gibraltar in twenty-nine charts, so it necessarily lacked detail. However, it did show the two passages out of the northern part of Quiberon Bay: the Teignouse and the Béniguet. It also showed the entrance to the Gulf of Morbihan.

'I don't know,' said Beazley, shaking his head. 'I'd rightly want a pilot to take us into the bay even in daylight, but here we are, and we must make the best of it. It looks certain that he can't go pell-mell across the bar and into the Morbihan, at least. We'd be upon him before he was in range of the batteries, just look at all these soundings,' he said, pointing to the scattered figures indicating shoal water.

The entrance to the Gulf of Morbihan was narrow, just half a mile wide, and with all the transports for the Duke d'Aiguillon's invasion force anchored inside, it was certain that he'd have placed batteries to cover it. The approach to the narrows was if anything even more hazardous, with a two-mile-long, twisting passage to be navigated before the safety of the batteries.

'Can you still see him, Mister Gresham? What do you make of his course?'

'I can see his sails clear enough by the moon, sir. He's still full and by and we're catching him. He could fetch the Gulf on this heading, but it's also the right heading if he's making for the passages.'

'Watch him, Mister Gresham! I want to know the moment he looks like tacking.'

'Now, Mister Beazley. Either way, we've some interesting pilotage to be done. He's a timid fellow, I believe, and I guess he'd rather be in the Morbihan than out at sea with the whole Channel Fleet hunting him. If that's the case, then I'm going to stay right on his heels and engage when he reduces sail for this channel.'

He pointed at the chart, to the channel leading to the Gulf of Morbihan. Beazley looked doubtful. With this sea running and the gale increasing in ferocity, he wouldn't feel safe without five fathoms under his keel, and that much water was hard to find either side of the narrow channel.

'I want our best two leadsmen in the fore chains. They'll need a good arm to throw far enough ahead at this speed, and I'll need them to act quickly when we get into shoal water.'

Beazley unbent from his study of the chart.

'Sir, I must state formally that my knowledge of these waters is insufficient for pilotage, and the gale is too strong for careful soundings. It's not safe to follow into the Morbihan Channel, sir.'

Carlisle pursed his lips. He couldn't criticise the master for his caution and for his formal statement of the facts; it was after all his duty. However, at this moment, he needed more willing support, and Beazley was still the best qualified to provide it.

'Thank you, Mister Beazley, and I understand your objection. Would you be so kind as to note it in the log, then we can get down to the business of pursuing the enemy.'

The master didn't look happy, but his caution had been effectively countered. In the same way that Carlisle couldn't criticise his advice, Beazley had nothing to say to Carlisle's determination to obey the admiral's last flag hoist: engage the enemy!

\*\*\*

Despite the sheltering chain of islands and reefs, Quiberon Bay was a weather-tossed wasteland of blown spume and spray that stung like hail. *Dartmouth's* leeward gunports were underwater most of the time. On the lower gundeck, the water was forcing its way through the gaps where the caulking had been removed to ease the ports ahead of being needed. Despite the shelter of the poop deck – a new luxury that Carlisle was still becoming accustomed to – all those whose duties kept them on the quarterdeck were soaked through and through. The chase was just two miles ahead, still on the larboard tack and still heading for the passage into the Gulf of Morbihan. They were closing fast but was it fast enough? Carlisle watched the tops'ls and t'gallants as a squall hit them, he felt the strain on the windward mainmast lanyards. He studied the sails and rigging while Gresham and Beazley studied him. They had a shrewd idea of what he was considering.

'We'll shake the reefs out of the t'gallants, Mister Beazley.'

'Aye-aye sir,' he replied without a pause. It was what he was expecting, and he was resigned to it. They could lose a topmast, certainly, and then the chase would be over, but with constant care of the helm, they were unlikely to broach.

Ten minutes later with the topmen safely back on deck, *Dartmouth* was hardly heeling any more than before. Her speed, however, was noticeably greater. They were all caught up in the chase now, and there was a feeling of invincibility. They all knew – they knew for certain – that they'd catch the Frenchman before he could come under the protection of the batteries.

'Here it comes,' said Beazley, 'luff her a little,' he added to the quartermaster.

The squall gathered force slowly this time. There was perhaps a minute between the first tentative indications and the full howling reality. The quartermaster eased the wheel over and *Dartmouth's* bows moved a point or so to windward. It wasn't much, but it was enough to spill a little of the wind and blunt the savagery of the blast, and it gained a few yards to windward in this race to the death.

'Chase is tacking, sir!' shouted Gresham, whose fighting instinct had kept him focussed on the enemy, leaving the sails to the master.

Beazley raised his speaking trumpet ready to bring the ship about. That was the correct thing to do in a stern chase such as this, to tack at the same time as the quarry. Carlisle raised his hand.

'Wait!'

What was the Frenchman doing? Had he detected a shift in the wind that meant he needed another tack to reach the entrance to the Morbihan? Or was he making for one of the passages out of the bay into the Atlantic? The loss of her main t'gallant didn't appear to have hurt her ability to claw to windward and now that the wreckage was cleared away, and she'd struck her fore t'gallant, it was hardly noticeable.

'Has the wind headed us at all Mister Beazley?'

The master tested the wind and looked at the binnacle. He exchanged a nod of agreement with the quartermaster.

'No, sir, dead westerly. It backs a point in the squalls, perhaps, but otherwise it's steady.'

'Very well, we'll tack in his wake. No, a cable before, we point higher than he can without his t'gallants.'

'You think he's heading for the sea, sir?' asked Gresham.

'I do believe he is, Mister Gresham. He's heading for the southerly of the two passages, the narrower one, and we need to be close to him as we don't have a pilot.'

'Which way will he go once he's through?' Gresham asked of nobody particularly.

'North, Mister Gresham, he'll go north. He'll have seen Commodore Duff's squadron escape to the south and he won't want to go that way. North for sure unless he has some particular errand to the south.'

Gresham smiled; his teeth white in his mahogany-dark face.

'He doesn't look like a man with an errand, sir, except to save his skin.'

'I hope he knows the way through,' said Beazley. 'All I can make out is that there are seventeen fathoms at low water, but how wide is the passage? And can it be navigated with a foul wind?'

'Where he leads, we can follow,' said Carlisle studying the Frenchman through his telescope. 'He's made a good job of clearing away his t'gallants, so I believe he's a seaman at least. Mark his track, Mister Beazley, mark it well, for that's our safe passage.'

\*\*\*

*Dartmouth* tacked smoothly in the space between gusts, and now, even though they'd come about earlier than the chase, the French ship was a point, maybe two points, off their leeward bow. They were winning the race, but it was clear that they wouldn't come up with her until they were through the seventeen-fathom passage.

'She's just going through now,' said Beazley.

'What's her course?'

'Sou'west by south, sir, as near as I can tell. The wind may have veered a point.'

'Follow right in her track, if you please, no luffing. If I were her captain, I would be close to the windward side of the channel so that I can get through without having to tack until I'm well clear.'

'The channel between Belle Île and this island – Houat Island it's called – is six miles wide,' the master said after quickly consulting the chart.

'He'll hold on until he's right under the lee of Belle Île unless he tries to escape to the south.'

Carlisle was beginning to understand his adversary. The French captain wasn't thinking far ahead, just eliminating each danger as it came up and hoping for a change in his fortunes. After all, it would only take a bad squall to dismast his pursuer, or for her to strike the rocks on this tricky passage, and then he'd be free. But if *Dartmouth* survived, then he would be overtaken and he'd have to fight or strike, and two better-matched opponents it would be hard to find.

A wedge-shaped rock with an outlying beacon passed so close to starboard that even in the dark they could see it. Close enough for a heaving line to reach the beacon. As Carlisle had guessed, the chase had kept to windward. The danger to leeward was further away, perhaps, but who knew what submerged horrors lay between the beacon to larboard and the Frenchman's track? The passage was no more than three cables wide; if the wind had been anything south of west, it would have been impassable. However, the Frenchman showed no nerves at all. Perhaps he had a pilot; almost certainly this area was known to him being so close the main Atlantic seaports. He achieved it, however, and he was through, but only a mile ahead of *Dartmouth*.

'You may breathe, Mister Beazley,' said Carlisle. 'Our task is easy now. He can't lose us, and he'll have to fight, whichever way he turns.'

\*\*\*

To the east, the sky was lit by flashes of gunfire. Incredibly in this gale, a major fleet action was being fought in the dark in a rock-bound bay. Hawke must have pushed through between the Cardinals and the Four, regardless of the dangers. Carlisle could only imagine what scenes were being played out. Which great ships were being forced aground, and which – God forbid, in this sea – where capsizing as they tried to manoeuvre in the confines of the bay in a rising westerly gale? There was no way of knowing which side was winning, but it was hard to imagine Hawke coming second-best in such a chaotic struggle. If ever a man was born for this day it was Edward Hawke. Better to ignore it and concentrate on his own little battle.

The Frenchman held his course as Belle Île became a looming presence just a mile on his bow. By now, *Dartmouth* had head-reached on the chase and gained somewhat to windward.

What was in that French captain's mind? Carlisle looked again at the dog-vane and at the binnacle. The wind had hardly shifted. He must know that he couldn't avoid a fight. Was he merely putting off the inevitable in the hope of a miracle? But why didn't he want to fight? His ship-handling didn't give the impression that he was short-handed, so what else could it be? He studied the chase again, an idea forming in his mind.

'Mister Gresham, Mister Beazley. Does the chase appear a little tender?'

They both studied the ship on their bow.

'Why, yes, sir,' said Beazley, 'now you mention it, these squalls are laying her over a trifle more than us, even without her t'gallants.'

'She may be riding a little high,' said Beazley.

'She's armed *en flute*, gentlemen, a guinea on it,' declared Carlisle thumping the binnacle. 'She's landed her lower tier of guns so that she can embark soldiers for England. Her twenty-fours are probably gracing the batteries of the Morbihan as we speak. That's why she appears rather shy of us.'

Beazley smiled. Gresham looked blank, disappointed. There was no glory for a first lieutenant in taking a ship of equal rate but a third of the weight of broadside.

'That changes things. He can't escape capture. Probably he would prefer to run his ship aground, but not today,' he said, pointing at the surf on Belle Île that even on this leeward side was soaring mainmast-high. 'Then I do believe he may turn south and hope that he can strike to an overwhelming force, for his honour's sake, rather than to a single fourth-rate.'

'The chase is paying off, sir,' shouted Enrico, 'she's coming off the wind.'

'Follow her, Mister Beazley, don't let Duff's squadron have the pleasure. Crack on now, don't worry about our t'gallants, just lay me alongside to leeward of her.'

The chase was short. With *Dartmouth* surging up on her leeward side, and Duff's squadron not in sight, the Frenchman fired a broadside to windward, backed her main tops'l and lay to. It was dark, but not too dark to see the white of France hauled down from the ensign staff.

\*\*\*

> *…and thus, she struck her colours, one of the most ignoble actions by a Frenchman that I ever saw, for as you know, they are for the most part heroic fighters. She was a British prize, built to the 1751 establishment, almost the same as Dartmouth, and she was armed en flute as I suspected. No lower deck guns at all, but she had a full complement and was only a week out of dock. She was fitted to take a*

*battalion of infantry all by herself, and she had provisions for her people and the soldiers for two months. It appears that her captain was bringing her round from Rochefort to join the ships that were already in the Gulf of Morbihan. He had slipped past Bobbie Duff's squadron when they had to cut and run with Conflans' fleet approaching, and he still had high hopes of escaping unnoticed when the two fleets met. I was just in the right place at the right time. Unhappily, it will do nothing for Matthew Gresham, an action such as that is hardly noticed by their Lordships. However, she is a fair prize and it being dark and the battle well to the east, there were no other ships in sight. Admiral Hawke will have his eighth, of course, but the rest is all for Dartmouth, less the percentage for Hawkins & Hammond. Prize money, head money, gun money, perhaps, and the not-inconsiderable value of her stores should come to a respectable amount, which will be useful as you told me in your last letter that the purchase of the house on Governor's Green is progressing satisfactorily. Gresham will not get his step from this, but he will have a sizeable sum for that cottage that he is pining for. A cottage and a wife, of course. He seems to believe that one cannot go without the other and that the possession of a cottage guarantees that the wife will follow. I hope he is not disappointed.*

*Now for the even better news. Dartmouth will be taken into the dock tomorrow for her bottom to be scraped, caulked and payed. There are a few minor repairs to be carried out then I expect to be ready for sea by the middle of December. Whoever suggested that old Clevland at the Admiralty is an unfeeling automaton is way off the mark. He knows my family situation and has given me a convoy again, to Savannah and then to Hampton Roads where I will gather ships from all over the Chesapeake and take them north. That will be at least a week, possibly two weeks, while the ship is doing nothing more active than swinging around an anchor just a day's ride from the twin objects of my affection. With good fortune, when this letter reaches you by the packet, it will be less than two months before I see you again.*

*I must close now; there is a cutter sailing for Falmouth on the tide. With this easterly wind she can be there late tomorrow and catch the Thursday packet.*

*Give my regards to my father and to Barbara and Cranmer.*

*I reserve all my love for my dearest wife and son.*

*Dartmouth*

*At Portsmouth*

*27th November 1759*

\*\*\*

# HISTORICAL EPILOGUE

## Quebec

Quebec was a close-run thing. If Wolfe had been thrown back from the Plains of Abraham, it's difficult to see how he could have mounted another attack before the short Canadian campaign season ended. In that case, Quebec would have had to wait for the next year, and by then, King Louis might have been able to find enough men and resources to reinforce New France. Nevertheless, by luck or superb generalship – the odds will be argued for as long as people study military matters – Wolfe won his victory, at the cost of his own life, and the French had to withdraw upriver for the remainder of the year. It meant a hard winter in a shattered city for Murray and his soldiers, and another winter in Halifax for Commodore Colville. Meanwhile, the French in Montreal, with their supply line to France severed and their best general dead, could have been forgiven for thinking it was all over for New France. Yet, with commanders such as the Marquis de Vaudreuil, the Chevalier de Lévis and the Chevalier de Bougainville, and the remains of an army still in Montreal, there was still hope. As the Saint Lawrence thawed in 1760, it would be a race between a British relief force and the advance of the French downriver from Montreal.

## Quiberon Bay

The threat of invasion in 1759 was very real. King Louis was gathering armies at Vannes, Le Havre and Dunkirk and the British navy was stretched to blockade all those places as well as the French naval bases. By far the most dangerous was the Duc d'Aiguillon's army of seventeen thousand men and his transport ships which were waiting in the Gulf of Morbihan for a naval escort. With Britain's defending armies stretched across England, Scotland and Ireland, it only needed Conflans' fleet to bring out the French army and escort them to the Channel, for the landing to be a reality. The French had no intention of occupying England; they wanted only to hold an important piece of land to divert Britain's attention from Europe, the Americas and the East Indies, and to use as a bargaining chip in the peace negotiations. At Quiberon Bay Admiral Edward Hawke, in his dramatic attack in a rising gale on a lee shore ended those invasion fears.

Quiberon Bay also ended the life of the gallant Comte de Kersaint whom we met in *The Jamaica Squadron*. He took his seventy-four gun *Thésée* to the aid of his admiral in *Soleil Royale* and in a squall, with the lower ports open, she capsized and sank. Kersaint and two of his sons died along with all but twenty-two of his six-hundred-man crew.

## *Annus Mirabilis*

1759 became known in Britain as the *Annus Mirabilis*, the Wonderful Year. In North America, the French had been defeated at Quebec and Fort Niagara. In Europe, the Battle of Minden had secured Hanover for another year. In the West Indies, the important sugar island of Guadeloupe had been captured. While at sea, the Battles of Lagos Bay and Quiberon Bay had ended French dreams of invasion of England and had reduced the French navy to a hollow shell. The sea routes of the world were in the hands of the British navy. The seemingly endless succession of triumphs led to the famous remark: 'Our bells are worn threadbare with ringing for victories.'

## French Despair

The loss of Quebec was a financial disaster for France, with the government cancelling its debts and the merchants losing heavily. Not only was the future of New France hanging by a thread at the end of 1759, but in response to the financial crisis, the budget for the French army fighting in Europe was cut by more than a third. Saunders and Wolfe achieved effects far beyond North America when they mastered the Saint Lawrence and beat the French army on the Plains of Abraham.

## Saunders and Wolfe

Admiral Saunders is one of the unsung heroes of the great age of sail. His achievement in bringing Wolfe's army to the gates of Quebec and sustaining it through a long campaign is without equal. He stands almost alone as a self-deprecating figure in a time when self-promotion was the norm. Despite leaving such a small historical footprint, it's possible to perceive much of the character of the man, and I trust that I have done him justice.

In contrast to Saunders, General Wolfe was not afraid to blow his own trumpet, and since his dramatic death on the field of battle, his life has been dissected by many, many writers. I have just this to add. With the ebb and flow of fortunes in a long campaign, we should do well to remember that it's the result that matters. By that measure, Wolfe stands among the greatest of Britain's generals. And it's well-documented that Wolfe recited lines from Gray's Elegy on the eve of battle.

## Bougainville and Cook

It's a fascinating coincidence that two of the greatest names of the age of exploration fought against each other in the Quebec campaign of 1759. Louis-Antoine, Comte de Bougainville was a soldier first, but something in the campaigns of 1759 and in his voyage to France and back wrought a sea-change in him. His later expedition to the Pacific and his circumnavigation added substantially to the sum of our knowledge of the world.

James Cook was an unknown master's mate in 1759, and

it was his skills at surveying and cartography in the Saint Lawrence and later in Newfoundland that brought him to the attention of the Admiralty. He was one of the few sailing masters that achieved a King's commission, and his legacy is written large in Australia, New Zealand and the islands of the Pacific.

## The Pilots of Bic

Unlikely though it may sound, the incident at Bic where the French pilots were lured on board the British ships and persuaded to help their invaders really happened. One can hardly exaggerate when writing about the exploits of the navy in the eighteenth century!

## Old Killick

And finally, for those who've read and enjoyed Patrick O'Brian's books, *Old Killick* really was the name of the master of the transport *Good-Will* at the siege of Quebec. His casual dismissal of the terrors of the Great Traverse has been recorded for posterity in the journal of Lieutenant Knox of the Forty-Third Regiment. Who could resist adding that incident to the story? I couldn't.

# OTHER CARLISLE & HOLBROOKE NAVAL ADVENTURES

## Book 1: The Colonial Post-Captain

Captain Carlisle of His Britannic Majesty's frigate *Fury* hails from Virginia, a loyal colony of the British Crown. In 1756, as the clouds of war gather in Europe, *Fury* is ordered to Toulon to investigate a French naval and military build-up.

While battling the winter weather, Carlisle must also juggle with delicate diplomatic issues in this period of phoney war and contend with an increasingly belligerent French frigate.

And then there is the beautiful Chiara Angelini, pursued across the Mediterranean by a Tunisian corsair who appears determined to abduct her, yet strangely reluctant to shed blood.

Carlisle and his young master's mate, George Holbrooke, are witnesses to the inconclusive sea-battle that leads to the loss of Minorca. They engage in a thrilling and bloody encounter with the French frigate and a final confrontation with the enigmatic corsair.

# Book 2: The Leeward Islands Squadron

In late 1756, as the British government collapses in the aftermath of the loss of Minorca and the country and navy are thrown into political chaos, a small force of ships is sent to the West Indies to reinforce the Leeward Islands Squadron.

Captain Edward Carlisle, a native of Virginia, and his first lieutenant George Holbrooke are fresh from the Mediterranean and their capture of a powerful French man-of-war. Their new frigate *Medina* has orders to join a squadron commanded by a terminally ill commodore. Their mission: a near-suicidal assault on a strong Caribbean island fortress. Carlisle must confront the challenges of higher command as he leads the squadron back into battle to accomplish the Admiralty's orders.

Join Carlisle and Holbrooke as they attack shore fortifications, engage in ship-on-ship duels and deal with mutiny in the West Indies.

## Book 3: The Jamaica Station

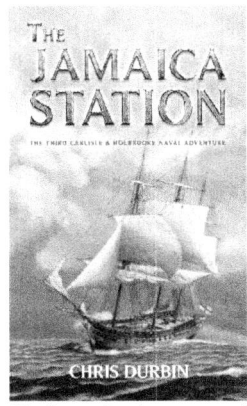

It is 1757, and the British navy is regrouping from a slow start to the seven years war.

A Spanish colonial governor and his family are pursued through the Caribbean by a pair of mysterious ships from the Dutch island of St. Eustatius. The British frigate *Medina* rescues the governor from his hurricane-wrecked ship, leading Captain Edward Carlisle and his first lieutenant George Holbrooke into a web of intrigue and half-truths. Are the Dutchmen operating under a letter of marque or are they pirates, and why are they hunting the Spaniard? Only the diplomatic skills of Carlisle's aristocratic wife, Lady Chiara, can solve the puzzle.

When Carlisle is injured, the young Holbrooke must grow up quickly. Under his leadership, *Medina* takes part in a one-sided battle with the French that will influence a young Horatio Nelson to choose the navy as a career.

## Book 4: Holbrooke's Tide

It is 1758, and the Seven Years War is at its height. The Duke of Cumberland's Hanoverian army has been pushed back to the river Elbe while the French are using the medieval fortified city of Emden to resupply their army and to anchor its left flank.

George Holbrooke has recently returned from the Jamaica Station in command of a sloop-of-war. He is under orders to survey and blockade the approaches to Emden in advance of the arrival of a British squadron. The French garrison and their Austrian allies are nervous. With their supply line cut, they are in danger of being isolated when the French army is forced to retreat in the face of the new Prussian-led army that is gathering on the Elbe. Can the French be bluffed out of Emden? Is this Holbrooke's flood tide that will lead to his next promotion?

Holbrooke's Tide is the fourth of the Carlisle & Holbrooke naval adventures. The series follows the exploits of the two men through the Seven Years War and into the period of turbulent relations between Britain and her American colonies in the 1760s.

## Book 5: The Cursed Fortress

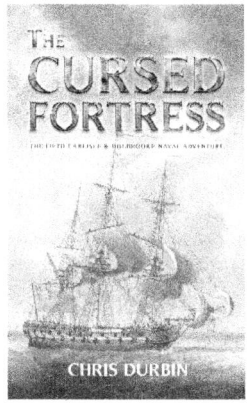

The French called it *La Forteresse Maudite*; the Cursed Fortress.

Louisbourg stood at the mouth of the Gulf of St. Lawrence, massive and impregnable, a permanent provocation to the British colonies. It was Canada's first line of defence, guarding the approaches to Quebec, from where all New France lay open to invasion. It had to fall before a British fleet could be sent up the St. Lawrence. Otherwise, there would be no resupply and no line of retreat; Canada would become the graveyard of George II's navy.

A failed attempt on Louisbourg in 1757 had only stiffened the government's resolve; the Cursed Fortress must fall in 1758.

Captain Carlisle's frigate joins the blockade of Louisbourg before winter's icy grip has eased. Battling fog, hail, rain, frost and snow, suffering scurvy and fevers, and with a constant worry about the wife he left behind in Virginia, Carlisle will face his greatest test of leadership and character yet.

The Cursed Fortress is the fifth of the Carlisle & Holbrooke naval adventures. The series follows the two men through the Seven Years War and into the period of turbulent relations between Britain and her American colonies in the 1760s.

# Book 6: Perilous Shore

Amphibious warfare was in its infancy in the mid-eighteenth century – it was the poor relation of the great fleet actions that the navy so loved.

That all changed in 1758 when the British government demanded a campaign of raids on the French Channel ports. Command arrangements were hastily devised, and a whole new class of vessels was produced at breakneck speed: flatboats, the ancestors of the landing craft that put the allied forces ashore on D-Day.

Commander George Holbrooke's sloop *Kestrel* is in the thick of the action: scouting landing beaches, duelling with shore batteries and battling the French Navy.

In a twist of fate, Holbrooke finds himself unexpectedly committed to this new style of amphibious warfare as he is ordered to lead a division of flatboats onto the beaches of Normandy and Brittany. He meets his greatest test yet when a weary and beaten British army retreats from a second failed attempt at Saint Malo with the French close on their heels.

Perilous Shore is the sixth of the Carlisle & Holbrooke naval adventures. The series follows Holbrooke and his mentor, Captain Carlisle, through the Seven Years War and into the period of turbulent relations between Britain and her American colonies in the 1760s.

# Bibliography

The following is a selection of the many books that I consulted in researching the Carlisle & Holbrooke Series:

## Definitive Text

Sir Julian Corbett wrote the original, definitive text on the Seven Years War. Most later writers use his work as a stepping stone to launch their own.

Corbett, LLM., Sir Julian Stafford. England in the Seven Years War – Vol. I: A Study in Combined Strategy: Normandy Press. Kindle Edition.

## Strategy and Naval Operations

Three very accessible modern books cover the strategic context and naval operations of the Seven Years War. Daniel Baugh addresses the whole war on land and sea, while Martin Robson concentrates on maritime activities. Jonathan Dull has produced a very readable account from the French perspective.

Baugh, Daniel. The Global Seven Years War 1754-1763. Pearson Education, 2011. Print.

Robson, Martin. A History of the Royal Navy, The Seven Years War. I.B. Taurus, 2016. Print.

Dull, Jonathan, R. The French Navy and the Seven Years' War, University of Nebraska Press, 2005. Print.

## Sea Officers

For an interesting perspective on the life of sea officers of the mid-eighteenth century, I'd read Augustus Hervey's Journal, with the cautionary note that while Hervey was by no means typical of the breed, he's very entertaining and devastatingly honest. For a more balanced view, I'd read British Naval Captains of the Seven Years War.

Erskine, David (editor). Augustus Hervey's Journal, The Adventures Afloat and Ashore of a Naval Casanova: Chatham Publishing, 2002. Print.

McLeod, A.B. British Naval Captains of the Seven Years War, The View from the Quarterdeck. The Boydell Press, 2012. Print.

## Life at Sea

I recommend The Wooden World for an overview of shipboard life and administration during the Seven Years War.

N.A.M Rodger. The Wooden World, An Anatomy of the Georgian Navy. Fontana Press, 1986. Print.

# The Author

Chris Durbin grew up in the seaside town of Porthcawl in South Wales. His first experience of sailing was as a sea cadet in the treacherous tideway of the Bristol Channel, and at the age of sixteen, he spent a week in a tops'l schooner in the Southwest Approaches. He was a crew member on the Porthcawl lifeboat before joining the navy.

Chris spent twenty-four years as a warfare officer in the Royal Navy, serving in all classes of ships from aircraft carriers through destroyers and frigates to the smallest minesweepers. He took part in operational campaigns in the Falkland Islands, the Middle East and the Adriatic and he spent two years teaching tactics at a US Navy training centre in San Diego.

On his retirement from the Royal Navy, Chris joined a large American company and spent eighteen years in the aerospace, defence and security industry, including two years on the design team for the Queen Elizabeth class aircraft carriers.

Chris is a graduate of the Britannia Royal Naval College at *Dartmouth*, the British Army Command and Staff College, the United States Navy War College (where he gained a postgraduate diploma in national security decision-making) and Cambridge University (where he was awarded an MPhil in International Relations).

With a lifelong interest in naval history and a long-standing ambition to write historical fiction, Chris has completed the first four novels in the Carlisle & Holbrooke series, in which a colonial Virginian commands a British navy frigate during the middle years of the eighteenth century.

The series will follow its principal characters through the

Seven Years War and into the period of turbulent relations between Britain and her American Colonies in the 1760s. They'll negotiate some thought-provoking loyalty issues when British policy and colonial restlessness lead inexorably to the American Revolution.

Chris lives on the south coast of England, surrounded by hundreds of years of naval history. His three children are all busy growing their own families and careers while Chris and his wife (US Navy, retired) of thirty-eight years enjoy sailing their classic dayboat.

# Fun Fact:

Chris shares his garden with a tortoise named Aubrey. If you've read Patrick O'Brian's HMS Surprise, or have seen the 2003 film Master and Commander: The Far Side of the World, you'll recognise the modest act of homage that Chris has paid to that great writer. Rest assured that Aubrey has not yet grown to the gigantic proportions of Testudo Aubreii.

# Feedback

If you've enjoyed *Rocks and Shoals*, please consider leaving a review on Amazon.

This is the latest of a series of books that will follow Carlisle and Holbrooke through the Seven Years War and into the 1760s when relations between Britain and her restless American Colonies are tested to breaking point.

Look out for the eighth in the Carlisle & Holbrooke series, coming soon.

You can follow my blog at:

*www.chris-durbin.com*

Printed in Great Britain
by Amazon